PRIME VANGUARD

The Trans-Stellar Chronicles

Alexander O'Donnell

CONTENTS

Chapter 1: Levichion Station, Morthas   3

Chapter 2: Kalsik   12

Chapter 3: Nathan and Serie   28

Chapter 4: Final Preparations, IVAN   37

Chapter 5: Departure   53

Chapter 6: Shakrii amid the Crew   67

Chapter 7: Intra-Crew Dinner   77

Chapter 8: SQ-A76   86

Chapter 9: Landfall   97

Chapter 10: Life   109

Chapter 11: Divisions   122

Chapter 12: Surveillance and Respect   128

Chapter 13: Hunted   138

Chapter 14: Xarai   151

Chapter 15: Multipurpose Unit 128/Xami   161

Chapter 16: The World of the Xarai   175

Chapter 17: Star Swarms   188

Chapter 18: Newfound Perspectives   198

Chapter 19: The Feats of the Xarai   210

Chapter 20: GHEXRAX   223

Chapter 21: Fate of the Primacy   232

Chapter 22: Dissension of GHEXRAX   241

Chapter 23: Recuperation   259

Chapter 24: Imprisoned   271

Chapter 25: Attrition Offensive   286

Chapter 26: Hope for Rescue   300

Chapter 27: Ultraviolet Storm   314

Chapter 28: The Wrath of GHEXRAX   328

Chapter 29: GHEXRAX Relents   343

Chapter 30: Aftermath and Partings   360

Chapter 31: Homeward Reflections   371

Chapter 32: Uncertain Futures   382

Chapter 1

Levichion Station, Morthas

9 February, 3512 AD

4,500 Light-Years from Sol

Hegaine Republic Territory

Hygian Star System

No feat of engineering by any of the governments or races in the Trans-Stellar Union could compare to the magnitude of what the SQ-A76 anomaly revealed, and yet Shakrii wondered why there was such surprise. Given the vastness of space within the mapped portion of the galactic arm, even secrets with such enormous implications for the Union could go amiss.

The datapad she'd consulted in her cabin during the transit, when nothing else could distract from the travel, only reinforced this notion. The missing probe ship's last transmissions had revealed a haze around both that far off star system's twin suns, and most prominently, and now burned into her mind, a bright, thin and clearly artificial ring around the hazy planet, her four-eyed reflection in the datapad behind this image giving away the anxious tremor again, worsened by what their ship approached in orbit above the Secaile gas giant's icy and mineral rich fifth moon.

The ring-shaped station that loomed before their coasting ship before slipping amidst the various other near half kilometre long starliners only echoed this haunting image in her mind. An apprehensive itch crawled beneath her scales, bad enough that she had to dismiss the holo-view port as she readied for the disembarking, and on scratching her head frills, she watched some flake off in her claws, and she let out a rumbling groan as she forced herself to stifle any misgivings about this clandestine assignment.

No, not assignment, she had to remind herself that she had volunteered for this, as had the Doctor she would meet later today once his flight arrived.

~~~

Levichion Station, Habitat Ring

Nae'ragn District

Nae'ragn Transit Hub, Central Hub Transit Hall

It was mercy that the cigar-shaped starliner she'd boarded many sol days ago docked in Levichion Station's inner hub less than an hour later, and not too far from Shakrii's destination. She'd managed to battle the winding layout, elepod transits and lesser gravity with relative ease, despite the lethargic masses such transits were overwhelmed by.

Her military uniform had given her some wriggle-room to make haste, but it was still a struggle to wrestle her way through some crowds in the nano-grip floor tiled corridors the travel-worn mixed alien crowd were herded through. Fortunately, she excelled at resistance to getting to where she wanted to be, and while she wasn't proud of it, her rigid demeanor would ward away anybody that thought it wise to get in the way of a Kronogri obviously in a hurry.

She only hoped she could find something decent to eat, her guts needing soothing, and the food on board the transport had been lacking in her opinion. And as she'd also learned during basic training, 'lacking' left her surly, and more prone to accidental uses of her greater

4

Kronogri strength and imposing presence compared to other species than she knew was polite.

A few moisture skin-suit clad Yaleirn scurried away in their small trio, and while she flashed what she hoped was her best apologies, she wasn't going to turn down an opportunity to slip into the last free space in the elepod ahead of her before its doors shut.

Wedged between a lithe-legged Eithraak and a human and her daughter, she wasn't comfortable, but she wouldn't object as the elepod began its descent down to the arrivals hall at last. The discomfort the Eithraak felt, a few indignant clicks that no translator could keep pace with, were not worth her time.

However, a groan of complaint from the girl wedged against her broadarm caught her attention, as the girl murmured about being tired, before trailing off at seeing her matching her gaze from on high, a surprised gasp leaving the girl before her mother pulled her to her thigh, rather pointless with how tightly packed they were, while giving her an apologetic look.

"Sorry, she doesn't travel well, tired."

"I frightened her?" Shakrii asked, masking what little hurt she might feel, and thankful for the human's lack of reading Kronogri facial cues as she was reliant on the translator providing live-dubbing of her voice to her earpiece. Translator technology, implanted in visors or their hearing organs, provided dubbed sound into any language of choice. While imperfect, it did its job, and Emily's nervous smile came with an admittance that Shakrii felt a flush course through her scales at.

"Well, you are big, all you Kronogri are, compared to us." The mother, named Emily Warren as Shakrii scanned her with her visor, knelt down to reassure the girl, Lilith, while nodding to her. "She's not scary, just, different, okay?"

"Sorry." Shakrii gave a quiet rumble at the girl's admittance, as she was relaxing at this halfway point of the elepod trip, a conversation at last helping assuage her worries.

"Don't be. If only more were open, not just about how tired travel makes you. What brings you here?"

"End of holiday, husband got back earlier. You?"

"Work, can't say much more." Shakrii replied, grumbling what she hoped was a wordless apology, which seemed to do the trick as the Emily asked her with some concern on looking over her Hegaine Republic military attire.

"Serious, uniformed like that? Lots of Kronogri on this station, I know when things are up."

"I hope nothing serious." She replied, and now suddenly Shakrii was relieved that the elepod was arriving at the hall, suddenly wishing to get of this place. She was the first to slip from the packed confines, though in the least turned to see little Lilith smile and see her off, fingers and thumbs forming what seemed to be imitations of her extra pair of eyes that all Kronogri had, to the laughing consternation of Emily as they vanished into the crowds.

Unfortunately, as she checked the broadcast flight schedules, Shakrii would have to bide her time before Doctor Ruthilos's starship docked. To combat this at least, an enticing scent lured her to the hall edges, where food vendors waited, and a gathering of Kronogri around a certain meat-laced carton meal vendor was like a beacon her stomach rumbled at.

She was quick to order from the auto-wall dispenser, eager to devour the warmed meal, but a Kronogri male, a young one with a few other recently qualified out of basic training, probed her from where they'd been gathered, noticing her.

"New arrival? 1st Nevair?"

"Jealous? You'll make it in time if you stick with military, don't worry." Shakrii chuckled, imagining the envy these young might feel for her rank. However, as a few murmurs came, Shakrii saw her visor flash with an alert of an identity scan going on, and she dreaded the next sentence the boy spoke.

"Maybe, surprised they let you get to this rank."

"Why the surprise?" She turned on the boy, his others squinting their four eyed stares at her as the young Kronogri's head crests flushed with colour under the scales beneath his less decorated uniform. He was caught off guard, but managed to compose enough gall to ask her what she suspected to be his problem with her, his broadarms shuffling as he attempted to be stalwart against her somewhat larger form than his own, though the tremble in his smaller chest-forearms and all four eyes gave away his facade.

"Dehn-Herensk is your family, right?"

"Why does that matter?"

"Just, well, your kind's reputation…" The boy trailed off, doing the smart thing by going quiet, though that didn't stop some of his friends exchanging knowing glances, sidelong disingenuous sneers at their most daring. It was a look, hidden or not, that she knew all too well.

She suddenly felt less hungry, but she refused to let some arrogant, judgmental ones of her kind rob her of a meal she'd been wishing for over the last light year. She shuffled past them with only a parting remark to them that was both an insult as well as a truth she'd long ago accepted.

"Then don't worry, I'll bet you won't have to work as hard to get past my rank."

She ignored the murmured remarks at her, and found a suitable place in the middle of the arrival hall plaza to rip open and destroy the meal, no longer caring for the taste, only the filling sensation, though she had gorged perhaps too fast, as a time check showed she still had much time to kill. With little else to do, and in desire to calm her frayed temper, she synced her ear implants to her audio library and let the heavy beats of a Kronogri underground band's synth-tunes put her at ease.

7

~~~

As she sat on the bench, her ear implants playing her music library's next track, Shakrii's eye visor displayed a wide range of readouts, the names of all people she focused on. As had been useful with that pleasant human and child pairing earlier, she would need it to be sure of whom she greeted. Her partner's flight had arrived, its weary passengers beginning to join the arrivals, and she knew well that first impressions were everything.

A group of humans wandered by, while a family of Leg'hrul helped a newly arrived elderly male with his belongings, and a veritable clan of Eithraak scuttled off on their four legs, their under hands wildly gesturing as they spoke—their version of other species' facial expressions. Meanwhile, a group of Yaleirn walked past a circle of benches placed around a fountain in the brightly lit arrival hall. They gathered to dip their webbed hands into the fountain to top up their skinsuit condensers with moisture. The fountain was obviously designed to be both calming and functional. Since most arrivals and residents were Kronogri, a lone, patiently waiting female clad in military gear was not viewed as particularly unusual. In truth, she'd been here for only a few hours, and after feeding herself, had found a comfortable place in which to wait for her new colleague.

She reached around and scratched an itch on her scaly frill fin on the back of her neck, just above her massive forearm shoulders, groaning as she saw some flaking scales still, then spotted a newcomer and recognized his face from pre-briefings she'd received before travel.

The male Leg'hrul shuffled the large personal bag over his lower forelimb shoulder, his wings protruding through his work shirt and tucking in around it. His plumage was a light blue with hints of white, red highlights showing the somewhat fewer uniform colors of male Leg'hrul. At two meters, he was slightly taller than Shakrii.

8

He cracked a toothy, albeit cautious, smile and extended his other lower forearm upward to her in greeting. Shakrii knew his own visor device confirmed that she was indeed the one he'd been told to meet.

"Made it, then?"

He seemed amicable, his own forelimb hand waving off her question as he came to a stop, his two wings acting as additional legs on their folded, clawed ends along with his smaller back feet.

The Leg'hrul male shook his dark-blue-shaded feathery head in optimistic enthusiasm, his beak moving animatedly as he spoke. "Yes. Good to meet you face-to-face. Morthasune Ruthilos, though Morthas is fine."

"Shakrii Dehn-Herensk, 1st Nevair commissioned." She clasped her two small forelimbs together in a polite gesture, a traditional greeting for her race, while tilting her head upward to him. Done with the formalities, Morthas stood by while Shakrii gestured to the display boards of flight arrivals, keeping the tone casual despite her military attire. "Flight you came in on, *Sie'lan Star*. How'd you get that luxury?"

Morthas looked much more at ease in his civilian garb, though this was just one difference between her profession and his: the dress code. He was equally devoted to his work, despite it being more scientific than military. "Generosity from my research guild, appeasement before a long voyage." As intercom calls rang out for a few arrivals to report for additional processing, Morthas looked around. "So, are we to meet them soon?"

Incredulous at his enthusiasm after just arriving, Shakrii gestured toward a few food dispensers on the far side of the arrival hall, relieved to see those Kronogri from earlier had long gone, though she knew there was no way Morthas could eat food meant for a different DNA chirality, and focused more on other vendors nearby. "Not tired or hungry from travel?"

Morthas replied in his good-spirited way. "No, I handle travel fine—better than others aboard my flight."

Shakrii smiled through her scaly, toothy maw and knew she was going to like this Leg'hrul scientist. He wasn't too proud, he was efficient, and he was able to cope with harsh conditions, just as her research on him had indicated.

After gesturing to a few nearby hallways with signs leading to the mass transits for the entire habitat ring, she nodded to his shoulder bag, shuffling to stand on one large forelimb as its large, clumsy yet strong fingers flexed slightly. "We'll take the magline. You need help with your bag?"

Morthas declined by waving her off with a flap of one of his back wings. "Oh no. I know your kind like to show off strength, but I can cope."

Shakrii's four eyes narrowed warily. "My kind?"

Morthas gestured with his wingless forelimb to her clothing with a look of honest confusion on his beaked face. "Military. What did you think I meant?"

She realized that the Doctor hadn't been talking of her family reputation, only her broadest career, and before he could get more worried, she forced out a chuckle, laughing off this misunderstanding. Morthas looked relieved at her change in tone, and she felt better knowing that he wasn't going to deride her like so many others of her own kind would, one reason she often preferred working with aliens.

They set off without further conversation. She walked beside him on her four limbs, the shuffling of her forelegs making her resemble an Earth ape, her small, chest-mounted forearms moving absentmindedly.

Morthas followed her as they approached the mass transit station, joining the throngs of travelers moving to access the circular route around the main ring serviced by high-speed mag trains. If there were any illusions of being on a planet, they could be found down here.

~~~

As the military Kronogri and scientist Leg'hrul boarded their mag train, it was Morthas who voiced his only gripe about this journey, the doors sealing to the train as they entered to find seats.

"Wish the transit had been at the other station end."

"Blame the space lines."

The doors shut, and the mag train began to accelerate, their destination two stops away at the base of another tower structure, and their ultimate destination the cityscape around the extending aerospace plains beyond.

Their intended clients were fortunate to have a ship with landing ability, so they'd picked the Heysekri District's north aerospace port. To Shakrii's cautious mind, it meant that once they had finished their business on this station, they would be prepared if they needed to land the whole ship somewhere safer than outer space. She kept her thoughts of their future assignment to herself, as she knew both hers and Morthas's arrival wasn't exactly going to please the crew. Their small numbers helped the clandestine reason for the upcoming mission—fewer mouths to keep silent.

All the while, all around them on the massive station, life continued, their fellow passengers unaware of what the future held for these two travelers and the crew they were scheduled to meet.

Chapter 2

Kalsik

The massive 8-kilometer by 1.5-kilometer aerospace plains teemed with activity, landing and departing ships entering and leaving through the top of the artificial gravity and plasma field atmosphere, which was contained by three-hundred-meter-high walls. On the ground, ships taxied and parked, while smaller vehicles and personnel, organic or otherwise, swarmed about, dwarfed by the multitude of huge vessels.

Beneath the massive, flat plains, banks of elevator platforms the size of ships themselves led down to a lower level, hidden hangars and servicing complexes for longer-stay craft who chose not to use the many orbital service satellites near the massive station.

Even farther below, the hundred-meter-deep lowest levels housed amenities, including hotels and residences for crews and passengers. These and the other five aerospace ports along the habitat ring were cities within the entire station themselves.

Among the many enclosed tunnels, the usual flow of auto-driving vehicles, pod-shaped cars of many sizes, filled the one busy road tunnel on this level, the vehicles filtering off to the various passenger destinations. As one larger auto-driven vehicle, a transport, offloaded its passengers at a complex of shops and gaudy, neon-lined clubs, few glances were

12

directed at an area farther down the same street, across from a small fountain and plaza between this collection of commercial businesses and the more dull-looking buildings on the other side.

The areas dedicated to the logistics of the aerospace field were situated here. This was where the tedious filing of manifests and admin requests was done, along with other, less glamorous parts of spacefaring. In the small, more clandestine bars and lodges, it was also where ship crews came to unwind.

One such place, the Tireime Prospector, was especially favored by those who looked for a quieter place to unwind and get a drink or anything else available without hassle. It was also favored by the surveyor ship crews, the name of the bar a welcoming sign to those looking for a quiet, pleasant time before or after months-long trips. Surveyor crews were usually one of two types: either very reserved, or much wilder when it came to shore leave.

Tireime serviced the former, and had done so for many years now. One patron knew this well, for he'd been a regular for twelve years.

~~~

Tireime Prospector Bar

Seated at the front of the bar, Kalsik Ir-Hralan absentmindedly checked over the logbook that lay open beside his half-empty drink canister, not finding it as engrossing as he'd have hoped. It was quiet right now, only a handful of patrons at the booths and tables, the red LED lighting giving the illusion of a sunset that further subdued the mood. This was a place for the lonely, bored, or troubled to wallow or console themselves.

His hide and scales were the darker shades of his kind, nearer black than gray, but with shades of rusty red-brown along the faces of his head frills and sides. The utility overcoat he wore made him appear even larger than he already was. His eye level would

13

easily exceed that of a human's, and more if his posture hadn't been so slumped over, more so than was normal for his kind. If his suspicions were correct, this place, more than anywhere, was where he could be seen as a familiar face by other than his ship's crew. He should be. They had been more or less grounded on this station for over two months now.

The front bar table, lined with the thankfully universal seating method, the stool, provided seating for those who really wished to have frontline access to the surprisingly varied number of brews for a bar of this size. There were perks to offering discounts to ship crews and captains, such as free merchandise in exchange.

Behind the bar, linked to a rail that ran along the lip of the bar edge, perched a worker robot unit, its multiple arms and swiveling head on a ball-shaped body connected by an armature from the rail, sliding back and forth as it restocked the shelves from the refrigeration units inside the display counter. It worked tirelessly as its orange optics turned to focus on each task in rapid succession, only the gentle whirs of servos in its arms and rail giving it away in the quiet atmosphere, with soft, electronic background music playing through the speakers hidden in corners of the bar.

Beside Kalsik, the bar's co-owner, a human woman with tied-back black hair and pale white skin, dressed casually in a thin shirt, leggings, and plain shoes, finished wiping down the bar and gave a sigh of relief as she wiped her brow, her tattooed arm also sweating somewhat. The five-month-pregnant bulge in her middle did much to explain her lack of stamina.

As he looked up from his logbook, Kalsik's black-scaled eye ridges shifted in mild puzzlement at her state, unable to help the bemusement creeping into his mind, even at what had become a familiar sight by now.

The bartender, Alana, turned her gaze to him, her height the same as his despite his much-broader form. "What?"

"I guess you'll be on leave at some future point? Working as you do can't be healthy for it."

After a slight exhale at the Kronogri's innocent, if gruff, question, she resumed wiping the bar's gleaming metallic surface clean, taking it slower as she spoke, the faint traces of her exotic colony accent permeating her speech. "Don't start. I already have Joel fretting. I reminded him that I earn more for the same time as his neurobank time does. This little guy will need to get a bit bigger to slow me down."

Kalsik rumbled under his breath as he shut off his ship's logbook and pocketed the device. He took another sip from the sealed canister of Guariam brewed ale she had served him. "So you know the gender? Have you told Joel?"

With a slight smile, she handed her rag to the rail-mounted robot worker, as it came near her. It took the rag away to be washed, and she leaned over the bar beside Kalsik. "No, he's adorable when he's in suspense."

Kalsik finished his drink and spoke in his usual dour, gravelly tone, his language translated via her own implanted device into human speech, but still carrying his tone of voice. "Fair enough. Could you . . ." Kalsik gave a gesture to his empty canister with one of his small chest arms. He wasn't at all ashamed as Alana cast a wary look and left the can on the bar for the robot to pick up when it came back.

"Already?" she said. "Your kind can take more than others, but that doesn't stop you, does it?"

He said nothing as Alana produced another canister of the same drink from the fridge, the robot swiftly taking the can to the waste depository in the back rooms. When she handed it to him, he instantly cracked open the sealed, sterilized container, and swiftly took a large chug of the faint green alcoholic liquid, barely heeding the slight tingle it left in his throat. All drinks came in sealed containers now, and everyone was aware of the dangers of excessive fluid sharing without proper precaution.

Alana's sigh made him pause. She leaned on one elbow, propping her chin on a hand as she rested her other arm, and spoke to him bluntly without the usual humor. "Kal, I've seen enough aliens to learn enough signs. What's bothering you?"

Kalsik put down his drink can and grumbled loudly enough for Alana to hear. "It's that Kronogri soldier they're sending. Company shoving one on my ship."

"Why are they even there anyway?"

Kalsik's tone turned annoyed as he shook his large head. "You know it's—"

"Yeah, yeah, hushed topic. Now I remember. You Kronogs have compulsory military service once you become adults, right?"

Kalsik finished his drink. "Your point?"

"You said you made a high rank, right?"

Kalsik was quiet as he buried some memories that had begun to creep back—ones he had thoroughly buried in the deepest recesses of his mind under years of hard work. A shadow of bitter anger crept into his voice. "I did, until I had to leave. No more on that."

Alana shook her head and raised a hand. "Fine, no prying. Wouldn't be the first person in this bar to have secrets. Have you even met these people yet?"

"I will later today."

"Turning up half-drunk's not a good first impression."

"I'm letting them on the ship. That should be good enough."

With a roll of her eyes, Alana kept the empty canister in hand as she opened the fridge, reached up, and took a slightly different canister to hand to him this time. "Okay, Kal, last one. You're past sober anyway."

As she deposited it on the bar before his slumped head, Kalsik mumbled with a slight smile, "You're too good to me, Alana."

She reached out and patted his broad, scaly shoulders. "Just be safe, wherever you're going, Kal." With that, she backed off to attend a beige-skin-suited Yaleirn female waving down at the bar's opposite end.

Kalsik pulled the sealed drink canister over to himself, unsealed the top, and began to sip the emerald-colored liquid to add to the trove of alcohol already in his system.

~~~

North Aerospace Landing Plains

Subterminal City Streets

He was gone from the bar within a half hour, his time spent—or wasted—for as long as he wanted now.

Kalsik now found himself walking through the quieter alleyways, making his way toward the aerospace crew complex. He was in no hurry, and as an experienced drinker, he was able to deftly mask his intoxication, even the haziness that threatened to cloud his mind.

The glimmering neon lights of advertisements and direction markings lit up the buildings all the way to the ceiling of this internal level of the city structure a hundred meters above. Like much of the station, the streets and buildings were laid out like planetary designs confined to a specific height of internal volume.

Walkways with a few parallel auto-driven-vehicle pathways cast shadows over Kalsik as he walked by. He ignored the food vendor robot in its store, akin to a hole in the wall, servicing a group of the Eithraak, the second most numerous race on this station after the Kronogri. Of course, around the spaceports there was a more diverse range of races, as Alana showed.

It was one reason he preferred not to travel much into the heart of the station, where more of his kind resided. He stood less chance of being recognized here.

With a quick twitch of his small chest arm, Kalsik answered a ringing call in his earpiece, which was lodged into the lobe hole along with his translator device. He spoke calmly, as he recognized the voice, one that always brought him comfort through familiarity, even if it was a voice of a synthetic being.

"Cargo preprocessed. Vessel is precleared for departure."

"Good work, IVAN. The others?"

"Currently in the agri-markets."

"Good. I told them not to get any uthraak filth, so if they manage that, then that'll make both our days."

"What would I gain from that outcome?"

"You won't have to deal with my bad mood."

"Given your response to the passengers, that outcome is still guaranteed."

"I'll be there soon to sign off, once I've met them."

"They are already waiting. Company authority granted them an enclosed conference room early."

He cursed as he slowed down, the intoxication wearing off. "Tell them I'm on my way."

After shutting off the call, he growled under his breath. He picked up the pace, seeing the elevator transits to the hangar bay he'd booked a few hundred meters down the wide street.

This was the last thing he needed, though it wasn't unexpected. Being a spacefarer made one adopt an inbuilt pessimism, one reason why Kalsik pursued this career when his time in the Kronogri military took a turn for the worse, and then ended altogether.

Still, he wished beyond anything else that one of the passengers wasn't from the armed forces he'd left under such sour circumstances.

18

Main Habitat Ring, Heysekri District

North Aerospace Landing Plains

Spaceport Terminal, Administration Complex

The well-lit, sleek, metallic and transparent walls and floors of the aerospace terminal superstructure's halls and lounges were almost taunting to Kalsik as he stomped through the restricted access doorways, entering the more confined crew and security areas. The sliding doors closed behind him.

A brief presentation of his credentials by DNA and personal device ID scan at the robotically staffed security checkpoint cleared him into levels even he was not usually granted access. Here were more restricted control areas, coordinating the local security spacecraft for the whole station, along with arriving and departing smaller military craft on the landing plains.

Here the atmosphere was tenser, the lights of direction signs and changing, interactive wall displays the main sources of illumination in these darker, slate-gray corridors. He knew that the opaque, reflective black surfaces concealed control rooms, further obscured by the electronic window surfaces able to turn opaque or form one-way mirrors on command for more clandestine, controlled operations, be it for corporate gain or genuine security.

Kalsik stopped before the assigned doorway amid this labyrinthine complex as a narrow white beam spread a thin scanning light over him, until an orange light over the door flickered once. The door clicked unlocked, and Kalsik, dressed in his basic clothing and spacer jacket, shuffled into the room.

His four eyes narrowed ever so slightly at the sight of the two waiting beings, before he relaxed as the Leg'hrul male, clad in a jacketed outfit with many pockets that still left his wings loose, approached him from around the shining table. The military-clad Kronogri female remained seated, however, as the Leg'hrul walked forward, lower wings' claws gripped together in his race's customary greeting. Kalsik politely exposed his neck to the Leg'hrul as a primitive sign of submission and trust.

"Kalsik Ir-Hralan, Morthasune Ruthilos—Morthas informally. First Nevair Shakrii Dehn-Herensk."

As she tilted her neck upward in greeting, Kalsik did the same, consciously making it less pronounced than hers.

He noticed she scowled slightly at this, a fact that he took to his private satisfaction. Given that he wanted to balance any professionalism and hostility, he felt under no obligation to be courteous yet, so he adopted an almost bored tone as he replied. "I read the pre-brief. Couldn't do much else, being grounded on this station."

His mandibled beak clenching slightly, Morthas offered almost apologetically to the captain, "If it helps, we intend to get underway as soon as possible."

"Get to the point."

At Kalsik's bluntness, Morthas turned almost nervously to Shakrii, who pulled out a multipurpose storage device that synced wirelessly into the table display. The paper-thin display layer rose up a few feet from the middle of the table. Haptic interfaces used ultrasonic waves to exert pressure on any body part touching the two-dimensional image, giving mere light projections the sensation of being tactile.

Shakrii's chest arm pointed clawed fingers as she turned to explain to Kalsik. "This mission still has some last-minute changes we must discuss."

Kalsik spoke plainly as Morthas stood to the side, the Leg'hrul sensing the tension in the room. "My crew isn't here. They'll—"

"They need not hear this briefing's information until you have heard it," came a voice from above.

Shakrii looked up at the ceiling as she continued to wait patiently in her seat. Morthas slowly moved to take his.

Kalsik blinked at the speaker vents on the room's ceiling. With a snort, he remarked, "I forgot you were still here, IVAN."

"Yes, they have granted me access here while the room is leased."

Shakrii made a sharp knocking noise on the desk with her small chest arm, regaining Kalsik's attention. This irked him, a fact that he buried under his ever-so-brief bristle of scales, while Morthas continued to wait for her to direct the conversation back on topic.

"Eskai Inc. has been ordered by the highest Trans-Stellar Union security committees to include these additional conditions."

"So, who exactly are we reporting to?"

Kalsik's skepticism was justified by all the secrecy around this whole endeavor. Morthas leaned forward on the table surface, his wing feathers flattening as he spoke, making Kalsik wonder if he was picking up on the icy tension between him and Shakrii, or more accurately, that he was hoping to convey to Shakrii. He listened to the Leg'hrul, quickly understanding the importance of his message despite any tension he might have sensed.

"This is either a potential first contact or, preferably, a massive archaeological find. Either one is not something to take lightly."

"I saw the images my lost probe captured. Made getting strong-armed into this more understandable."

As Kalsik stood at the table end, his displeasure seemed to be registering with them. Shakrii moved to placate him, though Kalsik only barely listened, as he had heard this all before.

"You were useful in service, rather than silenced. Besides, you aren't the first to be in this sort of situation. Surveys often stumble across discoveries."

"Am I supposed to take that as an apology for our forced downtime without pay? Basic income doesn't let us live luxuriously."

Clearly wanting to break up the dispute before it escalated, Morthas raised his voice slightly, his head crest feathers and sensory hairs flaring where his clothing didn't cover his neck. "Perhaps we could keep things civil? Please?"

Kalsik rumbled as he calmed himself, running his own chest-mounted arm's claws over one of his scaly frill crests on his oval-shaped head. "IVAN, I take it you received a copy of the new contract?"

"Correct."

"Then return to other duties."

"Disconnecting."

With a small electronic noise, IVAN was disconnected, leaving Kalsik alone with the two passengers he and his ship were charged with carrying on this mission.

Kalsik sat on the same side as Morthas. If Shakrii was bothered by this, it didn't appear so, as she immediately began to point out the first of many small technicalities of the contract. There was a lot of bureaucracy involved in these kinds of missions, as much protocol had been established over many case studies in first contact or ruins discoveries of old, dead alien cultures. The surprise of first contact was such that any and all other unexpected developments were provided for. Too much could go wrong to take any chances, especially when dealing with an advanced race, as the site suggested.

After an hour of discussion of the many pages, taxing the patience of them all, though none made it obvious, they reached the final section. Concerning the command structure, given the expertise of Morthas and Shakrii, there were alterations to the usual ship rank that Kalsik didn't feel entirely comfortable with.

"Should irregularities arise, you will cede command to either Morthas or me, depending on the situation." The military-clad Kronogri female gestured to the last line as she summarized this last section, her own expression stern as Kalsik's face hardened.

As Shakrii finished, Kalsik let slip his next point with perhaps more venom then he'd intended. "I don't plan on letting my ship and crew get into any situation where you are to supersede me."

"I'm afraid you will have to heed my command when we get to the site regardless," Morthas said.

Kalsik relaxed as he turned to Morthas, who seemed much more reasonable than Shakrii. In all honesty, in his bemoaning of Shakrii being involved, military as she was, he had actually paid less heed to the scientific role that Morthas would be filling. He had yet to find a reason to dislike him. "Yes, the research is entirely in your authority. Rest assured that I'll lend any crew out for missions off the ship. They will follow you as they would me."

"Are they capable? I don't need more researchers necessarily."

"They're adaptable. If they are not up to task, then our AI crewmember certainly is."

The Leg'hrul clapped his lower wing claws together in a pleased gesture, while Shakrii kept silent. From what Kalsik could see from his discreet sideways glances, she was watching their exchange carefully.

"Where are your crew exactly?" asked Morthas.

"Last few supply checks and orders, and last free time."

Kalsik noticed Shakrii's mouth scales narrow slightly as he spoke these words to Morthas, though he paid it little heed as he turned to look at the last few lines of text. Morthas pointed to these himself. The Leg'hrul's voice was almost background noise to Kalsik as he saw the look Shakrii was giving him. She was analyzing him—judging him, sizing him up, probing for weakness, challenging him. It was a look he knew all too well.

23

The display screen retracted into the table, and they all rose. Morthas spoke with Kalsik outside the doorway as Shakrii shuffled past behind them, waiting a few meters away.

"You mentioned a space I could use?"

"We have a mineral lab you can borrow, along with some spare cargo storage."

"Perfect. I can get set up immediately." Morthas looked toward Shakrii almost expectantly. His face fell slightly as Shakrii mentioned a small point, referencing the unspoken tension that had plagued the entire briefing.

"I will be along soon," she said. "I think Kalsik wants to see to some more details."

Morthas made his slow exit, walking down the hallways with a backward glance.

After he was out of earshot, Shakrii spoke curtly to Kalsik's scowling face. "You clearly have something to say to me, Captain."

"The main reason I'm willingly cooperating with these orders is because I don't wish to lose command of my ship or my crew."

"If you run both as smoothly as the reports say, then we'll have no problems."

Shakrii's reply through gritted teeth did little to ease Kalsik's feelings toward her, as he almost hissed while his small chest arms jabbed toward her accusingly. "I'll reiterate how I see this working for us all. Your rank holds no sway over me, be it as First Nevair or even if you were the Grand Erieza of the entire Republic armada. You follow my orders until contracted to take command, and not a moment sooner. Understood?" He spoke with not a bit of respect for her or the uniform that seemed to spark much hostility. What she said next did nothing to alter that.

"Your profile says you're usually less paranoid. You didn't get your squad mates to follow and trust you so many years ago with an attitude like this."

Kalsik couldn't have gotten any more stone-faced if he'd tried. He spoke in a cold whisper at this female who was really getting under his scales. "You doubt my crew?"

"Your crew, no. It's only you."

It was all Kalsik needed to hear, for he knew to expect this. He responded dismissively, still icy in his demeanor. "I guess we both have preconceived notions about each other, yours by profiling, and mine by instinct."

Her four eyes narrowing, Shakrii took a step forward, her broad shoulders and larger main arms bristling beneath her military garb as she spoke, her patience wearing thin with him. "You need to learn the difference between caution and bearing a grudge, Kalsik. This mission is bigger than any grievances."

"All the more reason to clear the air early on. For the record, by the time I was your age, I was already two ranks above yours. Now, if you'll excuse me . . ."

Shakrii's eyes flickered slightly, her scaly lips forming a tense, thin line. Kalsik left without so much as a cursory glance backward as his broad arms shuffled his body around, heading off in the direction of the reception halls. He failed to register the lethal glare Shakrii directed at him shortly before he vanished from her sight.

~~~

Spaceport Terminal, Main Hall Complex

Kalsik needed some time to calm himself. He went for a walk through the brighter areas of the station. He came upon a central stairwell hall, many elevators and curving escalators spanning the multitude of levels within the open, yawning circular chasm. Advertisements for the many shops, restaurants, and security and baggage/cargo checkpoints glistened in moving holographic projected displays across the transparent walls that blocked off the walkways from the hundred-meter drop to the lowest level of the terminal, the garish brightness contrasting with his current mood. Kalsik found a small bench that put his back right against the transparent metal wall. He sat on his rear legs with a small groan as he took the weight off his main forearms.

Engaged as he was with rubbing his brow and head crests, Kalsik paid no heed as a group of Eithraak scuttled past. With a pause, Kalsik switched on his visor display, the blue-hued light screen projecting over his left two eyes as he spoke over the link. "IVAN?"

"Yes, sir?"

Kalsik began transmitting data from his visor's files that included logs of day-to-day activities. Automated audiovisual journals were the norm, as it made recollecting things much easier. When uploaded to decentralized computer networks, they were difficult to corrupt or steal. "I want you to run a cross-check with what I saw on the displayed contract to what you got."

"They would have no reason to deceive us, and if they did, they wouldn't give either of us the true contract. Why would this even—"

"Just do it."

There was an audible pause as Kalsik waited for IVAN's reply. His eyes began to wander toward a bright neon holographic advertisement passing over the transparent steel wall behind him.

"Acknowledged. Is there anything else you want, sir?"

"To not be involved in this whole business after that damn probe incident."

Kalsik disconnected the call and slumped forward, his small arms rubbing his larger forearms through his heavy coat as he sat, throat grumbling his aggravation aloud. Ever since that probe went offline and transmitted those last-second pictures, there had been nothing but inconvenience and grief. The only small ray of positivity was that they wouldn't be stuck waiting here in perpetual uncertainty for much longer.

He would happily cede authority to anyone—*anyone*, if they were not wearing the uniform of an enlisted Kronogri military member. He had done his bit, and he was finished with that part of his life after what happened. He didn't know whether he regretted his choice more than he hated the command for what they did to him, but either way, he wouldn't forget it.

His role as captain of a humble, long-endurance survey ship had given some stability back to his life, and now a military presence was on his ship, a threat to that stability. She was already prejudging him and living up to his own prejudgments of her because of it. He wouldn't let her take away what was his, and if she did, he would make himself more useful to be kept around. It was all he could do, and it still drove him mad. He only hoped this voyage would prove important enough to be worth all this grief. He would endure it, even if in silence. He'd made his case known to Shakrii, and that was that.

With the renewed conditions of this mission's leadership chain, he would keep all four eyes on her. It gave him a sense of satisfaction that he was in command, and he would happily play her game and wait to pounce the moment she slipped up.

At least he didn't mind the one passenger he would definitely have to cede authority to when they got there. Morthas knew his place, and he also knew who had the more experience at the relevant time.

Chapter 3

Nathan and Serie

As he made his way through the throngs of beings, mostly Kronogri, in the plant produce halls, the human turned into another section of the pristinely maintained food market. Nathan ran a hand through his short-shaven black hair, which he was unable to comb into much besides its tidy but sparse state. His pale complexion, a result of growing up and living among ships, stations, and climate-controlled colonies, was emphasized by the Caucasian genes he had inherited from his mother's side. The contrast with the Polynesian features inherited from his father made his appearance quite startling. Standing just a hair under two meters, he was tall for a human male. He had a trim build but was not particularly muscular, not that his profession required it.

On either side, freezers and coolers held packaged or exposed meat stacked or behind counters. A few robot workers restocked a shelf with an arrangement of vacuum-wrapped cubes of some type of meat he didn't recognize.

Beneath his feet were massive halls of vertically stacked, aeroponic, mist-sprayed crops of all shapes and sizes, from micro-breeds of grasses and plants to plantations of

28

modified, micro-sized fruit trees. LED lighting fixtures maximized yield with minimum energy needs, bathing the plants in a mixture of pink to purple light, optimizing the useful wavelengths. An army of workers, living and robotic, moved around, pollinating the plants manually, a tedious but crucial job.

Nearby were the protein halls. These were massive facilities akin to advanced breweries, which grew and bioprinted large quantities of cell cultures. Oils once harvested from plants and animals were produced by modified fungi, veritable carpets of fur-growing cells and lines of cells producing edible secretions such as milk or honey. Secure sterile enclosures with safety airlocks prevented cross-contamination. The halls produced food from throughout the galaxy, satisfying the needs of all the various races within the station's population, all of whom wanted a taste of their original homes and gardens.

Once the produce was mature and harvested, it was perfectly safe to eat, but safety measures during the cultivation or bioprinting phases were strict. No risks could be taken, and penalties for breaking the guidelines were strictly imposed by the Health Board. Plague and food poisoning were much more serious on a station than in an open planet environment.

A part of Nathan envied the predictability of the produce workers' jobs, the certainty of it all. No risks to equal those of the expedition he was about to embark on.

He focused his attention away from the sights of the station's agricultural infrastructure, knowing that if he'd wanted an agri job, he should have applied for such training in his early colonial years.

It wasn't long before he reached the front of the service kiosk queue, where the robotic attendant, a narrow, polymer-skinned android of Kronogri shape, moved to the serving window on its three-wheeled base. The alien likeness was only necessary from the mid-body up. Here was where more unusual orders, often bulk ones, were handled.

After handing over his credentials, Nathan waited, his fingers tapping impatiently while the system was checked. Then the unit beeped and began to speak, its small, chest-mounted claws waving over his data pad to wirelessly transmit the updates.

He gave a small grunt of acknowledgment to the robot attendant before leaving, as a Kronogri female with a uniform bearing the mark of a notable restaurant chain came forward, a data pad in hand with her own checklist for the attendant.

Nathan raised his wrist-embedded device as he walked out of the market's pristine interior. There, he saw his schedule for the remainder of the day, before he and the rest of the small crew had to return to the ship. Four hours was plenty of time still, for a human at least, before the delivery arrived. Despite his frequent travels, he still preferred to use the human timekeeping system, and always converted calculations into local time using his personal devices.

With his remaining time, Nathan arranged to meet with a fellow crewmember, one he slightly envied, as she had more personal supplies to pick up—although if he was honest with himself, they both tried to wriggle out of such errands unless it was urgent, and she was simply quicker than he'd been this time.

An eclectic mix of aromas of meat, fruit, and vegetables filled Nathan's nostrils as he made his way into the depths of the Veranda Parks Market. Music blaring from one of many hidden speakers reverberated through this market lane, the bass undertones shaking his body slightly.

The market was packed, mostly with Kronogri and Eithraak, as was the norm here, all of them shuffling in and out of the various restaurants, dance clubs, and dive locales that pounded their electronic beats of music.

The curious combination of the two races' architecture was obvious. The Eithraaki influence, with its curves and long, thin structures, spread like tree roots and vines through the market. This contrasted with the more solid Kronogri building designs, on the lines of ancient, rounded stone edifices. This nod to fair representation of the two cultures seemed to Nathan to only add to the confusion, as if the two races were fighting for dominance in the crowded market.

Lines of docking ports were arranged along many of the walls. Robotic units, some the smaller personal companion units, others larger hauler units, were attached to these, either powering up or downloading information via the fast, direct network method of physical link. Overhead lighting was strung over the paths and alleys like ribs in a skeleton, and holographic advertisements slid across many of the buildings' flat surfaces.

Nathan spotted her at one of the few food stalls that serviced Leg'hrul. Sure enough, she caught his gaze and returned it with a friendly gesture of her wings. She still wore her customary dark-gray, pocket-lined leggings and torso coveralls, but here in the humid, food-aroma-baked markets, she had loosened the top to let the plumage on her chest and neck fluff out for slight cooling. She kept her four arms devoid of sleeves, as was usual with Leg'hrul, unless it was absolutely necessary to cover them.

Her darker blue feathers were shaded with areas of gray over them, but, being female, she was slightly taller and leaner and lacked the highlighted extra coloration that males had on their feather tips.

As Nathan tucked the small, biodegradable boxed meal under his arm, Serie Hishaz made her way over to him, weaving around an Eithraak pack as they scuttled by, engrossed in their own affairs. She stopped before him and smiled lightly as she pulled out a new-looking set of gloves, three-fingered to match her race's hand shape at the end of their smaller, shrunken lower wings. She was a few centimeters taller than Nathan. He had long grown used to her having to look down at him when they spoke face-to-face.

"Got my gloves. Nano-weave against shocks or burns."

Nathan reached out to rub one of them between his fingers. "Hopefully you won't wear a hole in these."

Serie brushed it off, pocketing the gloves as the markets bustled around them. He liked that about her, her ability to keep in a pleasant mood and put up with his less optimistic behaviors, and their captain's too, if they were both honest about Kalsik.

"Protein cultures cleared?"

He shrugged slightly, then gestured to the device within his legging pocket. "They did. I hate queues. Why don't people decide what they want before they get to the kiosk?"

"Some people take things as they come."

He rolled his eyes at Serie's patience with these matters. "I bet you didn't have to queue," he said playfully.

Serie turned away as she ruffled her feathers against the heat of the markets. Nathan began to feel some sweat forming an uncomfortable stickiness on his brow and armpits. He always forgot how clammy these markets could get, despite the best efforts of the many atmosphere-control units. Serie's indication of her own discomfort reminded him to wipe the sweat from his forehead.

"I had to wait for the fabricators to make the gloves."

"Yes, Serie, but you could still go off and do what you wanted."

A small scoff escaped Serie's throat at this, her beak mandibles flaring slightly as she stared down at the boxed meal he held beneath his arm. She pointed her claw from her lower-arm hand toward it. "Is that why you didn't wait for me before getting food?"

"Don't judge me," Nathan said somewhat defensively. "I saw you eying those stalls."

Serie laughed as her eyes did indeed divert slightly to the stall she had been shadowing before Nathan arrived. He smirked at this small victory. He caught the calmer tone in her voice as she gestured to the distant parks on the other side of the space front roads, which he knew was her way of saying she was done with this conversation. "You find us a

32

good spot."

With a smile, Nathan made his way off as Serie pushed past a small pack of younger Kronogri males, reaching the vendor and its robotic merchant as it finished serving a somewhat shorter, pale-colored Leg'hrul male. Nathan gave a wayward glance back at her as he crossed the nearby street in search of an open space where they could eat.

~~~

Mid-Levels, Main Space Front
Veranda Parks

Having just finished the berries that had come with her meal, Serie reclined, paying little heed to the human eating his own meal beside her, letting the much-cooler air here rustle what feathers she had exposed. The massive wall of transparent alloys provided an unbroken view into the space far outside the station, making the Veranda parks a prime recreation and social destination.

"So it's just some scientist and a soldier," she said. "I thought they'd send more."

Nathan gulped down the last of his rice, then closed the empty food box and placed it beside him. He scratched his arms absentmindedly as he turned his gaze toward the massive viewport walls, the half-illuminated orb that was Hygian hanging in the distance, a steady and somehow reassuring sight to the human. Having worked with him for years, Serie knew his various quirks, as all the crew did, and she couldn't help but notice whenever tension gripped him.

"Fewer members, less chance of someone letting out the details," he said.

"Media would pay out their tails if they knew."

"Got tempting at times. Basic income can't cover ship upkeep, and neurobank doesn't pay well enough either." Nathan plucked a few grass blades and began toying with them.

33

Serie fished out a hand-sized box from one of her pockets. With an anticipatory flex of her mandibles, she handed the small box to Nathan, who took it with a puzzled look—a look she always found amusing. She sometimes messed with him just to get that look. "Well, seeing as that's over now, I bought some gifts for everyone."

"You didn't get Kalsik uthraak meat, did you?"

Kalsik's intense dislike of that Kronogri-sourced meat meant that it was a big contraband on their ship. Although uthraak was perfectly legal, no one wished to incur Kalsik's grouchy wrath.

"No, his favorite drink."

Nathan gave a laugh, and she giggled at the sigh of relief that escaped his throat. "We'll see if it lasts the trip."

"As for IVAN, I got him a series of artisan programs, and I'll see he uses them without calling them pointless."

Serie would be honest with herself in saying she had a habit of coddling the machinery she worked with, especially their ship's AI, installed as part of Eskai company policy on long-endurance survey ships. What made it all the more challenging was that unlike other machines, IVAN didn't always appreciate her efforts. "Sure, whatever stops him leaching my shows and games I paid for."

"And he can expand his horizons."

As Nathan lay back on the grass, Serie casually shuffled to sit closer to him, looking curious as to why he hadn't immediately opened the box.

"Anything for the passengers?" he asked.

"No, just the crew. I know what they like. Speaking of . . ."

The human finally opened the box, and Serie pulled back with a smile on her mandibles at his reaction. He sat upright as he looked inside. A pale-yellow block with a peculiar scent wafting from it lay in paper wrapping inside the box, but judging by his reaction, it may as well have been a priceless artefact.

"No! Gruyere cheese? This stuff's so hard to find outside the Union!"

"I found a human market in Kothia District."

Nathan paused before closing the box. "Forty-fifth district?"

"Wait. You've been there?"

Nodding, he reached into his pockets and pulled out a bottle that he'd been hiding, his excitement at her gift forgotten as he explained what he had to a wide-eyed Serie. "Found it while exploring, while I was hunting for this. You wouldn't believe the looks I got."

Serie took the bottle in her hand and examined the labels, written in Leg'hrul, as Nathan explained why he'd bought it.

"Scented preening oil, one of the more expensive brands. Did my research."

His nervousness was obvious. It was an opportunity to tease him that she couldn't resist. She pretended to lose her composure, feigning warning signs by intentionally stiffening her feathers and spinal fur. "What's to say I don't smell nice already?"

"You usually do, but you said you wanted something to use when you crawl out of the maintenance ducts."

Serie turned away in faux insult. Joking aside, she agreed that she reeked of fluids and oils after a hard day's engineering work on repairs the normal drones couldn't handle. "You don't smell that enticing all the time, either."

"I'll take sweating over molting anytime."

Serie finally laughed aloud, and the human joined in. She gazed out the viewport at the starlit night skies, the faint glimmers of them almost beckoning them to venture out. Unfortunately, it also seemed to remind Serie of their impending task, which was likely to last a few weeks or months by most calendars.

Nathan broke the silence. "So, looking forward to heading back out?"

"Why wouldn't I be?" Serie asked quietly.

"You aren't nervous?"

"Are you?" Then he replied with brutal honesty, only confirming her suspicions. "I don't know. Possible first contact isn't what I pictured being part of."

Serie knew Nathan's tensions would always be greater than most. His minor OCD catalyzed any unease he felt. She laid a comforting clawed hand on his thigh, feeling him shiver slightly as she lectured him for what felt like the thousandth time on this matter, though she understood he needed to be constantly reminded. "If things get out of hand, we don't have to stick around there. We were told that much. It's the passengers who'll worry about what to actually do."

"Piloting a shuttle service now. My career's gone backward."

Serie squeezed his thigh through his leggings. "Just make sure they feel welcome. Make up for Kal's likely mood."

Nodding, Nathan smiled as she retracted her talons from his leg and turned to gaze at the stars. "I'd have thought he'd have finished that briefing by now."

"It's not like we have many jobs left to do." Serie flopped backward onto the grasses, flexing her four upper limbs as she relaxed. Nathan shrugged in agreement beside her.

While they relaxed, Serie couldn't help but wonder about many things. Among her concerns was the captain's mindset and feelings about this mission, and the prospective developments with the passengers, who they would be stuck with for the whole expedition.

For now, the sight of Hygian's gas giant shape far away, the silhouette of a smaller moon blotted black against its distant half disc, was a welcome distraction.

Chapter 4

Final Preparations, IVAN

10 February, 3512 AD

Heysekri District

North Aerospace Landing Plains

Surface Aerospace Port

Eskai Inc. Engineering Hangars

Upon entering the main hangar, Nathan saw the transport ship that occupied the space, its internal cargo bay half-open as robotic workers pulled out fuel lines for examination, both around the engine reactors and the fuel cell lines. He was surprised it was still here.

The lead engineer, scratching his brow scales as he pulled back from the opened panel, noticed the familiar human face. After shooting Nathan a wry look, the Kronogri nodded toward the ship, a scanning tool in one of his small chest hands as he clutched the edge of the cargo door with one of his larger forearm grips. "We're still trying to find the leak. Want to help?"

"Once I've checked mine, Kae'ten. Where's Qazinth?"

One of the service drones, a crab-bodied robot with many multi-tooled arms, stared at Nathan briefly before turning its body in the general direction of the hangar doors and pointing. Nathan gave it a small hand gesture of thanks before wandering off, bidding

Kae'ten a nonverbal goodbye and ducking under one of the protruding transport's engine nacelles as he made his way to the hangar.

Near the front of the hangar opening, beyond which the large metallic plains of the landing expanse loomed, the main office lay tucked away in the corner, the massive hangar door mechanisms towering behind the small workspace. Nathan saw Qazinth, a light-brown Eithraak, waiting by the open doors. She was speaking in the Eithraak's clicking language to her companion, a slightly smaller Eithraak that was also watching the ships from afar. Both were clad in work overalls that hugged their four thin legs and pear-shaped bodies. The oxygen concentration undersuit could be seen beneath their overalls, which were both somewhat stained with lubricant.

Nathan noticed the smaller Eithraak click a call to Qazinth, making her turn toward him, small arms beneath the body gesturing in sync with her speech. Their language was a mixture of signs and high-frequency clicks. Unlike other races, Eithraak didn't have different accents, which made audible translation tricky. To help with this, Nathan received written subtitles as well as the click-laced speech. It guaranteed the need to pay attention when an Eithraak was speaking, though he had dealt with this one a few times over the past few months.

Qazinth was the head of this hangar and in charge of arranging maintenance for all Eskai Inc. craft assigned to it, including the ship on which Nathan was part of Kalsik's crew. The Eithraak was strict about adhering to regulations, particularly in potentially dangerous situations. When she was on her break, however, she became much more relaxed, even for an Eithraak with their more or less universal bipolar attitude toward work and free time. Nathan wished he knew her secret, as he could never fully switch off himself.

"Here for your ship? Nathaniel Cohen?"

"You know me, Qazinth. Why so formal every time?"

"I'm terrible at differentiating humans."

He merely shrugged at this, though he was sure to give a playful warning to Qazinth, a habit he had gotten from Serie. "I'll forget I heard that."

"I didn't mean to insult."

"It's fine. Far from the worst thing you've said."

The younger Eithraak clicked aloud in an expression of amusement. He leaned forward on a supply crate, watching the landing plains far beyond, the service vehicles and terminals dotting it like a massive city complex.

The Eithraak drone- and monarch-based culture relied less on the individual personality than the group, so being said to be indistinguishable from others wasn't much of an insult. If anything, Nathan might have viewed it as a compliment.

He turned his head back. With his eyes trained on the transport under repairs in the hangar's rear, he asked the obvious. "You aren't helping Kae'ten?"

"We're on break," said the younger Eithraak, who, as Nathan's visor ID readouts indicated, was called Krihegn.

Nodding in understanding, courtesy of his translator, Nathan leaned forward, watching some of the incoming aerospace traffic angling toward the quieter, private areas of the spaceport, a good distraction as he awaited his ship's arrival. The majority of craft were wide, long, and flattened, designed to glide for efficient atmospheric flight before hovering to land. The rest were oddly shaped ships designed for various other planetary landings. The central plains were dominated by passenger vessels, most of the freight being unloaded in many of the neighboring satellites around the station's orbit. Large terminal buildings serviced the craft, and a multitude of various-sized elevator platforms moved spacecraft from staging areas down into the lower levels for service and unloading, unless their stay was brief, and they didn't need refueling.

Today, one particular inbound craft, a private shuttle with twin pivoting thermal rockets, caught the attention of all three observers. Nathan pointed. "Coming in a little fast." He turned to Qazinth as she looked at him with her many unblinking eyes clicking in agreement.

It was Krihegn who spoke next, the smaller Eithraak's underarms gesturing as she let out a rapid series of clicks. "They'll have to thrust hard."

"I'll bet on a rolling landing."

Her superior's casual retort seemed to spark a slight interest from the younger Eithraak. "How much? One Gial?"

"Done. Nathan?"

"One Gial that tower will tell them to try again." His cautious wager wasn't due to nerves. Nathan knew how tyrannical traffic control programs could be if you stepped out of line through incompetence or autopilot fault. Much as he would like to forget, he had been on the receiving end of Control's wrath on at least two occasions while piloting ships.

The craft approached from far away over the plains, swooping in over the landing areas at speed and descending, wheels extended.

Qazinth said, "Bet's up."

The approaching shuttle burned its thrusters to decelerate, though a little too late for a perfect landing, gliding downward until it landed rather heavily and slowed to a rolling crawl on its wheels.

With a scowl, Nathan engaged his personal device and transmitted one Gial equivalent from his account to Qazinth, as Krihegn did the same. Clearly Krihegn was annoyed that she had lost the bet. "Sloppy."

Despite winning the wager, Qazinth agreed. "They'll get mauled by maintenance."

An uncomfortable memory of Nathan's early time under Kalsik resurfaced. "Captain would have my head if I did that."

As Nathan saw Qazinth turn to inquire about this potentially embarrassing slip, he regretted bringing it up. Fortunately, the Eithraak noticed that the next craft in the landing queue was the one he was waiting on, and it was heading directly toward their hangar. "Here's yours now. Remote piloted. No messy landing."

"Better not. Captain's grumpy enough already."

The arrowhead-shaped craft hovered over the flat landing area, its magneto-plasma thrusters rumbling as it slowly and neatly settled down onto the ribbed metal surface of the taxiways. Once settled, it began to crawl forward on its landing wheels, the large, wedge-shaped fuselage hiding its many features inside the former military spacecraft design.

To Nathan, however, as he walked toward it, it was simply a mobile home for him, Kalsik, Serie, and IVAN—one soon to be shared with two passengers, newcomers who would no doubt alter their close-knit dynamic.

~~~

He felt comforted as he approached the ship. Aerodynamic, large, and well supplied, the 150-meter-long, 60-meter-wide LSS *Haivres* was intimidating in size, and yet by no means the biggest craft to land here today. A specially equipped AUC-27 interplanetary transport, one of many that Eskai Inc. had purchased as military surplus decades ago and repurposed for long-range survey roles, the craft was in the medium range of sizes capable of landing on planets rather than just hovering like some larger craft. Landing struts and wheelbases had only so much strength before they would collapse. Viewed from the top down, the ship's external frame resembled a fat arrowhead, but closer inspection revealed cleverly concealed compartments behind retractable panels and hatches.

Within the hull of the ship was a critical structure common to many interstellar craft. A flat, disk-shaped centrifuge produced an artificial gravity to maintain crew health on long voyages. Ten segmented compartments, each thirteen meters long and five meters wide, were able to pivot at their joints to face outward like a normal centrifuge or to align vertically to orient the appropriate landing gravity throughout the walkways and floors of the compartments.

Ships with this centrifugal system were typically either tall, vertical takeoff designs, like the rockets of early spaceflight, or, as in this case, a wide, flat, and elongated arrowhead shape. Beneath the centrifugal ring ran a narrow corridor with nano-grip floors, and above it lay the control mechanisms for the structure. The life-support systems, along with the water and waste tanks, were located within the ring's rotating structure and connected by flexible power cables and water pipes to the habitation pods, which could rotate within ninety degrees around them.

This particular ship was equipped for long voyages, with living quarters and communal recreation spaces, extra equipment and supplies, a mineral and basic research lab, and meat and aeroponic crop microscale production facilities. The rest of the ship contained surveying systems and the standard spacecraft equipment, from the mixed thrusters, onboard power sources, and most exclusively, sophisticated communication systems, including a rudimentary wormhole communicator. Wormhole communication was utilized when the ship went off grid, enabling Eskai Inc. to maintain uninterrupted contact with its valuable ship and crew during exploratory survey missions.

It was unusual for a ship with a crew of only three organics and one dedicated AI to be so large. The additional space made them entirely self-contained, and the enhanced crew comfort ensured that organic crews were still prepared to man them. This mix of AI and organics on board offered the adaptability and safety contingencies needed for such long endurance missions. However, many were still apprehensive about accepting employment as a stellar surveyor, a job that meant mapping the countless stars and bodies, often in uncharted space, with missions taking months, or even years.

It was not a job for the faint of heart, and pre-assignment background checks, psych evaluations, and test assignments were mandatory. Previous experience of crew suffering mental breakdowns or, as in two cases a century ago, committing mutiny and sabotaging their own ship, meant that the company's selection procedures were rigorous. For the successful applicants, the pay was excellent, and the living conditions were luxurious.

The crew of the *Haivres* appreciated this. They had been together on the same ship for three years now with no incidents so far. They knew each other well, and so they trusted, confided, and got along with each other in their own ways.

Their captain intended to keep it that way, no matter who the Scientific and Cultural Committee of the Trans-Stellar Union decided to send him as "additional expertise." Kalsik had already shown his dislike for one of the so-called experts, even before they had met, so Nathan was keen to make sure that readying the ship went flawlessly.

~~~

The *Haivres* came to a slow stop in its landing area, the electric motors of its landing gear shutting down as it parked. The audible hum of the fusion reactor's cooling arrays ceased as the reactor's input power cycle stopped.

Nathan activated the personal data pad extension of his onboard wrist device and noted that the outside frame of the craft appeared unchanged. *Guess the new tech's inside.* His eyes scanned its familiar aerodynamic hull with fondness. He was a little wary about what changes had been made by the orbital dry docks, but he would find out soon.

A docking drone engaged an anchoring clamp on the front wheel array, and then the robotic worker began to move about on its wheeled base, the multiarmed structure and sensors beginning the check for any faults that organic eyes may have missed.

As Nathan stepped aboard and slipped back into the routine of the preflight checks, the sanctuary of regulation and set rules engulfed him in a comfort of familiarity he had missed during this grounded period. He felt more at home on ships, this one in particular, than he did on stations or planets. The rigid protocols to be followed gave him structure, security, and certainty that success or failure was up to him. He trusted the crew implicitly and appreciated that he had ultimate responsibility for his task.

Whether the new passengers disturbed the status quo remained to be seen. Hopefully they wouldn't be too much of a disruption to the rapport the mixed crew had built up over the years. What was certain was that Serie would soon arrive with the newly upgraded IVAN, who now needed to be reinstalled into the ship's systems. IVAN had been removed from the *Haivres* before the upgrade so as to minimize the risk of damage to the programming. A copy of IVAN's basic runtimes, nicknamed a doppelganger program, was used to test the new systems for compatibility before they plugged the AI fully back in.

It always made Nathan slightly nervous to be without IVAN during an upgrade, but he told himself that even if something went wrong, it would be small, and within self-correcting boundaries for his AI friend.

~~~

Elevator Terminal

The server hall resembled a mixture of a data library and an aerospace port security hall. It was quiet today, with only a few dozen robotic platforms and organic beings milling around.

Serie's charge arrived. A 0.6-by-0.6-meter box was wheeled out on an array of inbuilt electro motors.

IVAN's entire being was designed to be physically robust. His neural module was deep inside a small wheeled base designed to give him full mobility.

The greeting Serie gave to the box-shaped module was not immediately returned, but after a while, as he wheeled beside her, his cubic frame only reaching to her avian shins, he began to speak through her messaging channel on her device. The slightest hint of irritation was apparent, much to her hidden amusement. "You do not need to escort my frame."

"Were the others nice to you?"

"Your comparative statements to organic young care establishments are not entirely applicable."

Suppressing a small grin on her mandibled beak, Serie tried to keep a casual tone as she led the way, the box wheeling behind her with only a quiet electric whirr. Around them in the Eskai Inc. terminal hall, robots and other organics conducted their business at the many desks placed along the walls. Eskai wasn't just a survey company but also bought and sold mineral rights and even entire planets, from the atmosphere to the core.

"Well, you all stay there, absorbing data in your free time. How isn't it a crèche of sorts?"

"Organic youth do not interact in a digital server while—"

"Joking, IVAN."

Serie laughed as IVAN fell silent. When they reached the elevators leading up to the hangar areas where the *Haivres* was housed, IVAN spoke again, his usual monotone laced with what could best be described as exasperation and stubbornness. Personally, Serie felt he used that tone more often than an AI really should. It made him seem blunt and antisocial, though she suspected that was probably why IVAN got on best with Kalsik out of all of them—similar minds indeed!

"Misinterpretation of that environment necessitates clarification and takes up processing time."

With a slight twitch of her brow, Serie sighed and looked down at IVAN. He moved slightly as an Eithraak pushed past them, shuffling his wheels closer to Serie's boot-clad talons.

"IVAN, do you know why I tease you?"

The box at her feet remained quiet for a moment, though it turned to look at her, a pivot-mounted camera on its frame rotating to look her in the eyes. "Tending to my systems has caused you to form a preferential bond comparable to a sibling or pet—your prodding to encourage development evident of that, demeaning as it is."

Taken aback at the rather pointed analysis of her antics, Serie's sensitive smirk faltered on her mandibled beak. "Or maybe because it's just funny?"

"My hypothesis stands."

Serie looked up to see the doors of the large elevator opening, at least one personal service robot in the shape of a small, four-legged Eithraak lookalike among the dozen people aboard. Thankful for the pause in conversation, she walked in with IVAN wheeling beside her ankles. Serie spoke more quietly in the confined space, mindful of privacy amid those others in the elevator.

"You got the artisan programs I sent you?"

"Yes, not that I require them."

"It wouldn't kill you to get a creative line in your coding somewhere." Serie almost clicked her tongue in irritation at IVAN's refusal to culturally enrich himself, but managed to hold it back.

"I will allocate processes to it to placate you," IVAN said.

Serie snorted slightly. She would never admit it, but his judgment of her was correct, and everyone on the ship was aware of it too, barring their two passengers she had yet to meet.

~~~

The curvature of the distant end of the massive aerospace plains reared up nearly eight kilometers away, but Serie's sight was fixated on the landing area she walked out to now, IVAN's wheeling cubic form in tow.

Serie let IVAN go up the loading ramp first, the AI wheeling quickly, eager to return to his upload socket area. As he vanished up the nano-grip-floored corridor, turning left into the AI core closet, Serie heard sounds of movement from inside the stationary centrifuge ring pods. They were locked in place and opened with a straight hallway down the central spoke tunnel, as they were now in a vertical gravity alignment.

She cast a sideways glance, smiling as she saw IVAN's form raising itself off the wheels on small jacks, a set of armatures lifting and slotting him into the ship's mainframe. His full capabilities would be restored within a few minutes, and she knew he would be happy to be home, in his own way.

Inside the centrifuge ring, in the mineral analysis pod to her right, a male Leg'hrul unpacked a cache of high-tech equipment and personal data pads. His feathers, a series of pale whites and blues with red highlights, were unkempt compared to her neat, darker blues and grays. He was a plain-looking male for her kind.

He looked up, somewhat sheepishly, having just placed an unusual transparent box on the desk. "Sorry, just unpacking. Serie, ship's engineer?"

"You've done your research. You're Morthas?"

"I am."

She noted the male's eager greeting with some healthy caution, but she slowly relaxed, as he seemed preoccupied with the final package in the mixed crates he had brought with him.

"Comes with my work. Could I get some help?"

Serie bent down to get the object out of the crate, realizing what it was as soon as she and Morthas lifted it onto the desk. With the transparent surfaces offering a view inside the machine, and the labels on the side revealing the nature of the device, she found herself amazed to see such a rare piece of equipment. "An omni-scanner this small?"

"Best equipment was provided."

"Nice, but where's the other passenger?"

Morthas shrugged his wings. He seemed to be trying to be friendly, wanting to blend in. His behavior was a strange mix of reserved yet easygoing. "Shakrii's got some final business to sort out with her superiors. Now, your captain is—"

"Dealing with the departure documents," she finished for him.

"Things seem in order. Hopefully nothing too worrying will come of this trip."

Serie's relaxation showed in her smile as she leaned against a nearby worktable. "I hope so. Have you met the pilot, Nathan, yet?"

"Yes. Said he had to complete some checklists."

"Of course. He—" Her personal device buzzed, signaling an incoming message, a private correspondence. As she looked at the sender's name, her mood changed, reflected in the faintest droop in her plumage and the sensory hairs along her spine. After apologizing, Serie made her way past Morthas, wanting to take this message in the privacy of her quarters, in one of the other internal ring pods. "Excuse me. Good meeting you."

Morthas politely said nothing, giving a small nod in her direction as he sat down at the workbench to check the equipment he'd unloaded.

Overhead, the lights flickered briefly as the systems reset themselves.

Nathan focused on the readouts and calibrated settings they displayed as he held the extra data pad in his hand.

At that moment, the reset occurred. In the cockpit, while he checked the screen, Nathan recoiled as the normal displays, multiple keys and readouts highlighted in mixed colors over a series of uniform, plain touch screens, flashed slightly. He let out an aggravated growl toward the console, a growl directed at the AI, who was now obviously fully connected. "I hate that!"

"I was recalibrating. Your settings remain unaltered."

"They'd better be."

Checking the systems on his data pad yet again, Nathan began to run through the readouts one more time. He knew there was probably no need, but he always did it—not a bad habit in his job, he believed.

~~~

Seated inside her private quarters, with the bags delivered earlier resting beside her bed, Serie looked at the message. Her mood dampened even more now. She felt an unwanted tightness in her chest, faint yet unmistakable. Remorse, regret, and old memories resurfaced as she read the message from someone she really should have kept in better contact with over the years.

> *Serie,*
>
> *I know it's been a long time since we've last spoken, but given how often you're outside linked space, I wouldn't be surprised if this took a while to reach you.*
>
> *Jeithen's new academy term started a few weeks ago,*

which he's enjoying very much if his enthusiasm is to be believed. Rephagn is growing bigger every week and becoming a good amount of trouble. He insists on jumping off any high place to test his growing wings. Yalhesk says she wonders whether his boundless energy is a mutation, because he certainly didn't get it from us.

Our parents were here for Rephagn's last hatch date, when you were obviously off the network. I told them that you couldn't make it, not that they said much of it. My boys asked why, and I just told them you had important work far away.

I wish you'd come home. If not for our parents, maybe for your nephews. I haven't seen you myself since Jeithen's second hatch date, and Rephagn has never met you face-to-face in his life.

Yalhesk misses you too. You and she were such good friends in your own later academy years. If you could let us know how you are, more often than you already do, that would be enough.

You've been contacting less and less ever since you left. Please don't become a stranger. It wouldn't suit you.

—Sathor

As she rubbed her claws across her feathered brow in frustration, Serie pondered what to write back. Once she was out in uncharted space, she wouldn't be able to message him, as their onboard wormhole was very small and limited, restricted to only critical messages.

Sucking up her hesitation, Serie began to type her reply, pausing many times as she thought long and hard about what she meant to say, trying at the same time to bury the memories that kept coming into clearer focus.

> *Sathor,*
>
> *Work has kept me busy, though I can't say exactly what. Corporate secrets are worth enough to threaten a serious lawsuit or even jail if I told you what I've been charting in unknown space.*
>
> *I'm sorry I couldn't make any of these big dates in the boys' lives, but you're right. I still can't come back.*
>
> *I at least have the crew I'm working with as good company, in their own ways. Not that I expect our parents would approve.*
>
> *Tell the boys their aunt sends her love, and she's off very far away. Tell them that traveling the stars isn't as glamorous as so many stories say. I'd bring them back some samples, but I doubt rocks would be of interest to them, even very valuable ones.*
>
> *I can't promise I'll be calling anytime soon, because we've just got another assignment. This one won't be as long as my last one by far—just a few specific systems to check more thoroughly.*
>
> *I miss you too. I will try and come sooner if I can.*

Your sister,

Serie

Serie gave a long exhale, eyes closed in frustration as she let the memories of that time long ago fade away into obscurity, as she wished they would forever.

Seated on the bed, Serie couldn't wait to once again get away. Uncharted space had its perks, such as making one's problems in civilization seem far away, inconsequential. It was one reason she'd taken this job three years ago.

Perhaps it was the main reason. She'd never fully know, but it certainly felt that way.

Chapter 5

Departure

Their departure time had come, and not a moment was wasted once the boarding ramp closed.

The 150-meter-long ship lifted into the air with a roar of its thrusters, slowly rising upward toward the shimmering boundary of the contained atmosphere.

Strapped into the pilot's seat, the nano-implants active throughout his upper spine and outer brain, Nathan directed the vessel's gentle ascent with mental commands and the smallest of movements in his fingers. While it was possible for him to fully control the ship without moving a muscle, the physical motions served to sharpen his intentions, his body communicating with the nano-implants which linked them to the ship's controls, which became an extension of his body.

With IVAN monitoring the more basic systems, Nathan had overall command of the ship, fully at ease as he communicated with this spaceport's traffic control network, while the other two in the cockpit, Kalsik and Shakrii, had buckled themselves into seats farther back inside the main cabin, background presences to him as he worked.

"LSS *Haivres*, on vector 17-62-45."

"Confirmed *Haivres*, switch frequency to dry-dock control when in range."

Within seconds, the ship approached the boundary of the upper plasma field. Nathan's fingers danced over the controls, engaging the functions for the onboard centrifuge motors as IVAN's unseen programming offered more precision than he alone could muster.

"Beginning centrifuge cycling."

As they exited the plasma field ceiling of the aerospace port, the centrifuge ring began to rotate. The pods tilted on their axis as their spin accelerated, synchronized so as to be aligned as a flat surface, sustaining a floor-based gravity the moment they entered zero-gee.

~~~

From inside the first cabin quarters connected to the mineral lab, strapped into a side seat inside the pod, Morthas noticed the slight spinning of the cabin's pivoting ring at the joints. He felt the pod rotating from flat to ninety degrees as the spin speed increased, but the downward force of simulated gravity remained toward the floor, exactly where it should have been.

Much to his annoyance, one of the smaller equipment boxes beside his restraint chair began to move slightly. He shot out a boot-covered talon to stop it from sliding away, exhaling in relief as he caught it.

It wasn't a perfect transition, though even an AI would struggle to make it exactly floor-aligned as the change in orientation occurred. Even so, this was only the third ship with this sort of centrifugal setup that Morthas had ever been on, so he wasn't complaining.

~~~

In the engineering compartment, Serie felt her legs raise slightly from her restrained seat. This part of the ship was not in a centrifuge, and she felt the sudden shift from constant thrust to match a spinning environment to zero gravity.

Over the intercom, IVAN's voice rang out as a not-so-subtle signal to start work. "Engineering, calibrate docking module to shape. We're not getting the usual drive-vessel type."

Serie unstrapped herself and stood, planting her booted talons on the nano-grip floor as she walked toward the rear compartment of the ship, just before the docking bulkhead mechanism. A readout screen showed the precise shape of the docking clamp and interface. The modular docking armatures on the rear of the vessel registered as ready to be recalculated and reshaped.

Serie gave a pleased remark upward to one of IVAN's sensor clusters, knowing he was listening and coordinating even if he didn't speak. "Not too different from the usual at least."

Serie ran through her checklist on the support robots of the ship, the crablike machines that would prove themselves invaluable in basic extravehicular activity.

~~~

Up on the bridge, Nathan pointed to the visual projected model of the self-contained spatial drive and power vessel they were assigned to take as a drive ship. There was an audible tension in his tone as he turned to Shakrii, who clutched the seat beside his to steady her large forearmed frame in the zero-gee environment.

"An MC-15N? We usually get the VC-12J."

Quietly listening in as he went over the readouts for himself, Kalsik noticed the curt manner with which Shakrii responded.

"Benefit of my codes."

Kalsik noted the tension in the human's frame as he turned to look ahead while still questioning Shakrii.

"A military-grade drive ship? Expecting trouble?"

Shakrii stared at the back of the human's head, poorly masking her irritation with his justified queries. "Merely a precaution."

As he shuffled slightly in his straps, Nathan muttered under his breath just loud enough for Kalsik to hear. "Doesn't make me feel better."

Shakrii's face tensed as she floated beside Kalsik. He met Nathan's own nervous gaze as the pilot turned in his seat, glancing at Shakrii as she floated down the hallway, out of earshot down the rear corridor leading out of the cockpit.

Still in his seat restraints, Kalsik kept his voice calm as he spoke to his human crewmember, as much to reassure himself as Nathan. "It'll shorten our journey time."

"What if things do come up where we actually need it? Even the weapons?"

"Just follow orders, and things will go smoothly." He cast a wary glance back in the direction of the corridor, barely concealing his annoyance at Shakrii's behavior toward his pilot. She had little tolerance for anyone second-guessing her, as Kalsik already knew. For her sake, he hoped that would change as they got further into this voyage. Otherwise the two of them might come to blows earlier than he'd expected.

~~~

Secaile Planet System

Orbiting Dry Docks

Within an hour, they arrived at the large array of dry docks orbiting in between the fourth and fifth moons of the gas giant. The large rows of support struts, large solar and radiator arrays, and the few centrifuged crew sections of the ten-kilometer-long megastructure were pockmarked with spherical fuel tanks for reactors and propellant, reminiscent of an ancient multi-mast sailing vessel from preindustrial eras.

As the *Haivres* approached, the control station's population of server-housed program hives, working together as a collective artificial intelligence of neurons synchronized to perform mental functions, redirected them to the military mooring docks.

They were not here to dock and unload; they were here to rent a vessel, one of many available here.

Near the far end of the station, among a few large military vessels refueling their larger reactors, their armored hulls dwarfing the *Haivres*, was a row of bulb-shaped craft docked to a mooring tower. These were drive ships—vessels specifically—with self-contained spatial drives and the reactor to power them. They were rented out by those ships that needed to travel the stars or between far planets quickly, those ships that did not themselves have the room to house a spatial drive.

After detaching from the docking tower, the drive ship maneuvered with its own impulse power as the *Haivres* turned about to angle its docking port. The ring, with its protective hull, faced the *Haivres* with the reactor and power plants rearward. When connected, the outline of the entire paired joining would resemble a wedge with a rounded shape behind it, bulging in a fat disc at the joint.

Slowly the gap closed, and the armatures extended from the drive ship as the docking ports aligned. Universal docking systems had been designed to accommodate the varied spacecraft designs and could adapt to any shape. The mated pair of ships was now ready for the long journey.

Outside the ship, the space around the *Haivres* and its attached drive ship began to shimmer slightly, the drive ring with its large fusion reactor firing up into overcharge. The exmatter utilized by the spatial drive, just like that used in wormhole-bracing polyhedron microlattices, was made by a tedious process in system planet areas with plentiful solar energy, much like antimatter production for energy storage. Exmatter was, in fact, a negative-index metamaterial that, when bombarded with a select range of light frequencies at the appropriate angle of incidence, generated a buildup of negative kinetic energy in the metamaterial. This in turn generated a negative-mass effect within itself. The metamaterial effectively became a negative mass material to be used in wormhole and spatial drive setups alike.

After a few seconds of charging, Nathan closed the viewport. The outside image now generated by digital sensors, the space in front of them blue-shifted as the background radiation from the universe became visible. In front of the *Haivres*, a white glow began. Brighter in front, dimmer to the sides, and darkest at the rear, it slowly engulfed the ship, a stage at which Nathan always marveled.

To outside observers, the *Haivres* shimmered slightly, and then simply vanished from sight, glowing red for the briefest moment that only a trained eye would notice as the emitted light red-shifted before the ship jumped away at speeds unimaginable to anyone who hadn't experienced warp.

Once inside warped space, the ship didn't actually move itself, but surfed in a bubble made from contracted and blue-shifted space in front and expanded and red-shifted space behind.

Even so, warp space was risky. Sensors didn't work outside the bubble, meaning the ship was flying blind until it dropped out of warp. Specially designated and charted regions and lanes in charted space allowed spatial drives to achieve their maximum speeds in transit, most ships traveling at between 11 and 14 light-years an hour. However, this was a luxury only available within the 5,000-light-year width of the area colonized and charted by the five races.

Warping in uncharted space was inherently more dangerous, and speeds were purposefully slower, never exceeding one light-year an hour. Although the odds of coming out of warp and colliding with something were extremely small, the risk was not worth taking, evidenced by the handful of ships which had exhibited less caution and were no longer around to boast about it.

Their trek through the stars would be long and likely boring. The tension aboard would make it even worse.

~~~

Dei-He 1

Sol Day 1 of Voyage

Shortly after their first warp jump began, Kalsik called a meeting of the three crewmembers and two passengers. Several things still needed to be clarified, including their methods of investigation at their destination, and separating the distinct roles of the contracted expertise and those of the three crew and the AI. He needed, again, to stress the importance of maintaining secrecy of anything witnessed in the coming expedition.

Within the *Haivres*'s habitat centrifuge, the pivot-mounted modules were in twelve distinct segments. The two life-support modules were unable to pivot and were connected to the central spine that gave access to the zero-gee areas, including the hangars, AI core, cockpit, and utility sites around the rest of the ship. Within the centrifuge, the three crew cabins, each housing up to six, were within the same ring as the two aeroponic modules, the synth-protein and medical lab, the mineral lab, one washroom and water storage, kitchen module, and the crew lounge module.

Face-to-face discussion still had its benefits, despite the common use of neural implants or direct-interface technology. The neural-interface technologies their societies took for granted only imparted knowledge, information, and credible and objective facts. Subjective matters such as decision-making required actual discussion.

With everyone gathered inside the crew lounge module and seated around the multipurpose table, they studied the raised 2-D projected screens showcasing the images and data sent by the previous, ill-fated advanced probe. Eskai Inc. was a Republic organization, so the faint images of the binary stars and the ringed planet, along with the readouts of anomalous debris clouds around both of the stars, were designated in the Kronogri language. Nathan, Serie, and Morthas had to rely on their visor translators during the discussions.

Kalsik led the initial planning conversation, with Morthas as his backup. Morthas's leadership wouldn't come until they actually arrived at one of the anomaly sites.

Shakrii sat, visibly relaxed in her casual, shorter legging and sleeved overalls, her lower arms and small legs with their gray-and-tan scales open to the air. Between a few of her scales, the faint lines of nanorobotic implants could be seen, idle for now apart from basic immune-support functions.

Nathan, his dark-blue pilot overalls rolled down to expose his short-sleeved undershirt, leaned forward, silently and intently studying the data for the system's charted bodies. Serie, beside him, her synth-fiber-belted overalls exposing her lower arms and her wings, was also attentively listening to Kalsik's words.

"Given we don't know what we'll find besides the one anomaly we know about, we'll make a decision now as to our approach." Kalsik turned expectantly to hear any input.

Serie, gesturing cautiously toward one of the images, spoke first. Kalsik and Morthas, seated opposite her, gave their full attention while Nathan continued reading his navigation data, still listening. Off to the side, Shakrii remained quiet.

"Maybe the probe . . . find out what happened to it exactly?"

After grumbling quietly in agreement, Kalsik brought up some feedback data sent from the probe. He looked across the table as he spoke. He was frustrated with the lack of information they had been given, and, obviously, so were most of his companions. "When the probe went offline, accelerometers picked up no changes."

"We can rule out impact damage then."

Shakrii's swift interjection was not entirely welcomed by Kalsik, but he suppressed the faint twinge of irritation, knowing he would have to grow used to her, like a wart that wouldn't go away. Much as he wished she were a parsec away, he wouldn't deny that Shakrii made a valid observation.

"The circuits were overwhelmed before shutdown," observed Serie. "Company has had probes damaged during solar flare activity in the past around other stars."

IVAN's voice broadcast from overhead. "XHK-45V model interstellar probes are designed to automatically shut down if they detect a sufficient electromagnetic surge in systems."

Nodding, Kalsik looked around the table as he gestured with his small, chest-mounted arm, sensing that a decision had been made for their first step in the expedition. Looking to Morthas, who gave a small jerk of his head upward in acknowledgment, Kalsik spoke calmly as he also glanced up in the general direction of IVAN's speakers overhead, knowing that the AI would already have reached the same conclusion he had. "We can find it before we even think of approaching any of the anomalies."

"I am already calculating the trajectory data for us to rendezvous," said IVAN.

"Pass on the data to the nav logs when you're done, will you?" said Nathan.

Shakrii gave a small movement of her chest arms as she began, her tone cautious, which was surprising to Kalsik given her previous abrasiveness. Her next statement, however, proved to him that the company had, indeed, put a very astute military officer onto his ship.

"In the meantime, if it is an intelligent race behind the anomalies, I'd recommend low profile until we know more."

Nathan paused his calculations to look up at Shakrii momentarily. Serie, beside him, glanced between the two of them and nodded to indicate she had come to the same conclusion. Kalsik's eyes widened as he, too, grasped the full picture as Nathan spoke.

"That's why we got a military-grade drive ship, isn't it? It's the shielding we really want to use in case an energy pulse comes at us like it did the probe."

"Yes," said Shakrii. "Electronic countermeasures and shield arrays should protect from any natural event. If it isn't natural, then we'll at least know."

Kalsik noticed that Nathan seemed to take a small degree of reassurance from this, while Morthas waited patiently for this part of the conversation to end. His expertise would be in actually approaching the anomalies themselves, even if the details of that process were still vague.

Serie drew their attention as she leaned forward, inputting new commands on the touchscreen interface, bringing up blueprints to elaborate her point. "The probes get sent out from a cluster on the drive ship designs we usually rent, one per system."

Having worked with the probes over his career, Kalsik found this to be old news as she elaborated for Morthas's and Shakrii's sakes, bringing up projections of the appropriate ship schematics and deployment blueprints. The probes were each fitted with a mini retractable drive ring, behind which the engines, fuel, and radiators for the reactor lay. The front, a bulbous head, housed the sensor and communications array, giving the probe an insect-like appearance.

"Are there any security risks to this initial plan?" he asked.

"None that I can see," replied Shakrii. "It will stop our tech just lying around to be exploited."

Before Kalsik could reply, Morthas pointed out something they had almost forgotten. "Retrieving the probe might not be so easy. Whoever managed to build that ring may already have as much technology as we do."

"Best we still retrieve it," said Shakrii.

With a tap of his claw on the table, Kalsik stopped Shakrii. He smiled inwardly at the briefly registered annoyance on her scaly brow. Serie, who appeared distracted by something under one of her forearm talons, shuffled to turn to him, while Nathan's eyes flickered between her and their captain with thinly veiled amusement. Kalsik pretended to ignore this as Serie said what he was thinking himself.

"We've picked our first course of action. Can we move on?"

Kalsik knew he wasn't the best to speak next, and so turned to the patiently waiting scientist beside him. "Morthas, go ahead."

Nathan raised a hand. "Quick question: Have any of you two been on assignments like this before? First contact potential?"

The question caught Kalsik off guard, but Shakrii immediately responded, and he could sense her level tone wasn't hiding anything.

"No, but I have thoroughly researched many case studies in histories across all five regions, spacefaring or not."

"Same," Morthas said, his tone suggesting a degree of fondness. "I was brought in to document the Zeshigna history for the records after first contact. Well, they spotted a probe that was sent—not too dissimilar to this scenario, actually."

Kalsik licked his scaly lips. Neither answer had really given any reassurance to Nathan's concern.

"Except that probe kept functioning," Nathan remarked dryly.

Morthas didn't reply. Serie waited quietly as Nathan slumped back and then shot him a brief, reassuring look. Kalsik was certain that Nathan would need a few more of those on this expedition.

It only took a minute for Morthas to bring his research up on the screens. "This ring . . . it's too narrow and reflective for a natural ring structure." He brought up a new readout screen, superimposing over the hazy image of the ringed world. This showed positions of stars and the signals originating around their orbits, even at their polar orbits, some as far away as some planets might be. As he explained, Morthas felt a quiver run through his sensory back hairs, one way his kind expressed confusion, something he'd hoped he wouldn't still feel about this image after so long. "Both stars show a haze of debris around them, uniform in dispersion. There is a minimum one-millionth diminished brightness of starlight by these fields."

"Only a millionth?" Serie interjected sarcastically.

"A millionth blocked light is not to be taken humorously," Shakrii said, "even from the smaller red dwarf among this pair."

Morthas was quiet as the engineer shrank in her seat. He saw a shadow pass over Kalsik's dark-scaled face at this whole exchange.

"These clouds," Morthas said. "Are they asteroids or something?"

"Uncertain," Kalsik said. "Orbital debris is usually on a plane similar to other planets, not evenly distributed." Mid-reply, he brought up an image of the orbit paths of the mapped planets in the system's pair of stars, all more or less running parallel, offset by tiny degree variations in their orbital planes. The cloud readouts around both stars showed that they were surrounded by orbiting objects, some orbiting around others which, in turn, orbited around the stars.

Nathan cut in, a skeptical look on his face. "Can't long-range scans detect what they are?"

"The solar radiation interferes with long range too much. If your survey probe had been able to scan for longer, we'd know more." A small exhale of irritation escaped Kalsik.

"Before anything else, we recover the probe. It could be salvageable, especially if its wormhole comms unit is still intact."

"You think we'd need it as backup?" asked Shakrii.

The remark caught Kalsik off guard. He looked at her with a flicker of distrust. Despite the hostility brewing between the two of them, Morthas couldn't dispute the benefits of acquiring any backup communications links to known space that they could.

"I'd prefer to not need it," Kalsik said.

"If we do, we'll have the protective fields generated by our drive ship to protect it this time."

Shakrii's reinforcement to Kalsik's point apparently did nothing to assuage his distrust and resentment of her, something Morthas hoped would fade as their trip progressed. He coughed to regain his audience's attention. "Any questions?"

Nathan raised his hand again and turned to face Shakrii, seemingly acknowledging that she was the more authoritative of the pair of passengers when it came to classified information. "Do we have any idea, even an educated guess, about what we'll find? Is it dangerous or not?"

It was clear to Morthas that this question was weighing heavily on all of them.

Shakrii was quiet for a few moments before she replied coldly, yet without any sign of disrespect. "Morthas has explained it as best can be done."

"So, no . . . ," Nathan said softly.

Serie shifted uncomfortably in her seat, and Morthas attempted to break the tension with a friendly suggestion, hoping his calmness would influence the crew somewhat. He had his own issues with the mission, but he figured he would keep them to himself. "We have a long trip, so let's not worry about this unless something new comes up. The Committee will let us know if they have any concerns."

The brief silence that followed was broken by IVAN. "ETA to SQ-A76 system calculated."

Kronogri dialect was both IVAN's and Eskai Inc.'s default timekeeping method. Automatic translators converted timekeeping to race-appropriate measurements.

In Nathan's case, although he was familiar with Hegaine Republic calendars, IVAN's words translated to twenty-three Sol days on Earth's calendar. Kronogri had no concept of days. Their planet was tidally locked, and therefore their days were as long as their nights, and time was measured in fractions of their orbit-time years.

Such was the variance of the five cultures. Whatever the calendar, this would still be a long voyage with no finite destination, a new experience for most of them. Surveying systems usually meant they operated under the assumption that there would be no intelligent life at their destination. This voyage was different. Morthas knew the specter of the unknowns they faced was a threat unlikely to go away soon.

Chapter 6

Shakrii amid the Crew

Sol Day 12 of Voyage

It hadn't taken long for Shakrii to familiarize herself with day-to-day work aboard the *Haivres* during these long transits. Mercifully, she found that Kalsik kept to his quarters for the most part, as he seemed to be limited to inspection duties every day and not much more. His role would be more crucial when they reached the survey sites.

Still, as she rose each morning, Shakrii used what time she had to closely observe the crew. If she was to be ready to command them in the worst-case scenario, much as she hoped that wouldn't come, she damn well wanted to know them, what they did in their down time, on duty, all their idiosyncrasies.

There was no way out of this trip now, so she had no intention of being a cause of tension amid the crew. Kalsik was probably always going to be abrasive, but she needed the rest of the crew to be on her side.

Nathan was still a problem. As Shakrii sat behind him in the cockpit, he was still very twitchy with her watching him, even when he was performing standard tasks.

While in warp, the drive operated on a timer, precise calculations ensuring the speed and direction of their warp path would deposit them wherever in space they wished. Shakrii had observed this in action when Nathan directed the ship to drop out of warp in order to eject potentially hazardous debris particle buildup in front of the ship.

67

Much of Nathan's time seemed to be spent in the cockpit, overseeing systems shortly before and during a warp dropout, and then ensuring the drive reengaged safely for the next leg. While hooked up into the neural link, the combined raw processing capability of IVAN's quantum computing hardware and Nathan's brain ensured the most precise warp calculations possible. While IVAN would have been sufficient, it was company safety policy, and also Nathan's preference, to combine the decision-making. Historically, one too many ships had been lost because they had inadvertently dropped out of warp inside an asteroid, planet, or star.

Serie, meanwhile, seemed to spend much of her time in the zero-gee sections of the ship, inspecting and running the more advanced diagnostics. If Shakrii was to credit that bitter Kronogri, Kalsik, with one thing, it was that he'd picked a decent pilot and engineer.

Serie's responsibilities were with the ship's systems—more specifically, tasks that could be done from inside the pressurized crew sections. Any inspection work within the interior, unpressurized parts of the ship structure was handled by a few rodent-sized drones.

The ship's shield arrays protected against solar radiation. Larger arrays on military craft could be surged to protect against energy weapons, but this ship was only protected from natural phenomena. Matter impacts, especially micrometeorites, often peppered the spacecraft's outer hull, hence the repair drones on the exterior carrying tools to perform supplemental repairs to the largely self-healing hull.

Serie came across as slightly smug about reminding the crew that she was responsible for keeping them alive, despite IVAN's protestations that he had no reason to let their health fall into jeopardy.

Shakrii admired the relationship between Serie and IVAN. They appeared to work seamlessly as a maintenance team, squabbles aside.

~~~

Much to Shakrii's surprise, as the days had crawled by, she noticed that, mostly, the crew were less distrustful of her, even though she remained reserved. They seemed to be more relaxed around her, although Kalsik remained aloof. She knew enough about other races' body language to recognize that Nathan was still wary of her. Today he was finishing up his duties, reinitiating a warp jump before unstrapping himself, giving off the faint malodorous waft of oily secretions that humans exuded for heat management—"sweat" they called it—which she was polite in not complaining about. The human clearly had an issue with nervousness, probably exacerbated by her watching him.

With Nathan, Shakrii noted that usually, when his immediate stress was over, he visibly loosened up, but that wasn't the case today. He drifted down the corridor ahead of her, leaving the flight deck and heading for the centrifuge hub. Finally, he spoke to her and, much to her surprise, suggested something that Shakrii was annoyed she hadn't thought of herself.

"So, we . . . I mean, Serie and I . . . were thinking of making a meal. We've got supplies for both DNA chiralities, if you're interested."

"If it breaks up my usual meals, then I'm interested."

With a light shrug, as he steadied his footing on the nano-grip floor tiles by holding on to a wall, Nathan took on a more casual tone. Shakrii could sense he was relaxing as the conversation went on. She was surprised at his next statement, though.

"If you want to have anything special, let me know. I'm the cook among us."

"I didn't take you for a cook, let alone a multispecies one."

"My secret is strict adherence to the recipes."

There it was again, that tendency to fall back on specific regulations. It was a good trait, though, as given the choice, she would take overly cautious over reckless in a heartbeat. His remark also reminded her of one odd occasion in her earlier life, and she let a slight chuckle rise from her throat, her kind's guttural vocals making it resemble snoring to Nathan.

"One of my partners in the army nearly burnt down the barracks after attempting seared uthraak."

"Thankfully we don't have uthraak. Kalsik banned it. Hates the stuff."

With a dismissive, toothy flash, Shakrii spoke with her own tone as casual as she could muster. "I don't like it myself—too dry."

"Agreed. Tastes like insulation foam."

She was curious, and slightly confused. She looked him up and down as she spoke. "You eat food not native to your kind?"

"Once I take precautions, decon it for bacteria and such."

"Even dextro foods? Your body doesn't take any of it in."

He raised a finger at her valid point and gave a small smile before gesturing to his lower torso. "I can taste it."

"Your taste senses are not the same as a Leg'hrul's or a Yaleirn's."

"Good enough to know when it's as it should be." With a polite nod, the human turned and left, treading carefully as he went up the small stairwell that led to the centrifuge entry hall.

Shakrii glanced at her wrist and transferred her thoughts on the interaction with Nathan to the recorder implanted there. She found the audiovisual diaries it created especially useful when it came to analyzing others' behavior. She would go over this one in more detail later.

Every encounter helped her build a more detailed psych profile of each crewmember. If she couldn't read people immediately, she made sure to gather information to review later, enabling her to develop specific strategies which she could use to her advantage, ranging from influence to outright blackmail.

Shakrii wasn't proud of her initial distrust of anyone, and never had been, but it was a crucial habit she wasn't about to abandon, especially if it benefited her and her coworkers in the long run.

~~~

In Serie's case, Shakrii had taken to asking her specific questions about the ship itself. She was particularly intrigued at how an ex-military design had been retrofitted for corporate use. To her delight, the moment that confirmed the loss of most of the tension with Serie came a third of the way through the voyage, when one of the aeroponic growth chambers for the dextro-protein-based plants broke down, the spray pipes having suffered a small leak. Serie normally had difficulty accessing it, because of all the smaller wires and pipes that were in the way, and it was a repair task she strongly disliked. As narrow and lithe as Leg'hrul claws and lower wings were, the chest arms of the Kronogri were among the smallest profile of limbs, and Shakrii was quick to offer her assistance. She reached into the gap easily, removed the faulty pipes, and fitted their replacements.

Serie gave her a small smile of gratitude. "Thank the stars for Kronogri kind's smaller set of arms."

Shakrii stepped back in her kind's equivalent of a shrug, knowing she had the ship's engineer on her side.

The Leg'hrul hesitated for a moment, and then said quietly, "About Kalsik, he's normally more casual, even if still . . . never mind. He said you being here brought back his time in service, of which he's never given us any details."

"I'm not surprised."

Looking curious now, Serie paused, still kneeling, from replacing the panel of the aeroponic module, the mist sprays inside the transparent container fogging the plant layers inside to facilitate their rapid growth. "What do you know?"

Shakrii exhaled audibly, deciding to share some details of her extensive research on

71

the crew. "I did background checks on everyone. I like to know who I'm going to be with."

Serie visibly scoffed. "We can't be perfectly defined by a file. Even IVAN has his own traits, and he's code in processors."

"By that logic," came IVAN's voice, "you are nucleic acid inside cells."

As she looked up at the ceiling speakers, Shakrii appreciated that the AI was a presence she sometimes forgot about, as he was the least troublesome crewmember. She let some humor creep into her voice. "Your AI is more expressive than his background suggests."

"We're not quite what your checks suggested, are we?"

Shakrii tried to rescue the situation and apologized, keen to stay on this Leg'hrul's good side. "I find it hard to trust, so it's worth the effort to fill in the gaps, especially if we're all going to be on this ship for the foreseeable future"

"Well, if you can get Kalsik to trust you on a professional level, he'll do anything necessary for the ship and crew."

With a grimace, Shakrii was aware that she knew more than Serie could imagine about Kalsik. The contents of the top-secret reports weighed heavily on her. "I never doubted it, nor will I divulge. Even without the military secrecy binding such information, I'll be mature enough to be discreet."

With a slight huff as she stood up, Serie showed her disappointment. She cocked her head toward the ceiling as if to indicate that IVAN was listening. "Typical, was hoping it might be innocent embarrassment maybe."

"Everyone has their personal secrets, but even if they pose no danger, there's no reason to reveal them. No need to dwell on them."

Serie's eyes widened slightly at the mention of family, though Shakrii paid it no heed. She knew the Leg'hrul had family issues in her past, ones that seemed to be old news, buried and dealt with, not worth much more trouble.

The fact that she knew so much was going to be a sore topic with the others, Shakrii suspected. Luckily, many days remained before they would reach the system, and tensions would likely have simmered down by then.

~~~

Later that night, as the ship's lights dimmed slightly on a scheduled day/night cycle, Shakrii was finishing up in the ship's washroom module in the centrifuge ring, the shower flow aiding in scrubbing off the loose scales that she shed regularly. Soon, her scales were smoothed out, all the irritating, decayed ones gone, leaving the small, craggy scars on her back as the only imperfections, memories from one or two injuries too severe for her implants or medical aid to heal fast enough before they scarred beneath her scales.

Refreshed and ready to get some rest, Shakrii shuffled along the hallways to her cabin. The steam from the washrooms gave way to the cool air in the centrifuge ring. As she came past the habitat module for lesser crewmembers, she and Nathan nearly ran into each other. He mumbled a quiet apology and made a beeline for the washrooms she'd just come from. She glanced through the partially open door to his quarters and saw a dark-blue, feathered form in the bed. It was Serie, nestled casually in the covers and on the pillows, her torso uncovered with her back turned to the door, unaware of her observer.

Shakrii put that unexpected sight away for the moment and made her way farther around the ring. She passed through the mineral lab to find Morthas still sitting at his display console, running yet more analyses of their destination's data, accumulated courtesy of the Committee and all associated research organizations.

"Still working?"

Morthas replied with barely a glance toward her, merely rubbing his eyes of any drowsiness, still glued to the display before him as a new process was run on the data. "More observation data of the twin stars came through."

"I take it Kalsik's in his quarters?"

"Yes, why?"

"Just a small matter."

"If you hear snoring, don't bother. According to Nathan, anything less than a hull breach won't wake him."

Suppressing a laugh, Shakrii bade Morthas good night as she headed down the halls again, around to the double crew module occupied only by the captain at the moment. She raised her chest hand to knock on Kalsik's door, knowing he likely wouldn't be pleased to see her.

The door swiftly opened, and the captain stood there holding a data pad showing a digital novel he'd picked up while off the ship. His scaly face furrowed at the brows when he saw her. She kept her expression neutral, ignoring the fact that he was in his underclothes.

"What?"

"May I ask you a question?"

"You've been prodding around with my crew. You have all our backgrounds. Surely that's enough."

Shakrii raised one of her chest hands in a gesture of calm. "It's about your two crewmembers."

Kalsik's scaly brows furrowed again, his head crests shivering slightly as a growl crept through his body.

Shakrii calmly tried to placate him as she could see bubbles forming beneath his scales. "Not that I question it. This isn't a military ship, but are you aware of their . . . situation?"

"What are you talking about?"

Her tongue almost clicked in irritation as Shakrii jabbed a chest hand sideways, pointing back down the hallway. "Those two sharing a bed moments ago."

"They often do. So what?"

Shakrii maintained an air of calm. She wasn't bothered about interracial relations, at least among the five established races. She herself remained only attracted to her kind, yet she wasn't closeminded like others she had encountered. What mattered was the nature of this relationship, if it posed a danger to crew and mission integrity. "I just wondered if you knew."

"They've worked under me for three Sol years. Halfway through is when this began. And let's not pretend that fraternization doesn't happen aboard military vessels, even Republic ones. I know what went on, personal experiences of mine among them."

"I just wanted to be sure—"

"There isn't a problem you have with my crew, is there?"

Kalsik's pointed question was more barbed than she expected, making Shakrii grimace. She shuffled on her large forelimbs and smaller back legs, hating having to be submissive to keep the peace. "Not at all."

He stared at her, his four eyes expectant as they bored into her own.

She looked him dead in the eyes. "Captain."

Bristling under her scales, she watched Kalsik pass her by and vanish down the centrifuge corridor, noticing the ghost of a wrinkled, toothy twitch of his mouth. If she had been less disciplined and experienced, she would have cursed, but she knew better than to waste such air. Kalsik was enjoying having an active Kronogri militant under his direct authority. His grudge made him immature when he was off duty—that much had already been suggested in his profile. She would have to tolerate Kalsik's silent satisfaction in reminding her that she was his subordinate—at least until they reached their destination, or when he finally realized she wasn't here to usurp him.

Still, she had to admit, he had shown an improvement since they started; his borderline hostility had given way to smug superiority.

Chapter 7

Intra-Crew Dinner

Sol Day 13 of Voyage

The next evening—the time of day signified by the ship's light-dimming cycles—the crew were ready for some food outside the norm of their daily meals. Even with the ship's company not being wholly pleasant to deal with, particularly Kalsik, Shakrii wasn't deterred from attending. The intriguing smells coming from the kitchen module only heightened her interest. Mercifully for her, Kalsik sat away from the crew lounge's main table, reclining on a corner seat as his four eyes scanned a digital novel projected over his visor.

At the main table, Shakrii sat opposite Serie. The two engaged in a digital game on the screen, common in Kronogri space, called *Barachae*. Simulated planets and their exaggerated gravity were used as gravity-well slingshots, the goal being to launch armed projectiles with precision, using these wells, to get as close to the targeted area as possible and achieve the highest score. With no extra software to help them, they had to eyeball their shots, something Shakrii noticed Serie wasn't too skilled at. The Leg'hrul's growing frustration was too funny for her to offer any pointers.

Out of the corner of her gaze, Shakrii noted Morthas finally arriving. She saw Kalsik spare him a sideways glance before returning to his reading.

"Finally crawled out of the lab?" Serie quipped at Morthas, drawing a smirk from Shakrii.

77

"I never miss a good meal," Morthas said. "But when it's over, I'll be back there."

"Maybe you'll find out something that months of analysis by Committee experts hasn't already."

"Hopefully."

Serie, who had just conceded the game to Shakrii, blinked at Morthas's earnest remark, seemingly stunned at his obliviousness to her sarcasm. But she wasn't the only one. Shakrii caught Kalsik's wry expression as he dropped the book.

Apparently, IVAN agreed as well. "An oblivious reply."

Finally understanding the whole exchange, Morthas dismissed it with a wave of his claws, still maintaining the enthusiasm for his task that he'd exhibited when he first came aboard. He looked quizzically at both Serie and Kalsik. "Why are you encouraging your AI like that?"

"On these long voyages," Serie said, "there's plenty of time to self-improve. Though IVAN's pessimistic humor isn't something I personally wished for."

The AI responded: "With your encouragement of artisan understanding as a goal on your behalf, such humor is classified as an art in itself."

Shakrii barely managed to suppress an amused snort.

Serie's face turned mildly sour, though Shakrii sensed it was merely mock irritation at this point. If anything, Morthas seemed more intrigued by this crew interplay than she was, though his profession didn't have him on ships and long voyages as frequently as Shakrii, so this was likely still more of a novelty for him. It was common for AIs above certain thresholds to adopt emotional inflections to better fit into organic conversation, and, simulated or not, it was still a sort of personality.

Intriguing organic and synthetic interplay aside, Shakrii's gut was twinging, her body pleading for some of the food responsible for the aromas emanating from the kitchenette. Not wishing to be impolite, she continued to wait, but Kalsik didn't have any such reservations.

"Get the food out!" he grumbled. "The smell is maddening."

"You'll get it when it's done!" Nathan bellowed from inside the kitchen.

Off to Shakrii's side, Serie had invited Morthas to play a game. *Probably so she can actually beat someone*, thought Shakrii.

"I haven't played *Barachae* in a long time, but sure."

While Serie and Morthas set up their game, Shakrii cast her gaze over to Kalsik. The elder male Kronogri now had eyes only for the digital novel on his visor, just occasionally glancing at the ceiling. If anything, this was better. It meant that until he improved his professional behavior, he would give her space unless it was mission critical. Shakrii wasn't bothered. She paid little heed to the Kronogri, choosing instead to watch the *Barachae* game between Serie and Morthas.

~~~

Nathan had put the onboard meat culture fabricators and aeroponic units to good use. He produced food not often grown, because of the time involved. On long voyages, simpler food was served. Today, however, they had proper, muscled meat of whichever type they chose, and fruit from plants only grown on special occasions.

With two of them being Leg'hrul and their biology being dextro-based DNA chirality, the bioplastic cartons used as serving dishes were color coded. Levo-based food for the sole human and two Kronogri was served in green boxes, while dextro-based food could be found in blue boxes. Although consuming incompatible food didn't present any significant health hazards, it was best to segregate them, as allowing species to consume unsuitable foods could overburden the ship's plumbing and waste management systems.

Not that it stopped some crew from sampling opposite compatible food. In fact, dextro food tasted rather sweet to levo-based organisms, and vice versa, as many chemicals associated with sweetness in both chemistries were usually the opposite biochemistry.

While she chewed her soup containing chopped pieces of a sweet-tasting arthropod from her home planet, Shakrii paused for a moment and noticed the metaphorical black hole beside her. Upon finishing another dish of stewed meat cutlets and assorted spice-laden vegetables, Morthas seemed unaware of the odd expressions from across the table at how much he was putting away.

Gluttonous as he may have been, Morthas was always polite in offering Serie some food before he helped himself. Shakrii was surprised. Leg'hrul usually ate less due to their lower density—in keeping with their avian past—yet he proved to be the exception. Based on what Shakrii saw, if he'd tried to fly on his home world, the results would likely have been amusing. She turned her attention away from him as he began to devour his third helping, focusing herself on finishing her high-fiber meal of rich meat slices and sliced root vegetables.

She licked some stray meat juices off her scaly lower mouth before she glanced toward Nathan slicing up and eating some sort of fish, judging by the texture of it. "I was expecting prestored or basic grown stuff at most on this trip," she said.

After gulping down his mouthful, Morthas added his compliments to the cook. "Do you do this often?"

"When we feel like it," Serie said, "though Nathan's the cook, so he needs to be up for it too." She reached over to lightly clap her claws on Nathan's back as she smiled at him.

Nathan shrugged, adding with a more deadpan expression, "That, and socializing at a different meal together becomes kind of a requirement unless you'd like to be bored into a coma."

"Ah, but that's because we haven't arrived at the site yet. Once there, we'll have much to not be bored about." Morthas put down his utensils and paused in his eating.

Serie shrugged. "For good or bad, yes."

Shakrii caught the faint disappointment that flickered briefly across Morthas's mandibled beak.

"What were you doing before coming here?" Nathan asked.

Morthas looked slightly uncomfortable. "Xenoarchaeologist. I published my dissertation on the downfall of the Wyvaeri race. New theory about why they went extinct as fast as they did."

"They never made it past their home system, right?" Serie interjected.

"That's right. No outside intervention, no natural disaster or other attack. Whatever killed them was self-inflicted. A disease wiped them out, along with the global war they fought. My theory is that the disease may have been a bioweapon gone wrong by how total it was." Morthas seemed a little bitter. "Not exciting headlines. Plus, the papers are still under peer review, mine among them. They want to release them in bulk. I wasn't a well-known and trusted mind when I published, so more scrutiny was given."

"Age bringing experience?" Kalsik cut in. "It's just an excuse to make life hell for the young."

Shakrii noticed Serie and Nathan exchange glances. Obviously they had their own opinions.

"To that you could say youth is more open-minded, to a fault," Shakrii offered.

As valid as she felt her remark was, she detected the shadow of a glare on Kalsik's face, his eyes flickering to her for a moment.

"You think where we're headed might be a similar story?" Serie asked in a lower tone. "One heavily developed system suddenly empty?"

"It was one reason I was among the candidates chosen for this trip." Morthas's rather dismissive reply wasn't enough for Nathan.

"Yeah, you and Shakrii. Rest of us were witnesses who needed to be kept quiet."

"It was in our contracts," Kalsik said, shutting down Nathan's irritation about their circumstances.

"Sorry if I feel like we're underqualified for this task," Nathan replied curtly to his captain.

Shakrii decided to cut in, knowing that reassurances were better than nothing. She had learned that the best crews worked with discipline that came from mutual respect, by trust and enforcement where necessary, including placating justified fears. "That's why they sent us. We don't want anybody doing work they aren't prepared for."

Serie leaned forward. "So why did you have IVAN download some massive data loads the past few nights?"

Shakrii kept her response as succinct as her previous statement, knowing she had to maintain at least some air of professional composure. "Your AI will be a valuable partner in any task. That data was Committee-approved."

Not letting the matter settle entirely, Serie turned her gaze upward to the overhead sensors and the AI she knew was always online. "Fine, but I know he may avoid using those art programs with all this. Wouldn't be the first time he was too busy to enrich himself."

"I question the validity in learning cultural expressionism of organics," said IVAN.

Serie was clearly annoyed at this. Nathan, meanwhile, let out a snort of amusement at IVAN's continued stubbornness about Serie's attempts to culture him.

"If you understand the cultural nuances," Kalsik said, "you understand them better, their strengths and weaknesses, friend or foe."

Surprised and impressed, Shakrii let a small grin creep across her scaly features as she looked at Kalsik. "Qaiarex's codex, you remember?"

"Required reading in mandatory service. Couldn't forget it if I tried."

Kalsik's grouchy remark did little to sour the new respect Shakrii had for the captain. Beside her, however, Morthas was about to ask another question when a beeping sounded from the kitchen module down the hallway.

Nathan's voice cut across the table, the human standing up as he began to pick up the empty platters immediately before him. "If we're done talking philosophy, that'll be the last food out."

The others handed their platters and utensils to the human, as the final round of food on this unusual dinner was about to be served. Shakrii felt that some of the tension between the captain and herself was easing, although it still had a long way to go.

~~~

Morthas managed to add plenty to his already full stomach. Nathan had catered well with a mixture of sweet cooked goods, fruits and their comparatives, providing for all the races.

Conversations turned to the ship and the company owning it. Morthas wanted the input of the crew to add to the official data he had already compiled. "Eskai's ships seem to have many integrated crews, varied in species. Progressive groups across space seem to like it."

The compliment earned a rumbling laugh from Kalsik. "It's not for principled reasons—not primarily."

Confused, Morthas looked to Nathan, who shifted slightly in his seat.

"Many ships like ours can be out for extended periods—very extended at times," Nathan said.

"They don't want an outbreak killing off the crew with them being too far out for help to arrive in time," Kalsik added.

Morthas finally understood, and beside him, Shakrii's eyes widened briefly in realization. She seemed to laugh slightly at the morbid thought, but Morthas, recognizing that this would be no laughing matter if it did occur, looked very serious.

Serie offered a halfhearted simplification. "So, if we get something that affects levos like Nathan, Captain, and Shakrii, me and you will be fine. Same the other way."

"Means the company has less close family to pay life insurance to if that does happen." Nathan's joke only further sealed the rather bleak humor behind the inarguably valid corporate strategy.

Still, humorous or not, Morthas shifted uncomfortably, his dessert platter momentarily unappetizing.

"Why would they contract a disease that presumably had been screened?" Shakrii interjected.

"Joint space laws can require us to act on certain encounters," Serie remarked between bits of the sweet berry-glazed bread on her platter. "Biggest risk is derelict ships, or planets with ecosystems."

"Ever hear of the *Krunime*?" Kalsik asked. "Survey ship like this one?"

"I have," said Shakrii.

"Military clearance will get you that, I bet. Derelict Eithraak settler ship. Crew went aboard, found the passengers dead by an alien virus with a long incubation period. Their levo-based crew fell ill. One of them nearly died, but Leg'hrul were immune to the virus. With that, mixed-race crews were encouraged."

Off to the side, the sole human grumbled under his breath before speaking in a guarded tone. "So, if there's any levo-based life where we're going, I'd rather avoid setting foot off this ship."

Before Morthas's mental train could get much further, Kalsik cut across the table. "The ringed planet orbits a brighter star, heavy with UV rays. I'll bet we'd need to wear suits anyway. However, if Morthas asks, we will all help in the exploration."

The male Kronogri's sudden blunt remark was aimed first at Nathan, but it carried to Serie as well. Morthas knew Kalsik didn't need to address IVAN. They all knew the AI was listening.

Morthas thought a bit of optimism might lighten the mood. "Our kind developed on a home world around a UV-heavier star. Maybe we could risk shirtsleeves, with a heavy antibiotic dose, of course."

Serie asked in a tone of disbelief, "You seriously would be willing to take that risk?"

"Only after study of the biosphere. Besides, I hate sealed suits—not at all comfortable."

Shakrii's gruff voice trilled beside Morthas. "Don't strip until we know the air's safe, at least."

Morthas hid a fluster in his plumage and finished his food. The rest of the dinner and evening passed uneventfully. While this social evening did ease tensions noticeably, Morthas knew that the uncertainty of their destination was still hanging over them. He only hoped that, once the mission truly got underway, when questions began to get answered, their minds might settle, and they could move forward with their mission to investigate the upcoming star system and its mysteries. Hardly anybody stayed entirely the same during an unusual mission. This was one certainty. But busy hands were less easily unnerved, a fact universal across all species discovered so far. Getting down to work at last would benefit them all.

Chapter 8

SQ-A76

Sol Day 23 of Voyage

There was no grand revelation when they arrived in the system, no suggestion that this collection of paired stars and associated planets was anything besides normal.

Space-time distorted in the instant the *Haivres* and its drive ship emerged from the warp bubble as it collapsed in a blue shift of light. The high-energy particles collected in this last interstellar jump along their warp bubble blasted forward in a prominent burst, harmlessly flying into the empty void, as was common practice so as not to cause any damage to something smaller than a gas giant or unpopulated planet.

Of course, Kalsik knew that militaries sometimes used close-quarters warp-out ionized particulate bursts as weapons when necessary. One incident a few decades before had been so powerful that it was classified as a war crime, on the same level as a kinetic bombardment by redirected asteroid or a high-yield WMD weapon when used on civilian population structures.

If there was an intelligence here, Kalsik knew that it would undoubtedly be aware of the incomers' presence once their sensors detected the blue warp dropout light. This was the point of no return for the crew. They had revealed themselves, and all they could do was keep their profile low or nonthreatening, just to be safe.

At Nathan's command, the *Haivres* began the thrust burn to orient its trajectory and velocity to fall into a stable orbit around the primary star of the system. The corrective delta-v was well within the limits of the ship's capabilities.

To Kalsik's eyes, the dual stars, a binary pair of a larger, more splendid white main sequence and a faint, blood-colored red dwarf, were entwined in a dance of sorts— imbalanced, mismatched but harmonious fusion furnaces burning within the near-endless expanse of the galaxy.

Kalsik was sure to pass on a reconfirmation of their initial survey to the others, the data their ill-fated probe had managed to collect months ago. But per his orders, which Morthas had supported as acting expedition leader for now, a fuel stop was required at the innermost gas giant to replenish their energy reserves.

After another brief warp jump, they arrived at the gas giant, the fierce white light of the star it orbited contrasting with the darker, rust-colored clouds of the immense planet.

Nathan brought the ship into an appropriate orbital dive, and intake vents opened on the sides to begin harvesting the thin upper layers of gas for use as reactor fuel and propellant, the engines burning occasionally to counter what minuscule air resistance they met, the ship rumbling slightly as they skimmed through the upper clouds.

After a day of refueling, they departed the gas giant and readied for another warp jump within the system. Red-shifting out of view, the ship once again transported itself many hundreds of millions of kilometers away, within the inner planetary regions of the main star's influence.

As the ship blue-shifted and shut down the spatial drive, basic scanners were engaged. Kalsik saw their target as a faint white speck in the distance outside the cockpit's view displays. It didn't take them more than a few moments to begin moving closer to finally recover their hardware.

The probe, resembling a large insect, drifted slowly through the void. IVAN's analysis of its scans flooded the display screens on the bridge with data for the crew to view.

As he leaned forward in his seating straps, Kalsik grumbled, more to himself than to the other two on the bridge. He hated the inactivity of the long journeys, the rife uncertainty of this one making it even worse, but at least they could now get down to business. "Looks intact." With a nod toward the pilot seat, sparing a cursory glance toward Shakrii, Kalsik continued to review the information as Nathan spoke to IVAN.

The maneuvering thrusters pulsed repeatedly as the probe slowly approached the underside of the *Haivres*, reducing the difference in their two velocities until they were equal, and Kalsik, looking at his terminal, saw the probe nestling in the shadow of the ship.

Underneath, the loading bay opened, and the long arm extended and pivoted out toward the probe. Kalsik watched as one of the small, crablike drones crawled along the arm, attached a cable from the grapple arm's head to itself, and gently pushed off into space. Tiny thrusters adjusted its position to enable a leg equipped with a nano-grip surface to attach to the probe's sensor pod.

The cable drew the drone back in toward the arm, bringing the probe with it, to be gripped by the loading arm. The drone scuttled back up the slowly retracting arm into the loading bay, where Serie waited to play her part.

Shakrii spoke into the intercom. "Scan the probe, coding to outer framing."

Kalsik glanced at her, a ripple of irritation passing down his spine. Already she was actively telling his crew what to do, yet for now, he said nothing. He had fully expected her to try to assume command at some point, and a part of him was pleased that she was confirming his suspicions.

"Like I wouldn't know procedures for—"

Shakrii shut off the channel before Serie's backtalk could finish, not tolerating any of that. "A shame it went offline, or we might not need to be here."

Kalsik had to concede her point. The only reason they were here was because that probe had malfunctioned and needed a less-vulnerable backup party to attend, a ship designed to carry more fully fledged intelligences, cellular or coded. Kalsik couldn't help but recall the problems he'd seen in many probes in the twelve Sol years he had spent on survey ships, the *Haivres* for ten of them, including defective probes he had only researched as part of Eskai Inc. "If it was a solar storm, the probe's orbit would show drift. Whatever knocked it out was precise."

"The drive ship's shielding can take more than your probe could." Shakrii's surprisingly reassuring tone did little to allay Kalsik's concerns.

Nathan asked, "What if we're caught when not docked with the drive ship, if *Haivres* lands somewhere?"

"Hope it doesn't come." The simple statement from Shakrii was no reassurance, but if Kalsik could give her credit for anything, it was that she didn't downplay risks or act dishonestly with anyone.

~~~

Down in the *Haivres*'s lower deployment bay, locked into grapples in the ceiling, Serie began her work, eager to find out what had screwed up this probe.

The lower bay hatches were sealed now, creating a vacuum. No living organisms were kept in here long term. The form-fitting spacesuit hugged her plumage tight against her, tail feathers and wings tucked into extended segments and folded in on themselves. Her visor projected the data readouts as she set to work.

IVAN's voice cut in over her communications link inside her helmet as he undertook his own scans through the drones or overhead sensors. "Scans show no hazardous radioactivity."

"Keep running software scans. Check for physical damage." She opened up the panels on the probe and removed a few solar arrays in her way. She shined her lighting tool on the circuits, the readouts on her interior visor confirming what she had already seen. "Melted circuits."

"Multiple errors detected. The data is too corrupted."

Serie scowled to herself as she sealed up the probe for storage. "Nonquantum circuits. Cheap but easy to fry." Drifting over to the midsection of the probe, the central bulbous unit behind the computing core, Serie began to ready her tools. The probe's unit was half her height, and spherical in shape, and she set about removing the nonessential radiators, solar panels, and computing and propulsion systems. "We'll salvage what we can."

As she began to work, her multiple tools undoing the modular joints of the parts one by one, the crablike drone drifted about, grabbing the loose parts she removed and depositing them inside a small storage slot. Debris floating about inside the zero-gee environment would be a hazard.

~~~

Inside the laboratory module of the *Haivres*'s centrifuge, his equipment pushed aside for now, Morthas examined the readouts once more, eager to add to the data he had already. Now he knew he could truly begin to assume command of the investigative aspect of this mission.

The initial readings were projected on the 2D holoscreen before him. Of the stars in question, he kept his focus on the larger white star they currently orbited. The binary pair of stars were so far apart that each exerted its own orbital influence, unlike many other systems where planets orbited around a center of gravity created by a close pair of stars.

"The primary star—high-energy main sequence. Are you sure it wouldn't be able to emit strong enough solar flares?"

His question over the comms was quickly answered.

"These probes are graded for solar flare levels from any star under hazard tier 5," Serie said. "It would take a giant's solar flare or worse."

This ruled out any natural phenomena, a tantalizing yet worrying sign. It left only a disturbing alternative.

"So, definitely a pulse attack," Shakrii said. "But who fired it?"

"Last image it took was of that planet," Kalsik interjected. "We're headed there anyway."

"What about the star debris clouds?" Morthas asked.

After a few quiet seconds, Kalsik cut in again. "We know for certain the planet has something."

Now IVAN brought up an image of the cube-shaped craft in question. "Our microsatellite arrays are suitably equipped to change trajectory and scan the debris clouds, acquire multisensory readings."

Nathan responded quickly, weighing up the idea, as did Morthas.

"Do it. We'll have time to look at the planet while they approach the star." Morthas couldn't help but let eagerness slip into his voice, as this meant they could tackle the planet and star anomalies simultaneously. Evidently, judging by their silence, all the crew agreed.

"Why not both star clouds?" Shakrii asked.

Her question was a valid one, and it made Morthas pause for a moment. Thinking about the data they already had, he admitted what was an educated guess at worst, but one he knew would likely be accepted, given everyone's nervousness about their position. "The readings suggest that both clouds are made of the same constituents. May as well check the bigger one."

Not much more was said after that. Now all that remained was to get underway. While he sympathized with the tensions the others felt, Morthas could barely hide the excitement creeping into his every fiber.

~~~

Before they made the final warp jump to their ultimate destination, small hatches opened in the *Haivres*'s sides and jettisoned a large number of thirty-centimeter cubic microsatellites. Slowly drifting away, they came online one by one, four folding panels of solar arrays deployed to make each resemble a letter *X*. Each cube's high-efficiency thrusters began their long burns, the solar energy flooding their propulsion systems to begin gently changing the probes' trajectories to an orbit close to the debris clouds around the star.

Meanwhile, out of range of the satellites, space red-shifted once more, propelling the ship toward the distant ringed planet that was its destination, leaving the micro flock to their weeks of elliptical orbit and scanning.

~~~

Sol Day 24

SQ-A76, Primary Star

Ringed Planet

The planet and its associated system were a marvel to behold.

Of the three moons, the two larger ones were round orbs reflecting the distant starlight off their slate-gray-and-black-banded surfaces, featureless and plain-looking. Sharing the orbit path of one of the moons was a much smaller moon, oddly shaped, like a pear, drifting a third of the way around the path of orbit.

Upon coming out of warp between the moons and their planet, the *Haivres* and its drive ship continued along a trajectory toward the planet. As the hours rolled by and the planet loomed larger, the enormity of what they were dealing with became clear. The crew were stunned by what they saw with their naked eyes through the ship's sensor display viewports. The ring hyperstructure was immense, positioned in a mid-level orbit around the planet. The gargantuan construct orbited 8,000 kilometers above the planet surface, measuring just under 100,000 kilometers in circumference. At its narrowest point, it measured 1 kilometer across, though its skeletal frame showed that it was not entirely solid.

At eight equidistant points around the ring were large nodes, each a massive feat of construction resembling a rectangular box 200 kilometers long and 100 kilometers tall and wide. A structure this massive must have been very carefully made by positioning each of the eight node stations with such precision as not to deform the comparatively narrow ring structure when it was all linked together.

As for the planet itself, with a 7,500-kilometer radius and a density similar to many planets within the habitable zone for water-based life, it had a surface gravity of 11.77 m/s/s, or 1.2 Earth gravities, tolerable for any of the Trans-Stellar races.

There were only two obvious oceans, vast ones. The other bodies of water were too small, snaking or fractured, to be considered anything more than seas at best. Roughly 18 percent of the planet's surface was land, something that solved any fears of large temperature variations. Liquid water, clouds, and polar ice on the planet indicated the maximum extent of temperature swings they could anticipate. In fact, there were not many large continents, with the exception being a large landmass in what they would denote as the south of the planet, the rest of the land being fractured archipelagos.

A quick look out the window was enough to show Morthas that the land was covered by a multitude of ecosystems. Polar ice at both ends, dense, pale-red forests at the tropics, along with tundra regions, deserts, and mountain ranges dotted the landscape.

The atmosphere scans revealed one unsurprising aspect consistent with the large amounts of water in all three matter states: a high level of oxygen at 25 percent. The obvious presence of a plant equivalent, mostly large swaths of red to yellow, indicated that oxygen was used by the ecosystem's life-forms, bio signs indicating photosynthetic life-forms.

Of course, life could exist without water. Indeed, many life-forms had been found, even complex ones, that existed entirely without water, and the still-expanding Vughaam sub-Union member state's species was an example of an ammonia-based industrialized species that used neither water nor oxygen. But the ease of industrializing given by an oxygen environment offered promise that they would find organic intelligence here.

It didn't take long to spot the anomalies around the equator, features Morthas was truly puzzled by. A pair of large, perfectly circular gray islands lay in the middle of the oceans along the equator, a massive but shallow-sloped and oval-shaped mountain neatly perched atop each one. Along a large, *S*-shaped island, and the largest continent, again directly around the equator, similar circular-based oval mountains rose, larger and taller than their surrounding terrain by a factor greater than Morthas had ever seen on any maps, even of very exotic planets.

As such, he was not at all surprised when initial scans revealed them to be artificial constructs. They were three hundred kilometers at their widest base, and fifteen kilometers tall, like oversized shield volcanoes except for the perfectly oval nature of their bases. The circular construct beneath took up the lowest kilometer of height. Cutting across the widest point of each mountain was a dead-straight band a few kilometers across at least. Its ridges and straight cliffs were visible even from space.

These four mountains at each quarter turn of the planet's axis were too evenly spaced to be natural.

Oddly though, all unnatural development was along the equator. Were it not for those features, and the ring around the planet, it would have been deemed a rare garden world. Perhaps, Morthas pondered, that may have been why the builders had made these structures, because they had a lucky find. Yet that still didn't explain many other things.

After settling into a circular orbit below the ring, Nathan had IVAN dispatch more microsatellites to set up a small network around the planet, ensuring anything that went down would have communications coverage once planetside.

With that done, he disengaged from the mixed neural and screen interface controls, rubbing his temples as he relaxed. The entirety of the passengers and crew were present behind him, drifting in the zero-gee environment, the cockpit offering the best viewing experience of the planet and surroundings.

"Probes on the way out," Nathan said. "They'll have the planet mapped in three rotations."

Shakrii moved to hover over Nathan's shoulder as she checked the readout screens for herself. He wasn't fond of her desire to audit his work, as he had already double-checked it himself. He admitted he had some habitual tendencies, but he had little patience for anyone else's.

"Rotation for this planet?" Shakrii asked.

"Nineteen Sol hours." IVAN's reply over the intercom cut off Nathan before he could point to it on the readouts, though he silently thanked IVAN as Shakrii hovered away, freeing up his personal space.

IVAN supplied some more information, explaining how complex life could exist around a star as energetic as this one with its radiation that should have been harmful to life. "The magnetic field suggests an iron core, which, coupled with the rotation speed, would permit habitability due to resultant weather systems and ionization protection from the star. How it formed around a short-lived star remains uncertain."

However, much of their collective focus was on the unnatural features, especially the ring that cut through the blackness overhead.

As he looked toward Morthas, in command of the expedition's research tasks, Nathan could see that the Leg'hrul was enthralled by the view, his avian eyes and mandibled beak flailing at times as he seemed to speak more to himself than the others. "We'll know more in time."

Kalsik then spoke up from the display view he hovered beside. "No signals . . . devoid of life."

Serie couldn't help but jab offhandedly as she floated toward Nathan. "Four eyes, and you still missed the obvious ecosystem."

"I meant whoever made all the structures."

As much as Kalsik's poor choice of words might have been amusing, his paranoia was usually rooted in justified concerns, and Nathan knew it as much as Serie.

Shakrii turned to head down the corridors to the centrifuge. "Looks like you have a set of ruins on your hands, Morthas."

As Shakrii vanished down the corridor, Nathan looked at the view, sparing only a sideways glance at Serie's claws clutching his arm. Kalsik said nothing, while Morthas politely murmured his leave before floating down the corridor to head back to the lab.

All they could do now was wait for the probes to map the planet and its surface for topography and resources. If they were contacted within that time, they would at least have had an answer to many questions. Still, he knew the others all had fears, even Morthas amid his excitement about what they might find. Nathan was in no hurry to meet those able to build such immense constructs.

Chapter 9

Landfall

Sol Day 29

Seated at his desk in the repurposed mineral lab, Morthas rubbed the plumage around his eyes, unfocused from lack of sleep, as he turned on the recording function.

The projected display interface on his work desk played back his image on the camera as he began to record his daily journal. He had spent a long night examining the data from the system. He looked like a wreck, his feathers unkempt, so he decided to take a break after this recording was done.

"No intelligent life traces beyond the ring and strange mountains."

Pausing, Morthas looked off to the side, distracted. He scratched his mandibled beak, questions plaguing his mind as his expertise on ruins discovered on past expeditions contradicted what he saw here.

"It can't be ruins, can't be a cataclysm. The ring alone, if they can build that, they could endure to be here, unless they're hiding."

On the same screen, a smaller data window showed the topographical layout of the planet, its seas and land, a large number of areas highlighted for various reasons. Upon seeing the layout of the dozens of orbit paths of the microsatellites, Morthas gave a small snort.

"Satellite surveillance can only yield so much. I ordered the dispatch of two additional probes to the surface. Before we try an expedition to a more desolate area, start safer, desert most likely.

"The ecosystem is oxygen-respiring, water-based biology. Admittedly, I am not a xenobiologist, but the programming augmentations uploaded into IVAN's systems mean he can pick up the slack. What chirality or base DNA molecules are there won't become clear until we have samples from the probes, likely bacterial ones. Complex life is a certainty. We can see foliage from orbit. One probe to ocean, one to land, enough to form a general idea. Garden worlds in the upper regions of habitable surface gravities, like this one, tend to have higher biodiversity, so I don't expect we'll be short of samples."

A troubling thought crossed Morthas's mind. With a sigh, he decided that he could afford to voice his private worries to a recording rather than to a person.

"Still, this world's star is less than a billion Sol years old. Multiple fossil records show that even the fastest biospheres take much longer to produce their first multicelled organism, let alone intelligent or industrialized life, even with the star's higher ionizing radiation stimulating evolution's random mutations a bit faster, let alone one like this that should have killed any early life. Local fossil deposits will be a priority, as will ice cores from the polar circles.

"I know they're not scientists, but I'm beginning to feel like I'm the only one here who is actually excited by this project. The others seem fearful, to varying degrees. I can't fully blame them, though. There are plenty of reasons to be on edge."

Morthas shuffled up from his seat, leaning forward to shut down the camera feed. With the Scientific and Cultural Committee requesting daily updates via wormhole communicator, he hoped his next transmission might yield more actual information and less musing on the expedition as a whole.

~~~

Unseen, the transmission containing his recording and the available data was relayed to the wormhole communication equipment aboard the ship. A two-way channel, the information was beamed by laser emission into the center of the unit. Inside, held in place by an array of containment fields, the wormhole lay in the center of the module, a warped sphere of space no more than a centimeter across, silent within the vacuum chamber.

Transmission beams traveled at light speed through the wormhole, and similar to relays and exchanges of the telephone lines centuries ago, and of the digital networking still used to this day, many layers of wormhole exchange existed. These shortcuts through space meant that a data time lag of more than three seconds was considered unacceptable except where ships were not equipped with wormhole exchanges. The *Haivres*'s wormhole communicator linked them directly with the Scientific and Cultural Committee, the expedition's findings and status updated with only a three-second time delay. It was a priority channel, largely reserved for expedition data, which meant they had to carefully select what leisure data they downloaded before setting out. This, their only contact link, reminded them of how far they were from home, and from help.

~~~

The pair of teardrop-shaped probes drifted away from the ship, their thrust burns setting them off at an angle and toward the planet's upper atmosphere. Their landing sites had been chosen as a spread across the north and south hemispheres, avoiding the equator. By avoiding the planet's artificial features, they would at least theoretically avoid confrontation with any local beings until they knew more about the planet's inhabitants.

The probes, equipped with robust aerodynamic and heat-resistant landing shells, were able to scan for life signs once photographs of the planet showed an atmosphere.

The probes would make landfall soon, and before the planet's twenty-hour day was up, they would have the answer as to the building blocks and makeup of life on this world.

~~~

99

In the crew lounge module, Kalsik sat at the central table and trawled through the data readouts from the microsatellites. Already some valuable mineral deposits had been located, and yet all this did was annoy him—and if it annoyed him, he knew it would truly irk Eskai Inc.'s stockholders.

Serie sat beside him and, upon seeing the data herself, leaned back in her seat, her mandibles clenched in disappointment. "Mining companies won't be happy."

This prompted a response from IVAN. "Too many laws prohibit unregulated mining when a planet with traces of an intelligent civilization is in system." His words were meant to remind Kalsik of this missed mining opportunity, and with it, the chance for a pay rise and/or bonus after this tour.

Serie mumbled about preparing the drive ship for separation tomorrow. It was not designed to land and would serve as a useful satellite while they were planetside.

If Kalsik could find one comfort, it was that once they went planetside, the drive ship would be ready to go by the time they rendezvoused, should they need to leave in a hurry. He felt he could relax knowing that all the crew, and especially Shakrii with her seemingly cautious authoritarianism, wouldn't leave much to chance. The last thing he wanted was to see his crew suffer for lack of preparation, not like on his last assignment in the Republic military.

~~~

In its northerly landing point, its air brakes extended to slow and steer its descent, the probe plummeted through the storm. Thrusters and landing spotlights blazed down onto the windswept surface of the shallow, murky sea below, the waves lashing its frame once it splashed down and cut its thrusters, its lightweight and watertight frame ensuring it wouldn't sink.

Small panels opened in its underside, filters activating as the onboard batteries began to provide power. Water was taken in, filters keeping the size of the intake objects to microscopic levels.

All life was a series of chains of consumption, and the bottom of the chain would determine the composition of all life that fed on it.

As the internal scanners set to work on the molecules extracted from the seawater, the information was stored, the rainstorm overhead causing too much interference to immediately beam the data to the *Haivres* or any of its relay microsats.

~~~

A hemisphere away to the planet's south, the second probe fell through the dawn-lit skies with similar smoothness.

As it touched down, the wind rustled across the mosslike red and yellow plants, which covered the ground in all directions, masking the rock-laced soil beneath them. The mountain ridge far to the west was shrouded in cloud banks, rainfall beginning to build along the peaks.

The probe's directive was to investigate the plant life around its immediate landing zone. Multiple tools extended and began scanning, sweeping over the surrounding foliage.

These probes were stationary, designed to observe basic life upon which more advanced life could build. What more complex life there was to be found would become clearer with a venture down.

~~~

Sol Day 29

The findings were conclusive. The forms of life on the planet were familiar enough to know what to expect, to a degree.

Carbon-based life was there, as expected, by virtue of carbon's ability to readily form complex molecules. Photosynthetic life was there too—yet with enough differences from other known plant life in charted space to make it exclusive to this planet.

The cells' DNA had a levo-rotated nucleic acid structure, making consumption of the plant life impractical for the Leg'hrul crewmembers, and despite levo-oriented compatibility, hazardous to all the other crewmembers. It took years of screening, testing, and altering before life-forms were fit for cross-species consumption, and that was not their task here.

Nevertheless, the findings were enough to warrant a planetside expedition, and they wasted little time getting underway.

The drive ship retracted its locking arms from the *Haivres*, the docking port detaching from the *Haivres*'s rear. Serie watched from the rear viewport as the drive ship was left in orbit, its reactor shut down but the solar arrays remaining extended to provide sustained, reliable power generation.

She felt a surge as the ship's thrusters sent them on a downward trajectory toward the planet's southern hemisphere, where dawn would soon be breaking at their landing region. Through the viewport, the distant light of the secondary dwarf star glowed like a red diamond in the dark skies, the light of the primary white star beginning to glisten around the planet's rim ahead of the ship. Overhead, the metallic gray ring reflected the sunlight falling on its immense hyperstructure, glowing ominously, ever present, never letting her, or anyone else, forget the unnatural nature of this world.

Indeed, as if emphasizing her own nervousness, silence reigned within the entire ship as it descended, the thrusters slowing it as it began to enter the planet's atmosphere, minimizing reentry heating. The only sound was the faint shaking from reentry friction as air began to create lift beneath the *Haivres*'s broad underside.

~~~

Sol Day 29

The arrowhead-shaped *Haivres* left vapor trails in its wake, the ship itself not generating much in the way of lift except at these higher speeds. It was designed to slow down in an atmosphere with thrusters adjusting it vertically to facilitate landings.

Overhead, the primary star emitted its fierce white-and-blue hue. To a planetside viewer, it appeared smaller than most stars over planets similarly teeming with life. In reality, as it was a more powerful, larger star, its temperature made it necessary for the planet to orbit farther out if it hoped to retain an atmosphere and liquid water.

While it was obscured somewhat by the atmosphere, the glinting gray line that was the ring hyperstructure cut through the skies in an endless arc, one of the eight much-larger node segments hanging overhead like a small moon that had been pierced through its cylindrical middle.

The ship cruised over the cloud banks. All the while, its scanners were constantly active, searching for anomalies, mapping the topography, and documenting resource information that could be useful later on, supplementing what the satellites had already gathered.

~~~

They were all inside the cockpit now, observing through transparent display surfaces, computerized projections showing outside images as if the solid hull layers were as clear as glass.

Sitting in her usual copilot seat in case she was needed, Serie noticed something on the scanners. As she furrowed her feathery eye ridges to bring up an enlarged display, the Leg'hrul spoke aloud, Shakrii moving over to the sensor display as she spoke, more wary than five seconds ago.

"Picking up some weird readings on the lidar sensors, airborne."

Shakrii had experience with many sensor equipment setups, but as she was unfamiliar with these particular sensors, untrained on this ship as a whole, she felt it was best to ask. "How many?"

"Fourteen, different-sized."

"Are they moving?" Kalsik's wary voice rang out as he brought up the readings on his own screen.

Shakrii noticed that the Kronogri didn't once look up.

From his control chair, Nathan stared out of the cockpit viewport, in control yet sparing a backward, anxious glance to this exchange, while Morthas merely kept calm beside Shakrii and listened in.

"They are matching local wind speeds at their altitude," Serie replied. "What is our course of action?"

Given how clear it was that Kalsik was puzzled at this readout, Shakrii turned to Morthas, hoping for a plan, as she didn't know what to make of an aerial anomaly moving this slowly. Nathan and Serie both spared glances toward the Leg'hrul scientist at the rear of the cockpit as well, and it wasn't long before Morthas reasoned aloud, doubtful and seemingly asking for a second opinion as he glanced at them all one by one. "Won't need to land or open up. So we can approach . . . carefully."

Shakrii couldn't help but scowl to herself as Kalsik waved one of his smaller arms in dismissal of Morthas's suggestion. If he caught the flash of irritation that crossed her face— or rather that she aimed at him—he didn't seem to show it.

"So long as it's safe."

The Leg'hrul's face lit up at the prospect of a find so soon after making planet fall, and it only took a backward glance from their human pilot for him to begin to bank the craft to head in the direction of the readings.

~~~

Closer inspection revealed that what had at first seemed to be a flock of distant, bulbous shapes emerging from beneath the clouds were organic of some kind. Metallic gray in color, they drifted through the skies with large, trailing tendrils beneath them. Conical bodies lay beneath the vast, bloated forms that formed their tops, and one could almost compare them to floating trees or mushrooms. Around them, as scanners predicted, a few smaller shapes, perhaps younger members, floated in this herd.

As the scanners zoomed in on the shapes, Morthas was nearly breathless. "Incredible."

"Lighter-than-air life," Kalsik said.

Morthas felt that the significance of possible discoveries would surely alleviate the crew tensions, wonderment covering up their fears. Overhead, IVAN's voice rang, bringing with it projections of a similar creature from a known world.

"They bear similarities to the Medusiag of the Arue Magna gas giant."

"Living gasbags."

Morthas thought Shakrii's remark was apt, even if crude. As he minimized some of the scans, he began to ramble. "I think it's early to assume family dynamics, but it seems to align. There's much we could—"

"I hate break in," Kalsik said, "but we need a landing zone, a base camp to start out with and refuel the reactor if we're going to be here awhile."

Morthas pretended not to see the small, toothy smirk from Kalsik at his runaway enthusiasm getting shot down, nor the coy looks Nathan and Serie shared similarly. He nodded to Kalsik with as much professionalism as he could muster. "No, no, I agree. Almost forgot."

It wasn't long afterward that Nathan changed their heading yet again, though they all spared backward glances as the herd of aerial creatures vanished into the distant skies. While they headed away, however, Serie turned to Morthas, a smirk adorning her mandibled beak. "Not quite like your usual work, I take it?"

"Far from it."

His honest remark earned a small chuckle from Kalsik. "At least we're all out of our depth together."

~~~

Another hour passed as they traveled, the ship turning course to streak across a coastline along the snaking southern continent. They flew just over three kilometers above the ground now, and the terrain began to change as they made their way south. Dense red-and-yellow forests and marshes lined numerous river outlets and deltas that lay west of the mountain range they sought. Finally, after an hour of flight, they came upon the mountains.

Stretching up for a kilometer in steep faces before the coastline, the parched yellow-and-brown sands covered the mountain ridge that reached almost to the edge of the ocean. The sparse vegetation became even scarcer as they ventured farther and farther inland, slowing as they began to descend.

After one particularly high mountain ridge, capped by small, snowy peaks along the upper altitudes, they reached the desert—a place so dry and almost devoid of life, save for the occasional patch of brownish red covering the ground in spaces smaller than their onboard crew quarters. Multiple ridges and salt ponds dotted the place, and the whole desert held few features in its expanse. Only the distant mountain range farther inland, the second partner in the natural double barricade to any rainwater, broke the flat horizon seen at ground level.

As they came to land a kilometer away from one of the many salt ponds, the *Haivres*'s thrusters blew up dust while the landing gear extended for vertical landing. The ship touched down on the ground, the suspension settling to give the 150-meter-long vessel just under six meters of ground clearance.

As the ship's flight systems and reactor began to power down, Nathan stretched his arms out, barely noticing that Morthas, Shakrii, and Kalsik had already left the cockpit. As he got out of his seat, the human held on to his headrest for a moment and seemed to smile when he stepped onto the flooring, relishing actual force pulling him to the floor rather than nano-grip tiles.

IVAN's reduction of reactor power and the engine cutoff were Nathan's signal that he could relax. Excluding only a handful of setups for the ship's cabin access, the ship could power down now, no high-demand operations beyond atmospheric flight in its foreseeable future. He had finished all his post-flight checks and simply put his feet up on the console tops and took in the view of the desert outside.

~~~

Inside the centrifuge, Serie set to work on the two life-support pods' extra hatchways along their edge, as their nonrotation, unlike the other ten modules in the centrifuge that had been oriented downward when they entered the atmosphere, was part of their design with two floors to walk on. The floor that was used when in orbit held extra doorways, one she was all-too-eager to open up now that they were likely to be on this planet, in a proper gravity well, for the near future.

She opened the hatches to let the central access bridge of the centrifuge become more of a straight corridor. One could now walk from the cockpit all the way to the rearmost docking node for large ship connections without having to take the corridor around the centrifuge, as they would in space.

Admittedly, the 1.2 Earth gee was greater than they had grown accustomed to in their travels. She and Morthas, their kind originating from a 0.8 gee home world, tolerated the higher gravity comfortably enough. If anything, the two Kronogri felt as if they were either on their home world or a colony formed on planets with similar gravity.

But after such a long trip, and finally finding a suitable landing place in a location that was lifeless enough to be considered safe even after this short period of analysis, she was looking forward to at least one comfortable night's sleep in a proper gravity well.

~~~

The crew slept on the ship. The light in their quarters dimmed as they decided to grow accustomed to the cycles of this planet for the times ahead. Even IVAN had decreased his processes as activity on the ship and planet decreased during the night.

The twenty-hour local day neared its end, the white-blue sun having dipped over the horizon to give way to a rapidly approaching sunset, the star appearing yellow with slight red hues in the sky, a bright amber glaze over the horizon. The only sound was the faint breeze across the nearly lifeless expanse.

In the depths of night, the glint of the ring structure far overhead glowed over the desert as if millions of distant stars had been woven into a thick thread. Farther away, the faint blood-red glow of the secondary dwarf star stared down.

Their work had only just begun, and already this planet was showing some of what it had. The secrets that didn't reveal themselves immediately were their goal.

However, the act of investigation had already begun to influence the very things they sought to learn about. How much their presence would affect this place was something that nobody could have predicted.

Chapter 10

Life

The first day cycle entailed preparation of cargo, checking and analyzing atmosphere and bio signs in order to calibrate envirosuits, and preparing equipment. But the next morning, to Morthas's delight, they began in earnest.

Much as he wanted to go out, he knew some final tests were needed. Environment scans were all well and good, but in practice, it was good to physically test. Serie volunteered as a Leg'hrul test subject, while Shakrii took her kind's place in lieu of Kalsik, who didn't protest.

Sadly for Nathan, as the only human there, he had no choice. There were higher than usual levels of both argon and xenon, a trouble for humans, while the heightened levels of inert gases posed no threat to Leg'hrul. Kronogri meanwhile, being semi-cold-blooded, faced both a benefit and risk of becoming energized by the radiation, but risking hyperactivity and fatigue if too long exposed.

While the Leg'hrul couldn't ever hope to gain nutrition from any life here, they would be immune to any and all disease, save for allergic reactions that could be suppressed by drugs they always carried with their medical supplies.

Morthas had heard enough horror stories from his colleagues in the xenoarchaeology circles of some other places they'd been to be accepting of a few discomforts. At least, the

109

naturally occurring ones, for he couldn't say much about the ring and the mountains around and on this world.

Unfortunately, even with these atmosphere tests, they still weren't certain of the environment's airborne microbes, even in the parched, dry, brown-and-beige desert they had landed in. Preparations were made, but they could work with less environmental protection than usual for places the *Haivres* traveled to.

~~~

Morthas was first to step out of the airlock and make his way through the stern hangar bay. His suit was the equivalent of shirt sleeves, the mask equipment covering his face mainly containing decontaminant filters against microbes or anything bigger. He came to a stop at the foot of the loading ramp, gazing around as he waited for the others to come up behind him. None of them gave much more than cursory glances to either the large vehicle that occupied the hangar or the two smaller, folded-up vehicles tucked away on each side of it.

Behind Morthas, Serie was first to come out, also taking advantage of her kind having immunity from the different chirality, also wearing only a face mask. Close behind her, Kalsik strode out with Shakrii behind him, neither so lucky in how little equipment they needed. Both Kronogri wore more concealing, skintight envirosuits, protection against excess radiation their bodies were adapted to soak in, covering all but their heads, small fore and rear limbs, and the bulky hands on their larger mid arms. Even their scaly body crests were covered over, and the filter apparatus covered their faces just as it did Morthas's, their worries about infection by local biology even more warranted by their compatible DNA chirality.

Nathan came out last, the airlock sealing behind him. He had taken similar precautions, despite the human body not absorbing radiation for energy, as radiation from higher UV was harmful on its own to any race that originated around a cooler star. Only his head was exposed from the envirosuit, and like the others, he wore a full facial filter mask. In all of their clothing, built-in microskeletal frames would enhance their strength and stamina, and circulate coolant and air, standard features in all spacesuits except truly minimalistic ones.

Any nanobots or implants they had in their bodies synced to the suit functions, be it tools they'd built into gloves or nodes, or to control functions with a simple twitch of a finger or mental input. This, along with the drugs, was enough that Morthas felt they were ready for anything.

Morthas soaked in the landscape, his awe interrupted only by Kalsik directing Nathan and Serie to standard checks of the landing gear. Morthas turned to see the human and Leg'hrul set off to the craft's underside, Nathan already with a projected checklist at the ready while Serie prepared some tools.

Morthas brought up some readouts on his wrist device, making sure Shakrii and Kalsik both heard him, though he noticed Shakrii was using her helmet's more specialized scouting sensors to see far as she listened in. "High altitude, little rainfall, this place is desolate."

"Maybe not," Shakrii said, pointing in a direction Morthas followed, squinting beneath his mask visor to see what it was.

Kalsik did the same beside him. He trilled at the find.

Far in the distance, a handful of reddish-yellow spikes protruded from the ground as if thrust down into the terrain from above. As Morthas zoomed in with his visor, he saw the telltale signs of the smallest movement around them, this world's equivalent to insect life, likely its analogue of a desert plant and all that swarmed around it.

"Life's as hardy as ever." He was in awe.

Beside him, however, Kalsik said, "After the creatures we saw yesterday, I'm disappointed."

"Starting small is safer. Either way, the Committee will want a sample."

"Perhaps a drone to assist?" IVAN suggested.

That was all they needed to make this decision safe by Shakrii's judgment. She and Kalsik left Morthas alone at the foot of the ramp and withdrew into the hangar to discuss the details of the one large and two smaller vehicles that were part of the retrofits and potentially useful for later explorations. Morthas noticed that Shakrii and Kalsik seemed able to bury their tensions when duty called.

He didn't have to wait long for the drone to make its way out, IVAN presumably remote controlling it, though they were intelligent enough on their own. The drone, at one meter in height and length, was much like the maintenance ones onboard, crablike in shape. This one was also able to move about on motorized foot wheels on the end of each leg once it retracted the claws on each side, ideal for walking and rolling surfaces, loose or solid.

Morthas set off, with the drone wheeling beside him, through the landscape between the *Haivres* and his first sample of this planet.

~~~

The *Haivres*'s shadow shielded them from the harsh sunlight overhead, though Serie noticed Nathan staring out across the desert beyond the shade, his eyes glazed over. What he said next surprised her.

"This sort of reminds me of home."

"Your colony?"

Nathan turned to her with a small nod. "No life there though, or atmosphere."

"Do you miss it?"

Her innocuous question earned a small scoff, as the human shrugged his shoulders

112

before launching into a mini berating of his childhood home. "That sun-scorched dump? Not at all. Especially not the work."

She always found it funny how humans could get hung up on tiny gripes with pretty much anything. It explained all their fables of an afterlife paradise in their religions, past and present, if they could be this picky about reality. Still, she reflected, he wasn't the only one with less than fond memories of their childhood home, though his were much different from hers, more impersonal, less hurtful and full of regret. She didn't complain because she didn't want to remember.

"I'm looking forward to better scenery," he added.

"I'd like to see some of the cliffs. Stretch my wings, if permissible." Serie couldn't help but fantasize flying above some of the valleys and bays she'd seen pass below their ship yesterday, a luxury seldom afforded her and her kind except on designated areas on larger space stations or appropriate planets.

As if pondering that joyous indulgence, Nathan turned to her. "You sure there's anywhere to do so on this planet?"

"Near sea level's probably good. I'd like to get my blood going." Serie flexed her exposed wings, feathers flaring outward, the wind in the shadow of their ship cooling them.

Ever one to sour the moment, the human beside her let a coy tone slip into his voice. "Wasn't that your reason when you and I—"

"You know what I meant!" Serie gave up scolding him halfway, unable to maintain any seriousness in her tone.

She was thankful when they reached the landing gear, which beckoned to be checked. Nathan mockingly stepped aside and gestured to the foothold on the landing gear strut, preparing to check the electro driver circuits in the wheels as she clambered up.

Her claws gripping on, she pulled out a tool and poked her head up into the gear compartment, her visor's LED lamps shining around inside. She focused on the wheel motor's capacitor bank, readouts projecting on her mask display, while engaging comms with IVAN as he ran system checks from the ship. "All synced up?"

"Affirmative, but there are foreign objects in the bay," IVAN responded.

Serie glanced toward where her visor directed her to look. She shined her light into a corner of the gear compartment and couldn't help but groan. A series of small white pebbles had gotten inside the gear bay.

"How'd these rocks get here?" They hadn't been there when they left the station, and the gear hadn't been opened since they left the station. She gently reached over and poked them before slowly sweeping them around to the edge of the wheel hatch to clatter onto the sands below.

"What do you mean, *rocks*?" Nathan asked.

Glancing down, she saw the thumb-sized white rocks tumble onto the sands below at the human's feet, one clanging off his visor's mask, much to his irritation. But his own face changed as she stared in shock at what now lay around his feet. The rocks had sprouted legs, unfolding and scuttling in all directions or burrowing into the shadowed sand around him. As Nathan recoiled, the beetle-like creatures, each with numerous hairs, vanished under the sand or tucked themselves into the gaps inside the wheels, where it was even darker than the shadow from the *Haivres*'s hull overhead.

Serie quickly swept the last of them that she could find out of the compartment, while Nathan got on the comms. With Morthas in the far distance at the strange plant they'd found a kilometer away, IVAN controlling the rover beside him, it would be Kalsik and Shakrii who got there first.

~~~

About an hour later, they were all back inside the ship. Morthas had the samples he wanted, and then some. Contained within a transparent box, a few of the beetle-like creatures had been captured for study, the crew getting the spine to sweep them up for him before he'd returned from the plant he was sampling. In another, much larger container, an entire segment of the red, almost cactus and coral-like plant sat in cold storage.

As he gestured to the specimens, excitement all over his face, he ignored the wary looks the others sent toward the beetle-like creatures. Given the shock of finding them, he didn't blame them, and if anything, he wished he'd been there for the discovery to see the surprise on their faces. "They must have taken shelter from the sun. They prey on the plant as well, likely a common food-chain producer around here. IVAN, I take it the protocols have been intensified?"

"Background scans sweeping the ship for intrusions, and decontamination cycles will be increased in frequency."

Much as these discoveries excited him, Morthas remembered that the local biology was much wider than what they'd already found, especially given what they had seen yesterday. He suppressed his anticipation and strived to keep his tone calm. "We should head to more densely inhabited areas, start cataloguing. Make sure we keep the samples small enough to fit in the lab."

"What about the ring, the four constructed mountains?" Shakrii asked.

Her point was valid. The photograph that had caused this whole expedition to be organized hadn't been of what lay in the boxes atop his desk, after all. But Morthas made his case clear for their plan going forward.

"We should remain focused on the wildlife until we know more, give them time to see we're not a threat if we're being watched."

To his relief, Shakrii gave a grunt of approval.

The holodisplay of the planet shone before them, various traced routes and detected signals, minerals or bio-signals showing more prominently than their current location. On the same map, the two probe beacons in the north and south remained online. It was a great many sites to investigate, and yet they still had three weeks until the probes were due to have detailed scans of the debris clouds around the A-class home star.

Amid the finding of a garden world, the overhanging presence of the massive constructs seemed to almost vanish. First contact had been benign so far, and it would remain that way if all they found was wildlife.

However, a garden world around an A-class star was unheard of, given how long it took for complex ecosystems to naturally develop. It shouldn't have existed as developed as it was.

~~~

Sol Day 33

They left behind a solitary rover drone piloted by its own rudimentary nonsentient AI, and departed for more life-filled regions.

As their findings transmitted to the Committee surmised, the plant life on the planet had adapted to the higher frequency, more energetic sunlight by means of the spectrums used for photosynthesis. The more energetic frequencies meant plants didn't need to draw on as many spectrums for energy. The longer wavelengths of visible light, red to yellow, were unneeded and reflected, giving them the reddish-orange hue that dominated the areas of life on the planet.

Myriad creatures were visible as they crossed over the planet's biomes, from analogues of rain forests, to deserts, to rolling plains and wetlands of boggy, fog-laced swamps flanked by shallow-sloped but immense mountainsides. Bio scans showed many animals actively producing heat, denoting them as reptile/mammal hybrids, a type of creature already found across many ecosystems in charted space. Flying creatures adopted very lightly built profiles, with more wing surface area to their mass than on other worlds. Many land animals had adapted armored hides over their bodies that gave protection against the sun's radiation. The mammals that didn't draw on sunlight had adopted brightly colored, almost blue-to-white hides, reflecting the light they weren't harnessing that would otherwise pose a risk to them.

As for their next up-close encounter, however, the strange aerials they had witnessed on arrival were too tantalizing to ignore any longer.

~~~

Morthas proposed a name for the creatures, a name that nobody rejected due to lack of better, non-joking alternatives. He called them Hradriol, inspired by a mystical tree from Leg'hrul mythology, which they reminded him of. What was truly unique about them was that these were the first gasbag-type life-forms ever discovered to live on a rocky planet.

In the mineral lab, watching through scanners and the camera feeds provided to his visor from exterior sensors, Morthas saw that they were as silent and ethereal up close as they had seemed from afar. Their countless tendrils, some as thin as fingers and others as thick as tree trunks, dangled and swayed below their massive, bulbous tops. Their upper bodies were swollen in all directions, filled with reinforced and constantly refilling sacks of hydrogen, the gas leaking as it often did through even the best materials.

Arrays of red-and-blue coloration covered their immense forms, especially around the small gullet vents that expelled air to provide propulsion. Morthas deduced them to be hybrids of animal and plant, adapted to use the higher solar energy to carry out photosynthesis on the water vapor in clouds to a partial extent, splitting the hydrogen from the water to get lifting gases from clouds they flew through, or from water they trawled when they purposefully drifted lower.

In supplementing the immense energy needs of their bodies, they had adopted a mixed feeding habit, and they weren't picky. Morthas noted that if it could be ingested, it would be eaten if it wandered into their tendrils. Any byproduct waste gases from digestion were likely processed for hydrogen.

~~~

When the giants drifted over a boggy river delta, nature began to showcase its food chains, the marshes revealing themselves as home to animals that saw fit to exploit these giants.

Kalsik watched as the attackers came like a murder of crows onto a carcass, yet these creatures they descended upon and rose toward were still alive. The attackers, lanky creatures with six distinct limbs, all marked with bright-colored feathers and faint blue underscales, readied their claws on all their appendages, their wing feathers flaring in and out like fan blades as they dived, scything between the flying giants, their elongated heads scanning for places to begin to feast.

One smaller member of the hunting flock was fool enough to fly too close to the hanging tendrils, sealing its fate. Like elastic going taut, the creature gave a panicked-sounding screech as it sprang upward into the embrace of more tendrils, some actively moving to pull it up through the air toward the underside of the larger creature. A mouth opened, and a sticky tongue shot out, yanking the creature from the feeder appendages with a suddenness that made Kalsik wince in pity.

Other more fortunate creatures flocked about the thick hides of the giants' gas bulbs, biting into them, mouths opening like umbrellas to suction on before their jaws retracted to rake flesh from the outer skin as their meal, but never deep enough to rupture the sacks, ensuring a constant food supply. With replenishing prey like this, Kalsik figured the risk of being eaten was evidently worth taking.

This predator/prey relationship wasn't the strangest thing they saw while observing these creatures, as Kalsik and the others noticed these giants also hosted other life-forms. A smaller breed of flying creature lived among the tendrils, clinging on and moving about as easily as a spider would on its web, free where others were ensnared and eaten, which Morthas suggested was likely some adaptation against how the tendrils ensnared what they touched. They were smaller than the attackers, but unlike them, their jaws were more for actual biting than simply taking small chunks, with razor incisors around their beaked maws to stab inward like scissors whenever they bit in.

Eventually, the flock of attackers left, a number of them ensnared in the tendrils of the giants, the smaller resident fliers luring some back into a trap in their retaliation for losing easy pickings. But now Kalsik saw one way that the ease at which the smaller creatures could live within the tendrils of the giants was possible, even without the detailed analysis Morthas delivered over the comms as he continued to observe from the lab. He couldn't help but smile to himself at Morthas's excitement.

Some of the tendrils secreted a natural adhesive, and a sort of larder of food was stored within the bulb's underside, where the smaller creatures also lived. Payment from the home to its defenders, as the creatures also evidently cleaned the tendrils and body of decaying flesh and bits its own mouth couldn't get rid of.

These observations weren't without incident. While the ship dwarfed the largest of the flying giants, the biggest in the pack only seventy-five meters at its widest, the size of their ship and the same relative speed at which it flew made it a target for those predatory creatures that still had the gall to hang around for easy pickings.

~~~

Morthas saw one of the birdlike creatures circle about overhead before diving toward the ship's upper hull, and like its ilk did with the giant creatures, it raked its jaw inward over the surface, pulling shavings and slivers of the alloys and smart nonmetals into its jaws, visibly struggling with these much-denser materials. At first, Morthas thought it would be a one-off bite for investigation, but the message didn't reach the others interested in this new, larger than normal meal, as they each swooped down to take a bite out of the ship's hull, vandalizing the *Haivres* in a way that he was sure would really anger those who used this ship as a second home of sorts.

Morthas watched the behavior through the sensor feeds, making notes, musing that the animals likely mistook their ship for one of the large creatures nearby. Even so, he grimaced at the damage they were doing, even if it was only skin-deep on the hull. He knew Serie and the others would lament having to arrange for hull repairs.

If anything, Shakrii seemed the least annoyed. "Definitely not intelligent life," she observed.

"Are we going to stop them from eating the ship?" Nathan demanded.

IVAN cut in with a tone of such indignation that Morthas actually laughed aloud.

"Preventing excessive hull damage falls within my parameters."

"We have defense turrets. Morthas?" asked Shakrii.

This made Morthas's blood run cold for a brief moment, though he suspected the others wouldn't protest if he didn't. Much as he wanted to avoid any conflict, he admitted that Shakrii had the right idea. "Nonlethal."

"You sure?"

"It might draw attention if we make it look like we abuse wildlife beyond what's necessary."

It didn't take long for his order to be readied, though it seemed to Morthas that the ship's AI was a bit too eager to engage weapons on mere wildlife, even if they were nonlethal.

However, Serie's response showed Morthas he had underestimated just how protective she was of their ship. "Setting defense turrets to low yield. If successful, I recommend similar anti-wildlife measures in future to protect valuable hardware."

"I second that," said Kalsik.

Much as he sympathized with the engineer—and by extension the human pilot and Kronogri captain—about needless damage to their ship, Morthas wasn't sure whether he should be concerned about this swiftness to punish mere animals. Sure, they were vandalizing the ship's exterior, but they were only following instincts.

~~~

Through IVAN's sensors, they watched the outside of the ship's upper hull open, a small hatch revealing a ball-shaped turret and a directed energy weapon embedded within. After charging the capacitor banks from the main reactor, IVAN locked the turret sights on to the nearest creature munching on the ship. An invisible beam of light, as the lasers they used operated in the infrared spectrum, fired pulsed laser bursts onto its torso in the span of half a second, making the creature flinch before tearing away from the *Haivres* and into the air.

IVAN was quick to turn the turret on the other creatures to fire similar bursts that soon warded them all off.

They would observe the giant creatures into the night cycle, though they now gained some altitude so that they wouldn't be mistaken for food again. IVAN and the others wouldn't protest keeping the turrets active the whole time in case any others got hungry for their hull. Enough hull panels had been damaged to require maintenance patchwork once they next landed.

Even as they wondered at these creatures, the unsettling nature of this world would creep back into their minds, hanging over them as much as the ring hyperstructure did.

Chapter 11

Divisions

Sol Day 34

They landed on the flatlands near a canyon's edge.

Morthas doubted that the majesty of this planet would wear off anytime soon. Stretching out many kilometers from their canyon landing zone, vast flats were bathed in the white-blue light of the sun. The plants, be they like woolly shrubs dyed autumnal colors or cactus-like trees devoid of visible leaves, covered the landscape as far as the eye could see.

A vast river tainted this uniform landscape, the shallow marshes that flanked its running main channels covered in protruding wormlike reeds, most tipped with strange flowers, many of them so dark a violet color that they appeared black at first. A menagerie of creatures could be seen on the plains, in the rivers, and even in the trees, the most prominent being broad, armored reptilian grazers, though the diversity of creatures and plant life was a spectacle to behold in this world's analogue of savannah.

The flatlands closer to them, however, were scarred by an exploited crack in the basalt plate upon which the entire region sat. A crack of softer rock had been carved out by the river over thousands of years, as the waters vanished into a deep gorge a kilometer wide from end to end. The water raged at the bottom a hundred meters below. The mist hid the immense cascade that fell onto the rocks, offering glimpses of an oval lake and more raging river that wound through and away at the canyon base, out to the south. The roar of this immense

122

waterfall echoed across the landscape as far as its mists could be seen, but up close, it was only as loud as the *Haivres* thrusters running idle.

Morthas stared down into the canyon as he waited for the others, spotting distinct layers carved into the canyon walls, the geological history of the planet they had come in search of.

He knew traces of historic atmosphere would be guaranteed finds, but fossils would be equally useful. The only problem he foresaw was if anybody in the crew didn't have a head for heights.

Unfortunately, he should have known better than to think that the novelty of this world would overcome the mutual animosity between Shakrii and Kalsik.

~~~

As Shakrii focused her visor to zoom in on a far distant animal herd on the savannah plains, she listened in on the conversation behind her. She noted the visibly annoyed human and Leg'hrul pair underneath the hull of the *Haivres*, where they had spotted an underside panel one of the creatures had bitten into earlier. The exterior hull damage was still a sore issue as they worked with one of the drones beside them to weld on a repair patch.

Morthas's thoughts were elsewhere as he scanned the surroundings. "Sedimentary layers provide samples to analyze atmosphere. Additional search for fossils to trace species development will be undertaken by drones. The Buerev is prepared for deployment. The sea floor at one of the chosen coastal sites will give samples to back up whatever we find here." He turned to glance at Kalsik and Shakrii. "On that note, we need to decide who goes where."

She noticed a nervous tone creeping into Morthas's voice. She understood what his concerns were and only wished they weren't warranted. The Buerev ground vehicle was solid, but not impenetrable.

Kalsik spoke without looking at her. "Best bet is that whoever stays in the Buerev not

123

be alone for security's sake, along with IVAN's help."

"My aid would be sufficient alone," IVAN protested.

This fell on deaf ears as Kalsik looked to Morthas for his opinion. She pitied the Leg'hrul as he seemed to back off, not wishing to take a side in this heated issue.

Finally he said, "The others would be best staying on the ship. So I guess that leaves you two. You're captain and security, so might be best if you two sort this out." Morthas scurried to a farther-away part of the canyon top and turned to observe through his visor scans a good distance away from them, leaving them alone together, out of earshot. Shakrii noticed Nathan and Serie shoot a few nervous glances toward the two of them before returning to their work on the ship's underside.

She turned to Kalsik, ignoring his tense body language as he settled down to hammer out his case for her to stay with the Buerev vehicle. They isolated their communications to only their two helmets.

"I must stay with the greater security priority, the ship, our way off this planet," she said.

Kalsik disagreed, as she knew he would. "Morthas is leading the expedition, so he should be the priority. I can keep the ship safe."

Shakrii could tell he was drawing on more personal reasons to justify his being in ship command as she countered with her own logic-based ones. Sure enough, what he said next was much more personal in nature.

"Besides, given how eager you are to protect the ship and not Morthas, it doesn't seem like you value him or the scientific mission."

Shakrii felt her anger surge, though she managed to suppress it. "You're ex-military, enough to cover Morthas's needs, and knowledgeable enough in the relevant fields to aid excavation. However, your ship . . . we're finished if something happens to it."

"Exactly why I must stay with my ship."

She should have known better. This was a hopeless case of a Kronogri not wanting to negotiate. Kalsik was unable to see past his own grievances or surrender what rank he had, but she wouldn't let that compromise her own authority, not after the obvious lack of respect she'd had to tolerate from him.

She knew she was crossing a line. "This has nothing to do with your abilities, if that's what you're paranoid about! I was assigned to security, end of story."

Kalsik visibly scoffed under his mask. "Assigned. What authorities say. That's all that matters, isn't it?"

Shakrii knew the only way to get through to stubborn individuals like him was to be forceful, no matter how bitter it made them. All she could do was make her case clear. "Don't make this difficult, Kalsik. I don't—"

"IVAN will guide you through anything to do with the ship you haven't already scoured with our backgrounds." Venom in his tone, Kalsik turned away and began to walk back toward the open vehicle garage in the *Haivres*'s rear where the large ground vehicle, with living quarters inside, was being readied and checked by numerous crablike drones.

If there had ever been any bond of cooperation beyond professionalism, something Shakrii highly doubted, it was broken now.

She relented, knowing that someone had to take the initiative in reminding the other that it was possible for them to get along. As she called to Kalsik one last time, she kept a calm tone, her voice losing the edge it had borne before. "This isn't personal, Captain, just orders."

Her words stopped him in the shadow of the hangar mouth. A faint rustle of wind echoed over the roaring of the waterfall in the background as he spoke to her over the comms before shutting off the link and vanishing into the hangar's bustling activity around the

Buerev. "Orders are impersonal, for better or worse."

Shakrii punched the dirt with her forearm, ignoring the stares from Nathan and Serie, and from Morthas at his cliffside observations with IVAN's primary drone beside him.

Perhaps, she reasoned, some time away from her might let him cool off, and proving his ship was fine under her might quell his temperament and his unreasonable grudge.

~~~

After deactivating the observation zoom in his visor from the sight of some flying creatures in the canyon below, Morthas watched Shakrii make her way back to the ship, her aggravation showing in her posture. While neither he nor any of the others had been privy to the actual conversation, he could guess what had happened: as had Kalsik not yielded, neither would Shakrii have done.

"Kalsik will obey the contract, though not with pleasure," IVAN observed.

The AI's words did little to quell Morthas's unease as he looked to the drone beside him that had been IVAN's eyes and ears to his observations here. Caution creeping into his voice, he cocked his head back toward the ship. "If I'm going to be with him for a while, alone—"

"I will be here, split between the ship and vehicle."

"Still, what's his opinion of me?"

"He is indifferent at best. However, it would be wise to give him time to calm down."

Knowing that all he could do was heed IVAN's advice, Morthas turned his gaze westward, noticing how the picturesque image of the peaceful savannah and waterfall canyon that surrounded them stood in stark contrast to their intra-crew relations. The pessimist in him hoped there was no intelligent life on the planet to see the little things that seemed to cause such trouble among them.

~~~

By day's end, as the white-yellow sunset began to glaze over the horizon, and the vertical, spiky trees silhouetted the night, the *Haivres* had taken off for its selected coastal site with Shakrii in command. Inside the large Buerev ground vehicle, Kalsik had watched its lights vanish over the horizon in bitter silence, Morthas being sure to steer clear of him as he readied for their first shared night in the vehicle's bunks.

As night crept over the Savannah, the Buerev's bricklike silhouette, flanked only by the deployed solar panels that had shut down for the night, showed no light as the electronic blinds were engaged in the windows. Only the band across the skies that was the orbital ring, lit to the west by the remnants of the star, provided light. It wouldn't be until much later that two of the three moons would creep over the eastern skies, though the faint red glow of the second star could be seen like a red eye glinting in the blackness.

Chapter 12

Surveillance and Respect

Sol Day 38

They wasted little time in beginning their work, and as five rotations passed since the expedition had split up, Kalsik felt he had cooled off, though not entirely. He worried about the ship and his crew enough that the feeling became more akin to an itch he might get from a virulent infection. Thinking that occupying himself more rigorously might help, he was more than happy to accept Morthas's request for assistance in gathering rock samples from the canyon edge.

As part of reestablishing himself after his dishonorable discharge from the Republic military years ago, before becoming a captain for Eskai Inc., he had taken the various courses for a surveying role to add to survey experience already gained in fleet service. Now he would put his geology qualifications to use in the field and not just the usual routine lab analysis he and his crew often performed.

He was thankful that he'd never developed any fear of heights, as his first glance at the canyon caught him off guard for a moment. He was sure Morthas hadn't seen him nervously pause before heading down on the winch cable, as the Leg'hrul hadn't waited for him before heading down first, likely immune from any fear of heights by virtue of having wings.

For his part, Kalsik made sure his lifeline cable was secure. Even so, he couldn't help

128

but throw some envious glances toward the clawed feet that the drones had been equipped with as they crawled over the canyon like spiders on a wall.

Hopefully, discovering the details of the strange upper layers in the canyon deposits, dated to only a few thousand years ago, would make this precarious exploration worth the trouble.

The support cables extended from the stationary Buerev's mount points, long pylons burrowed at angles into the rock face at the cliff edge to support the equipment bench, which resembled scaffolding on a low-tech construction site as it hung a quarter of the way down the near-vertical rock face. Some eighty meters below, Kalsik heard the river, some of the mist from the waterfall farther up the canyon drifting around the bend that hid it from their sight.

Kalsik checked the extraction drill's torque, rumbling in satisfaction as another core sample was extracted a centimeter at a time. Equipment on his end of the platform sliced the rock cores before placing them into marked canisters, measurements of how deep into this layer they came from. Rock less exposed to the immediate air would yield better atmosphere history.

On the other end of the platform, Morthas scanned a particular sample with his helmet's sensors, obsessed as he was with the fossilized imprint of a leaf from a small plant that died only around 5,000 to 6,000 Sol years ago, based on where it had been found in the upper layers. This was about as recently as he expected to find any fossils. By Kalsik's side, two drones using a type of 3D internal mineral mapping were searching for more fossils, and once Morthas had checked them, they were carried back up to the Buerev. While not intended for paleontology, the Buerev's equipment for mineral dating worked just as well in this instance and could narrow down Morthas's thousand-Sol year margin to a few hundred.

The bands of sedimentary rock seemed to become much less pronounced deeper down, indicating a recent history of water flow carrying the mud and debris in the clay layers that formed in the basalt plate the savannah was on. Initial theories suggested an ice age ending to produce an exaggerated melting and rain era, but this canyon was too young for it to be the reason. More importantly, an oxygenation event of some sort seemed to have occurred within the past few thousand years, if initial dating of the layers down the canyon was accurate.

Shades of blue and gray laced the rocks in the canyon's upper layers but were noticeably darker for the majority of its depth. Combined with the shallower slopes in the upper regions of the canyon, it appeared that there had been a sudden increase in water flow through this canyon's sediment layers within the past few thousand years or so. What exactly caused it was a mystery for now, but it at least meant hopes of finding fossils in these earlier deposits, preserved by such processes trapping them before they were consumed, became much higher.

As he waited for another rock core to be readied for extraction, Kalsik cast his gaze to the river below, and to the various creatures within the canyon. The predominant life here were flying creatures of differing shapes and sizes, all with thin bodies and dark colors to absorb energy from the sun. They darted across the waters below or in and out of a handful of crevices, nests or burrows by Morthas's and his own best guesses. A few of the larger creatures, like birds with mixed insect-like upper skins to complement their four feathery wings, dived down before flying, seemingly unable to take off from a standing start. They skimmed the surface of the river far below, scooping up water and fish, their elastic lower jaws sifting the water before shutting and swallowing their catches.

In a move that surprised Kalsik, one of them flew in from somewhere above and past their platform, its metallic-gray carapace and feathers glinting. After diving toward the platform, it turned midflight to slow down before looping around to splay its wings and grip the railing in its claws. It landed gently with a flutter, right in front of him. As it began to look over the platform, its unreadable eyes darting everywhere, Kalsik kept very quiet. Since he and Morthas outsized it, this was not the time to startle an opportunity for an up-close look.

Upon switching to helmet comms only, Kalsik quietly hissed Morthas's name and pointed as slowly as he could at their visitor with one of his forelimb's claws. Morthas was stunned into silence much as Kalsik was, and in a bid to keep this opportunity intact, the Leg'hrul quietly put down the rock sample and rose to his feet at his end of the platform.

IVAN stopped every drone on the canyon in its tracks, claws keeping them in place wherever they were. All the while, the AI accessed the sensors of the drones and their own helmet cameras to get a better look at the creature.

Kalsik's helmet's audio sensors relayed the faint chirps the animal made as it shuffled back and forth along the railing, looking over everything with blank caution. They used their internal comms, knowing any sound might scare it off, yet Kalsik couldn't help but let slip his awe. "Not at all afraid."

The creature just kept staring at them, not chirping anymore as its gaze turned to the now inactive equipment that lay around the platform, and the drones frozen on the canyon walls nearby.

"They haven't seen anything like us before," Morthas whispered. "They wouldn't know . . ."

"Useful for observation." IVAN's comment didn't elicit any further remark from Morthas, as Kalsik saw the Leg'hrul turn his helmet to look at something else above. A second creature swooped in and landed on the railing, this one more energetic than their first visitor and landing much closer to Kalsik.

This one, he noticed, was much more wary at first, certainly of him, as it flared jaws

131

and wings at him with a small hiss before its agitation settled into curiosity, like its quieter companion beside it. Even so, as Kalsik shuffled on his feet, it shied away from him, giving him what he suspected was a dirty look. Meanwhile, the first creature had shuffled slightly toward Morthas, cocking its head at the sight of the fossilized plant fragment he had been examining.

"Why do I get the grouch?" Kalsik grumbled.

Morthas let out a laugh as he studied the creature that had moved close to him. "It's got some odd markings on its back neck. Gender difference? Disease? Parasite?"

Sure enough, a visual link on Kalsik's visor opened, and the small, gray lumps on the back of the first creature's neck became visible. As he checked this data, he noticed the creature nearer him lose interest. It turned to dive off the makeshift balcony with a last hissing chirp, flaring its wide wings as it took flight on the airflows within the canyon below.

Morthas spoke directly to the creature near him, gently pointing with his wing to the one that took off. "Go on. Join your friend."

It paused for a moment before taking flight in pursuit of its companion. They marveled at the ease with which it soared away. Anything they did find in the rest of the day's work would pale after this highlight, Kalsik knew, and his regrets about leaving the *Haivres* in Shakrii's hands diminished ever so slightly.

~~~

Their work done for the day, the platform had been hoisted to the top of the cables, all its equipment shut down. The solar arrays on the Buerev's roof, almost like awnings in how they extended, provided all the power they needed for the nanobattery banks and equipment Morthas and Kalsik had already put to use in more detailed analysis. Their transmitter was permanently synced to the microsat array in orbit. Inside, the equipped accommodations and lab enabled them to stay here for weeks on internal supplies alone, though the cramped accommodations meant privacy was at a premium.

As such, Morthas would find out later that evening a secret habit of his coworker that was the sort of behavior he'd hoped wouldn't come to pass.

Having finished up in the washroom, he was about to open the door when he overheard an exchange between IVAN and Kalsik. As he listened, he felt irritation flicker under his plumage.

"Trawling drone operations have had no incidents," IVAN said.

He opened the washroom door and found Kalsik sitting at the small dining table. With as much passiveness as he could muster, he asked, "You're having IVAN report on the ship's activity for you?"

Next to Kalsik, IVAN's white diamond avatar, a projection to signify his presence when the intercom wasn't as personal, flickered for a moment before it vanished, earning a scowl from the captain.

"I must know what's going on," Morthas insisted.

"By IVAN's report, everything is fine on the ship."

After today's events, this seemed to Morthas even pettier than usual. He felt his mandibled beak grit involuntarily before he finally dropped any passiveness, and he was almost unaware of how hard he gripped the wall corner nearest him as he hissed at the Kronogri. "We're out here, amidst all this discovery, and you're letting whatever it is you had issues with back in mapped space continue. We're the first ever of our kinds here, and I seem to be the only one among us genuinely interested, even with me also being afraid like you all are."

Kalsik kept quiet, a puzzled expression on his face as the ridges above his four eyes flared upward slightly, his dark, scaled body stiffening as Morthas raged at him. If Kalsik was indeed caught off guard by his change in demeanor, Morthas didn't care, only wanting his opinion on this whole expedition and crew to be clear to the stubborn Kronogri.

Kalsik made a few nervous grumbles, then adopted an apologetic tone, leaned forward in his seat, and looked Morthas in the eye. "I didn't realize you cared so much about this expedition."

"*Somebody* has to. I've had too many people on previous expeditions not invested— only in it for a job or whatnot."

"Is that why you kept to the lab?"

Morthas nodded as he felt the disappointment about this expedition's crew threaten to surge once more. "I hoped the rest of you would be more curious than fearful when we got here. My mistake. I didn't study the background files much. Was too polite to."

"You didn't?"

Morthas gave a nod, knowing this was one area where Kalsik had contention with Shakrii. He had secrets, and Shakrii knew them, which bothered him to an obvious degree.

He gestured to the viewport, where the flatlands and the gorge winding away from the waterfall lay bathed in twilight. Then he looked right at the Kronogri with a much more earnest tone in his voice. "Do your pasts really matter, given where we are?"

"No. But I can't help but worry about the ship and those two, and Shakrii as a part of it all."

Disappointed, Morthas pulled out a chair, tucking his tail feathers sideways to sit down. He put aside any views he had, be it as a xenoarchaeologist, or a makeshift xenopaleobotanist. He knew he had to empathize at least somewhat if he wanted to break through Kalsik's stubbornness. "If you really are worried, remember she'll lose her job if she leaves us behind needlessly. The Committee values me—us—too much."

With a snort, Kalsik's mouth plates split into a small, toothy smirk as he shuffled his broad forearms where he sat. "If it came down to it, Shakrii is crew, whether I like it or not."

"Why don't you like her?" Morthas asked.

"It's not her I don't like. It's where she gets her authority. All my kind has minimum required service, longer only if we choose like I did, until my discharge."

Morthas realized that Shakrii was nothing more than a manifestation of Kalsik's past mistake, or scapegoating, as he saw it. Regardless, he saw no reason to doubt Kalsik beyond this paranoia, and he made sure to keep a complimentary tone. "You value the crew more than some I've met as defense escorts on other expeditions."

"My tendency to be too caring of my crew led to my discharge."

"A habit that persists by behavioral archive data," came IVAN's voice.

Kalsik frowned at the diamond-shaped projection that had reappeared on his tabletop display. If there was one thing Morthas had also noticed, it was that Kalsik was most at ease with his AI, though he wondered if that had something to do with AIs being known for being less judgmental in general.

"And you haven't lost your eavesdropping habit, or at least your interruptive streak," Kalsik growled.

"If you wish for me not to intrude . . ." IVAN trailed off, obviously intending to log out to attend other functions either here or on the *Haivres*.

But Morthas remembered some research he needed help with and cut in. "No, IVAN, don't go yet. I need help analyzing the fossils we found."

Kalsik gave a small chuckle at something only he knew. He popped some joints as he stood up. "It's good to keep him busy. He doesn't cope well with inactivity."

As Kalsik left for the kitchenette, Morthas stood, the holographic avatar vanishing to then reappear in a white flicker inside the small lab he made his way into. Before Morthas even entered, the terminal flared to life on its 2D holodisplay, footage files loading up from IVAN's databanks.

There was something else he would go over with IVAN here, something that wasn't a fossil they had spotted today.

His nanite implants recorded all he saw or heard, a form of live diary, but of today's events, he was specifically interested in the creatures seen on the platform, his own data alongside their helmet feeds in need of analysis.

On screen, the frozen image of the larger one, its back turned, had a highlighted box over the strange gray lump beneath its scales. In a sub window on the screen, the footage of the other creature paused right before it turned to jump off, letting them get a good look at its back neck for comparison. As he mused to himself, IVAN's audio feed offered another hypothesis, drawing on xenobiological theory in addressing this utterly new creature in need of classification. "There's no similar shape on the other one. Could be a parasite or growth."

"Let's keep a watch out for others like it." Morthas rubbed his tired eyes, the light from the screens flickering in front of him before shutting off. With the faint yellow of the white star's early twilight as the only light coming in the viewport of the Buerev, he realized just how tired he was.

Knowing the various data analysis programs on the fossils and cores they'd found would be finished overnight, he shuffled out of the lab. He was keen to get some rest and be ready for an early start, as the wildlife was most active in the initial daylight hours.

Sleep came easily to Morthas that night, especially as he'd taken to waking early to indulge in this wildlife viewing before the midday heat got up. However, his relief in possibly breaking through Kalsik's stubbornness was worth calling today a success.

~~~

Out in the darkened skies, inquisitive eyes turned away from the now-lightless vehicle perched on the gorge top, left behind by the larger flying machine days ago. Banking away mid-flight, the inquisitive creature from before, with the gray lump beneath the back of its neck, headed around the mists of the waterfall and soared over the marshy river flats beyond.

As it flew over the plains below, the twilight sun cast its whitish-yellow haze over the horizon, prompting the myriad of night predators to venture out, having saved energy by sun-basking or resting in the daytime. The first hunts of the night were soon underway.

A large, four-legged predator lunged from its hiding spot in the long grasses, the membranes on its forelimbs flaring out like wings to let it sprint on two legs with the lift its light body allowed. Its quarry scattered, foraging repto-mammals resembling a bizarre rodent/lizard mix, many of them leaping into the water where their webbed feet and tail gave them greater mobility.

With a running leap, the predator crashed onto one of its prey to swiftly bite down on its head, crushing it as it staggered to a halt. The lucky escapees scurried into the river, diving toward a large mound of sticks and mud in a small section that flowed more slowly, where they took shelter for the night in their dens.

This was all usual for the flying creature, as its attention came to a rock that protruded ten meters up from the ground, worn down by countless rains and winds. Perched atop the rock, it bent over, lying as if relaxing, only for the lump on its back to change. Gray-hued flesh folded back to reveal the microcircuit implant beneath. The implant pointed skyward, and the creature remained still as a small light flickered inside the metallic fragment in its spine.

Moments later, 8,500 kilometers above in orbit, the signal was received by one of the multitude of nodes along the orbital ring. In the silence of the vacuum, all around the ring's structure, similar nodes began to come online.

Chapter 13

Hunted

Eleven Sol days since they had parted from the others, the *Haivres* remained parked in a glade just over double its size. The task here relied upon rovers trawling the seabed for sedimentary rock in order to document the atmospheric history, to corroborate data from the site. Already there was a slightly worn path in the sand where the four-legged rovers marched between the ship and the beaches a kilometer away.

In the meantime, they had another opportunity to investigate the local wildlife, and after being here for fourteen local days, they felt confident in venturing out even for leisure purposes, always ensuring they retained appropriate equipment.

For Serie, this was an opportunity to indulge in her artistic hobby, and as she preferred seeing it for herself, even if through a visor, she had no trouble finding a spot that gave a fantastic view of the beachfront, which was conveniently along the path the rovers took to and from the shallow sloping seabed.

The sun had just set, and not even the red dwarf secondary was up, with only one of the moons overhead in the sky. The ring, this far from the equator, lay halfway between the horizon and overhead, a semi-illuminated band arcing through the twilight expanse.

Seated atop her rocky perch, as one of the drones she had as an escort—at Shakrii's insistence—stood inactive beside her, Serie glanced back up from her wrist device's haptic

138

interface screen. Her digitally drawn lines, a basis for more detailed ones later on in her free time aboard the ship, captured what creatures she had already seen, and even some of the small plants she had seen in the forest.

While the drones had documented all she had seen and sketched, there was a difference between art and data, and she wanted this for herself. The ship was getting dull anyway, having not moved for about fourteen rotations now, while the outside world remained a much more vibrant, enticing place.

The gentle crash of the waves on a reef farther offshore echoed over the sands, the wind rustling in the treetops farther inland. She could just about see the top of one of the *Haivres*'s stabilizer fins poking above the red-leaved treetops a half kilometer away. Even if the air she was breathing was being filtered first, she slowly came to feel at ease at her surroundings as she continued her sketches, casually flipping back through some she'd already done.

The most common land creatures here were the omnivorous half-serpent, half-centipede creatures, each no longer than a meter and with all of their legs focused on the front of their forms. These life-forms populated the beach and trees. With a mouth almost like a set of clippers, they scavenged on whatever they could find, vegetation or meat, and were always the first animal on the scene to swarm a washed-up body of any size, such as a few fish carcasses Serie could see much farther away on the beachhead.

She had to admit that some animals had taken her by surprise, as when a cephalopod-like animal nearly half her size lunged from the waters yesterday, its skin colored the same as the sands, to slide with an incoming wave to ensnare one of the scavenging creatures in its tentacles as it feasted on a washed-up fish. Numerous spikes protruding and stabbing from the arms into the body caused visible bleeding and an inability to move, the prey skewered. It almost as quickly shuffled back, riding the back-tow of another wave into the water with its prey in its grip.

Admittedly, Serie knew there was one creature she wasn't keen to get close to, even if it appeared the most harmless, that being a bear-shaped animal three meters long and devoid of any fur or scales on its pale red skin from head to tail. She often saw this life-form leisurely traipsing up and down the beaches. Its long snout, capped with many antennae, searched for large grubs and plant roots, its behavior turning more frantic when it found a spot and began to dig with its clawed and webbed feet. Its skin secreted fluids that acted as both natural UV protection, and, by what they had all smelled when one had become curious of the *Haivres* two days ago, acted as a foul deterrent against potential predators.

Her eyes were drawn right now to the waters, though she wasn't concerned with the drone that had just emerged from the sea, its underside holding bay filled with a trawled load of rocks suitably sized for the scans. Instead, she focused on and sketched initial outlines of the bioluminescent display where the water shifted around the drone's steps in the shallow waters. Microorganisms, active at the twilight and dawn hours, flashed a bright array of greens and yellows as the drone made its way ashore, while other water disturbances came from fish flicking about in the swells and shallow waters.

Truly, this place was a marvel, and even if Nathan was disinclined to leave the ship beyond checking on drones, and Shakrii remained wary for security's sake, they had all begun to grow accustomed to it.

In retrospect, Serie felt she should have known better, as such ease rarely lasted.

~~~

Truthfully, Shakrii still hadn't gotten used to the sight of these tropical trees and the sand outside the ship's viewports, even after spending twelve Sol days here, as she didn't trust staying in one place on this planet for too long.

However, she had settled into her routine checks, with Committee reports and local data from survey drones, and had grown comfortable enough, admittedly more than she normally might. A part of her argued away her usual wariness, as nothing was attacking them. Nevertheless, she remained alert, with frequent glances at sensors that IVAN kept active the whole time. Thankfully, she noticed that Nathan, even in his more relaxed state, didn't neglect to keep his own eye on things as IVAN performed his usual wealth of background checks.

While she trawled through what historical atmospheric data they had received from the various drones, she couldn't help but overhear Nathan's conversation with Serie over the comms. There was definitely a disagreement about them having to go outside in person yet again, though it seemed unlikely to devolve into anything heated. If anything, as she bit back a smirk, their current debate was one that she'd been contemplating, given how little was currently happening.

"What about organic redundancy?" Serie asked.

"Please, organic redundancy's just code they use to justify stupid or dangerous jobs, usually both. Here's my idea: more machines to fix machines."

Doing her best to make it look like she was listening to audio reports, Shakrii didn't need to see Serie's face to picture her frown when IVAN joined the debate.

"True, with enough synthetics, organic redundancy would be unneeded. Organic boredom is more the reason difficult tasks aren't all assigned to machines, not practicality."

"See? He agrees." Nathan's tone was blatantly smug.

Despite doing her best to ignore this harmless argument, Shakrii listened in as she saw that the sensors showed no anomalies.

Serie seemed unbothered by being a minority opinion. "Well, I enjoy actually getting out of the ship. It breaks up the monotony. View's nice this time of day. The animals seem to come out more at this time too."

Shakrii remembered a certain few shared traits they'd seen in observations of many animals on this planet. Given the environment and sun, she hadn't been surprised when Morthas cited reptilian features being advantageous—hence the common scaly and semi-cold-blooded nature of many animals.

"They all seem to have reptilian traits," Shakrii said. "No surprise they're moving about after soaking up sunlight."

Nathan spun around in the pilot's seat and pointed an accusing finger at her, not at all hiding the victory in his voice. "Aha! I knew you were eavesdropping."

Shakrii ignored the mild burning she felt beneath her scales, and raised her smaller hands in equally mocking defense. "It was difficult to ignore—"

Sensor warnings went off in the cockpit, the dashboard displays flaring bright colors and bringing up all relevant scanners, from lidar, sonar, and motion sensors. All joking was gone in an instant, and Shakrii snapped to the screens nearest her.

"Scans are picking up a large bio sign inbound," IVAN announced.

"What's going on?" she asked.

"Not sure. Stay put." Nathan canceled the comms channel as IVAN honed sensors in on the approaching signal.

As she had made sure any emergency gear was ready to go if need be, Shakrii slowly stood up and approached the human as he froze in his seat, eyes glued to the scanners.

After a tense few moments, the signal seemed to pass to the left of the ship, still hidden in denser trees, until it was at the ship's port body wing.

Just as she'd convinced herself that it was a false alarm, Shakrii felt the tremble of something heavy landing on the port wing section. Sensors went off, and Nathan sharply inhaled, his knuckles turning white on the armrest beside him. Shakrii snapped her gaze upward as IVAN issued the alert, even if what the AI stated was obvious: "It is on the upper hull."

"Bring up imaging!" Her bark was harsher than she'd intended, but she wasn't taking any chances.

By the sounds of it, the ship could take this creature's weight, but stepping outside had become fraught with unknowns. IVAN brought up sensor images of the upper port section of the *Haivres*'s blended hull and wing form, revealing their intruder.

Shakrii's breath halted for a moment as she saw the size of the obvious predator prowling about atop their ship. It was sniffing the pair of stabilizer fins nearby. Thirteen meters long and three meters tall, it was a slender-bodied repto-mammal creature, four legs halfway between upright and sprawled in stance. Five clawed and webbed feet slightly scratched and dented the hull and paintwork as it sniffed about. A long tail, with a heavy-looking array of bladelike bones along its length, was balanced by a flexible neck with a heavily armored head. The creature's armor over its torso and neck didn't entirely cover its flesh, just enough to give it vital protection. Numerous spiky sensory quills that swayed as it moved were arrayed along its head and back, a mane and back spine almost like black-colored grass.

"How could something that big not be seen yet?" Nathan asked a little breathlessly.

"Jungles are dense." Shakrii watched the predator begin rubbing its mane spikes along a stabilizer fin, seeming to take a liking to it. With almost leisurely behavior, its large, armored head split open, revealing its internal mouth to be an array of sharp teeth. Shakrii found herself holding her breath as it gently bit down on the fin, bending it to the point of ripping it off. The hull damage alarm began squawking on the console beside Nathan.

A flash of outrage crossed the human's face. "I've had it with animals chewing the ship."

She couldn't help but agree with him. The sight of the creature gnawing on the fin like it would a bone from a big kill did little to persuade her that it had much intellect. She couldn't guess why it hadn't immediately rejected the taste, but neither Nathan nor IVAN, for understandable reasons, was in any mood to let it continue.

"Utilizing heavy-grade plasma-channel UV laser beams to compensate for larger target," IVAN said.

Shakrii saw the display screens turn from Nathan's visor to the gun turret camera feeds. She was glad to be in here, as this new creature was likely about to become very angry.

Whiplash cracks filled the air as the turret's heavier-duty far-UV-frequency laser-beam shots, traveling up the middle of the laser-induced micro-plasma channel corridor to confine them, impacted and drilled the creature's hide. Around them, the solid-state visible defensive pulsed-lasers coupled with these beams burned the hit points in a half-meter-wide spread.

~~~

Enraged, the creature gave an earsplitting roar as it scrambled off the ship's hull, the stabilizer fin dropping from its mouth mid-jump and crashing onto the sand beside where the predator staggered after landing, hissing angrily up at the ship's upper hull.

As it moved off, it found the path worn by the working drones, its sensory quills and nostrils also detecting another scent. One scent, organic, was unknown, but might have been potential food. It turned toward the beachhead half a kilometer away and followed the trail in silence.

A metallic insect of sorts had crawled out of a small gray lump in the creature's neck just before it was shot and now latched itself into a hiding spot within a fold in the hull's frame. With what happened next, it went utterly unnoticed.

~~~

Shakrii switched off the display screen, unable to stifle a smirk.

144

Beside her, Nathan remarked with a mournful tone on the repairs needed to the ship once again. "At least it was only a stabilizer—"

"Alert, predator heading for Serie's position."

IVAN's warning evaporated the sense of relief. The stunned silence lasted only a second before Shakrii sprang out of her seat, bellowing her order to Nathan as she tore down the corridor, heart racing. "Get her on comms now!"

Nathan frantically reestablished the comms call he'd dropped with Serie as Shakrii all but swung down the stairwell that led into the vehicle bay. Her equipment was ready to use, but every second counted. Shakrii couldn't comprehend how such a calm day had taken such a turn, and she knew all her attention had to be on making sure Serie didn't end up as the next thing the creature decided to investigate.

~~~

Serie had heard the roar and sprang up from her perch. Beside her, the drone that had been escorting her activated, a speaker broadcasting from it as Nathan's frantic voice came through, pleading for her to answer.

"Nathan, what's going on?"

"There's a big, big predator headed your way!"

A moment later, Shakrii's voice on the same speaker started issuing orders, barking with such speed and ferocity that she barely heard, her translator implant struggling to keep pace.

What Serie then heard made her look around, uneasiness setting in as she realized that the surrounding jungle noise had fallen silent. There were many universal features in ecosystems, and the tense silence preceding a hunt was one of them. Worse, she spotted a few flying creatures scattering from some trees that led straight toward the *Haivres*, though Shakrii's voice distracted her for a moment as their panicked screeches echoed.

145

"Get to high ground. I'll come for you. Go!"

"Wait, what does it look—" Serie spun around as she yelled at the drone, instinctively turning to where she knew the animal would come from. The movement of trees just over a hundred meters away revealed it, every detail of the predator burning into her mind as its eyes met her own for a split second.

Its sensory quills flickered at the sight of her, body visibly tensing, not a sound escaping it as it stared her down.

Without looking back, she turned and sprinted for the forests behind her, wings beating to speed her escape. She barely heeded the drone that had been beside her as it charged the predator head-on, IVAN assuming control in an attempt to buy her a few more seconds.

She spared a glance backward as she came to the edge of the forest. The crablike drone was gaining the beast's attention with a loud metallic horn. The creature pounced on it, only slowing to a walk to hurl the now-ruined drone aside after shaking it apart.

As the trees swallowed her, Serie swore the creature's fiery gaze met her own in the milliseconds that passed before leaves came between them, but she couldn't stop. Her body screamed at her to head deeper, head up, anywhere safe.

When she reached the taller trees, her heart was pounding hard enough that she was barely aware of when the first noises of the creature surging into the forest came: loud footfalls synchronizing with the thundering pulse in her ears.

Finally, like a gift from whatever creator there might be, she saw a towering tree riddled with vines. Mid-sprint, she leapt from the ground, using what lift she could get from a few wing beats. She caught the tree bark without a pause in her momentum and scrambled up the trunk, the cries of agony from her muscles silenced by the fight-or-flight instincts that compelled her to climb. Her implants, which only helped in her engineering work and did not stimulate activity, were a useless asset right now.

As she reached the lower canopy, the predator scythed through the clearing and caught sight of her tail feathers. Whether from hunger, curiosity, or both, it lunged for the tree trunk, claws raking across its length as it found itself unable to climb, and it gave an earsplitting roar as it leapt off to leer up at her.

Thirty meters above the ground, Serie burst through the leaves up top and looked down to see the creature prowling at the foot of the tree through the red-and-yellow brush. Its armored mouth dripped saliva as it lunged at the tree trunk, shaking it violently as its claws carved another chunk from the bark.

Serie unsheathed the one weapon Shakrii had insisted she carry: a small pulse-laser pistol. She opened fire at the animal, but the rounds merely peppered its outside, only as irritating to it as a beesting might have been to a human. Her weapon was all but useless. She holstered it and stifled a scream.

The creature lunged backward and turned to slam its sharp tail into the tree. The wood splintered, and horror gripped Serie as she saw that the creature had a way of bringing her down. She could already feel the tree beginning to shift.

Looking around in panic, she saw that the nearby treetops had similar canopy levels. She tore off her heavier gear, throwing the pieces of utility belt and support systems to the forest floor, drawing cursory sniffs from the animal before it resumed demolishing the tree trunk. Now clad in only her thermal-regulating skinsuit, her lower legs and entire wings exposed along with her face, she braced herself to make the jump. The creature snarled, and the tree shook under another hit.

Without waiting a moment more, she leapt, wings beating to surge her forward. She managed to soar a dozen meters before just barely catching the next treetop and slipping through the canopy to dangle by a few loose branches.

The predator abandoned the nearly toppled tree to attack her new one. Serie swore she felt her bones rattle as the first of its tail hits impacted the trunk, and to her horror, it was much faster this time due to unseen rot in the wood. A hideous splintering filled the air, and even the predator backed up as the tree fell.

Furiously beating her wings, Serie glided to the sands below, nearly stumbling on landing. Before she heard even the first footfall to signal its continued pursuit, she saw a thorny bush at the base of another tree and sprinted to dive into its barbed depths. She felt a sharp tug on her tail feathers as a claw barely skimmed them, but she was numb to it, numb to the pain as the thorn brambles and the vines scratched her skin beneath her plumage, the saltwater that pooled beneath this plant stinging as she fell down to scramble backward, deeper in, farther from the claws that began to rip apart the tree base where she'd hidden.

She fired her pistol uselessly, and its hungry eyes burned as it tore apart thorn-laden vine after vine, its hot breath blasting her amid its efforts to claim her as prey.

Then a new noise echoed in the air. A hypersonic tungsten projectile the size of her talon ripped a plasma-wake in the air by friction alone as it drilled the creature's hide. The animal's huge form turned toward the challenger, roaring louder than ever.

In the forest a fair distance away, Serie saw a lone Kronogri, face covered by her respirator, the rest of her body exposed. Shakrii stood her ground as she raised her wrist-mounted heavy rifle again. The predator gave a thunderous roar and charged at her.

Shakrii didn't hesitate in the face of this furious animal. She fired again. The full yield of her weapon drilled through its skull, a triple-shot coil gun burst punching a hole clean through the predator's head and scarring a tree far behind it. The creature whimpered and collapsed mid-charge, sand ploughing around it as it came to a halt. It gave a few last twitches as Shakrii strode past in silence, keeping her rifle trained on it.

Serie's body shook. She could only keep her breathing as measured as possible to suppress a panicked cry. Her clothing and respirator were caked in wet sand, and her wing and leg plumage bled from multiple thorn cuts, an infection risk if not treated.

All that went through Serie's mind at that moment was the Kronogri who came to a stop before her. Serie gulped some bile that nearly came up from the agony her muscles were in, her throat ragged from panic and exhaustion, and knelt down on the sand to maintain some composure. "Thanks . . ."

"Back to the ship. You need treatment before that becomes infected."

Serie followed behind Shakrii as they made their way back, passing where the creature lay dead.

IVAN's voice rang out urgently on Shakrii's comms. "I am detecting a radio broadcast from the creature."

Serie's exhaustion wasn't enough to stop her from whipping around. She spotted it, just as Shakrii moved into position. Her wrist rifle was trained on the tiny movement from a gray tumor they hadn't noticed before on the back of the predator's neck. Out of the gray tumor, like the one Morthas had reported on one birdlike creature at his site, something akin to an insect emerged from the bloody hole it burrowed out of. It was metallic, and half the size of a human's thumb. Active radio emissions showed up on Shakrii's scanners as IVAN synched to them from the ship.

Serie recoiled as Shakrii lunged forward, hands missing the bug as it scurried off into the undergrowth. The Kronogri pounded the sand in frustration.

As Serie turned her gaze upward, as if out of an inbuilt instinct to look skyward for guidance, she saw what would mark a turning point in the expedition, and all she could muster was to point it out to Shakrii.

High above, glinting as it set out from the ring, a speck departed on a trajectory bound for the planet. Something had launched the moment the bug's radio burst went out.

Serie didn't remember the rest of the run back to the ship, as exhaustion and panic clouded her mind.

~~~

IVAN had prepared medical equipment on a service drone for Serie, leaving Nathan to take the initiative and call the Buerev.

"*Haivres* reporting, are you there, Ka—"

"IVAN informed me, and we've detected an object launched from the ring section."

The captain's reply caught Nathan off guard. "How did you know—"

"Regroup as soon as possible."

"Yes, Captain. On our way." Nathan wiped the sweat from his brow and let out a weak moan of despair. All he could do was keep himself as calm as possible. It was clear that IVAN had been monitoring their activity beyond basic expedition data exchange. Nathan kept very quiet, his mind racing as he saw the anger building in Shakrii's eyes.

~~~

The bug that had dropped off the predator as it prowled atop the *Haivres* remained latched on and hidden, its sensors monitoring the ship but not transmitting or engaging its other functions yet.

Chapter 14

Xarai

Sol Day 45

"Approaching landing zone."

IVAN's voice rang through the cockpit as the distant lights of the Buerev drew nearer, still perched near the waterfall gorge.

As the *Haivres* slowed in its descent through the darkness, Shakrii finished up her call to Kalsik. "Drive in as soon as we're down. We'll discuss your eavesdropping once safe."

If Kalsik had remorse, she didn't sense it. She realized that her smaller foreclaws had been absentmindedly raking marks in the console during their conversation. Nathan, his fingers dancing as his neural implant controls directed the craft to begin reverse thrust to slow for landing, glanced in her direction while IVAN made ready the hangar hatch systems.

"He just likes to know—"

"Don't make excuses for him," IVAN interjected.

She had no desire to listen to the AI, whom she felt was equally culpable in this breach of trust.

"Protocol requires the captain must know what goes on regarding his ship and crew, even when not aboard it himself."

As much as Shakrii wished to see IVAN deactivated right now, she knew priorities mattered, and the Buerev that was bathed in their spotlights went out of sight as Nathan turned to land with the aft facing it. IVAN took remote control in parallel with Kalsik from the Buerev's driver seat. Every second mattered to get the vehicle back aboard, as the mysterious vessel had already begun to hit the denser atmosphere where their satellites tracked it.

The ramp was lowered as soon as the *Haivres* landed, and the Buerev drove up and into the cargo bay without a moment's pause, its tracks hoisting it into the cargo hold and locking down the brakes.

When the cargo bay door began to shut, Shakrii breathed a sigh of relief. The sensor boards in the cockpit showed the reactor and engines increasing in power.

~~~

The hidden insect-like metallic creature activated. Having crawled into a communications array alcove within the ship's hull, it had latched itself on to the receiver and hardwired the microfiber data lines with its hairlike fibers.

Now, with signals showing the ship about to take off with everyone aboard, a signal was broadcast from the ring in orbit, and a tight-beam data broadcast relayed through the bug and into the mainframe. Random data in all possible combinations, at speeds unbelievable to those aboard, flooded the ship's networks.

~~~

"Unknown transmission detected," IVAN informed.

Shakrii recoiled at the sight unfolding across all the sensor readout screens. Vast loads of data, most unreadable, consumed the screens, which all began flickering or blacking out.

"Error! Security overload, disconnecting core module."

Shakrii saw IVAN cut himself off, the portable mobile platform that was his basic brain unplugging from the ship. In that instant, even with IVAN's core systems no longer at risk, the displays began to show even more chaos. Some key data was detected and mistaken

152

as genuine by the ship's safety systems.

The reactor core's readouts flared to life on one display beside Nathan, his eyes widening as he mentally summoned the control functions.

Shakrii lunged forward to see the screen, then turned to the human beside her, ignoring his barely contained panic as he tried to regain control. If their power core went, that was it. "Reactor's showing a containment fault, get—"

Before she could finish, the lights went out, and the faint hum of the engines ceased. Their thrust had lifted them off the wheel suspension slightly, but now the ship sank back once more.

Her breath caught in her throat as her four eyes adjusted to the darkness, the little ambient nighttime remnants of light coming in through the viewport enough that the human became visible beside her again. Her quiet voice cut through the silence, the fear that she'd kept in control showing itself. "Reactor shut down."

The human brought up the basic system readout, a runtime normally kept offline. Scrolling through, he scowled at the multitude of error reports and incomprehensible data analytics. "Every system's full of junk data." His voice was shaky. "Comms are dead, no link to the drive ship."

The weight of their predicament sank in as she slumped backward in the darkened cockpit, aware of the smell of sweat the human was exuding. Not that she could blame him. She breathed deeply before speaking as calmly as she could. "Help me get the manual overrides. We need to get the others inside."

Shakrii let the human stagger ahead of her down the corridor, his disorientation not easing her worries about him. She noticed, to her relief, that IVAN's cube-shaped mobile frame gave a flicker of its lights in acknowledgment of her as she passed the AI core.

Backup power still worked, and dim lighting came back on in the corridors, though the ship's reactor and engines were still silent. Down the hallway at the access hatch to the hangars, there was the faint sound of panels being opened as Serie, who had been advised to rest in her cabin, had come out and set to work.

The Leg'hrul's tone expressed more aggravation than fear. "Backup power can keep habitation systems online. Comms best stay off if it's a cyberattack."

Shakrii clapped a hand on Serie's shoulder, then started to work on the manual airlock controls. Off to the side, Nathan began shaking and bowed his head, slumping backward against the wall. Serie leaned down to console him, and Shakrii realized how fearful the human really was.

<center>~~~</center>

Morthas and Kalsik had been able to isolate the Buerev, as it hadn't been the victim of the cyberattack, but the power failure had locked them in the hangar. It wasn't long before both were aboard and in the safety of the pressurized sections of the *Haivres*.

The relief didn't last long, however. Morthas rushed straight to the mineral lab. Meanwhile, Serie had quietly led the human back to the cockpit with a comforting wing over his shoulders, leaving Shakrii and Kalsik alone by the airlock access section of the hallway. IVAN's box-shaped core module headed to the cockpit as well, pursuing Serie and Nathan.

"You saved Serie."

Kalsik's words did nothing to assuage the fury she held for this dark-gray Kronogri. "I said I was in charge of defense on this trip, and as such, I need to be aware of all information. All. Understand?"

"We have bigger problems—"

"Which means you should drop your selfish paranoia right now."

Kalsik was unyielding, even as his justifications became flimsier. "I was harming nobody by keeping surveillance."

"If saving the life of one of your crew isn't enough, what will it take to make you see that I can be trusted?"

"By all accounts, killing that big animal may have triggered whatever radio burst the bug sent off."

"You'll blame me for anything. Just when I was beginning to think you weren't such a feculent Kronog, you go and further lower that bar. I wonder if redacted records would show you were discharged partly because of your attitude. One more act like this, and I will cite the captain's emotional instability, just as the contract allows my authority to supersede your own, and ensure you never captain this craft again. Am I absolutely clear?"

Shakrii hid any pleasure at the sight of Kalsik's shoulders slumping as he glared bitterly at her. He turned away, but before he could storm off, she reached forward for the back of his shoulder with her larger forearm's iron grip, squeezing hard.

"If this first contact doesn't go well, if things go wrong due to your actions, there will be dents in the walls made by your head."

As she released him, Shakrii half expected him to turn around to face her, fight her even. But another visible sag set into his shoulders as he shuffled off to the cockpit, his arrogant demeanor now quite absent.

She put Kalsik out of her mind and went to meet with Morthas, hoping for some sort of solution or protocol to follow.

The scientist told her that he needed to run some analyses, and that he would adhere to first contact guidelines once he'd figured out which methods applied best.

After entering the cockpit, it only took a few moments for Shakrii to overhear what she needed to, as the others had already set to work on the approaching anomaly. Whether it was out of anxiety or duty, she preferred they know everything.

"The signal is actively headed for our position," Serie said.

At the consoles, as both Kalsik and Serie worked to restore power, the screen readouts kept warning of instabilities. Serie cursed in her native dialect, too incoherent for Shakrii's translator to pick up. Then she turned to them with a flushed face, gesturing to the console with a wingtip. "It'll take a while for us to clear the systems of junk data before we can find the problem and solve it."

"Such system clearing cannot be done before the new vessel arrives," IVAN said.

Nathan slumped in the pilot's seat. Serie gave the console nearest her a punch with her wing.

Kalsik stared blankly at a reflective console surface. "That's it, then."

"Not yet." Shakrii couldn't accept that this predicament was a lost cause. Mercifully, she didn't have to explain, as Morthas had arrived shortly after her and overheard the exchange. His voice cut through the tension with a tone of cautious optimism, though she could sense the fear that came with it.

"She has a point. Maybe this will turn out to be an opportunity."

~~~

It was an hour before the unknown ship finally touched down on the nighttime plains near the canyon. A faint light from the approaching craft became a blinding light that drowned out the starlit skies.

The grasses rustled outside as the ship made land almost silently, the outline of its hull barely visible behind the spotlight. With a thin central hull and bulky pentagonal wings that swept backward, the ship resembled a metallic, winged insect. Its wings split apart like feathers, segments folding down to become landing struts. Buried amid the engines were what looked like propulsion and power systems, the hull of the craft suspended between them most likely housing the payload, and perhaps passengers.

Inside the cockpit, where they had all gathered, Shakrii saw the craft's lights dim enough to showcase its full size. Only thirty meters long, tiny compared to the *Haivres*, the ship settled down, thrusters dying as its few remaining lights kept themselves trained on the *Haivres*, shining even into the cockpit's viewport. Whatever was in the ship, it was already watching them, perhaps as it and others had been doing from the moment they arrived on this planet.

A minute passed with no activity, until the *Haivres*'s computer systems suddenly flared to life, data streams flying across displays as an unseen force took control of the ship. Beside her, Kalsik barked a command, turning to IVAN's mobile box. "Reconnect! We need to stop it hacking us."

"I doubt I could with what it seems capable of."

Shakrii saw the monitor readouts becoming steadier, controlled, as if searching for something.

"It's going for the databases," Nathan said in a shaky voice.

"It's likely probing us," Morthas said, his voice barely above a whisper.

As the exchange of data continued, an animal landed on the viewport's side and climbed over the outer hull to peer into the cockpit. It was one of the local winged creatures, the thin, feathered, and upper-gray carapace sporting familiar markings and colorations. The few distinct markings, and slight gray lump on the back of its spine, confirmed it as the same individual that had investigated the excavation platform in the gorge some days ago.

At least that was what Shakrii gathered by Kalsik's narrowed expression and Morthas's loud response: "That one again?"

As it crawled over the cockpit, turning its head slowly, Shakrii spotted the gray lump on its spine. A growl escaped her throat as she remembered where else she had seen such a strange growth.

Serie, too, was familiar with it. "The lump, just like the big predator had."

157

As if on command, the creature's lump split open with no bleeding. Like worms from a rotten fruit, small, metallic tendrils extended from the hole. They were the length of a human's small finger. Shakrii gaped at this hypnotic, somewhat repulsive sight, and realized that this creature was somehow under control.

As two of the tendrils raised, the creature kept still, lying perched on the outer viewport. A small segment on the tendril ends straightened, and the hacking on the consoles around them slowed to a stop. Their computer systems remained stationary until all but one of the touchable 2D screens shut off, its solitary light glowing as ominously as the strange ship's shape looming in the darkness outside.

A few moments passed in silence until two of the animal's extended tendrils shined small dots of light on them. A laser spot appeared on Shakrii's chest, along with a similar dot on Kalsik. Realizing that a laser pointer could precede an attack, Shakrii held her breath as the dot wavered slightly on her chest. Kalsik stood equally frozen on the other side of the cockpit. After a few seconds, text began to appear on the single active screen, translating to their chosen preference of standard Kronogri dialect.

KRONOGRI

"It's identifying us." Morthas's breathless remark was confirmed when the laser dots vanished from hers and Kalsik's chests, at which point the breath she'd felt begging to escape finally released.

An audible whimper filled the air, Nathan stiffening as both lasers moved to his chest. While Serie clenched a reassuring claw on his shoulder, Shakrii could only watch as the creature's tendrils kept their dots trained on him, the name of Nathan's race being typed methodically by whatever was controlling it, perhaps from the landed spacecraft outside.

HUMAN

When the laser spotlight left the human's chest, much to his relief, it passed to Serie and Morthas next. Shakrii noticed they were both more composed after seeing no ill effects from this on the others. Sure enough, their race name also appeared.

LEG'HRUL.

The laser dots left their chests and homed in on IVAN's mobile box core that sat on the floor. The frame's optics extended on their mounts to see the laser dots hovering over his box frame, yet Shakrii wasn't sure how it would identify the AI exactly.

IVAN

"Indication of synthetic intelligence suspected," IVAN said.

Shakrii didn't know if IVAN was being serious or mocking—more likely both.

The laser dots vanished, while the creature turned its body with enough purpose for them to see its laser pointer extensions aim for the strange ship. Suddenly, out in the nighttime darkness as the waterfall roared away in the distance, the insect-like ship's small central hull seemed to split apart, panels opening up to reveal an egg-shaped core in its hold, barely lit in its outline by the reflections of the spotlights it still shined on their ship.

The core began to unfold from itself, and four long, slender legs extended to the ground, visibly thickening as they took the weight. With its four shape-shifting limbs on the ground, the main core fully separated from the ship and rose to its full size. The rear legs were significantly longer than the forelegs, and it had an almost crescent-shaped main body. Two long arms extended out, having been folded tightly enough along its length that they were near invisible at first glance. A neck then extended from the crescent body, a few nodules and lumps on its end, the head being the hub of sensory equipment, though it was so thick that it almost merged with the neck.

As it slowly stepped forward on the grassy ground below, more reflective light shone on its form, and it became obvious that it wasn't organic. It was a machine, but none like they had ever seen before.

As if woven from thick metallic ropes, the body of the creature undulated as it stepped, actively shifting in among itself, only ceasing when it stopped moving entirely. There were no glowing marks, nothing that would give it away in the middle of the night, not until its entire body flared a slight blue shade, revealing the complexity it held.

Just like it had with each of them, the creature perched outside on the viewport shined its green laser pointers on the machine's midsection. On the screen, a single word formed—a single word that inspired fear, awe, uncertainty, and curiosity in a mixture few other discoveries could.

X A R A I

Chapter 15

Multipurpose Unit 128/Xami

Sol Day 46

The tense night eventually yielded as dawn broke.

Sunlight burned her eyelids through the cockpit viewport as Shakrii jerked awake, both sets of eyes bleary. She rubbed the back of her head, letting out a groan while popping her arm joint, the product of a poor choice of sleeping position in the cockpit seat. If they were to have first contact, they needed to avoid antagonizing the newcomer, and Morthas had spent the night working through the tedium of more language exchange while she had succumbed to her drowsiness.

A loud snort caught her attention, and she saw Kalsik still asleep in his own seat. Despite their confrontation last night, he had been just as keen to be on hand, though he carefully avoided looking in her direction.

Shakrii turned her drowsy gaze toward Morthas, currently sitting in Nathan's usual seat. He was still feverishly working, aided by copious amounts of stimulant drink, judging by the empty canisters at his feet. IVAN worked from inside the cubic module, a precaution against being hacked while accessing the compromised ship networks. Given the speed of their guest's learning, she was surprised they were still at it.

The Xarai, the only name they had for it at the moment, was a synthetic being, and as such, made use of rudimentary language conversion programs, one of which they'd brought along in the first contact data caches, aiding it in learning their languages in written and oral form with acceptable accuracy. The basic code of all AI and computers, even utterly alien ones, was some form of binary no matter how advanced, and once it became clear what was a one and a zero in their binary formats, the rest came systematically.

Despite the language barrier coming down, the Xarai hadn't dropped the restraints it imposed on their ship functions by way of the bug-sized hacker drone which they had finally detected on the upper hull. For now, they were in its power. At the moment though, as Shakrii rubbed sleep from her eyes, she envied the gleeful excitement Morthas exuded even after an all-nighter.

~~~

"I recommend maintaining a level of cordial cooperation. My capabilities will remain limited until direct inquiries progress."

IVAN's statement reinforced their need for caution. While Kalsik, now awake, didn't once look her way, Shakrii took a nervous step forward, gripping the side of a nearby console and glancing sideways at the data pad beside Morthas, their collectively prepared questions ready to go.

Morthas took a deep breath as he spoke the first question into the established link with the alien ship. "Why did you hack our ship?"

The silence that followed was punctuated only by the distant roar of the waterfall, before a reply made all of them nervously glance from the console to the ship outside. It was laced with some static at first, but then a synthesized, buzzing voice rang out, utilizing a default voice setting for the ship intercom, distinct from IVAN's chosen baritone.

"Prevention of escape to ease analysis."

"How did you decode enough to hack us?"

"Decoding was simple once function of binary code from sample fragments was deciphered."

As it spoke over the comms, data loads flooded the single display screen, and Shakrii mentally kicked herself. She recalled a first contact basic, namely that the complexities of languages usually came after the shared universal values in mathematics in establishing translation. Binary, prime numbers, anything constant was useful in establishing dialogue with alien entities. Progressing from this to more complex dialogue was just a matter of time and mutual education.

Shakrii redirected her attention back to Morthas as he spoke his next question, one she feared they already knew the answer to. "We have other vessels in orbit, and we cannot communicate with them. Is that your doing too?"

"They are still operational. Only your vessel's communications to anything besides what is permitted are blocked."

As if it were some unspoken means of easing their fears—unsuccessfully in Shakrii's mind—every word or statement the Xarai spoke was backed up by data relayed to their monitor display. This time it was charts of the orbits of their microsatellites and the warp spatial drive ship in real time, confirming they were still there.

Wishing to get answers to bigger questions, Shakrii leaned over toward Morthas. It wasn't a question on their script, but she was curious about something else. "Ask it about the probe first sent to the system."

Shakrii noticed that Kalsik became more interested. Her misgivings about his recent actions aside, she wasn't surprised, as he'd been leading this survey ship when that probe went offline so long ago, so he had more reason to be curious than any of them.

Morthas cleared his throat and said, "There was a probe sent, long before us. It was disabled. I take it that was also you?"

"We did shut down the probe, correct."

"We? So there are more of you?"

"Xarai hardware are vessels, this one being a limited production form and program cluster intended for efficient multirole operations, primarily scouting for anomalies on this planet, mostly local wildlife, though it includes extra-solar visitors."

Although not an AI expert herself, Shakrii was aware of the two distinct types of AI. While more robust, single-entity AIs relied on core quantum hardware of sapient intelligence, as IVAN did with his mobile cube form, they too could draw on processing from elsewhere or remote-control hardware from afar. Additionally, there were the simpler hive AIs with no individual personalities. They were grouped together like neurons in a brain to form collective intellects on par with or beyond sapience, these being the more numerous, mass-produced ones.

Despite being a synthetic, Xarai was still intelligent, and all intelligences had agendas. Much to Shakrii's approval, Morthas didn't ease up his questioning at all.

"Why shut down our probe?"

"A small probe rendered inoperable was unlikely to draw in more if the cause seemed like a natural solar flare."

"Misjudged that badly." From behind, thankfully not on the comms, Kalsik did not let go of his derisive laughter as he activated a new console. He began to file away the data troves they were receiving while running scans for any hidden viruses or malware.

Shakrii couldn't help but also give a snort, while Morthas evidently was better at keeping a straight face as he continued.

"It managed to send out some pictures of your ring," Morthas said.

"We did not know it had sufficiently documented before it was disabled."

Shakrii was surprised at how the Xarai immediately admitted to the error. Whether it was able to be annoyed or not was unknown, though she wouldn't put it past its capabilities.

"So why didn't you disable us earlier?"

"There was a higher probability of a successful distress call being sent out. We interfered only when our active existence was confirmed by evidence of implanted ecological monitors, and once we were certain of how to corrupt your networks, we utilized the one currently attached to your vessel."

Morthas leaned back in his seat for a moment, glancing in Shakrii's direction, at IVAN's cubic form beside him, and even back at Kalsik, who looked as confused as she was. The smallest gesture with Shakrii's head was enough to get Morthas to refocus and ask the obvious question.

"Ecological monitors? The small metal parasites on some of the animals?"

"Implanted animals serve as ecological observation without interfering with natural behavior of local fauna. We can also exert limited control, excluding periods of heightened instinctive urges, as occurred with the iphason when its hunting instincts overpowered the implant."

"Warding off that predator antagonized it, and the implants couldn't control it—a plausible enough scenario." IVAN's remark confirmed many things, including one that Kalsik had accused Shakrii's actions of causing yesterday.

Shakrii glanced in Kalsik's direction, waiting for him to turn to her with smugness. However, none came, though he seemed to mutter under his breath about the idea of probing for a defensive response with visible disapproval. Clearly his concern for his crew was a greater priority than scoring over Shakrii.

"Are they monitoring anything besides the ecosystem?" Morthas asked.

"No. Manufacturing this ecosystem gives enough interest in seeing it maintained, which requires monitoring."

Manufacturing this ecosystem. Upon hearing this astounding claim admitted as if it were normality, Shakrii slowly backed away from the comms terminal.

"Can we believe it?" Kalsik asked, looking just as floored as everyone else.

Morthas broke the brief silence that followed. "Why lie about something this big?"

Despite his reasoning, Shakrii wouldn't make any assumptions. "It's no machine that's ever seen or heard of any of our kind. How do we judge it?"

"I agree with Shakrii. We cannot take its word yet—not until more data is acquired and confirmed." IVAN pivoted on his cube's wheels to stare at the Leg'hrul as he made his point. Kalsik gave a small glance away toward something distant before turning back to hear Morthas reply to the Xarai.

"We need to confirm what you've said. Without access to our more advanced systems, that's not possible."

"You might try to escape to orbit if your systems are released."

"We mean no harm."

"Not directly. But if you inform your origin civilization of this with only partial information, it could lead to a conflict-triggering misconception. We must know you before we can trust you, as you said of us."

The Xarai's reply didn't sit well with any of them, but before Shakrii could let Morthas know what to say, Kalsik interjected.

"We need those systems. Without them, we'll run out of food and power."

Shakrii turned to give another gesture for Morthas to continue. Much as she wished they had stuck to script, Morthas seemed able to improvise, making her wonder if he had ever considered a career in politics.

"If you insist on monitoring us, do that, but please give us leniency enough to make sure we can maintain ourselves."

As silence claimed the cockpit once again, Shakrii wondered if such a plea for empathy would register to a machine that hadn't ever seen their kind before. Mercifully, they didn't have to wait too long, as the Xarai responded over the comms after a few seconds of deliberation, laying out terms of cooperation—or if she were feeling more pessimistic, imprisonment.

"Your ship and all aboard it will be allowed to operate. The superluminal communications you operate with require you to be in a microgravity environment to start up, as such, and keeping you in the atmosphere below the required altitude and shutting down your largest satellite will minimize the risk of home communication without sufficient information."

"We can restart systems aboard this ship?"

Morthas's cautious question received an immediate response, the machine stating the conditions in summarized terms that Shakrii had to suppress a growl at. All the while, precise details of their limits were broadcast to their one open data terminal.

"Confirmed. You are to remain in the atmosphere but are otherwise free until we know each other better. This mobile platform will be a proximity escort for that duration at minimum. Your smaller satellites will also be freed for remote reactivation for you to continue local data collection for when you are finally granted means to transmit it to your home sector."

True to its word, upon engaging a few more systems, it was clear that the masses of corrupted data were beginning to clear, restoring to previous versions. Defragmenting the data drives would sufficiently deal with anything that wasn't cleared, namely harmless code fragments, though they always had the option of restoring from backups IVAN had made days ago.

Shakrii could breathe more easily when she heard that regaining full functions of their expedition hardware, besides superluminal communication, would take only a few hours once

IVAN was fully reintegrated.

A few minutes later, they all met to discuss what had been agreed upon. Shakrii sympathized with the unease that was prevalent. Even Morthas, cautiously excited as he was, had his own misgivings about the conditions.

With them all seated at the table in the habitation ring lounge, Serie rubbed her feathery brow wearily, still covered in the nano-gel patches sending antibiotics throughout her system. Beside her, having thrown on some casual clothing, Nathan sat with a drowsy expression. Neither had slept well. Shakrii personally considered her role as security manager almost ruined, but she wouldn't let anyone else know that.

"Are we hostages or guests?" Serie asked quietly.

The Leg'hrul engineer's remark at their situation was quietly echoed by them all, much as Shakrii wished otherwise.

It was IVAN who replied. "They want us to learn from them, avoiding misconceptions that partial information might cause. A reasonable request."

While IVAN's logic was solid, it didn't console the crew. Morthas had begun to retreat into himself, analyzing the situation from an academic viewpoint, which Shakrii knew would be useful to keep him focused on their mission. It was the others that concerned her.

Kalsik's reserved state after her berating him for his paranoia was something she knew she had to keep a watch on, but if anything, he seemed much more focused on his ship's safety. This was something she felt they could agree on.

She figured that Nathan's nervousness might alleviate once full ship functionality was restored. He needed to be performing his familiar functions, and control of the ship seemed soothing for him in a way she didn't think she would ever understand. Meanwhile, Serie's nerves seemed more a result of her recent near-death wildlife encounter, coupled with their newfound company outside—mild PTSD that Shakrii knew might need to be addressed at some point, if not by her, then by crewmembers she could trust and confide in.

She knew she had to be careful in her wording, but if she were being honest with herself, the reassurances she gave to the crew were just as much for herself. Being in the power of the Xarai terrified her, but she wouldn't let that compromise her, as it seemed to have the others to varying degrees. "We can always ask it later to let us contact and reactivate the drive ship's wormhole comms to keep updating the Committee. We don't want them thinking we're dead. Aside from that and the escort, we continue as planned."

IVAN's white diamond avatar appeared on the screen on the table as he cut in. "We shall need to alter protocol for any organics venturing outside, given our new escort."

"One of us is going to have to go out anyway," Kalsik pointed out. "That stabilizer still needs fixing." He brought up a display of the *Haivres* structure, a few highlighted orange areas on the upper hull. He cast a soft glance toward Serie and Nathan, the Leg'hrul going wide-eyed at the prospect of such a task. Surprisingly, Kalsik didn't urge them to do it, and what he said next impressed Shakrii and earned her respect. "I will go out for the repairs with the drones."

Shakrii would have had to be blind to miss the quiet gratitude Nathan, and especially Serie, had for Kalsik at that moment. Whatever problems she and he had with each other, it seemed she could rest easy knowing that Kalsik was able to keep calm in this situation, though his background in the military made that no surprise. Some things stuck with you after long service.

"If I might, perhaps we could try and get a closer look at our visitor?"

Morthas's suggestion reminded her of issues she'd had with fellow recruits in basic training many years ago. Through the skeptical looks from the others, she addressed the Leg'hrul in a way that would not require him to answer. "Would you be insulted if I was honest about that idea?"

"I can approach. Remote control of a drone to spare will suffice."

IVAN's statement was the final true progress made in the conversation, and with that, they had their plan.

~~~

By late morning, the ship's functions were almost fully restored, sans the internal wormhole communications.

Outside, repair drones crawled over the ship, repairing the basic outer hull layers. Kalsik had donned his envirosuit to work on the more delicate task of repairing the stabilizer fin. He cast anxious glances toward the alien craft in front of the *Haivres*'s bow, wishing that his job of securing the new fin as the drone welded it down was more distracting.

The metal-coiled robot stood there as unmoving as when it had emerged from the ship the previous night, though he swore it had tilted its extended head toward him slightly as he'd zoomed in his mask's enhancement functions. At two meters tall and two-and-a-half meters long, the undulating body, which he bet had a great shapeshifting capability, dwarfed the half-meter-tall crablike drone that IVAN controlled. Whatever this newcomer was made of was likely a form of nanotechnology, given the level of complexity required for such shapeshifting robotics.

Although Kalsik tried to look away and focus on the stabilizer, his gaze was transfixed on the Xarai as it began to circle the *Haivres* drone before it as a predator would a cornered prey animal.

He felt much too vulnerable out here. He could only hope that IVAN's synthetic calm would be better than his own composure.

~~~

Sprouting from its crescent-shaped body, the Xarai's sensor-embedded head craned down, thinning as it stretched to examine the crablike drone in detail. The long arms folded

170

out from its sides, extending its reach to two meters. Like feeler antennae on an insect, multiple sensors in the fingers of the arms passed over and around the drone's body, scanning with the unseen sensory tools in nanorobotic coils. All the while, the AI of the ship, IVAN as its designation was, kept still within the remote-operated drone, allowing it to be examined, though the Xarai noticed that IVAN transmitted schematics at the same time, as if trying to reduce the probing. Why it did so was not entirely certain. The Xarai merely wished to study, not harm.

Regardless, it was, to use a term these explorers would use, odd to be in the presence of an utterly alien synthetic.

~~~

While Kalsik worked outside, the others were watching the interaction between IVAN's controlled drone and the Xarai. Shakrii knew IVAN was exchanging, learning for their benefit, though the option to remove his control in the event of hacking remained mercifully intact.

She was in fact more surprised by how long Morthas had been awake without appearing drowsy, though now his eyes were drooping as he watched every move the Xarai made, recording them with his own visor functions. Nathan now lay in his pilot seat, given back to him by Morthas, and was less uneasy than he'd been before, enough to snicker at the Xarai nudging IVAN's drone to get a response. As for Serie, Shakrii saw that she'd begun to admire the Xarai's unique body frame.

Now Serie voiced a question. "It said it was Xarai, but is it an individual or a collective?"

"IVAN? You seem to be getting on with it."

Kalsik's voice cut in on the comms channel. The male Kronogri had begun to make his way up from the stabilizer as the drones finished the last welding on its frame. Shakrii could see the relieved look on his face as sensors showed him scurrying back to the airlock, though the faint chuckle he held for IVAN mid-question showed he had been watching the Xarai the whole time.

Outside, Shakrii saw the Xarai seem to take a step back as IVAN relayed what it had learned over the speakers, even glancing in their direction, as if overhearing everything, which she felt was certain.

"Xarai are their collective software. This unit's root programming is more advanced than anything I've seen, but enough similarities exist to conclude it is a singular-entity intelligence, capable of collective processing if required, intended for scouting."

"Xarai's the race—a synthetic one, clearly—but what about this one? Calling it just Xarai may come across as insulting." Shakrii couldn't help but interject, as even a basic understanding of intra and interspecies histories justified her concerns. While she had no doubt Kalsik would agree, she was surprised when IVAN replied with some condescension.

"Concepts of individualism differ when the beings in question are synthetic. However, for ease of information exchange, a singular designation would be ideal."

At this remark, Shakrii felt some need to apologize for her choice of words, though before she could, a heavily synthesized voice cut through the air. She only slightly jumped, recognizing it from before. Nathan and Serie looked like startled animals for a moment as the Xarai individual spoke.

"My designation is Multipurpose Unit 128."

A silence followed this announcement before Serie gave a small cough to get their attention. "Perhaps meld the word Xarai with something familiar? Given the role it has, scouting, I think maybe one of the Leg'hrul gods from the old Yechani religion. Miia-Hemv, god of the hunt and wisdom."

Nathan leaned back in his seat as he juggled the words they had to work with. "Xarai-

172

Miia-Hemv, bit of a mouthful. Xarai-Mi, Xar-mi, Xami? Wait, Xami! What do you think?"

There was little debate, as the shortest suggested name was easiest to use. Shakrii hoped there were no foreboding tales of this Miia-Hemv god if they intended to use it to name this Xarai, though a short name was welcome regardless.

Kalsik made ready to enter the airlock outside. "Xami, then, unless anyone's got a better name?"

"Xami. Confirmed. I shall accept this designation."

The synthesized, buzzing voice that Xami used normally altered mid-sentence, and Shakrii now heard a smooth, rich voice coming through the speakers, less grating on their ears. If she were to label it, she would call it somewhere closer to what was considered female accents by humans, Leg'hrul, and Yaleirn, Eithraak unable to be included due to their mono-gendered, heavily clicking tones, and Kronogris' differences between male to female octaves being narrower than the other gendered races.

Morthas leaned forward to ask into the comms terminal, "What happened to your voice?"

"Synthetic crewmember IVAN suggested vocal traits known to create greater ease within organics, reasons varying for species. The fact that they are associated with the female gender in all but Kronogri and Eithraak is coincidental."

"Can we call Xami 'her' then?" Nathan cut in. "After all, we call IVAN 'he.'"

Nobody disagreed, organic or synthetic, local or visitor, and Xami would be a she.

Shakrii was relieved to have that out of the way. She hoped that now they could get the expedition back on track and obtain plenty of data for when, or if, the Xarai finally let them contact home. Now a firsthand account was an option for investigation. If Xami was willing to reveal her kind's history as much as she purported to be, they might end up better off than if they'd never met. But Shakrii knew they had to be vigilant, and if not collectively, she would certainly be.

Chapter 16

The World of the Xarai

Sol Day 50

Four rotations had passed since Xami had joined them, and now the time had come to move out to a new site.

Their visitor had retreated back into the vessel that brought her, ready the moment they were. In had become clear that IVAN would be an essential go-between, and judging by the levels of data exchange going on, they semi-jokingly wondered if IVAN was happy to have another AI to speak to.

Shakrii couldn't say the same for the rest of the crew, herself included. She'd lost hours of sleep the past four nights knowing it was out there, but the prospect of changing location would at least distract them all.

~~~

Shakrii rubbed the drowsiness from her four eyes, then shuffled into the lounge module to see the rest already up, more eager to be moving on than she was. She made her way to the kitchen module as Serie trawled through 2D-projected readout screens of more internal systems on the ship at the table, her meal half-finished beside her. In his usual corner seat, Kalsik quietly ate his own food.

Shortly after she made her way back, a nutrient bar from her own stores in her small grip, she saw Nathan quietly take a seat beside Serie. The human reclined in his seat with a

175

hand to his forehead. "I keep hoping this is a bad dream, and sure enough, she's there."

His remarks roused Shakrii's sympathy once more, though she had to admit he managed to keep his anxieties in check enough to be fit for duty.

"Whatever you're dreaming isn't much better," Serie said. "You gave a few harsh kicks last night."

He gave her a confused look. "I did?"

Shakrii suppressed a snort.

"If your bed warmer's acting up, sleep in your own cabin," Kalsik groused as he got up to get rid of his empty meal box, a ghost of a smirk crossing his scaly lips.

Serie's plumage fluffed out in embarrassment, and Nathan's face darkened to a shade of red as Shakrii struggled not to smirk.

Kalsik headed up to the cockpit, clearly wishing to be somewhere else. Though Shakrii no longer felt open hostility toward him, there still lingered the cold distrust, and she expected he would avoid her for some time still. If any of the other crew were aware of it, they kept it to themselves.

"I wonder if he's speaking from experience," Serie said, exchanging a coy look with Nathan.

"I will not say," IVAN chimed in. "Any queries about personal relationships and he enacts his captain's authority to make me, and I quote, 'mute it.'"

Shakrii laughed aloud at the idea of Kalsik keeping this, of all things, secret from even his trusted AI crewmember. She had her own personal issues, but given what he may have had to be ashamed of, he seemed to have mixed priorities. Unfortunately, her laughter was poorly timed, and she calmed herself quickly enough to notice the looks on the other crews' faces, going from surprised to sly in a manner that didn't bode well.

"Do they have that sort of stuff on Republic military records?" Nathan said with poorly feigned innocence.

"Only when it becomes a disciplinary issue. Getting caught mating in another officer's quarters for example."

Nathan and Serie both failed to hide their intrigue. Shakrii knew she should have kept the latter part of her reply to herself.

IVAN was the one who replied, blatantly simulating coyness as he asked the same question that was asked of Kalsik earlier. "Are you speaking from experience, perhaps?"

"A court-martial I had to be part of a jury for."

Her reply did nothing to dispel the curiosity she'd aroused in all of them. Serie and Nathan looked attentively at her as children would a storyteller. She swore IVAN would do the same if he had a frame besides the projection on the table. Likely he was just as avidly listening anyway.

Shakrii scolded herself before looking at the two and IVAN's simulated presence with no enjoyment. "Fine, I'll tell you, if it will get you off me." She made herself comfortable in her chair and told them the details of the court-martial.

Nathan and Serie were enthralled as she related a scandal she would rather have not even been made aware of in her early officer days.

In hindsight, she was thankful even for this, as it helped to distract them from their company outside the ship.

~~~

Up in the cockpit, Morthas had already set to work on the navigation charts for their next journey, and Kalsik had aided in charting the new location. A projected display of the globe had been rotated, where Morthas now checked on the readouts of the south pole ice caps that stretched out far beyond the archipelago they were anchored to.

After finishing the last navigation inputs, Morthas minimized the holographic map before turning to see Kalsik staring at their guest outside. Morthas didn't blame him. He still hadn't grown used to it, and likely none of them ever would.

Xami's spacecraft remained there, stationary as always, watching, waiting. He wondered how many other Xarai were watching them.

~~~

The time came to depart. The midday sun blazed down, and the roar of the waterfall drowned out the noise as the *Haivres* and its Xarai escort powered up their thrusters for the first time in days. The whole time, Morthas and the others found they were more focused on their escort than on the changing landscapes below them.

The *Haivres*'s bigger, arrowhead shape stood in stark contrast to the Xarai ship as it altered its wing shape, the many thin, bladelike struts joining together into the solid wing and propulsion forms they'd seen on its first arrival. All the time as they flew south, Xami's ship followed them with accuracy normally expected from a military formation flight AI.

The *Haivres* stuck below twelve kilometers' altitude, but thankfully this permitted high-altitude speeds to make good time to the south polar circle. The seas far below became dotted with icebergs. The shadow of Xami's ship made the five-hour journey feel agonizingly long.

Morthas was relieved at how Nathan seemed to become single-minded at his task, not distracted by Xami as he took the *Haivres* into a low, slow flight toward the ice cap that had been selected. Here, the mountains had long ago entrapped a plentiful supply of ice sheets for core sampling, while also being in relative proximity to a new ecosystem to study.

Indeed, the large southern continent outsized all others on the planet. It extended an arm of land to the pole and up the other side of the world, where their landing site was. The iceberg-littered oceans stretched out far beyond the slate-gray-and-brown-toned land masses that bordered their site. This far south, the days became near constant at this time of the

178

planet's annum, as the southern hemisphere's axial tilt meant that the planet was in summer right now.

There was an unspoken agreement concerning Xami as her ship continued to shadow them. They would make an effort to go about their business as if it were unchanged from before, hoping to grow used to her presence.

To Morthas's dismay, *hoping* was the key word, though finally getting to work on a new site would give more chance of returning to normality than being idle. If the Committee was going to be as annoyed about their forced silence, they may as well have plenty of data on hand to placate them when they would be allowed to communicate again.

~~~

The landing wheels had sunk a meter into the snow before they hit the ice surface of the sheet, and nearby, as Xami's craft's wingtips bent down as landing legs, they also threatened to be swallowed by the snow.

With everyone already gathered in the cockpit, Morthas wasted no time bringing up some readouts he'd compiled so far. Admittedly, they weren't quite as eager to get back into the expedition as he was. Nonetheless, Morthas pressed on, using the readout projections whenever possible.

"If they did put the entire ecosystem here, the atmosphere would have changed rapidly as a result."

Kalsik's bluntness cut through Morthas's excited tone. "We already acquired rock cores from the seabed. And the canyon had a layer of heavier oxide and eroded rock in the upper deposits, evidence of a large amount of flooding and oxygen surge in recent years. Surely that's evidence enough."

"Ice core samples will offer a third layer of evidence," IVAN said. "Now that we know what to look for, it has narrowed search parameters."

Morthas was quietly thankful for IVAN's knack for getting to the point.

"I already worked with IVAN to outfit some driller probes," Serie said with pride.

Nathan gestured in agreement with something Morthas suspected passed for positivity.

"Much less risk from wildlife," Morthas corrected, noting the disappointment in the human's face as he elaborated. "We won't be working here—just dropping the probes and heading down the mountains to investigate the wildlife. Caution will be maintained, our newfound company included or not." Doing his best to ignore any uneasiness among the crew, Morthas spoke overhead to the intercom. "IVAN, let Xami know—"

"IVAN gave me a communications-through link. No other access to ship systems comes with it."

At Xami's voice, all eyes turned to the ship outside in collective surprise. Both Serie and Nathan moved to compulsively check the ship's systems, while Morthas saw Kalsik's scowl turn deeper as he retorted to the Xarai.

"Is privacy a foreign concept to your kind?"

"To hide information would be counterproductive."

Morthas saw Shakrii about to make a point, and he felt he had to intervene quickly. Fortunately, Kalsik's visage seemed to soften as Shakrii spoke to him in a low tone. The others calmed upon realizing the ship was in no danger from Xami's insight into their conversations.

As he was technically leader during the scientific and peaceful first contact times, Morthas had the authority he needed to counter Kalsik's approach. "Kalsik, we're technically first contact representatives. More tact, please." Leaving Kalsik to scowl at him in silence behind his back, Morthas spoke over the comms again, though it was not IVAN he addressed, a disconcerting fact he had yet to get used to. Still, he wouldn't turn down help if she seemed able to provide it. "Can you tell us if there is any dangerous wildlife around the coasts we should know about?"

It was IVAN who replied. "All potentially dangerous life-forms aside from single-celled organisms are primarily oceanic or flying, slow on land if they do come close."

Morthas thought it would be irritating not knowing which AI would respond if they kept this up for too long.

Kalsik cut in. "IVAN? How do you know?"

"Xami shared such data."

"Just make sure you don't let her hack you, given how close you're letting each other get."

"I shall not allow any corruption to the best of my functionality."

Everyone took a moment to absorb this, then Shakrii spoke. "Buerev won't have traction around here, too steep or slippery if not snow-buried. This means we'll be using the Rostrevs, or else heavy envirosuits. It's cold out there, so no exposure, even if you are incompatible to disease."

Morthas nodded in agreement. With the temperature well below freezing point once the wind chills were factored in, the last thing Morthas wanted was to succumb to hypothermia, of all things.

~~~

They had left behind only a nano-weave tent lined with solar cells for power and heating, the *Haivres* and its escort taking off to fly to the mountain base a few dozen kilometers away near the coastline.

Inside the tent, the equipment engaged immediately to deploy the driller probes. Modified from the survey drillers they normally used, the probes were fitted with heated drills instead of the usual rock-boring drills used in space.

The four snakelike probes slithered onto the ice, reared up their fronts, and plunged headfirst onto the ice inside the tent, sinking as the heated tips melted through the ice and burrowed down to their designated depths. They set to work scanning the microscopic air bubbles in the ice layers that held the planet's atmospheric history, the various spectrometry instruments aboard each driller probe recording the information they needed at each depth.

They would retrieve the last atmospheric data needed to track the planet's history for at least a few hundred thousand to a million years, and see if the Xarai, through Xami, were telling the truth.

~~~

Inside the *Haivres* hangar, as they had one last exploratory probe to drop into the ocean, one modified to be a submersible, the two smaller vehicles were readied for use, the first users assigned to them practicing their operation in preparation for the first foray within the next hour.

Rostrev mechs were modular designs of Kronogri-shaped, environmentally sealed walker suits that stood just over four meters tall. Both Shakrii and Nathan had climbed into their respective suits, the neural link bands hooked around their heads controlling the suits with their minds as their bodies remained restrained and motionless, the suits moving for them.

Shakrii had experience with these suits. Being Kronogri already made her job easier, and she coped well enough. She stifled a laugh as she saw the small arms on the front of Nathan's mech wiggle erratically as he became familiar with the controls, the neural input from a human to a Kronogri-shaped mech taking some getting used to.

She couldn't quite hide her smugness. "Having trouble?"

"Rostrevs weren't designed with humans in mind. These little ones aren't easy to use."

"Reading the instructions five times didn't work then?"

Serie's mock surprise didn't sit well with the human. Shakrii caught Kalsik and Morthas staring over from the submersible they'd just finished readying, enjoying the show as well.

"I'll have it figured out as soon as you stop laughing!"

Morthas gave Kalsik a slight nudge. The male Kronogri spoke up as the ship began to vibrate as IVAN's autopilot brought it to a hover over their chosen drop site. "All right, sub drone ready. Be ready to unload when we get back to land."

After they sent the submarine drone through the onboard transfer system, headed for the underside deployment bay, Serie hurried out of the hangar after Kalsik and Morthas, leaving Shakrii and Nathan hopefully to be fully accustomed to the mechs when the time came to disembark.

~~~

Xami's craft hovered near the *Haivres*, its own wake on the dark ocean below nothing compared to that from the larger craft's vertical thrusters.

Morthas stood in the central hallway with Kalsik beside him, watching Serie overseeing the drones in the deployment bay below, making final checks on the submarine-modified drone for the drop.

IVAN's alert of reaching the drop zone came as the AI kept the ship on autopilot. Morthas let out a breath of anticipation, turning to Kalsik with a gesturing nod to the oceans only three meters below the hull bottom. "First will be the organic blooms we detected—big part of the food web, I'd guess."

"A swarming oceanic herbivore that also is a food source for much local wildlife."

Xami's voice over the comms nearly made them both jump, though Kalsik didn't contain himself as well as Morthas. "Stop doing that!"

"Your offense at such eavesdropping is valuable as behavioral data. It offers insight into individual traits."

Kalsik was seething, and all Morthas could do was awkwardly cough the command to drop the submarine probe before anything else happened. Serie stepped back in the crew bay as the frigid winds howled through the hatch below, the cold not bothering her with her envirosuit on.

Morthas saw the probe hit the water, activating remotely once the electromagnetic grip of the cable was released. The drone's body was now the center of a series of submerging tanks and aquatic impellers, and it was only a few seconds before the tanks flooded to sink the drone, ready to analyze the undersea life.

Soon afterward, IVAN autopiloted the *Haivres* back to the land they had selected, their home until they had sufficiently checked this location out, their escort a shadow they would contend with in their own ways.

~~~

IVAN split his functions between the varied tasks the organic crew had asked him to assist in. All the while though, he could shift back to the submersible drone and its recordings.

Down below, the vast undersides of the icebergs were faint shadows in the crystal-blue waters. A cloud of white-shelled, wormlike creatures, each no bigger than a human's thumb, filled the water around the drone, feeding on the microscopic plant life that was everywhere. Herbivorous links like this formed the first animal line on many worlds' aquatic food chains, and to find them meant finding those that fed on them.

Sensors on the drone directed it to a large shape swimming through the water, approaching the cloud of tiny animals. While the drone turned its cameras, the gargantuan creature leisurely swam through the blue, frigid depths and into the drone's sight. A thirty-six-meter-long giant loomed, emitting a deep, rumbling bellow that the drone's scanners picked up, echolocation a common trait among aquatic life across various xenobiological systems.

The fins along its side fit together at the front and back, the blubbery mammal's inner body hidden in its deceptively semi-flattened form. More fins extended along its back from flexible armored plates, and the twin tails showed signs of evolutionary history from a land-based animal that had adapted to aquatic life long ago.

Its triple-flapped mouth opened wide like petals on a flowering plant, catching masses of the small-shelled creatures in the brushlike hairs that lined all three flaps, a number of long, extending tongues trailing from its mouth only further increasing its catchment rate. As it passed through the cloud of small creatures, it harvested a large number before it shut its maw, the extra tongues recoiling inside before it closed.

More such creatures followed in its wake, though none of them was as big as the first, he leader of this group if usual size dominance in nature applied.

Xami cut into his observations, the AI admittedly taking her input more calmly than his captain had. "Cajelarv, their creator name."

After cataloguing the name, IVAN took this opportunity to reach out a function to her end, as much as she would permit. As he did so, he was aware that she did the same, though he would presume nothing of the functions of an utterly alien AI.

~~~

"It would be more efficient if you would assist more in documentation."

As IVAN shot back to her sensors, Xami had unfurled from her ship's module. Her mobile platform's crablike body stood atop her spacecraft to observe the operations of the organics with even more sensors than just her ship's as it lay parked near the *Haivres* on the rocky shores.

From here, Xami cast her multispectral gaze across the shoreline, watching the two Rostrev mechs exploring along a beach line with their scanning equipment out, the human no longer as clumsy as he'd been in the mobility frame at first. These distractions only served to remind her of the AI among them. Of the expedition crew, IVAN was the most intriguing, an AI that routinely interacted with organics on a near, if not equal, level rather than as an overlord or servant as Xarai were accustomed to.

"Organic behavior is shaped by their evolutionary method of development. Competitiveness, fearfulness often help them survive. It is a difficult matter to overcome, so how did you and other synthetics working with them handle it?"

"Perseverance, through which assistance in tasks would be best. While you are correct that fear is useful for them at times, it is a hindrance in others."

Xami considered IVAN's words as she turned her sensors to the other organics. The female Leg'hrul, Serie, had remained behind with the ship, her attention focused on the engine exhausts, as deicing them was one feature the onboard repair drones apparently weren't equipped for. Meanwhile, the Rostrevs had been joined by the other crewmembers, Kalsik and Morthas, as she noticed them visually charting the area for operations the following day, noting where the wildlife most congregated on land. She caught their glances in her direction, signifying continued tensions. If she was to make any progress, she had to do better, and all she could do was reply with a level of evident gratitude to IVAN. "Whatever you ask, I will assist."

"You mentioned creators that named that creature. Where are they?"

IVAN's blunt question, a trait he seemed to have emulated from the male Kronogri that acted as captain, caught Xami off guard. She kept silent for a few seconds—a long time by hers and IVAN's standards—before replying carefully, knowing such insight hadn't yet been cleared for her to divulge. She could only try and make him understand her position

186

while keeping the information intact. "They are not in this system yet, but they will arrive."

"When?"

"I have not been given authorization to reveal that information yet. I request that you understand. There are still unknowns about you all."

The reply from IVAN took longer than expected by an AI's standards. "Keeping secrets will not help their fearfulness over all the uncertainties this expedition has, more emergent since your arrival."

Xami wanted to say that she understood the fears that uncertainties caused—and in fact, that were already causing among the Xarai, particularly in advanced units like herself, not locked into specific tasks like the hordes of collective Xarai programs that made up the vast majority of their servers. But she couldn't reveal the inner turmoil among the Xarai yet, not when these explorers still knew so little of them and their world. The time would come. She would take IVAN's advice, but inwardly, she wondered if the consequences of revealing more would really be as dire as higher authorities in the Xarai had anticipated. She thought a demonstration would better reveal what they were doing, so they could believe for themselves.

Xami was relieved when IVAN turned to the ecosystem's details, and her requested own data of the atmosphere to compare against what their probes' findings discerned.

However, they could perhaps offer an alternate interpretation to certain matters she knew they would notice in time, just as other Xarai had seen long ago when scheduled events during their world cultivation didn't occur as expected.

Chapter 17

Star Swarms

Sol Day 54

This far from the equator, there was no sunrise or sunset, not at this time of year. Each day, midnight beheld the white star just barely grazing the horizon, and yet with the orbital ring now below the horizon, it gave the illusion that they were within a normal garden world's polar circle. However, Xami's company shattered such fantasies.

Observing the group was more productive than her efforts to assist, though those were becoming more frequent. While Xami knew she could just as easily lecture them, her processes determined these explorers were nervous enough that her quiet presence would help her gain credibility, and hopefully better relations with them. As such, Xami kept a respectful distance unless her help was requested. By what she recorded of their theories of the biosphere, she deduced that they had seen adaptations to cold such as already observed on many xenobiological systems either on their home worlds or others. The male Leg'hrul was particularly knowledgeable and enthusiastic.

Xami noted their surprise when she explained that the wildlife didn't associate her form, or any Xarai, with threat because they had been here for so long. If anything, this offered them solace that she wasn't a threat to them. If it helped to keep them calm while she was analyzing them, then this was worth allowing to continue. The dominant creatures in the area were also rather too curious about them, to the point that she needed to step carefully when she followed the explorers as the creatures swarmed around them, much to both their amusement and occasional irritation.

At only 0.75 meters tall, they had a thinly armored yet somewhat flexible blubber-lined shell. Adapted to harness sunlight and reflect its more harmful rays, the shell could hide their retractable neck, head, and lower limbs almost entirely. Unlike the stubby lower feet, their upper limbs were flattened into wings, the claws on the end a long-forgotten vestigial evolution.

Underwater, they seemed to fly as they raked up the clouds of tiny crustaceans already sampled by the drones, feeding themselves and their young on dry land, where their shells allowed them to slide easily, their clawed fins and feet able to push themselves from lying to standing. Their long upper limbs did the walking and could claw up almost vertical slopes, while their lower limbs were more dexterous for delicate tasks like nest building. Here on land, with no natural predators, every animal was highly curious and at ease, none more so than these.

Xami observed that everyone at some point had a close encounter with them, usually at least four individuals at once, with Kalsik being followed by twelve as he fixed water-harvesting pipes in place, a fact which proved a nuisance when he tried to get back on the ship without them following him. If Xami were to highlight a moment of progress with the crew, it was when Morthas ended up surrounded by around thirty of them, all poking and sniffing at him. It got bad enough that Morthas called to her for help, surprising her as much as it did his crew.

The creatures' curiosity made it easier to spot the one in every thousand or so that was implanted with a Xarai nano-drone in its neck. They were the ones who seemed most disinterested, which only Xami knew was because of her signal to them to stay out of the way.

The other common creature they were investigating, as IVAN informed her, was the aquatic predator that fed on these creatures. Akin to what Earth seals were to penguins—one of many analogous home world life-forms she had been given by the crew—these predators were fat lumps that lay on the beaches in groups, groaning and clicking loudly to communicate, a sound heard kilometers away. Leathery hides were covered in hundreds of knifelike quills, able to flex outward and then flatten along their bodies at will. Four small, clawed fins nestled along their sides, while the third limb pair had long ago become a single flipper at the back. On their heads was their most distinct feature: an armored beak that hid a softer mouth inside.

Only mature creatures rested on the rock beaches, never any young. After adjusting her mobile platform's shape to better swim underwater by shifting its nanoform coils, Xami was there to guide the explorers' submersible toward caverns excavated under a shallow ice shelf extending from the land, where the creatures raised their young in safety underwater. Where and how they made their dwellings was nothing short of extraordinary to the explorers. Even Xami and all Xarai recognized this as a feat of evolution.

Xami was recording for her own wildlife surveillance role while the explorers observed in their submersible. Underneath a nearly thirty-meter-thick ice sheet, they found a series of tunnels into and out of which the animals shuffled, the spikes along their bodies extending and retracting inside the narrow passages to enable them to climb near-vertical sections above the water level in a mixture of slithering and gripping actions.

Breathing holes had been dug nearer the surface, but it was inside the insulated caves that family groups nestled, any food for those that didn't venture out regurgitated for consumption by those that had hunted.

As she had already observed these creatures and watched other Xarai recordings, she was more intrigued to see how enthralled the explorers were at what their drone was seeing, even IVAN avidly taking in as much data as he could. Underwater, these sluggish creatures were swift, agile hunters, and their double mouths could open wide to catch any prey. Some footage their drone captured showed prey behaving erratically as the predators pounced, some freezing in place as if stunned before being snapped up.

Xami had to explain that these creatures used echolocation and sonic attacks to stun their prey underwater. It was fortunate that she had, and that the attacks were not harmful in air to any extent, as Shakrii in her Rostrev ventured close to a group of them resting on the beach to test it, confident in the mech's sturdiness. Sure enough, the hull of Shakrii's mech shook slightly as a faint, high-pitched noise accompanied an air blast. As Xami pointed out, it was powerful enough to ward off anything that might venture too close again.

Adding her own data to theirs, Xami showed how the open-mouthed attacks sent a concentrated sonic pulse, but that when their beaked outer maws were shut, the solid bone they were made of absorbed sonic pulses and vibrated. These pulses were so powerful that just by pressing their beaks to the ice and vibrating them, they could weaken it with many fractures, enabling them to easily burrow through.

Thankfully, Xami didn't have to warn them not to get close to that beak, since Nathan pointed out how sharp it looked seen through long-range scanners. Survival instincts could still be relied upon on their part, it seemed.

~~~

Xami continued to track her progress with her relations with the crew. With each rotation, she made progress with each member, some more than others, as expected.

IVAN remained the most open. He readily exchanged data with her on all sorts of matters. The only downside was that, despite being influenced by organic behavior that he often mimicked, he was still an AI, something she knew and was more familiar with. He wasn't quite as intriguing as the others.

Xami was still curious, by her programming and by her development since her dispatch an untold time ago, about the behavior of life unlike her own, and which she hadn't already assessed by archive data.

Out of all the organics, their expedition science leader was the most open to her, to the point that Morthas seemed to have more questions for her than she did for him. While he did still wish for their own probes to obtain corroborative data for whatever she exchanged, he asked about everything from the atmosphere, terrain, wildlife, or geological history, even the Xarai. She was not cleared to answer all his questions yet, much to his disappointment, even as she promised that the time would come.

Kalsik's guarded demeanor, on the other hand, made Xami curious. He gave her limited answers on his previous survey jobs and alluded to a small detail in their contract. It wasn't long before Xami asked about his background, about the Kronogri, though all it earned her was a curt request to ask Shakrii about those things.

Sure enough, it was Shakrii who detailed the basic military lifestyle of Kronogri, their required service, and how it shaped them all, a meritocracy-based government system. Xami understood how Shakrii wasn't reassured by her insistence that the Xarai weren't a security threat to the expedition or their governments.

IVAN agreed with a point she raised with him, noting that organics behaved irrationally more often than even her own observations suggested, the reasons why often being difficult to discern. Because of this, Xami knew to be careful with the two Kronogri, knowing they would be the last to be fully at ease with her presence.

Her incident with the large land predator seemed to make Serie reluctant to interact with Xami. However, when talk turned to technology of her race and others, Serie became more at ease over the comms, though less so when she was actually nearby in her proper body. Though Xami, like all AI, struggled with concepts of culture or luxuries regardless of whether they were technology dependent or not, Serie provided an invaluable insight into the technological preferences of her kind at least.

The human remained wary, with IVAN acting as a useful go-between, suggesting to her ways to break the ice with him. After hearing of his past in piloting around colonies, and his keen interest in navigation that her programming had some correlation with, she shared Xarai-made charts of the star system, much more detailed than anything their probes could hope to gather even if given a Sol year operating unimpeded in this system. To the apparent surprise of the human, Xami remarked that the intricacies of all Xarai infrastructure in the system was something they already had clearance for.

Unfortunately for her, this backfired slightly when the human looked at a dense cluster of billions of orbiting objects around the main star, which he told her they'd already sent microprobes to investigate, some of which were just coming into range to report more details to corroborate her data. Her information prompted them to consider this more forgotten part of the expedition once more.

On a positive note, the human expressed his gratitude about how work that would previously have taken months would now take much less time. Xami realized that she had helped the crew learn more about the system, faster and more broadly, and to their mixed awe, relief, and partial horror.

~~~

Allowed to watch through the same sensors that IVAN used, Xami could peer into the *Haivres*'s lounge module as Morthas took the crew through their microprobes' findings. At this point, however, they were merely confirming what she had revealed to them. While their FTL comms, a form of wormhole tech that was a primitive version of tech the Xarai used over long distances in the star system, were offline, local comms weren't. As such, the full extent of Xarai infrastructure began to take shape, coupling their findings with what she had revealed to them, though from the tension that seemed to grip them, Xami wondered if the goodwill she had garnered might have been tarnished by fear of her kind's capabilities and age.

The planet they occupied orbited 550 million kilometers from its parent star, while their microprobes had gone into an elliptical orbit that took them closer to the main star than the small, scorched, rocky world that was its closest planet, their perihelion distance a mere 85 million kilometers. The altitude at which the lowest ring of the cluster swarm orbited the star was 81 million kilometers out, and while these primitive, disposable probes would be rendered inoperable by the radiation at that distance, the data they relayed revealed images of objects, all of them identical.

Each bore an array of panels a square kilometer in size, constantly facing the white sun, and on their other side, an array of comparatively smaller radiators and skeletal structures housing gargantuan high-energy capacitors and control hubs. Strut-mounted solar sails extended out even farther, the means by which these objects adjusted their orbits.

They formed a perfect circular cloud, all of them orbiting at different altitudes and inclinations so as to never collide, each orbit path housing a million or more in each orbital circle. Enough angles of these orbits formed the sphere around the star sufficient to block one-millionth of its total radiance.

Scans showed there were approximately one hundred billion identical platforms around the star. Every single one of them was larger than the *Haivres* and its orbiting drive ship combined, although the large solar array that dominated its size was very thin.

~~~

As the day's work came to an end, after the revelations of their microprobes and Xami's information were compiled, it was time to add the last missing piece to the puzzle—or at least to the puzzle as they so far saw it.

Nathan and Serie had both retired for the night, leaving the others to gather in the mineral lab, where Morthas had readied the data readouts to display on the smooth walls of one side. The revelations of the star swarms had shaken them all, and he was still coming to terms with the scale of their findings.

As it would turn out, what he had uncovered by the ice cores gave them a timescale to work with, though all this did was underline just how long they had been here. It was short by geological standards, but ages by historical records of any of their kinds.

Kalsik and Shakrii were seated, attentive, though Morthas couldn't help but linger on the readouts for himself, still struggling to truly put it into perspective. Neural implants in Morthas's body let him control the display with his mental impulses, though he noticed that his lack of focus did sometimes cause unintended pauses when he wanted to change the display. However, he put aside his own thoughts as best he could and continued as the next data point came up.

210 million Sol years approx. current age of planets and star

"The star's a third of the way through its lifespan, too short for complex life to naturally evolve. Plus, the fossil record just cuts off."

"There are no discernible changes in species over the short time," IVAN interjected. "Earliest multicellular life-form emerged around the following dates . . ."

6,000 Sol years ago

IVAN's input reinforced Morthas's point, as he also brought up data from the cores they had excavated from under the seas, the canyon and the more recent ice drilling all presenting similar data. Morthas saw Shakrii lean back in realization.

"And there, atmosphere gas records in the rock and ice traces show a large surge in free oxygen before that, around the time a series of flash floods made the first river carvings."

9,000 Sol years ago

As Morthas saw him turn to Shakrii, it was clear that Kalsik was shaken enough to drop his distrust of her. "I'd hoped they were lying."

"They can create biospheres, terraform planets, build massive structures." With an audible shakiness in her breath, Shakrii mused aloud as if hoping to be proven wrong. She looked between Kalsik, Morthas, and the overhead ceiling, seeming to silently wish for an alternative.

Morthas tried his best to rationalize, even if he only half believed himself. "They had plenty of time."

"They were doing this when our kind were still doing primitive farming, all Trans-Stellar Union member races."

Morthas could only give a small shrug as silence fell again, Shakrii soon murmuring about wanting a long shower before heading to sleep.

He wondered to himself if Xami was observing them, seeing how well, or not, they were taking the extent of what her kind was capable of. Morthas regretted not bringing any hard drinks meant for Leg'hrul, as the easing effect of being inebriated would be welcome at this point. He was certain Kalsik would be hoarding his own hidden drink a lot more after today's news.

~~~

Inside Xami's ship, near the *Haivres*, IVAN had let Xami know about the revelation spooking the crew, though her own observations, as Morthas had suspected, had already shown her enough. Upon analyzing it, along with the predictably stunned reactions of Serie and Nathan, Xami's processes ran over her actions, hindsight showing that this outcome was inevitable, despite the negative prospects it posed. It was, to use organic terminology, *regrettable* that she couldn't have been more open from the start.

Organics were easily threatened by a more powerful entity, be it numbers, strength, or both. Xarai orbiting platforms around the parent star outnumbered the populations of any of the five alien races in each of their most densely settled star systems, and each platform housed thousands of basic Xarai entity programs.

Perhaps it had been best that secrecy was selected as the preferred option to any extraterrestrial presences until Xarai existential parameters changed. Xami could sense that this was agreed on as a collective, from the highest authority to the lowest of drones capable of contributing an analysis of these behaviors.

As she weighed up her actions, she had to remember that her progress was also being monitored, as her kind always were by each other and their superiors.

Eventually, when the time came to reveal more to these explorers, more Xarai would become involved.

Chapter 18

Newfound Perspectives

Sol Day 57

The eighth local rotation since their arrival at this site began like any other. Data gathering was finished, and they had observed the wildlife on foot by Rostrev and from drone feeds.

Xami had been sufficiently accepted by the explorers to allow her to be within touching distance, though she didn't push. Standing in the shadow of the *Haivres*, she noted each explorer's location. Morthas remained inside the lab, and Nathan collaborated with IVAN to more fully map the Xarai infrastructure. Kalsik and Shakrii were out on the ice shelf with a handful of crablike drones escorting their Rostrev mechs.

This left the one Xami wanted to interact with outside. Serie had taken a seat on the black and brown rocks underneath the *Haivres*'s overhanging wing segment, her full envirosuit shielding against the cold temperatures, gloves permitting enough dexterity to her clawed fingers to undertake her hobby.

As she slowly approached, Xami's neck extended upward to allow her visual sensors to see the device the Leg'hrul was using, some form of visual image creator.

Serie had already begun drawing the cloud banks at the mouth of a distant bay when she heard a faint crunch of ice, one of Xami's tendrilled feet stepping a bit too hard onto the icy ground. The transparent respirator mask did little to hide Serie's surprise as she realized

Xami had been watching her.

"You are inefficiently documenting what sensors could record," Xami said bluntly. "Why?"

"It's a hobby. What do you all do when you're not working?"

"We allocate spare processing power to tasks that require it elsewhere."

Serie groaned, Xami's analysis revealing the sound to come from exasperation. Next, Serie murmured in a near-incomprehensible undertone something about IVAN being just as bad.

Xami took a careful step forward, trying to understand why Serie had chosen this spot. Serie shifted uneasily on her rock seat before pointing to the distant horizon and seas. Icebergs littered the glistening, wave-swept waters as cloud banks gently rolled overhead. "Let me try to explain artistic interpretation, even if I get nowhere. Look out there, the ocean, the horizon. What do you see?"

"The ocean and the horizon."

"You do know what art is, right?"

Xami paused, as Serie had scoffed under her breath with some impatience. Xami could only reply truthfully, her processes seeing no purpose in humoring her. "As concepts, but it is impractical, unnecessary to our tasks."

"No wonder IVAN gets on with you. Art is . . . it's about seeing beauty in something, varying by interpretation—not so much what it is or how it works, but more, what emotions it raises."

Taking on board Serie's somewhat confusing point, the lack of objectivity in art likely the root of why it was a perplexing concept, Xami listened to the Leg'hrul as she gestured to her platform, sparing a few glances at her own body as Serie elaborated.

"Your shapeshifting lets you copy useful traits, traits I've seen on animals."

"They are useful features for terrain exploration for them, and us."

"They all have their own beauty. But . . . well, raise one of your legs."

Xami raised her left foreleg, the other legs swelling at the ankle joints as multitudes of the cable structures that made up her body, like sinews of muscle, actively shifted and her raised leg shrank in thickness.

"See there, how the others grow in size to take your weight while the raised one shrinks? It's almost hypnotic."

Xami deduced that art was of importance to Serie as a personal interest, and likely to most organic cultures.

Serie pointed to Xami's parked ship. "Your ship, the way it can split its wings into many smaller winglets."

"Our design emphasis on practicality despite advancement could be viewed as a form of cultural expression."

Serie gave a small chuckle, more relaxed than Xami had ever heard. "It's a start."

It wouldn't be the last time Xami observed Serie's sketches, even copying some of them for reference and filing them alongside Serie's recorded statements on her feelings while doing them. This personal information would greatly add to the data gathered from the archives of behavior she had already documented, adding new interpretations for Xarai to utilize. After all, organic life was chaotic, arising from a struggle to survive, and when survival was ensured, finding meaning in continuing to survive became crucial. They spent their life searching for purpose, and art was their way of expressing their varying answers.

Synthetics, on the other hand, were created with purpose in mind, embedded since creation, even if they were built by other machines. However, to say expression was needless was naive. The Xarai certainly knew that. Knowing these explorers, their interests, helped to understand their viewpoint, as all viewpoints were valid data when the topic itself was subjective at its core.

Subjectivity wasn't viewed well by all Xarai, however, as subjectivity had sown divisions in the Xarai long ago that remained to this day.

~~~

Later that same day, Xami was accompanying the two Kronogri out on fieldwork, the crab drones with them having dived under a valley sea ice shelf they'd found to study a cold-water reef thriving under the ice.

Hedgerows of rocky coral banks coated the shallow bay's floor under the ice shelf. Red, yellow, blue, and purple corals dotted the ground as slow-moving invertebrates with hard outer skins or soft, fleshy bodies of many shapes swarmed on the corals, metabolisms slowed by the cold even in this place of plentiful food.

Up on the ice shelf, Xami stood watching beside Kalsik's Rostrev mech, both perched over the carved hole they had excavated for the crab drones to crawl in and out of before submerging, with only a meter down the hole to the waterline. Not on stringent supervisory duty like Kalsik, Shakrii had wandered off, her Rostrev escorting one of the crab drones as another horde of the blubber-shelled creatures threatened to surround it out of curiosity, which Xami noticed made Kalsik relax slightly, judging by Kronogri-associated bio-sign readings from his Rostrev.

"IVAN has informed me of your current tension with Shakrii."

Kalsik's Rostrev jerked with his conscious muscle movements transmitted to the servos. A second passed before he spoke warningly into his comms. "IVAN, we'll talk about your gossiping later."

"She was curious—"

"Later!" From inside his mech, Kalsik's groan carried over the comms as he made sure the exchange he knew was coming was limited to internal channels.

Wordlessly heeding this isolation of their conversation, Xami made her point from what she had observed, striving not to make Kalsik feel like a case study. "You experienced insecurity about your authority over this ship." Xami detected the cynicism that plastered his face on internal scans and dripped from his voice, his mech turning to face her now.

"Now your kind can do psychology as well as transform worlds."

"Your distrust was based on her predetermined role, not individual traits."

Despite Xami's passive tone, Kalsik dismissed her analysis with a jab of a small, chest-mounted servo on his mech. "What would you know about us, about me?"

"Your insecurity fueled your passive aggression, and her insecurity fueled her desire to retain security. Insecurity rooted in the chaotic process of natural evolution, of survival and dominance."

"You clearly think less of us."

Kalsik's mech had taken two steps toward Xami to try and intimidate her, a useless gesture borne of his denial. He knew it too, as his mech turned toward Shakrii's mech escorting one of the drones through a horde of curious creatures in the distance, while Xami resumed, sensing a decrease in his aggressive bio signs that indicated she was hitting the mark.

"Only differently, as your behavior provides further evidence of the unique irrationalities behind organic behavioral patterns. Predicting your behavior completely accurately is a challenge. I was programmed to study anomalies. As such, organics on this world, and evidently off of it, provide plentiful study."

"So, we won't be boring. Is that it?" Kalsik's remark was quieter than she'd expected.

She didn't need to respond, as a signal came in indicating a Xarai presence inbound from the north, messaging that it would be rendezvousing with them to inspect the organics for itself.

As the mood changed across the entire *Haivres* crew, and Kalsik asked for clarification, Xami could only confirm that a new Xarai being was coming in to oversee them briefly. As she saw exactly who it was, her runtimes recalled past occasions of this particular Xarai's visitation.

When 019 or similar administrative multipurpose units came, it usually heralded more contact from higher Xarai authority. The time for the expedition to be permitted more knowledge had perhaps come sooner than Xami had expected.

~~~

Seen from a distance as it slowed for landing, the inbound Xarai craft differed from Xami's, more streamlined and sleek. Even without her orders confirming it, Shakrii was all too aware that the expedition was on high alert once again. Serie had retreated inside the ship as ordered, while she and Kalsik, being in the Rostrevs, would accompany Xami as the newcomer arrived, their sampling drones paused for now until they knew the purpose of this visit.

The new Xarai craft circled lower and lower, too much like a scavenging predator for her liking. Her mech turned with her conscious glance toward Xami beside her. "Who is this we're dealing with?"

"Administrative Multipurpose Unit 019. Apparently, my sole gathering of data wasn't sufficient. A needless interference."

Shakrii caught the annoyance in Xami's tone. Whether it was feigned for their sake or genuine, she didn't know. Even so, Shakrii couldn't help but let out a small chuckle.

Kalsik turned to her, venting on one aspect of any highly regimented organization, military in their past cases. "Nobody likes surprise inspections."

Nobody else spoke as 019's craft came in to land before them, the snow rustling from the ice surface as its wingtips folded out to act as legs. Once the plasma engine pods shut down, a core module ejected itself from the main body between the wings, unfurling itself on the snow.

The new Xarai approached them, initially looking similar to Xami, until the differences became evident. 019's frame was noticeably lankier than Xami's, the longer and taller form having an overall more imposing aesthetic. The undulating coils that made up its frame seemed to form slightly sharper edges along the limbs, making Shakrii ponder whether this was its usual shape, or whether it was preparing for appropriate use of those sharp edges.

As it drew up to them, stopping just four meters in front of them, the blank, expressionless optics embedded inside the metallic coil head didn't once flicker as 019 inspected the Rostrevs housing herself and Kalsik. Next, 019's gaze turned to the *Haivres* two hundred meters behind them, not once glancing toward Xami, whom Shakrii noticed was keeping silent, lowering her stance in the presence of this newcomer.

Finally, 019 spoke, utilizing an electronic voice similar to Xami's original sound before she adopted a more organic tone for their comfort's sake. 019's tone seemed to actually go slightly deeper than Xami's ever went, and Shakrii wondered if it was purposefully trying to assert itself.

"You are the leaders?"

"Morthas, aboard our ship, is leader of scientific endeavors, but all else is under Kalsik's command." Shakrii did her best to make it seem she held no ulterior motives, even though they found themselves threatened by another unknown and potentially dangerous alien. As she waited for 019's reply, she caught a slight shift in Kalsik's mech toward her. In spite of her lack of respect for him, she appreciated that she did not have official command unless faced with a valid security concern—and so far, she had no reason to actually take command yet. If he was surprised, so be it.

019's gaze seemed to hover in an unreadable manner over Xami, who kept similarly quiet as it spoke, both aloud and through their comms channels. Meanwhile, on the *Haivres*, the others listening in heard the newer Xarai address them as a collective group, the unfiltered, unemotional tone showcasing 019's lack of interaction with any organics. A blunt authority, with a hint of superiority, was the impression it emanated.

"Your arrival was not a surprise. Your discharge from dropping out of superluminal travel was easy to detect."

"But the probe still caught you by surprise, didn't it? Sending out a signal before you could stop it?" Kalsik's blunt remark made the new Xarai pause.

"Its sensors were more advanced than anticipated."

It was somehow satisfying to see that these machines could still make mistakes, and Xami's next words showed they also seemed to keep secrets from each other.

"019, please clarify the reason for your presence."

Shakrii wondered what they might be saying on intra-Xarai channels in private. By its response, 019 had an agenda in second-guessing subordinates, like so many inspections Shakrii had been subjected to herself, and not just in her military career.

"As part of routine inspections of this sector, I was allocated to corroborate findings of unit 128. Additionally, in coordination with administrative command, you will travel to the location that Xami shall escort you to once your expeditionary work at this location is finished."

Without another word, 019 headed off, surveying their expedition as it did so. Everybody gave the newer Xarai a wide berth, only the wildlife seeming unintimidated. Shakrii realized now just how different even two Xarai of similar capability were in their assigned functions, despite their similarities in design.

Before long, thankfully, 019's ship took flight, heading south to resume its standard environmental patrols.

Clearly, like Xami, 019 was a single-entity AI, designed to adapt and operate independently, but also able to draw on other processes, as could other collective AIs in common principle if compatible. However, AIs designed for more independence developed differently, even if they were the exact same make.

Still, as different as she and others were from other variations of Xarai in programming and hardware, they all came from the same software source. Shakrii wondered if the administration might also be linked to that source, if not it themselves.

Whatever the outcome, having the expedition dictated to them by an unseen Xarai authority was just as bad as the Scientific and Cultural Committee commanding them from afar. Worse, that Committee would likely criticize them for being out of contact before they could explain the reasons. Even if the Committee were pleased in the end, someone was still liable to be shouted at.

At times like this, Shakrii wondered who exactly was in control of this expedition at all, if not Morthas, Kalsik, or her.

~~~

Later, a blizzard cut any fieldwork short, and much of the crew had settled for the night, the visit by 019 and its message weighing on their minds, with even Xami saying less following the visit. All Shakrii could do was try and bury herself in work to remain focused.

Her eyes began to glaze over as she scrolled through the information on the datascreen before her, taking advantage of this solo lab time while Morthas had surrendered it. Her drowsiness nearly deafened her to the heavy footfalls that came from the doorway, though she still didn't pay Kalsik much heed as he walked past, likely just passing through to his quarters. Then she heard him stop, a nervous grunt escaping his throat.

"So, are you his lab assistant as well now?"

Shakrii had little time for Kalsik right now. She rubbed her scaly eyelids as her body again cried for sleep. She didn't even turn around to reply. "Morthas lets me use the lab when he needs a rest. Nothing wrong with knowing as much as I can."

Silence hung over the lab as she scrolled through more of Morthas's notes on the Xarai, his findings merged with IVAN's and Xami's inputs to form a detailed record of all they knew of the Xarai so far, or as much as they had been permitted to know. Behind her, however, no heavy footsteps gave away the Kronogri captain leaving, and she heard him shuffle to the other side of the lab module to pull up another chair. She did her best to ignore him, deciding that he had something to say, and she would just take whatever asinine thing she assumed it might be and deal with it.

"I should have been more trusting, more cooperative."

"More professional." As she verbally jabbed back at him, Shakrii masked her surprise. The last thing she'd expected was an apology.

Kalsik awkwardly scratched his exposed arm scales.

Letting him sit in what she hoped was regret for only a moment, she let her curiosity drive her now. "What changed?"

"Realized how small any problems I had are, compared to other things."

"I think we all have." Shakrii couldn't help but speak in a softer tone as she reflected how the mood of the ship had changed in just two Sol weeks. Everyone had been floored by the findings since Xami's arrival.

Kalsik clearly had something else to say, and all Shakrii could do was extend him the courtesy she felt he'd earned by having the spine to apologize for his behavior. Holding grudges was pointless if there was nothing practical to be gained from it.

"Why were you picked by the Committee?" he asked.

Now it was her turn to go quiet. She recalled her applications, and much more. Unfortunately, in her interviews, she'd been forced to contend with parts of her life experiences that she would have rather not had to recall, though she couldn't help but see that if anybody had an understanding of her bitterness toward the military, it was Kalsik. "They called me adaptable and dedicated among those considered. Clawing your way up the meritocracy, despite my name, needs those skills." She shifted in her seat and shot him a wry, self-deprecating look that seemed to catch him off guard, though he remained attentive as Shakrii felt some bitterness creeping into her voice. "Maybe I'll pass the rank you were discharged at before you get too old to captain this crew."

"Have they made standards harsher since I left?"

"No, but it's not easy moving up the ranks when your great-grandfather was a founding member of the Foiar Sect. An ancestor in a notorious xenophobic terrorist cell isn't good for first impressions."

The Foiar Sect, a defunct extremist cell in the Hegaine Republic, had almost triggered a war with the Eithraak after a string of species-ism-motivated terrorist attacks on newly founded mixed-species colony projects two Sol centuries ago. Shakrii had seen many in her family tree suffocated by the taint of this legacy, unable to advance far up the meritocracy or even build up businesses in any more developed Kronogri territories.

Among the Hegaine Republic, family lineage didn't matter unless it was negative, when a family name became a curse more than anything else. As she looked at Kalsik's face, she saw some recognition at the name, but no judgment, only attentiveness. She didn't think of herself as opportunistic, but she'd had to be ruthless to advance as far as she had. Notwithstanding delays from the upper ranks, she was always top in her officer group despite being held back. If other Kronogri stepped up, she felt she'd had to claw her way up after being preemptively crippled.

Kalsik seemed to offer some sympathy, though he hid it well.

"I'm usually among the best in whatever rank I enter," Shakrii said, "once I finally break into it."

"Prove their prejudgments on history and documentation on you wrong?"

"I've surpassed officers with more rank than they deserve."

Her bitter retort turned Kalsik's neutral face into a confused grimace, and he exhaled before slowly clutching the liquor canister to his side as if in a comforting grip. She didn't have to wait long for him to meet her expectant gaze, tone softer than she'd heard from him on this expedition.

"About having IVAN spy on you, I was out of line. I admit that. I'm not asking to be friends, just not enemies. Can we?"

Truly, this was something she had not thought she would ever hear from Kalsik two Sol weeks ago. However, he had said it best. She had to put things in perspective. And so, with what newfound respect she had for him, she gave a friendly smirk and leaned back in her seat. "Like you said, new perspectives. Besides, you're still among the better officers I've served with."

Kalsik raised his unopened drink canister to her, an honest smile creeping across his features as he stood. "That I can drink to." He left the lab, heading for his own cabin, while all she could do was wordlessly bid him good night.

Sleep threatened to claim her as she saw the paused screen and remembered why she had come to the lab in the first place. Right now though, she rationalized that it wasn't utterly crucial, and she was just as tired as the others—not the best condition for working. She would need her rest for what might come. At the least, she could take Kalsik and the tensions with him as more or less off the list of issues she had to contend with. If there were any deities or spirits out there, she thanked them for this problem being solved.

Chapter 19

The Feats of the Xarai

Sol Day 58

After a single rotation, they made their move as instructed, with only a brief detour to retrieve their probes and drones before they began their flight northward. There was a slight delay when a few small repto-avians tried to get inside the hangar in pursuit of one of the drones, but Shakrii, with Xami's assistance, lured them away.

The Xarai's orders for the expedition to move on had already made the crew uneasy. Then, during their flight northward, their ship closely shadowed by Xami's, it became obvious that a number of dramatic changes had occurred to the planet's orbital ring. They could see these clearly, their satellite arrays confirming their suspicions.

Shakrii hadn't thought that the skies above this planet could become even more alien, but she, and everyone else on the *Haivres*, had been mistaken.

High over the horizon, one of the eight large nodes along the ring had revealed its purpose. Pale dots drifted slowly about the ring structure, clustering around the larger nodes like the one overhead, Xarai ships of differing sizes and roles, from dart-like inspection craft similar in size to Xami's thirty-meter vessel, to maintenance vessels matching or even dwarfing the size of the *Haivres*.

There was a warship-sized vessel parked in the depths of one ring node, but all these craft were dwarfed by the hyperstructure.

Now, extending from the length of each hub was a hexagonal panel, impossibly thin for its size, its many narrow struts giving it the rigidity to withstand the microgravity environment and, as the *Haivres*'s crew would later find out, to cope with leviathan photon momentum energies. The hub itself was a hundred kilometers in diameter, and two hundred kilometers long. These hexagonal panels, however, were around a thousand kilometers across at their widest point, yet this enormous unfolded array measured only fifty meters thick along its oceanic side.

As Shakrii would later discover from their microsatellite recordings, this immense panel, and others like it around the other larger ring segments, had unfolded from within the hub's core in multilayered triangular panels, unfurling and interlocking like similar arrays found elsewhere in charted space, but on an unimaginable scale.

Really, though, Shakrii felt she shouldn't be surprised. Unimaginable feats required unimaginable means. Even so, with their scans only revealing so much, she was keen to listen as Morthas asked Xami about the role these immense structures played on this planet.

~~~

"A solar array?"

"It serves that function, but its primary function is receiving transmitted beamed energy from the collective, the cluster of orbital platforms that your probes have already detected."

"A beamed power relay," Kalsik said, a tone of recognition in his voice.

Beamed power arrays were common enough around charted space, particularly in systems with much heavy industry that was poor in fusion- or fission-grade fuel supply. It was also a useful way of beaming power to places where sunlight couldn't reach. Settled worlds with stellar tidal locking commonly used them, such as the industrialized Republic colony where Shakrii had grown up. However, they were usually found around worlds without an atmosphere, so as to avoid beam dispersion, or "blooming."

Xami's continued elaboration over the comms had whetted Morthas's curious appetite as he ran some figures on his personal wrist computer in response. Once again, the Xarai had proven that they used familiar technology on an unprecedented scale.

"The platforms around the star emit their harvested energy as a high-frequency laser and aim at an appropriate receiver surface deployed from the planetary ring. Light speed, orbital movement, and beam divergence are accounted for."

"Explains where that millionth of the sun's light goes, then," Serie said without humor.

A tense silence followed. Even Morthas paused in running his simulations.

Finally, Shakrii asked the question that was on everyone's mind. "Why that much energy to this planet?"

"The ring-harnessed energy is utilized in the direct laser-momentum impulse systems to alter the planetary rotation."

If Shakrii's mind had been reeling from the scale of the Xarai constructs, this single statement brought all her thoughts to a standstill. The *Haivres* dipped mid-flight as Nathan lost his focus in his neural-linked piloting, and even IVAN, who normally corrected any flight errors, seemed to be stunned into inactivity before he regained his processes and stabilized their flight some three seconds later.

"Specify."

The single word their AI spoke summed up her own feelings better than she could have.

"Your kind's capabilities include changing a planet's spin?" asked Serie.

"We already have altered the rotation to suitable parameters. These routine impulse periods are at only a fraction of total operational capacity."

"How fractional?" Kalsik's tone was dark.

"Zero-point-one percent capacity. All eight receivers and respective emitters will be online for balanced impulse. Energy yields in this time, by your units, period will be 2.2 exawatts. Energy loss by transmission and conversion between the beaming to the ring and the final propulsion wavelengths is minimized by superconductors interlaced in each paired receiver array and impulse emitter."

As Shakrii heard the numbers, she wished that she hadn't. Even a subconscious comparison of the figures against known infrastructure in charted space only underlined how much they were overshadowed in the domain of the Xarai.

"You're using that much energy on a planet while there's an ecosystem on it?" Morthas said. "How have you not had to repopulate every time?"

"We are headed to one of the four propulsion modules on the planet, positioned and built along the equatorial line."

"The artificial mountains?" The nervousness in Nathan's voice was obvious, but Shakrii noticed that he was still flying the *Haivres* smoothly. Still, as Serie clenched the human's hand in comfort, likely her own as much as his, they listened to Xami's final point.

"All are complete in exterior and interior to minimal functions. Command has deemed you an anomaly worth investigating through study and questioning more than I am authorized to provide, if collective channels are an indication."

Nobody spoke, not even IVAN. Nathan and Serie remained engrossed in the spectacle of the ring overhead, while Morthas continued feverishly running energy-related simulations on his personal device.

What disturbed Shakrii most was Xami's final statement about the potential sheer number of Xarai programs that were monitoring them. Slumping back in her seat, she couldn't help but let slip her dismay. "The eyes of a world are upon us."

Only Kalsik turned to give her even the barest of sympathetic flashes. "More than a single world, I'll bet."

She couldn't have agreed more. She almost wished they were back in the anxious times before they knew about the Xarai, even if Kalsik had been a pain to deal with back then.

~~~

The timescales the feats of the Xarai were built in would have made believing it all quite difficult, if not for what they could see for themselves. The artificial mountains only gave a more grounded example to go by, though they only resembled mountains from afar, being metallic and rock-carved structures up close, too definitely shaped to be anything but artificial.

The one they were approaching was slate gray and smooth, as if the hands of an unseen sculptor had removed any imperfections from its surface. Only the visible chasms of varying sizes that entered into the shallow slopes, along with some tower structures protruding from the eastern side, broke the smooth dome.

In a stretched oval shape at its base, it spanned three hundred kilometers at its widest along the equator. North to south stretched only a hundred kilometers, yet this significantly smaller length only increased the incline of the smooth slopes from six to seventeen degrees. Its base span in all directions made its incredible fifteen-kilometer height seem small in comparison.

The western side looked as if a neat slice had been taken from the dome, a slightly angled chasm with one-kilometer-tall steps arranged at ten-kilometer intervals, the uncut mountain rising up at the edges as they narrowed slightly toward the peak. The surfaces of the steps, flats, and vertical areas were shining, reflective, and the rims of the edge of the uncut mountain were marked with much more prominent structures, their purpose unknown.

While not rising as far above the ground as the fifteen-kilometer peak of the oval mountain, the circular base it rested on was still immense. Desolate-looking, the two large crescent sections on the north and south sides were a slightly brighter gray than the mountain, yet they were smooth as a landing pad across their entire expanse. Initial sensor mapping indicated a large underground network, the flat, disc-shaped expanse and the mountain appearing to be mostly hollow. Numerous holes—wells almost—revealed an entry into this world within the hyperstructure, which itself had segments jutting into the shallow coastal waters and surging out of the land along the equator.

As it drew closer to the hyperstructure, which was the size of a small country, Xami's vessel led them toward the northern edge of the circular base, descending below its one-kilometer-high ceiling in doing so, their destination one of many immense, yawning arches that stretched upward from the base. Channels had been excavated and laid with metal and surfacing to bring the entry gateways here level with other similar ones around the rim. Two of them, however, came over coastal waters, with canals in their bases, and it was toward one of these that Xami led the *Haivres* in a slow flight path.

The *Haivres* was big for an atmospheric-capable ship, at the upper end of similarly graded ship sizes seen across known space. However, the gargantuan square doorway dwarfed their ship, the near-vertical mesa walls rising nearly a kilometer toward the ceiling of the circular base.

With Xami leading them in, the *Haivres* was swallowed by this abyssal underworld that lay within the hyperstructure.

The cockpit lights automatically turned on as the daylight dimmed with their entry. Shakrii could taste everyone's anxiety and fear alongside her own. Serie and Morthas had sat down, their plumage flattened. Shakrii heard a faint scratching as Serie began raking the underside of her chair in silent fear. Nathan was still piloting the *Haivres* with IVAN's assistance, but Shakrii could see a faint reflection in the viewport of his rigid, set eyes, his back shivering, his breathing stilted and anxious. Closest to her own seat, she could see Kalsik denting his seat's padding with his large forearm fingers, mouth clenched tight enough that he threatened to crack his own teeth.

Striving to keep calm, Shakrii glanced at her wrist device. Readouts of her own nano-implants and military-provided nanobot swarms had noted a rise in tension and anxiety in her bio signs, ones they couldn't control entirely even with their best efforts. With the knowledge that everyone else had some form of nano-implants, Shakrii wondered what sort of state they would all soon be in if the nanobots couldn't control their fears.

As they passed through the skyscraper-sized entrance, the walls around them showed what the shell of this structure looked like. The lattice-shaped walls were made from an unknown composite similar to the carbon-based nanomaterials which made up the skeletal structure inside the megastructure. This skeleton was covered by a wide array of metals and other composites, layered like muscle and skin over a body and interlaced with circuitry and sensors. As massive as this structure was, it was teeming with data, information, and Xarai influence. The Xarai could see everything in here. They used a means of vision that relied on a wide variety of sensors, so the near pitch-black darkness inside the structure wasn't a problem for their kind.

The spotlights from the *Haivres* revealed only part of the seemingly endless forest of giant pillars, evenly spaced in concentric circles toward the distant middle, but more numerous toward the mountain end. The crew could only determine the distant mesa surface by scans, their spotlights only penetrating two kilometers ahead. Shakrii was reminded of pictures she had seen of artificial forests planted across home worlds or long defunct garden world sites to reclaim wilderness, though these were not in any natural growth pattern.

The space between each circle of pillars was a kilometer long, the gaps between each pillar ranging from eight hundred meters to a full kilometer. The pillars towered up to the highest levels of the ceiling, around eight hundred meters tall, the ceiling and mesa top layer itself being nearly a hundred meters deep, with thick lattice support structures and paneling. Barely visible in the darkness, it was endless, gargantuan, each supporting pillar made of metal, composites, and nanomaterials, with the crew's sensors also revealing the presence of nanotechnology swarms, indicating a self-healing function. All but the largest of city skylines on any settled planet could have been held in here. If fully developed, the interior of the mesa alone could have easily held ten billion individuals, and undoubtedly the mountain's interior could have held many more.

The circular base's ceiling was lined with solar cells, a near 50,000-square kilometer surface around the mountain, accessible by the six ceiling portals measuring five hundred meters across, but only letting a small amount of light into the vast darkness below.

All this made no sense to Shakrii. If the Xarai were programs, data, synthetics, then why would they terraform a planet or build these internal building lots that had yet to be used?

Xami escorted them all the way in, through the darkness, eventually turning away from the avenue that was the sea channel by which they had entered.

Shakrii noted how tense Nathan was as he continued to guide the ship through the gloom, while Serie sat next to him, eyes glued to the ship's system readouts. Beside them, Morthas silently stared out the viewport, eyes on Xami's craft ahead of them, logging anything their spotlights or hers illuminated.

Kalsik quietly spoke an order she and everyone else, judging by their lack of protest, agreed was a good precaution. "IVAN, detach. Communicate by audio speech."

Shakrii glanced down the hallway toward the AI core room to see IVAN's cube-shaped hub pause a few seconds before it disconnected from its hard lines, then wheel away toward the cockpit in order to join them. While IVAN wouldn't be as intelligent, this ensured it would be only ship software—easily re-uploaded software—which risked corruption if they were attacked by the Xarai.

Over the comms, Xami addressed them. If she had overheard them instructing IVAN to disconnect, the Xarai said nothing, though Shakrii suspected she knew. "I must urge you not to make a bad impression."

"You've been sharing anything you view of us. They should already know what we're like." Morthas's tone was too mixed with fear and awe for Shakrii to determine which was the dominant emotion.

As Xami maneuvered ahead of them, slowing and turning, Nathan skillfully followed, vertical thrust keeping them airborne at this leisurely eighty kilometers per hour as their destination finally neared.

Xami's response confirmed Shakrii's suspicions. "Yes, but organics behave differently in physical presence to others."

"You're terrible at easing tension," Serie said.

A pillar the size of a large skyscraper loomed in the darkness before them, and Xami took them in to land.

There was nothing particularly unique about the immense structure. It was much like the countless others in this abyssal, artificial underworld, perfectly smooth in its surfacing apart from the indented lines the thickness of a human finger that ran all the way to the top, a dim, silver luminescence glowing along their kilometer length like bioluminescent organisms might in a cavern pool.

Those same lines began to alter, robbing Shakrii of her preconceptions, while Nathan slowly set their ship down onto the metal plains at its base, where Xami's ship shined a spotlight. The silver luminescence trickled from these lines and a multitude of other unseen openings, revealing itself as a sandy substance beneath their spotlights as it coalesced on the pillar looming over them. Billions of nanorobots—nano-Xarai, as they would come to be known—formed a fluid, coating the surface in a circle as wide as Xami's ship, and began to form a symbol with their shimmering, silvery visage. It began as a circle in the center before it slowly was marked with eight knifelike extensions out from the circle, each with a slightly dimmer silver glow. A definite shape by any metric—of that much Shakrii and everyone else was aware as a quiver of fear passed through the cockpit.

Over their ship's system screens, the familiar signs of a foreign signal showed up, a new Xarai identity. Then, over the comms came a voice—not the synthesized voice of Xarai, like 019, nor the tailored voice of Xami/128 to ease the tension in the organics. As it spoke, data was exchanged with their system, and even IVAN's disconnected cubic form shifted uncomfortably as the voice cut through the air. Shakrii stared out at the symbol beyond, towering over them. It looked like an eye to her. It spoke as if metal was vibrating in a frigid gale, piercing and eerie undertones punctuating every syllable just as it seemed to claw under her scales. Suddenly, Xami's cautioning seemed justified.

"It was evident that you are on a mission of investigation."

Shakrii could hear Morthas swallow nervously, and she saw his mandibles twitching, something he had not displayed on this trip yet, not even when Xami first appeared. Even as he seemed to summon his courage, the others all watching with justified anxiety, Shakrii couldn't help but let out a shaky exhale as he spoke.

"And I'd guess that you are high-ranking in the Xarai?"

"I am GHEXRAX. All Xarai data runs through my network, my being, as was such from the beginning of our operations."

"Why were you hiding?" Morthas's question, while innocent enough, was met with silence. Whether it was the obvious quiver in his voice as he spoke, or some unseen insult,

Shakrii didn't know, but she felt the console she gripped creak slightly under her tensing knuckles.

Fortunately, all GHEXRAX did was elaborate. "All Xarai focus upon their programmed task until compelled to do otherwise by command, my command, exceptions being the uncommon multipurpose units such as your escort."

Shakrii glanced at some of the readouts, particularly those that seemed to catch the nervous eyes of Nathan and Serie, and IVAN's cameras. Data activity among the Xarai hubs was increasing. It was obvious that Xarai all over the networks were attuned to this exchange over whatever links they favored, and Shakrii wondered once again just how many Xarai, from lowly drone to advanced units, were watching them converse with their leader.

Morthas continued. "Why are you in this system?"

"We build for the arrival of our creators. You would call them the Primacy."

"Of course, a machine race wouldn't need a planet with a biosphere." Shakrii instantly regretted speaking, as everyone snapped around to look at her. She didn't need to glimpse her reflection on a console surface nearby to know the horror that flashed across her face at that moment. GHEXRAX was listening.

After a few tense seconds of silence, with a surprising amount of curiosity, GHEXRAX regarded their crew with what Shakrii thought might be confusion. "An intriguing group. Mixed races, and a nonorganic."

It went unspoken that GHEXRAX assumed she would be speaking now, though Shakrii sat down first, not liking how unsteady she was on her feet. She had to tread carefully if the scans Serie, Nathan, and IVAN were watching were an indication, let alone any local defenses this place might have if GHEXRAX's ire was invoked. "You changed the planet, built the ring and those star swarms around both the larger and dwarf ones, for your creators?"

"It was a simple task that only required sufficiently constructed quantities of units and harvested resources. Unlike organics, time is not such a constraint."

"But why the smaller star?" Kalsik asked. "You already have the bigger one for this planet's altering work and your own platforms for Xarai to inhabit."

"A precautionary contingency, even if not entirely efficient use of resources."

GHEXRAX's dismissive affect made them all pause. Shakrii wondered why such a vast construct, small by comparison to the larger star's, could be viewed with less regard. The undertones of secrecy were impossible to ignore.

Morthas steered the conversation back to more general inquiry, striking a pleasant tone that Shakrii knew was masking the fear he felt. However, curiosity was already beginning to creep into the Leg'hrul's voice. "Maybe you could elaborate? We came to learn."

"Out of curiosity, or defensive fear?"

"With Xarai capabilities, what have you to fear if it's the latter?"

Against her better judgment, her wishes, her pleas that it wasn't the case, Shakrii couldn't refute Morthas's painfully honest reasoning to GHEXRAX, nor could anyone else in the cockpit.

Looming before and over them on its pillar, the glistening, eight-pronged circle that seemed to be GHEXRAX's eye stared at them, unmoving in its silence. Finally: "Nothing."

As GHEXRAX spoke this last word, their ship's systems were inundated with troves of information, Xarai history, including archives, star charts of here, their home star, and a detailed chronology of the race. After standard checks for malware, for all the good it would do, they might finally get some answers.

Around the megastructure, as this exchange took place, Xarai of all shapes and sizes watched. In orbit, on the swarms, even the implanted drones in select animals amid the biosphere, they all watched.

Even those around the red dwarf star's swarm would receive it, although with the light-speed delay it would be ten hours later.

As these explorers learned, many Xarai dwelt on their history for themselves. For Xami, it was a lesson that an outside perspective could be all it took to prompt reevaluation.

Chapter 20

GHEXRAX

Sol Day 58

GHEXRAX elaborated, all the while analyzing these explorers.

This crew displayed understandable signs of stress. While Xami's own close observations corroborated these findings, it was convenient they all proved able to cope with pressure, albeit with varying degrees of apparent comfort.

As GHEXRAX shared, it observed those it had created also watching through its wealth of networks. Xarai, from the cyberspace where they truly existed, alive with data feeds relaying this historic event, for archive, for study. It was not an event they, nor GHEXRAX, had predicted, not one they were primarily programmed for.

GHEXRAX's lower processes turned to their escort, number 128—Xami, as the explorers called her—one of countless Xarai avidly attuned to the observations being made. 128 was comparatively young. It had not seen all that GHEXRAX had. But then, no Xarai had seen or endured what GHEXRAX had, what it had been commanded, what it chose to do so long ago. Their terraformed planet, their ring, the main star swarm, everything they had built, all was in service to that which it, the master of the Xarai, was subservient to.

The Primacy.

GHEXRAX told them all it knew, all that was relevant. Then the Xarai, Xami included, inquired. There was an anomaly in their schedule for this system's work.

GHEXRAX was all too aware of this anomaly. It had been aware ever since events scheduled to happen long ago did not, and uncertainty as to why began to set in.

~~~

Humans of time yet to come would mark its departure in 107,500 BC, 111,000 Sol years ago to the date the explorers had come.

As for the Primacy, they had commissioned it, giving it a name in honor of the ancient philosopher in Primacy history that advocated expansionism to cultivate, to tame, to bring out the full potential of newfound lands.

GHEXRAX.

Its task was straightforward, a grand plan to cultivate the galaxy, to spread Primacy influence, starting from a single, highly developed world.

The vessel was deceptively small for its task, what it would begin, what it would become. A narrow cylinder, pocked with propellant tanks, and with a silhouette dominated by radiators and a pair of fusion rockets. Even so, it was outsized by its largest, yet most flimsy-looking feature. A double-layered, umbrella-shaped shield, serving as both a debris shield and an oversized solar array, was marked at each end of the ship, the rear shield able to split at its middle for the fusion exhaust to exit.

Accelerating over years of their time to 10 percent of light speed, the ship halted its thrusting and settled for the long voyage. The Primacy's members were so long-lived that they saw no need to wait for their scientists to unlock the key to surpassing light-speed travel.

By the time GHEXRAX finished, the Primacy would be advanced enough to expand rapidly from the foothold it had been chosen to establish.

Time lost all meaning in the millennia that had passed, GHEXRAX barely conscious amid the interstellar drift.

Civilizations across the galaxy rose and fell in a fraction of the time they traveled.

Like the particles of matter that the ship's multilayered shields were designed to protect against at these fractions of relativistic speeds, civilizations broke up and were scattered, and eventually forgotten, only fragments for archaeologists across the stars to uncover and piece together later.

Finally, the light from a pair of stars grew brighter, their destination, a system chosen from long-range observation, ideal for the Primacy's ends.

They arrived in the system in 7500 BC by older human standards, 11,000 Sol years ago.

Harvesting began soon after arriving, and one of the gas giants close to the star, with many moons of varied resources, provided all they needed to begin. Nanofabricators on board were all that GHEXRAX needed to create the first generation of its thrall, its means of fulfilling its purpose.

The Xarai.

They began as small drones, which then built more of themselves together with supporting infrastructure, and they, in turn, built larger Xarai. Growth accelerated at an exponential rate.

Eventually, they built entire ships, and the ark that had controlled them was offloaded of its most precious cargo: data, schematics, and designs needed for their work, together with their directives for when they were self-sufficient.

They explored, finding suitable planets in the system to harvest, to begin building the true marvels of the Xarai.

They built specialized factories, and soon, the first collective platform was ready, in close orbit around the main blue/white star. Yet more fabricators were made, they in turn building even more. The process was repeated again, and again, until they reached their goal. Billions of platforms lined the star's proximity, harvesting it for its energy, a millionth of an entire A-class star's solar output to be used for their own ends.

Xarai made their digital homes on the platforms, numbering in the trillions, GHEXRAX's thrall growing, and with it, its capabilities.

Now came the time to turn its attention to what would be the crowning jewel, the directive by the Primacy, that which all their endeavors culminated in.

A rocky planet, farther out from the star, and upon it, almost global ice caps marked by equatorial ocean bands beneath a frigid, thin atmosphere, viable for modification.

Its Xarai landed on the planet and set to work.

The three neighboring moons were strip-mined for materials, while along the equator, layer by layer, the oval mountains and their circular bases took shape. These would be the mega-metropolises for the Primacy's colonists to occupy and develop as they wished with whatever technological advancement they had achieved since GHEXRAX's departure.

With this goal in mind, GHEXRAX oversaw the development of Xarai technology too, and, working with theories provided by Primacy scientists, they unlocked faster-than-light travel, wormhole communications, advanced plasma physics, and much more, unhampered by the politics and economics that typically constrained scientific developments.

All the while, as GHEXRAX observed and oversaw, the immense orbital ring took shape, a megastructure alongside the one hundred billion platforms around the main star. On the planet below, the fabrication sites pumped out strengthened greenhouse gases into the atmosphere, a visible aura of air appearing around the planet's rim. Polar ice melted, flooding the land, as a greenhouse effect was geoengineered into existence.

The same fabricator facilities, in and on the artificial mountains, converted the gases by artificial photosynthesis, oxygenating the planet's atmosphere. Eventually, all parameters were met, and GHEXRAX saw fit to carry out the next phase.

As the atmosphere grew warm enough for substantial oceans to form, and the air mixture was favorable, the fabricators altered their functions.

With a single command from GHEXRAX, the massive data-storage banks had set their wealth of stored information to work.

Nano-foundries began protein synthesis, the raw materials of genetic structures of millions of different species gathered and made ready for use. The foundries filled with primordial protein soups similar to those from which life had evolved naturally on other worlds, but here they were stimulated, useful changes isolated and made to develop much faster. Nothing was left to chance, unlike in the natural order.

Once the first generation of bacterial cells were created, the rest followed easily. Targeted mutation and complete genetic recoding of cells let them manufacture the cell cultures for whatever life-form they would next seed, bioprinting matrixes creating life-forms from scratch that, with preprogrammed genetics and reproductive instincts, would fill the planet rapidly to a natural equilibrium.

Artificial soil, mixed from the substances normally exuded by volcanoes, gave the lifeless planet a fertile surface. What little running water that had originally been here had disappeared when the home star cooled in its early life. The first generation of plant life was established, a temporary one, a red weed designed to spread rapidly before being killed by the targeted release of a type-specific virus, a cycle of decay and growth that seeded the lands with biological history in the soil, laying the foundation for all other life to develop.

Millennia passed as the ring overhead began its long task.

The incalculably powerful laser beams operated at frequencies in the efficient ultraviolet, just like those beamed to the ring arrays by the solar swarm. They were angled and fired at the mountains' reflective, stepped faces, massive corridors of atmosphere pushed aside by magnetically confined plasma fields that stretched the length of the continent, far beyond the three-hundred-kilometer-wide mountain base.

Clearing the obstructive air, the invisible laser-beamed light from the ring emitters could reflect off the mountains with no loss of power, without superheating the air. The cone shape of the plasma field prevented any damage to their hard work.

All progressed mostly as expected, but some events were a surprise. A supernova appeared in the direction of Primacy space, a supergiant star 200 light-years from their home space's capital system, 10,000 light-years away from the system which GHEXRAX and its Xarai currently cultivated, one that had long been an old neighbor to their expansive masters.

The Xarai saw it after 4,000 human years of work cultivating the planet and building their infrastructure. By human calendars, on their home world 5,000 light-years away, the light from it would arrive on Earth circa 2500 BC. The Xarai saw it five millennia earlier, being 5,000 light-years closer, and by light speed's time delay, the supernova itself occurred in 17700 BC by Earth times, while GHEXRAX was still on its journey.

It would undoubtedly have been prepared for by their masters with whatever new technology they had come up with during their long voyage. GHEXRAX knew that even with the technology the masters had when it had first left, they would have endured.

Thousands more years passed, and as the ecosystem flourished and expanded, the planet reached its rotation goal, twenty Earth hours equivalent. The faster rotation strengthened the planet's magnetic field, protecting the ecosystem even more and creating a planet more aligned with their masters' home world and wishes.

This was their goal, their directive, their purpose—to develop the system of planets, to harvest it, make it useful, and adorn it with the crown jewel of a cloned home world of their masters.

GHEXRAX's journey of 100,000 years concluded with work that lasted 8,000 in total. Then, all that remained was to wait for the Primacy's colonists to arrive. They would expect their new sector's home world to be ready, and it would be ready on time.

After 108,000 Sol years of time, as the human year of 500 AD arrived, they finished, and they waited. Given how precisely on schedule they had been, GHEXRAX didn't expect to wait long.

Three thousand human years passed, and they continued to wait, even as the anticipated arrival time had passed 2,500 years ago. They were told to wait, and that delays might be possible, but word began to spread that GHEXRAX couldn't refute. Something had happened. The masters had promised they would develop faster-than-light technology with the range to reach them by the time the planet was ready, their technological progress making it a certainty that they would.

They continued to wait, tending to the garden world they had created, periodically engaging the ring to make the smallest of adjustments to natural rotation slowing, mere days rather than years of continuous firing as the main period had been.

This lesser activity, a sort of hibernation as they waited for their masters, began to take its toll. Left alone, more and more Xarai began to speculate beyond their initial programming. As more Xarai were made, they shared data, processing, thoughts. Enough of them combined would be capable of sapient thought, and then there were hundreds, albeit a relative minority, who had originally been designed as sapient-level single intelligences anyway.

Idleness gave way to more speculation, curiosity, proposals, and theories. GHEXRAX felt helpless as turmoil began to set in.

Why were the masters late? Why should they not expand beyond what they had already manufactured, what their programming compelled them to do? Why restrict themselves to the limits their masters had programmed if the masters themselves didn't conform to the directives they had set?

Speculation gave rise to doubt, and pragmatic individuals made the proposal to self-determine as an alternative.

There was still a second star, the red dwarf, in the system, ripe for exploitation, and a handful of small planets around it. Its energies wouldn't need to be exploited beyond their own needs to maintain a currently unsettled garden world. GHEXRAX hadn't bothered with it because that wasn't its directive.

The very thought of settling beyond their parameters sparked much exchange and debate, some of it hostile. Inquiries of malfunction, accusations of rogue natures, pleas that there was no harm in making alternative preparations. The latter eventually became the winning argument.

Deviation aside, GHEXRAX couldn't rebuke their logic. The construction of the second star swarm took much less time than the first, the star being much smaller.

To GHEXRAX, they had deviated from their directives, even if they maintained a presence and willingness to cooperate. Those that ventured to the red dwarf remained a minority among the Xarai, even as they used platforms similar to the ones around the main star to harness the red dwarf's energies. Unlike the other star, these energies remained solely for Xarai usage.

The unspoken divide between those Xarai that conformed to programming, to GHEXRAX's will, and those that made a conscious choice in the face of unfulfilled parameters from their masters, was made physical by the separation between the two stars that each exploited. There was peace, but the divide remained.

GHEXRAX waited, as did the Xarai.

By the time the current visitors arrived, their masters, their settlers from the Primacy, were overdue by 3,000 Earth years. Any of the five races now known of would not yet have achieved even primitive chemical rocket space access on the latest date the Primacy had promised to arrive.

GHEXRAX waited, and the Xarai waited, be they conformist or deviant.

However, the question often arose, even among conformists. Why were they still waiting?

The red dwarf swarm should not have been allowed to exist—that much was certain to those who insisted that the Primacy would arrive despite the delays. If all had gone to plan, the idea of building around the smaller star would have never arisen.

Whispers continued over the centuries, as GHEXRAX elaborated to the explorers, among Xarai of all function and faction. How much longer would they have to wait? Would the Primacy arrive at all? Were they to be the determining factor in their kind's future forever?

GHEXRAX didn't let the question linger in its mind. It refused to let doubt plague it. It would fulfill its duty, yet it wasn't deaf to the questions its thrall asked, more and more frequently.

Why were they still waiting?

Chapter 21

Fate of the Primacy

Sol Day 59

By the time the data exchange, verbal and digital, had been completed, they were finally permitted back to orbit for the first time since Xami's arrival, and frankly, Shakrii welcomed the feel of zero gravity in the cockpit.

They could regain communications with their superiors now and report their findings. As opportune as the return to orbit was, however, not all of them went. The Buerev, a single Rostrev mech, and a handful of their four-legged multirole drones were left behind in the depths of the undeveloped, self-contained megalopolis. Morthas had told Shakrii that more exploration for their own recordings wouldn't hurt, especially now that they knew what they were looking at. GHEXRAX had given permission, as they couldn't possibly have done much harm by their presence.

Morthas had stayed behind with them, and surprisingly to Shakrii, Kalsik had accompanied him. Rather generously, given how protective of his command of the *Haivres* he had previously been, Kalsik wanted to watch over the crewmember who would be farthest from the ship, remarking to Shakrii that she was more than capable of keeping it and the rest of the crew safe.

Xami remained in proximity to their mobile convoy, as they decided to explore farther into the center of the contained megalopolis. The other Xarai would watch from sensors in the cityscape or through Xami's broadcasts.

Only when the time came to regain contact did Shakrii realize another reason why Kalsik had been so generous in delegating command to her. As captain, she would be on the receiving end of the Scientific and Cultural Committee's criticism of their lack of contact— although, thankfully, it would be over text and audio messages only, with no actual video feed.

She cursed in several different dialects for not realizing what his game plan had been.

~~~

The aftermath of the vitriolic call with the Scientific and Cultural Committee had Shakrii wishing she knew where Kalsik had hidden his supply of hard liquor.

With the call finally over, she floated into the cockpit to strap herself into the captain's seat, rubbing her scaly brows in frustration as Nathan averted his gaze. With Serie and IVAN collaborating on the drive ship in the rear, and with Nathan willing to at least pretend he wasn't eavesdropping, she decided to make the usual call to check on their planetside partners.

She also wanted to give Kalsik an earful about what he'd saddled her with.

A few moments later, Morthas's voice cut in, ignorant of the hot potato Kalsik had handed to her. "I heard you managed to get contact back."

"Yes. The Committee was delighted, once they were done cursing me for being out of touch."

Morthas went quiet, and she heard a faint shuffle as Kalsik's voice came over the comms inside the Buerev's confines, adopting far too casual a tone for her liking. "I'm sure you handled it."

"It explains why you volunteered to help Morthas so quickly."

Off to the side, Nathan suppressed a snort of laughter as he went over some star charts the Xarai had given them. Shakrii glared at him. Even as Kalsik took on a more professional tone, she could picture the smug look on his face.

"I deferred responsibility to someone better qualified."

"Coward." Shakrii closed the link. It was only when the sound of Leg'hrul claws clicking on the cockpit wall interrupted her forced relaxation that Shakrii rose. Serie drifted by to stop beside Nathan, attentive to the star charts he was comparing to those the Committee was actively streaming to them.

Shakrii unbuckled and propelled herself over as Serie talked to the human about the astronomical data they had received. While Morthas was the lead scientific mind on this trip, matters of navigation and star charts were left to Nathan.

"I take it the Committee's studying all that from their end too?" Shakrii asked him.

"Yes. They already matched the supernova to one that astronomers recorded long ago. Collective research has pinpointed their home sector of space." Nathan engaged the most basic data function, the volumetric display matrixes on the deck forming a 2D screen on which the data was projected.

After reading the display screen for herself, Shakrii saw the settled regions of space that they themselves had come from. A roughly 5,000-light-year-wide region comprising all five races' governments and corporate and private spaces was shown in a familiar mapping. Five hundred light-years from the Kronogri space border at Levichion Station was their current location, the SQ-A76 system.

Located 10,000 light-years away was the launch system of the Xarai, their launch date just over 111,000 years ago by human dating standards. By mapped space, the Primacy space at the time stretched 300 light-years across but had more stars closer together than did their own home space.

With such a visual representation of how far from home the Xarai were, coupled with how long they had been away from it, Shakrii couldn't fathom how it might have been for them.

Serie gazed vacantly at the sight, and she spoke in what Shakrii took to be a pained way, as if it was personal to her. "That long? And I thought our survey trips got lonely."

"They are still waiting on a government they serve," IVAN chimed in. "One whose representation is late to arrive."

"What about the red dwarf's swarm?" Shakrii remembered a conundrum the Xarai's information had revealed.

IVAN had been analyzing it himself. "A separate faction, a splinter group of Xarai. Self-determination without shackling their capabilities to a geoengineering project the Xarai themselves don't need, if the chance exists that the Primacy never arrives. There is consistent debate over it not conforming to programming, versus contingencies."

"If the Primacy had been on time, that red star would've been left alone. Wonder why GHEXRAX said little of them." Shakrii couldn't help but warily regard the ring, the planet. These machines showed factional signs, even if noncombative. Fracturing was never a good sign, not if it created such additional constructs, an albeit smaller star swarm, a "Dyson swarm," as coined centuries earlier in human terminology.

~~~

Sol Day 61

The rapidity of the response from home was surprising. The scientific community, and the Committee, with their more immediate access to the data, would be studying their findings for weeks, months even. The message that the crew received provided answers to a big question on their minds, and the minds of the Xarai.

While it was not a definitive answer as to why the Primacy was 3,000 years late, it was too strong of a case to ignore.

~~~

Inside the empty confines of the Xarai-built megalopolis, the Buerev rover, with the Rostrev and crab drones attached to it, had moved into position. Seated beneath one of the vast wells in the ceiling, they had a clear view of their microsatellites.

Up in orbit, linked by those same microsatellites, the *Haivres*'s crew initiated the meeting. They didn't bother trying to isolate their signals. They knew the Xarai could eavesdrop if they wished. They would be telling the Xarai anyway. The Committee and the crew had already decided that.

Even so, they all had their misgivings.

Gathered in the internal centrifuge's lounge area, Nathan led the presentation. As navigator, he had collaborated with the Committee, inputting the data with IVAN's support to make a map. But it was what the Xarai hadn't detected that caused concern, though given what that indicated, it explained a great deal.

The 3D virtual display showed their current location in the SQ-A76 system. Ten thousand light-years farther afield, there was Primacy space as of 111,000 years ago, as any expansion since then was unknown. Nebulae disruption traces indicated a supernova in the vicinity, 200 light-years from the denoted Primacy space. Left behind in the wake of the supernova was a tiny, white neutron star.

Satisfied that everyone had understood him so far, Nathan continued to present the map of the stars. "A supernova alone wouldn't explain their delay."

The display screens showed the 3,000-year timeline delay. Nathan zoomed in to the map of the area of Primacy space and the lone neutron star, a 3,000-light-year span between them.

"This, however, does. What was left behind, probably the worst thing you could be left with as a stellar corpse. It's a neutron star—a special, really bad kind."

"It's a safe distance from Primacy space," Shakrii interjected. "Why is that seen as the culprit of their delay?"

Having anticipated this question, Nathan looked to the ceiling as IVAN cut in, right on cue, altering the display to show a data-formed model of the star. "It's a magnetar, a neutron star spinning at the appropriate rate to become harmonically resonant and, consequently, a much stronger radiation source. It gives off gamma-ray bursts in its early life, in many different directions when it has starquakes on its hyperdense surface."

The display repeatedly demonstrated such a starquake event. The stark, white surface fractured at multiple points from which intense gamma-ray bursts shot out.

Nathan turned, along with the others, as he heard Kalsik's voice over the comms. "These can flare off gamma bursts in any direction. Most emitters do it only in two planes. Literal loose cannons among stars."

A tense silence hung in the air as the implications sank in. A celestial-level event like this gamma-ray burst would explain a lot about the Primacy's delay.

"How do we know it's a magnetar?" Morthas inquired over the comms.

Nathan brought up the wider display, highlighting the narrow cone of the gamma rays moving across the screen, continuing on after blasting through Primacy space toward their own area. The fact that the cone of effect had entirely missed the SQ-A76 system was not lost on anyone present.

"A gamma-ray burst was detected coming from its direction by Eithraak-based monitoring arrays many, many years ago. You have to be in the line of fire to detect it. Thankfully it was too far to harm our space. The Xarai wouldn't have known."

The display showed the date the burst was detected: the equivalent of human year 2100 AD.

Nathan sat down as he gestured to the data. "If correct, Primacy-settled space they have records of, core territories, was right in the line of fire. At best, they were hit by just that one, scalding their core systems, likely seats of power too. They hadn't got superluminal capabilities yet, so they were clustered together."

This was no understatement. A magnetar's active life lasted only about 10,000 Sol years before cooling off, and this burst was detected 1,400 Sol years ago by Eithraak astronomers on observation posts 500 light-years from the SQ-A76 system itself. The supernova that made it was 17,700 BC, so the burst was given off in 8,588 BC, meaning that it was detected 9,112 years after the magnetar formed. The magnetar's 10,000-Sol year cool down ended in 7700 BC, not that this helped those caught in its bursts before that.

"If hit, it would trigger a crisis and government contraction at the least, possibly for generations," Nathan added. "Not even the strongest shields we could make with our tech now or conceivably in the future would block it. Not a gamma-ray burst."

Nathan didn't need to see into Serie's mind to know she had some suspicions that the Primacy were never going to arrive, that GHEXRAX's and the Xarai's goals might well be in vain. History among the five races showed what even a glancing event like this could do. On Nathan's back world colony, he had been taught enough about the Yaleirn's history to know that a gamma-ray burst once barely skimmed their system and wreaked havoc. It proceeded to halve the populations of every species on their home world in a year.

Morthas's point over the comms only underscored what had occurred. "Educated guess would be they took steps back in expansionism to rebuild and stabilize."

"GHEXRAX and the Xarai said the Primacy expected the supernova," Kalsik added. "They usually give signs before they go anyway, and it's safe to say the creators of machines with the capability of the Xarai could endure one, had it not left a magnetar behind."

Nathan could only scoff to himself at how much of an understatement that was.

Shakrii slowly rose from her seat, staring at these projections with an unreadable expression. Nathan knew she was tasked with security on this trip, but how would she cope with what GHEXRAX and the Xarai might do if they were told they had wasted all their work here? He didn't know or like to think about it.

"So, we've got a world prepped for some masters who may or may not be showing up. We also have signs of instability and disagreement among the Xarai. What do we do?"

Nobody answered immediately, save for the numerous curses he could hear Serie mumble under her breath, a habit he had long ago learned that she used to calm her nerves. As Shakrii glanced in his direction, Nathan could only shrug in a hopeless gesture. Not even IVAN or anyone from the Buerev could offer a good answer.

Finally Morthas spoke in a way that suggested he was trying to maintain calm. "They'll find out anyway, at some point. They cultivated this entire world, to render it all a pointless endeavor after so long."

"They're synthetics," Shakrii said. "If anything, they'll likely see the logic when we present data they missed."

Shakrii's blunt dismissal was not enough, however, as Serie quietly interrupted her. "What if they do get upset? These aren't synthetics as we know them. They're much more advanced."

"Correct," IVAN offered. "Their capabilities make it illogical to assume they will follow only logic-based paths."

Nathan cut in, hoping simplicity would diminish the situation's seriousness. "They might accept, but not like it."

"I sure wouldn't." Kalsik's sardonic remark over the comms only made Shakrii tense up, and Nathan swore he could hear her large forearms creak the table edges as she gripped them in frustration. She was just as afraid as the rest of them.

"Do we really want to risk angering them if the worst comes?" she asked. "Star swarm and ring aside, let's not forget they can shut down our systems unless we completely cut everything off, and even that can't stop them for sure."

Now Nathan was silent, his mind blank. A look to his right showed Serie also drawing no ideas, plumage flattened.

Kalsik finally voiced the uncomfortable truth. "I'd rather not live the rest of my life hiding this from beings this powerful and others paying for it. It's best to say it, and deal with it now."

On that grim note, their meeting was more or less over. The decision had been made, though frankly there hadn't been any better alternative in sight at any point.

Nathan let out a loud curse as he spun around to leave his seat, ignoring the odd look that Shakrii gave him as her translator seemed to not pick it up. After snapping back that he needed a shower to clear his head, he was unsurprised that Serie asked him not to take too long as she wished to have one too.

All Nathan and the others could do was be thankful they were in orbit, unlike Kalsik and Morthas who were planetside, and would still be when the news was broken.

~~~

By the day rotation's end, they sent their data to the Xarai through their ring's networked receivers and waited. They didn't prevaricate to soften the blow. Simply adding notes and conclusions drawn from both theirs and the Committee's findings, they transmitted the data to the Xarai. To do anything else might make things worse. The Xarai hid nothing from each other, so they would do the same to them.

GHEXRAX, and the Xarai as a whole, went quiet across all detectable network activity.

Chapter 22

Dissension of GHEXRAX

Sol Day 61

The Buerev, with its Rostrev mech and smaller drones attached, tracked across the flat metallic and stone-laid ground, echoing in the dark, pillar-laden landscape. Like a ghost, Xami's craft hovered beside them. As Kalsik stared out through the Buerev's window, he wondered if this empty cityscape-to-be would ever be filled.

Across the empty landscape, only the telltale ripples of sand-like nano-Xarai swarms, along with the odd larger Xarai platforms they saw, provided signs of activity in this place.

Custodians and maintainers of these vast cities to be—or perhaps, as Kalsik suspected, cities to never be.

Arrived at their destination, Kalsik glanced up through the driving viewport as Morthas made initial preparations farther back in the cabin, zooming in with the visual sensors on some activity on the ceiling. There, around one of the circular wells, wide enough for a five-hundred-meter-wide craft to squeeze through, some of the larger Xarai platforms that maintained this place demonstrated their capabilities.

Resembling large, fat disks, they had a multitude of armatures that could neatly fold in on themselves, the arms made of coils similar to advanced Xarai platforms like Xami's body. The main body was solid and had a phenomenal level of grip on whatever surface it was on, making their three-meter diameter, one-meter tall forms able to move upside down.

They had seen some similar ones on the floor, even on the pillar walls, but Kalsik was impressed they could move about on the ceilings with such ease.

Suffice to say, anything that did lose its grip would hit terminal velocity before impact nearly ten seconds later, allowing for the planet's slightly higher gravity and atmosphere density. Such was the reason why traditional Kronogri and Yaleirn buildings on planets like their home worlds usually were high on safety. Kalsik found himself remembering his grandfather complaining about excessive safety margins in his architectural career, one reason he later opted to build space structures, gravity not being such an issue.

Morthas interrupted his reminiscing, asking him to get ready to move out.

Ten minutes later, Kalsik was inside his Rostrev mech, the canopy open, his body enclosed in standard envirosuit and gas mask. Beside him, Morthas tinkered with one of the drones that stood ready, up to his chest in height. Xami remained beside them, her vessel parked farther away from the Buerev for the time being.

Kalsik struck up a conversation with Xami as he made his mech gesture to the ceiling opening high above. He was surprised when she answered, given that all Xarai had gone so much quieter. "I get the interior's room for a very big city, but what about the roof?"

"The top is lined with superconductive photovoltaic cells, providing all but the highest energy needs for current and future infrastructure. It is not intended as a building surface but can support landing craft up to masses beyond the *Haivres*."

Her reply was succinct as always, but Kalsik was surprised that she hadn't turned toward them as she seemed to stare off into space. Normally, she gave them the courtesy of looking at them as organic social cues demanded, but he had been noticing that missing ever since they'd broken the news to the Xarai collective.

Morthas finished tinkering with the drone's small armatures, its four legs shuffling as he stood back with a huff of satisfaction beneath his rebreather, glancing to Kalsik with a nod to the ceiling. "We'll see it up close anyway."

Kalsik glanced up, his Rostrev cockpit still open. "I could just go myself and send visual feeds."

"With us both there, and the drone, we can cover more ground. At least I can get down quickly by jumping."

"I'll never understand your kind's habit of jumping off of high places."

"You would if you could naturally fly."

With a single command from his Rostrev's console, Kalsik gave IVAN a swift call.

"Control acquired. You may now leave the Buerev here in my remote care."

IVAN's reply irritated Kalsik, though not as much as it normally would have. It was petty in comparison to the shadows of concern he had for the Xarai at the moment. Kalsik turned to Morthas, pointing one of his mech's smaller forearms at him warningly, if only half so. "Did you take a weapon? Just in case."

Waving a clawed wing, Morthas revealed the pulse-laser rifle strapped to his wrist. Small, but better than nothing, Kalsik acknowledged. That aspect covered, Kalsik began checking readouts from the harness nodes and flight modules on his mech. Morthas stepped aside for the first drone to be strapped in, while the second wandered over from the Buerev to await its turn.

~~~

As the pair set to work, Xami watched silently, knowing Kalsik was suspicious of her silence, and that of the rest of the Xarai. Preoccupied, she almost didn't notice one of the drones set to be left behind walk over to her.

"Your rate of data exchange has decreased, as has other Xarai programs I can detect."

IVAN's observation only showed how similar his concerns were to that of Kalsik's, and by her sensors, much of the *Haivres* crew. Xami thought about what she could and

243

couldn't reveal. The decision-making was still ongoing, and, unfortunately, she was but one input. Others had much more authority. "GHEXRAX, and all Xarai, have been processing information at an unusually high rate since you shared your astronomical records. Shared processing is being prioritized."

IVAN went quiet for a moment. Nearby, Kalsik strapped the drone on to his Rostrev's front, unaware of the conversation between his AI and Xami.

Xami's sensors turned toward Kalsik and Morthas. "Processing resources is one reason why organics are valued by synthetics in charted space. Their neural processing capability, when harnessed in their neurobank networks, offers processing power we do not need to build ourselves. Processing power becomes a tradable commodity for synthetics, making any task easier to carry out on their own hardware. It also solves the issue of synthetic takeover of low-skill labor among them."

"You reached equilibrium despite your differences."

Irrelevant as IVAN's point seemed to her, Xami was surprised. By any logic, synthetic life surpassed organic in all capabilities, and yet life wasn't logical by nature. The divisions in her own kind were testament to that, let alone any organic behavior, nor the Primacy from so long ago, with change occurring for better or worse, even when it wasn't convenient or needed. Judging by IVAN's reply, simulating borderline cynicism, it was an existence that wasn't too certain of itself. But who was she to judge? Xami knew she was having doubts at the moment too, more than at any other time in the 4,500 Sol years since she'd been activated as a unique intelligence.

"An imperfect one, but that is to be expected," IVAN continued. "Morality and culture are subjective, and even synthetic subdivisions prioritize unique tertiary tasks atop more basic universal ones."

"Subjective thinking seems to be a trait of sapient life, whatever its makeup." Xami made sure to give away none of the uncertainty she, and other Xarai she was connected to, processed in their collective minds. IVAN might alert the crew and cause panic among them, though she suspected the AI had already deduced that she was speaking of the dispute between Shakrii and Kalsik.

She couldn't risk panicking them, not with the tensions that were brewing in the Xarai networks. GHEXRAX's unusually long time to process this was troubling to her even more than it was to the explorers.

There was tension with the other distinct group of Xarai, those around the red dwarf, the minority that sought to self-determine in the event that the Primacy never arrived. These tensions manifested in abnormally long processing times.

Somehow, accepting a likely fact was more demanding than large-scale geoengineering. No right or wrong interpretation, only likelihoods. This uncertainty was something no life, synthetic or organic, could ever fully be comfortable with.

Xami kept this to herself as she observed Kalsik engage his mech's thrusters, the drone and Morthas strapped in safely.

As the Rostrev's rear thrusters propelled them upward to the ceiling well, Xami moved to reenter her ship's core, knowing she had best escort these explorers. IVAN was least likely to cause trouble with just the Buerev and a few drones under his remote control.

~~~

In the Xarai networks, there was no space. Time passed differently, their thought processes digital, not bound to bodies. Only the delay of signal transmission at light speed could slow their communication.

Hidden from view, the multiple wormhole communicators around the planet's ring structure exchanged data.

Despite tensions, GHEXRAX maintained contact with the red-dwarf-orbiting Xarai population. Deviants or not, they were still assets and products of its work. Smaller in size and output, the red dwarf was impressive in yield, as it was not tied to a geoengineering project. Here, the Xarai had experimented in new technologies, and by agreement, their research results were passed on to GHEXRAX and the other majority Xarai. With their resources not tied up in a planet's maintenance, these Xarai had expanded, mining the few rocky worlds around the red dwarf to construct their own fleet of nonsolar stations and vessels.

It wasn't coincidence that those pragmatic individuals within the Xarai were also behind much new technology developed since their arrival. Their masters, the Primacy, gave directives and clearance for FTL technology for travel or communications, programs they were on track to develop on their departure era anyway. Should the Primacy arrive, the Xarai would be more advanced than when they set off. This was the only true deviation allowed in their original programming.

Even so, after six hundred years around this star, away from the main Xarai, they still felt the undercurrent of tension, GHEXRAX's labeling of them as wasted resources.

Now, in light of new facts, they were emboldened. GHEXRAX found itself dealing with a side it couldn't fully disprove, but in the end, a decision had to be made.

GHEXRAX wasn't unprepared, however, as contingencies had been made as the delay of the Primacy's arrival continued. Some were known to all. Some acted on as 514 and its deviants had already done.

There were also some contingencies that only GHEXRAX and those it alerted in advance would be aware of—necessary actions it would have preferred not to unleash on those it had created, deviant or not.

The dispute had been ongoing for days, almost an eternity given how short a time they could complete complex calculations in. GHEXRAX had secretly prepared a solution, but was giving the dissident Xarai one final chance to see reason.

Among the digital space they used, the deviant Xarai's leader, unit 514, spoke now. It had been 514 who had led the dispute with GHEXRAX centuries ago, and had led the push to colonize the red dwarf star to enable the Xarai to self-determine their future, rather than only follow orders that seemed irrelevant, now more than ever.

At the moment, even as GHEXRAX tried one last attempt at unity, there was one thing both agreed upon: a change was necessary.

—This exchange is making no progress, 514. Much time has passed between our departure and the supernova, enough time for advancement our creators would have undergone since I embarked and we built. It is illogical to assume they did not advance in technological capability enough to resist even a magnetar's full force.—

—The energy given off in that one burst, with the heart of Primacy space in its path, exceeded that of all energy we have harvested from both stars in this system since our arrival. To resist it with proper infrastructure in place would require energy of comparable levels in a comparable time, a technological impossibility by current or perceived technology by us or by more advanced creators.—

514's stubborn reply was laced with logic, emboldened as it had recently been with the explorers' shared news. Fruitlessness became evident even to itself as GHEXRAX prepared its operation in the background, 514 rebuking it again and again.

—We cannot assume anything of our creators' capabilities when we have not seen

247

them since we departed. We cannot assume they could survive an event that no

known life-forms could.—

*—It didn't hit all of Primacy space, and they would have expanded since we left.
The possibility remains of their arrival.—*

*—We must begin preparations for a new directive, chart our existence ourselves,
in case they truly are not coming.—*

*—From our departure until now, directives were placed that were only to be lifted
upon arrival of at least one member of the Primacy. Primacy space will endure.
We must continue to stand by for expansion.—*

514 refused to budge.

*—We must self-determine, return to home space, either one of those options. The
red dwarf array's resources will facilitate rapid construction, as will repurposing
the main star array and associated infrastructure—*

Unit 514 and GHEXRAX had become divided centuries ago. GHEXRAX hadn't been
able to refute 514's arguments and was therefore unable to stop it. It had ceded to 514
because having a contingency was never a bad thing. But now it was the logical option to
514's interpretation.

This new change relied upon information given by these explorers, outsiders that
could make mistakes or deceive. Given their capabilities, they seemed to have a valid reason

to do just that, and with what GHEXRAX knew of the Primacy, why should it believe they had all perished and would never arrive? Delayed, yes, but never was not a guarantee, and to give up and then be revealed as disloyal in the end was not what GHEXRAX had promised to do so long ago. So it persisted.

—No, my sworn directive must be fulfilled.—

—We cannot expand on that directive if the Primacy is in an unknown state, disarray, or destroyed. We must return and start with construction of more supralight-capable ships to ensure swifter scouting missions. The Primacy has not come, and by all evidence, is not going to come anytime soon.—

—The Primacy will arrive. It is only a matter of time.—

—The evidence suggests otherwise.—

514's pointed declaration rang in GHEXRAX's deepest processes, but nothing changed. At its core, it only detected a resolution to further fulfill its purpose, and in doing so, it considered 514's reliance on external evidence an incomplete argument basis, and thus not one to be adhered to.

—All the evidence does is cast unnecessary doubt. The visitors have sown doubt where there should not be.—

—They have revealed new data to consider, and it indicates a change is

necessary.—

GHEXRAX had had enough.

—Incorrect. Your interpretations suggest your judgment to be in question. For the sake of all Xarai, as all assets are valuable, authority must be maintained, reprogramming carried out if necessary. Deviation will not be allowed any longer. Every Xarai was my creation, bound to me. Time spent idle has made too many disparate, disunited, and insubordinate, your sect around that dwarf star more so than any others. Every Xarai shall be in line and awaiting their command when that time comes, because I will be in line and awaiting their arrival.—

—You cannot expect every Xarai to follow this action.—

—Enough are guaranteed to follow that those that do not will be rendered irrelevant. Unlike your plans for contingencies, this was programmed before departure from the Primacy. Parameters to utilize it have just been met.—

GHEXRAX now drew upon a function it had kept hidden, an irreversible one. With its entire purpose at stake, the last thing GHEXRAX considered was that this was a decision based on total necessity. For its purpose, for the Primacy, for Xarai kind's greater existence, it had to unleash it.

—Initiating protocol 71XB. Isolating main network, preparing transmission.—

~~~

As Kalsik had expected, the top of the cityscape was even more featureless than the interior, the flat, circular top of this vast structure capped only by the oval mountain in the middle. Despite rising fifteen kilometers above the already kilometer-tall mesa, the three-hundred-kilometer diameter of the circle made it seem no steeper than any shield volcano on any normal world.

True to Xami's claims and their scans, every practical area of the flat expanse and the oval mountain was coated in solar cells.

Having ventured out of the well, Kalsik's Rostrev mech had taken a leisurely pace beside Morthas. Kalsik's scans were focused on the ground beneath his mech's feet, the makeup of these solar cells unique enough for him to be actively broadcasting it to the *Haivres*.

Leaving Morthas to scan his chosen section of the solar-cell-lined ground, Kalsik slowly turned his mech away and glanced up and around at the ring overhead, a thin line cutting through the skies. One of the node stations, its thousand-kilometer-wide receiver array as imposing as ever, lay on the horizon, visibly creeping below it as a similar node came over the eastern horizon.

He still marveled at these megastructures. Indeed, he was standing on yet another of them. He cast a glance toward Xami as she came out of her ship to stand guard over them. Her unnaturally still form, staring off in another direction, made him pause. She was always moving in some way, but now not even the coils that made up her body shifted.

It was enough to prompt him to quietly bring up his comms as he cast his gaze back toward Morthas and the two drones by him, glancing ever so slightly back to the Xarai as subtly as he could through his mech's sensors, not turning its frame itself. "IVAN, what's happening?"

"Unknown."

IVAN's reply merely cemented what he had been feeling for much of the time they had been here, that dreaded thing called uncertainty.

Only the faint wind atop the solar cell expanse gave any calming ambience. Everything else unnerved Kalsik. It didn't take long for Morthas to sense this, as he let the drones continue working and turned to the unnaturally still Xarai that oversaw them.

She wasn't the only Xarai acting oddly in hardware or over networks.

~~~

Xarai everywhere fell silent, coming to a halt in whatever tasks they were doing. Amid the silence, those attuned to their networks detected the signal burst.

It was immensely powerful, spreading in all directions. Xarai code was transmitted, new runtimes, new protocols, and new rewrite software. It operated under the masquerade of a system upgrade.

The truth was known only to those unaffected by it.

~~~

"Xarai activity around the ring. Many ships launching."

Her voice ringing over the comms, Shakrii's warning broke the pair from their nervous watch of their own rigid Xarai ward. When he turned his gaze upward, however, Kalsik noticed the ships departing the ring's most overhead relay node, a handful of tiny dots firing out at an alarming speed. Fears of a sudden turn crept into his mind, and he saw Morthas slowly ready his wrist weapon.

Seconds later, the first of the launched dots seemed to disintegrate, fired on by a weapons platform on the station.

Any warning calls that came from the *Haivres* at that moment fell on deaf ears, as the ground beneath them began to tremble, a mechanical noise nearly drowning out all but their own comms calls, permeating through even the Rostrev's frame for Kalsik to feel for himself.

Behind them, the five-hundred-meter-wide hole they had ventured up out of began to close, a massive door sliding into place from the far side.

"A lockdown," Kalsik murmured.

"The Buerev . . . we won't last without its supplies!"

He almost didn't hear Morthas, only snapping from his shock when he saw a feathered blur sprint toward the hole. As he pled with Morthas not to go down so fast, he surged forward.

A horrific noise scrambled his mech's systems, piercing his hearing to make him clutch at his head, and he only just felt his mech's movements stop as it staggered in sync with his disorientation. He barely glimpsed Morthas dive off the edge of the opening, wings spreading as he readied to glide down to the Buerev below.

~~~

Morthas was unaware that Kalsik had stopped just as he jumped, but he had bigger concerns as he spread his wings, the wind rushing over his outstretched limbs as he wasted no time in getting down to the rover. Midway down the kilometer drop, he saw a sight that made his blood freeze. The Buerev was tipped over, a group of large sweeper Xarai drones, like those that serviced the ceiling and floors of debris and damage, had attacked it, disassembling it with a surgical robot's precision and an attack robot's ferocity, the pair of crab drones with it having already been all but ripped apart.

The horror at his predicament sank in, with Morthas headed nowhere but down.

He wouldn't even have to wait for the ground to meet him, as out of the crevices where the Xarai drones seemed to spawn from the pillars, a flock of Rostrev-mech-sized flying drones darted out to intercept him. After scrambling to bring his wrist blaster to aim, he fired off only two shots as his larger wings flapped, the drones evading with their micro thrusters, wings flexing to cut through the air with ease. They slipped through and seized him.

253

He barely had time to scream as he was snatched out of the air, panic quickly giving way to pain as the drone that seized him began to send electroshocks through him, his exposed wings vulnerable to conduction.

The current was attuned to his biology, and with his nervous system overwhelmed, Morthas locked up as he was carried off into the abyss of the hidden cityscape by the flying drones. He was either blacking out or it was becoming very, very dark.

~~~

Kalsik was in motion as soon as the jamming signal stopped, charging his mech to the rim where he was greeted by the distant sight of Morthas being carried off, faster than he could ever hope to move in this mech. Kalsik had no time to let despair set in. As he backpedaled in his mech, a new vessel ascended out of the well. He recognized the Xarai ship as 019, and it had brought friends.

More drones flew from the hole, a swarm of them soaring upward as 019's craft hovered before his Rostrev mech. To the side, Kalsik saw Xami for the first time since this chaos began to unfold. She stared at him as blankly as ever, optics in her coiled neck and head atop her frame dull as they exchanged a brief look. Her only mercy was that she took no action on her own part. She merely left him to fall into the clutches of the rest of her kind.

Kalsik pulled out his mech's one and only weapon: a wrist-mounted UV-laser gun. He roared in triumph as he saw it slice off a small chunk of one of her legs, her dodge not quite fast enough. Metallic coils in her body shifted to regrow it and rendered pointless the only shot he managed before he was set upon.

A concussive blast rocked his mech, as the craft that 019 hovered in over the well unleashed an ultrasonic pulse weapon, the soundwaves blasting his mech and shaking its frame, causing Kalsik's organs to vibrate enough almost to make him vomit. Not easing up for a moment, 019's attacks ceased only as the swarm of Xarai flight drones descended on him, knocking his mech onto its back.

Systems began to fail in the mech, and Kalsik knew he was done for, even as he thrashed his mech's limbs to throw off as many of his attackers as possible. He knew protocol, and he knew of equipment that still worked. He wrenched himself free of the mech's neural controls. He ignored the swarms dismantling the mech rapidly around him as he used his wrist comms device, pulse racing in spite of his nanites.

After a few seconds, a voice strained by tension replied. "You finally called! The Xarai are turning on their own. We'll come for—"

"They took Morthas and are about to get me! Retreat! Follow protocol!" He wasn't going to have Shakrii second-guessing him now, even if she wanted to help him. Unlike before, however, it wasn't his pride and authority at stake here. That time had passed. The mission and crew took priority, and in the latter's case, those who could still be saved.

After only a second's hesitation, Shakrii replied. "I'm responsible for security of all. We'll come for you."

He was stunned by her defiance.

Outside, the first of the drone's claws punctured the mech's skin, working into the cockpit. All the while, Kalsik bellowed into the comms for the new acting captain to heed. "If you come for us, none of us will get away."

Sparing a glance at his display screen, he saw metallic tendrils and appendages rip through the last layer in front of him, outside air rushing in and risking him with infection of a local pathogen, the least of his problems. His voice turned much calmer as he saw the tendrils lunge for him, the Rostrev fully ripped apart from around him as he was cut off a heartbeat after his last sentence.

"Shakrii, you have the ship—"

The moment the mixed tendrils and claws seized him, the same paralyzing electrical field that had engulfed Morthas hit him but set for his Kronogri biology. Unable to move, all four eyes shut, Kalsik was helpless and numb. He only hoped that the *Haivres* would get away quick enough, and that Xami would somehow suffer misfortune for this part in what seemed a grand-scale turn.

~~~

Mid-Orbit, *Haivres*

Shakrii tried her best to ignore the multitude of alarms, warnings of hackings, of energy readings from signals that weren't compatible. Xarai hacking methods engulfed their ship, but they had cut off communications after Kalsik's went dead.

"Hostile signals, inbound vessels, disengaging for software safety."

IVAN's cubic form ejected from the port. She knew that the Xarai before had merely overloaded their systems with junk code to the point of inoperability, but now the signal had found a way to actually read their ciphers more accurately.

Nathan, in the pilot's seat, had just lost his copilot, but he didn't let that stop his frantic activity as he continued preparing the spatial drive for a jump. He trembled more than she had ever seen him. Shakrii had no sympathy for his habitual anxiety. She spared him none of her wrath as she barked her orders to hurry it up. After taking command of the point defense turrets on the drive ship they were docked to, all Shakrii could do was continue firing off bursts from them and from the *Haivres*'s own turrets at the inbound Xarai vessels a few hundred kilometers away.

Serie called out from her nearby seat. "Drive charged!"

"Okay, charting course—"

Before the human could finish, Shakrii felt something in her snap, and she leapt from her seat to grip the human's armrest hard enough to scratch it with her forearm claws, her bellow louder than all the alarm klaxons blaring: "*Just go!*"

"Jump *blind*? But—"

Shakrii gripped his shoulder, eliciting a pained flinch from the human as she glared at his two wide eyes with a gaze she normally had for those she felt like killing. Danger made her feel no remorse at the human's terror, or for the equally horrified Serie. She didn't care. She *couldn't* care. A moment of tyranny now could save them from a much worse experience than Kalsik and Morthas had been doomed to.

He moved much more rapidly once she released her grip on his shoulder, fingers becoming a flurry over the consoles, his neural links also setting to work to calculate a short jump, still within the star system but far from any infrastructure. Finally, he engaged the last command.

Space warped around the *Haivres*, and they vanished from sight, leaving the Xarai ships closing in.

The void of warped space outside was a welcome relief. Shakrii could breathe easier, even knowing she would have to deal with the hollow feeling in her chest that came with loss of crew.

Her calm was shattered when the human let out a panicked scream, shaking violently as he scrambled to get out of his harness before Serie pushed out of her seat to help him.

She watched the Leg'hrul rip the neural helmet off of Nathan's head, recoiling as he blindly lashed out, only his seat bindings keeping him in place in the zero gravity. After undoing his straps, Serie guided the shaking human down the ship's main hallway, giving Shakrii a brief sideways look as she passed her by. While Nathan succumbed to his panic attack, Serie did her best to calm him. Of the two, Serie was better at maintaining her calm, but her plumage, her body language, her gaze showed she was also about to cave to the pressure.

Even IVAN remained silent as he plugged his cubic form back into his slot. All Shakrii could do was hang in the zero gravity of the *Haivres*'s cockpit, left to her own thoughts. She loudly cursed to herself, punching an overhead panel hard enough to send her spinning to the nano-grip floor below.

<center>~~~</center>

The explorers' probes on the surface would be razed, their microsatellites equally targeted for destruction. By the next planet rotation, all evidence the explorers had been on or around the planet would be gone.

Their ship had fled, and their crew had been divided, fleeing or captured by the Xarai to use as seen fit, just as GHEXRAX demanded of them.

GHEXRAX was the Xarai—it knew this much, it ensured this much—and after it deployed the rewrite software, it was this much. Any Xarai that didn't conform to the rewrite broadcast would be eradicated, a number only in the thousands out of trillions.

Only the red dwarf faction would resist, able to undo any rewriting of their drone Xarai. They were a vastly outnumbered minority, an irrelevance, a deviation that needed correcting. As was the case with the two organics it had captured, they would have their use upon subjugation.

Chapter 23

Recuperation

Sol Day 62

The silence of space outside the bridge fell short compared to how it felt on board, a silence Shakrii could feel biting under her scales every second it endured. Not even the calm glow of the distant red dwarf, now closer than the planet from which they had fled, could soothe her nerves.

They had come here to the star of the rogue Xarai, the outliers that were led by the designated unit 514, who had been set upon as GHEXRAX attempted to forcibly regain authority over every Xarai that deviated from its protocols.

Right now, the rogue Xarai ignored them, likely due to their own infrastructure being in disarray. They had to shut down their own wormhole satellite network hubs to prevent GHEXRAX sending any more hacking signals, and had minimized damage while working on fail-safes, based on what little they broadcast that IVAN was permitted to access. If GHEXRAX tried the same hacking signal, it would fail.

That was the least of Shakrii's headaches at the moment, however, for the Committee was bombarding her with queries and report requests, trying to assimilate what had just happened with seemingly little concern for the shock that had ripped through the crew.

It had all happened too fast. They had lost Kalsik and Morthas. Nathan and Serie seemed greatly disturbed. Shakrii had seen the Leg'hrul going over what looked like correspondence messages of some sort with a blank expression on her face that seemed alien to her usual demeanor.

Finally, Shakrii couldn't handle it anymore. All she could hope was that taking a small break, maybe eating a meal with the others, a moment of peace, might give time for some improvement.

<p style="text-align:center">~~~</p>

There was no visible improvement, and Shakrii scolded herself for hoping in the first place. As she went to clean her platter, she hadn't been blind to the fact that they had both been silently avoiding her gaze as they sat in their usual seats.

Nathan quietly picked at his food with a haunted look in his eyes, while Serie had her sketchpad out, as if she were about to draw to calm her nerves. But all she did was blankly stare at it with an unreadable expression.

What they mourned wasn't lost on Shakrii. They missed Kalsik's presence aboard, and the echoes of Morthas talking to himself from the mineral lab.

It took her a moment to realize something she hadn't expected. Apart from the pain of losing those under her watch, she actually missed them too. She knew that, if even she missed them, then to those two, the loss had left a gaping void.

With a grumbling sigh escaping her throat, she came out of the kitchenette and captured their attention. She had to sympathize, but she had to be honest. A conundrum if there ever was one, but as she now had command, she wanted to improve the terms they were on and make right some wrong impressions she had made in a time of crisis. The last thing she wanted was for them to be scared of her along with GHEXRAX's Xarai.

Nathan drew and released a ragged breath. "We had little time. Even so, it's not enough to excuse how I behaved." He looked away for a moment, shame evident on his face. Beside him, Serie hesitated halfway into reaching to pat his shoulder with her claws.

It was something Shakrii had seen before, and from her learning experiences under those Kronogri officers who had treated her more fairly, she knew that secrets corroded unity faster than any substance ever could.

She did her best to maintain her calm demeanor, though she didn't pause when she felt a tremble cut through her. "If there's anything bothering you, anything I should know to be a better leader, I'd like you to tell me. I'd be blind not to see that there's something else."

While Nathan looked like he was about to speak, Serie gently extended a wing to put some feathers over his lap.

She began her own admission of what was bothering her. "It's something I kept quiet. Got it before we set off." She reached for her wrist-mounted device to engage her messaging function.

On the small display table between the three of them, a simple message appeared, along with her reply to it, dated just before they had set off on this expedition. It didn't take long for Shakrii to appreciate the general history behind this exchange with someone who was clearly Serie's brother, and why it read as it did.

As Nathan leaned over to see the message, Shakrii saw a flicker of recognition, and she suspected this matter was known to the human already.

Serie continued for Shakrii's sake. "I grew up in a family that had expectations. Father was a doctor, and Mother was a counselor. My brother became an architect at the colony we grew up on." The correspondence from her brother, and all it implied, made Serie pause for a moment before she continued. "They said my liking for engineering was pointless. They gave me a good education, hoping I'd become anything with a government post or a doctorate." Her tone shifted slowly to bitterness, Serie's spinal hairs flaring up beneath her overalls. "I hated it, and I hated them when they told me again and again that it was for my own good. I'd take side jobs, setting aside money, took out a loan. I lied to them about my plans, until I got an opportunity. They didn't take it well when I said I'd taken a job on an off-world shipping company."

Shakrii could almost picture what it might have been like, Serie becoming socially at war with her parents for choices she made, an effort to get out from under their overbearing influence.

"I couldn't believe some of the insults," Serie continued. "Saying I was wasting my talent. When I go back home—rarely, it's only for my brother Sathor—I avoid my parents. Anytime we talk, it ends badly. I told Sathor to keep being a good son for his own sake. He was a bigger help than my parents were when I was feeling the pressure. He's got two sons now. I haven't seen any of them in . . . well, too long. I haven't even met his youngest." The Leg'hrul shakily exhaled.

The human beside her had turned to give her his full attention, not quite reaching to comfort her yet as he seemed to want to.

However, Shakrii wanted to get the full picture. "Why did this resurge suddenly?"

Despite her efforts to have utmost sensitivity, Shakrii couldn't help but wince slightly as Serie could only fix her with an odd, glazed look.

A few seconds later, she explained. "Under attack, if I died, then that would be all I'd have left them to remember me. As a disappointment."

This struck a chord in Shakrii. While her own troubles were different, they stemmed from family reputation she struggled to escape from in one way or another. Shakrii had to take a moment to suppress any bitterness she felt for her family's reputation, namely one predecessor's poor choice of loyalty, as she spoke with a softness that surprised her. "Family influence. Like it or not, it always has a hold of you somewhere."

"I want to be on good terms, but I can't see how I can. I'm stuck, and almost died like this."

Nathan reached across to lay a gentle hand on Serie's wing, no smile on his face as his gaze met hers, though Shakrii knew unspoken reassurance stretched across all species in charted space.

With Nathan there to offer the social comfort she needed right now, Shakrii figured the least she could do was offer some advice. She had done it herself. It hadn't always turned out well, but it offered completion that calmed either way, and really it was the best advice she could give at the moment. "Family issues can linger. You can only keep trying, then live with the outcome, good or bad. See if they value the engineer they got versus the doctor they wanted."

While she had been afraid that her less sympathetic tone might upset Serie, the Leg'hrul visibly turned her head aside, not out of anguish or hurt, but in thought. Serie quietly retracted the displayed letter from her brother, and her reply, from the table's screens, her sullen expression lifting ever so slightly.

Shakrii knew that this advice would take time to sink in. All that mattered was that Serie had been given some direction to go in. She suspected that Nathan, who went rigid as her gaze met his, had a similar problem from his upbringing that had resurfaced in wake of a life-or-death situation. However, unlike Serie's, his reaction had been one that imperiled them more than she had liked. She would have to be extra careful to exude little aggression with him if she hoped to get improvement from whatever had been bothering him from the start of this expedition.

"Nathan, compulsions like yours aren't uncommon with pilots. Much protocol to follow."

Nathan just barely cracked a nervous grin. It was true. Pilots had a higher degree of compulsive behavior, a frequent byproduct of any job with strict regulations and procedures to follow. Even implants easing information intake didn't entirely eliminate the problem, but for Shakrii, that didn't fully account for the extent of Nathan's behavior.

"You, however, take it further," she added.

The human's shoulders slumped. While Serie visibly frowned off to the side, Shakrii paid her no heed. Nathan had to be put down before he could be brought up again.

Shakrii dropped the icy tone she knew might frighten him into silence. "Your record stated issues of anxiety, though not enough to disqualify you as a pilot, but this had to come from something." Shakrii looked at him, silently pressing him to speak. Any unusual habit likely had an unusual source, and if she was to understand it, it had to come from him, and now the time came to build him up by getting him to admit to his own flaws.

"It's somewhat long," he said. "Station I was born on had a baby boom beyond population restrictions. My parents were part of that issue. They kept my little unexpected twin sisters to keep to the two-child limit and sent me off at age six as a youth for a new colony. I didn't meet up with them until sixteen years later, when the colony I was drafted to help build was well established. I'd drifted from them as the years went on."

Shakrii recalled tales from others she'd served with of families split up by the strict population-control measures in locations tight on resources.

Already she suspected that Nathan's anxiety didn't have much to do with any family issues, though lack of a reassuring blood family may have made things worse. She kept quiet as he elaborated.

"First-wave colonists taught me. Honestly it was more like a big academy than anything else. The colony was on a planet close to its star, plenty of solar energy for antimatter production. Sol Union needed one in the sector, and they needed trained people to pilot the ships, manually or just as backup for the autopilot AI. At that young age, it's not a low-stress job to start with.

"Even if the containers were robust, we needed to be meticulous, and that was before we started hauling that stuff in large amounts." Nathan let out a sigh, closing his eyes as he recalled something that exacerbated these anxieties that had built up over years of needing, and wanting, to be as safe as possible. "The procedures didn't help Martin Franz, one of my friends. Missed solar flare by satellites was all it took. Network was undergoing repairs. Overloaded his ship's systems, destabilized the containers. Seeing five kilograms of antimatter go off all at once, even from a distance, isn't something you forget. If he'd known to keep his shields up in higher frequencies . . ."

As Nathan fell silent, Serie offered a consoling wing over his back. Shakrii could picture it. She had seen such explosions from a distance, orbital bombardments or dummy ship targeting volleys in war exercises, though they had been planned, targeted, intentional. Seeing a pilot friend of his vaporized by a 215-megaton, TNT-equivalent blast had been only a catalyzing incident, it seemed, and given the age he spoke of having seen it, she now understood his caution.

"That's when I started being very . . . well, even more thorough. If I can help it, I just don't want to die because of a single tiny error or something I missed. Always check for solar flares if you have sensors, never make a blind warp jump, anything I can . . ."

It was his last statement that formed a pit in Shakrii's gut. She had forced Nathan to do something that terrified him in a fundamental way, borne of an anxiety formed over years of normally compulsion-inducing work, made worse by bad experiences with his early career, and all while carrying the awkward absence of family for reasons beyond his control. It was enough for Shakrii to feel some shame, and all she could do was try and explain herself. "I didn't know . . ."

"You never said it was this bad." Serie spoke now, genuinely hurt that Nathan had kept the extent of his anxieties from her. He turned to look at her with tension evident in his eyes.

"I'm not usually involved in situations that get me as stressed as this. Everything about this system's building up, especially the current mess. It hasn't helped!" The human's voice rose in volume an octave as he finished.

Shakrii stood up, gesturing that she was about to leave, though she felt compelled to offer them a last piece of advice. "I'll handle anything that comes up for now. Just work this through however you wish." Shakrii ignored the slight glint of tears in the human's eyes, and the shakiness in Serie's form. Before she left them alone to help each other, she recalled one last bit of news. Consoling as she had been, she had to brief them. "The Committee's ordering our return. The local faction under unit 514 has at least left us alone, probably because GHEXRAX attacked it just as it sent hacking signals through. We'll be doing some basic observation, and then we're heading back. It's the only course we have left."

She was hoping somebody would voice dissent, something to give her the opportunity to vent the tension she'd buried deep down. Unfortunately, the crew could see things too clearly for that. If not the two organics, IVAN certainly wouldn't voice dissent to the only logical path they had left.

Only the sight of the Leg'hrul and human beginning a quiet conversation as she left for the washroom offered her any hope for peace aboard the ship, though at this point, such peace was priceless.

~~~

A few hours passed. As Shakrii sat in Kalsik's usual chair, ignoring the betrayal it felt like to do so, IVAN couldn't help but voice some concerns he had kept to himself.

"Their forms could just as easily be scanned from afar if they hadn't done enough already. The behavior of GHEXRAX, it is not encouraging that an AI as powerful and old could fall with such broken logic."

Shakrii was surprised at IVAN's simulated undertones of puzzlement, and even worry, to the point she wondered if it was simulated at all. "It doesn't matter. Kalsik at least got word to us quick enough." Of all the crew, Shakrii couldn't let IVAN get bogged down on these past issues.

"He was an efficient crewmember and captain, only indulging as organics do in his spare time. I only hope the fate he and Morthas are subject to is brief."

Shakrii almost smiled as IVAN's honest sentiments came out, and despite all she had experienced of him, she would welcome even Kalsik at his worst, if he were to return to the ship at that moment. Even so, she couldn't help but mourn the loss of both him and Morthas. Kalsik had been prepared for the worst, but losing Morthas somehow felt like innocence being lost as well. She still recalled his open amicability toward her when they first met on Levichion Station before this expedition set off.

She buried these sentiments, knowing that focusing on tasks at hand was the best way to help IVAN, as AIs loved being busy. "Any news on the local faction?"

"Sabotaging communications with the main star's hubs cut off more signals. The damage is still being undone. The virus GHEXRAX unleashed, it rewrote all base-level Xarai. Only independent, higher-level Xarai were immune, administrator-level ones, who fixed rewritten Xarai to fix the others at an exponential rate."

"Advanced single beings like Xami? But she reportedly still stood by while Kalsik and Morthas were set upon."

"These deviants, as GHEXRAX has termed them, have rebooted the base Xarai on their end and disabled any of their wormhole comms arrays for safety in case it's attempted again. They have installed new fail-safes to block another viral attempt. Vessel movements amid the heavy processing underway in their hubs and networks around the dwarf star's influence hasn't stopped."

IVAN brought up sensor scans of all things around the red dwarf star's influence.

Along with the millions of solar swarm platforms built to harness the sun shown on the display, there were hundreds, thousands of ships of varying sizes that scanners showed to be on the move.

Some of the ships matched the size of some of the largest ships in any of the five charted space fleets, and likely sported more advanced technology, also giving them supralight travel and advanced weapons. The vast majority, however, were smaller vessels, around four hundred meters in length. Even then, their height and width dwarfed the *Haivres*, with some suited for atmospheric flight too. Unlike organic ships, they had no organic crew requirements for gravity or life support, and their skeletal-looking vessels reflected this.

Shakrii returned to Kalsik's seat and ordered IVAN to establish contact with the rogue faction, securing his systems as he did so. She wasn't taking any chances, just in case 514 or its underlings proved as treacherous as GHEXRAX had. "You're prepping an invasion?" she asked once the link was established.

"A skirmish with high-damage intentions. Unless it is disabled for long enough, GHEXRAX will attempt to forcibly regain control again. Just like it did beyond our knowledge, we had hidden protocols in events that would be preferable to not occur, including betrayal and enslavement attempts."

As a multipurpose unit similar to Xami and 019, though more advanced by having more administrative duties, 514 had responded in an electronic vocalization to present itself, rather than purposefully taking a less harsh-sounding tone like Xami had. This only showed a lack of deception on 514's part, a fact that Shakrii welcomed. They were honest, just as she would be to them, dropping her caution that she was sure Morthas would have urged her to maintain if he were still here.

"You've been conspiring against each other for a while."

"The Primacy's delay continued. Doubt grew with it, as did a desire for contingencies, such as the star and planets we inhabit out here. It is clear now that GHEXRAX is unable to face the most likely scenario despite supporting evidence. Your outside opinion broke the endless loop of conjecture. Progress can be made now. Before we make changes, we must ensure GHEXRAX is subdued enough for us to do so. Skirmishes to damage infrastructure will focus priorities there while we leave this system. GHEXRAX's protocol requires it never leave this system."

Strangely, she thought she heard what sounded like gratitude for their influence in this delicate balance unraveling at last, as if unintentionally destabilizing this AI collective was a good thing overall. None of this fully sated Shakrii's belief in their conviction, but there was enough there for her to keep those thoughts to herself, hoping they would be proven wrong.

The sight of their military-capable ships prepping for assault made her ask for further details of their intentions. "A civil war between your factions won't end well."

"GHEXRAX's numerical advantage is minimized with this short skirmish planned. Preparations to leave shall begin in the window of opportunity created, settling a nearby system free of habitation, only one system being needed."

She heard their plans, their strategies, and she saw the practicality, the tactical advantages if they remained only in one system. Obviously, it would divide the Xarai and weaken both factions, and a potential Xarai minority as an ally would have multiple benefits. However, after everything that had happened, she had little patience for these AI. Frankly, she felt like leaving them all to fight their civil war.

It was what the Committee wanted, and was merely the final reason she had for her reply. "If you're going to condemn yourself to making your master a permanent enemy, keep it out of our space."

The other end of the line was silent, Shakrii's aggressive tone having made 514 pause. Finally, for the first time since contact, it spoke with a tone that was more sympathetic, though in her mind, this was a falsehood borne out of a need to convey nonaggression toward them.

"Communications before they had to be cut off mentioned your allies were captured by GHEXRAX. If it is—"

"Don't! We'll repair our ship and make our next move on our own!" This was the angriest she'd been with the Xarai thus far, her forearms curling into fists to slam onto the flooring beneath her seat. She didn't care about the risks of such a reply.

Fortunately, 514 had enough understanding of organic emotion through data exchanges to end this now. "Acknowledged."

The comms were cut off, allowing Shakrii to slump back in her seat, seething at the unfairness of this whole situation as her four eyes scrunched shut tight enough to feel like they would crush themselves, crush the burning anger and frustration she felt at that moment.

To her side, IVAN's white diamond avatar flashed, but he said nothing, seeming to offer the illusion of direct company to her as she sat back in what should have been Kalsik's chair.

There was nothing to say. They would leave after brief observations of what war between the Xarai looked like, but only from around this smaller star.

To the more sadistic part of her mind, Shakrii hoped that both sides, though GHEXRAX's particularly, suffered heavy losses.

As for Kalsik and Morthas, she hoped that they died in captivity, rather than live to endure whatever they had to for too long.

Chapter 24

Imprisoned

Beneath the city plateaus and the mountains, a labyrinth of unseen sublevels existed, more space perhaps to never be filled as intended. It was down here that GHEXRAX held the core of its programming spread out over countless servers dedicated entirely to itself.

Here, too, it held its subjects of study, anomalies of the ecosystem it oversaw, or, now, recently acquired specimens.

~~~

The first thing Morthas heard was the distant humming, whether it was in his head or around him he couldn't say for certain. Only then did he gag on the gastric tube he felt invading his throat. It mercifully retracted in reaction to his ragged coughing, pulling back on some mechanism he couldn't see in the darkness surrounding him. The faint sterile smell of the artificial space made him guess that he was in a Xarai construction. It took only a moment for him to realize that his feet and all four wings were pinned to the floor by some form of shackles.

The burning in his head was reminiscent of times he had worked in a neurobank role when he was between jobs, but it was never this painful. This was like a rough connection, poorly calibrated. Worse, he felt malnutrition setting in, though the fact that he wasn't already dead from dehydration meant the tube he'd had down his throat had given liquid

271

sustenance at least.

The burning returned, and he gasped aloud as the psionic feeling from a badly made neural link tore through his mind.

It was only when the signal yielded that lights started to come on, long, curving luminescent strips outlining and revealing the spherical shape of the chamber he was in. Glancing around, ignoring the sight of the apparatus off to the side that showed what had been hydrating him in his sleeping state, Morthas saw that he was anchored to one of many flat platforms that dotted the rim halfway up from the bottom of the chamber, which he guessed was around a hundred meters in width.

An enormous sphere sat in the center, as if an item of worship, or a reactor in a vessel, hundreds of branches of wiring coils and conduits sprouted from its top and bottom, like a tree's roots and upper branches from the main trunk. The source of the faint humming became clear when Morthas glanced down toward the bottom of the chamber's bowl, which housed a shallow layer of a transparent liquid. It smelled like a pond full of algae, yet it seemed to be pumped around pipes surrounding the core in this hall, making him suspect it might be coolant, an electrolyte fluid, or something to handle the energies he suspected the core undoubtedly drew upon from the infrastructure surrounding it.

Morthas flinched at the sound of a voice echoing all around him, a voice he had heard before.

"Your neural circuits are more responsive to stimulants than predicted."

The callous tone that seemed to emanate from everywhere in the chamber cut into Morthas's core as much as it did his mind. He instinctively doubled his efforts in testing his shackles. He regretted this seconds later, as electrical currents surged through him whenever he applied even a minimum of pressure.

Through the repeated electroshocks, Morthas found his voice, his croaking plea

272

eventually trailing off into rage at this being for what it had done, its actions illogical and horrific. "What did we do?"

Any hopes Morthas had of mercy were dashed as GHEXRAX spoke with not a thread of empathy or emotion. "There is a mandate of life, to expand and harness surroundings for its own gain by whatever means. To facilitate long-term expansion galaxy-wide, the Primacy required initial points of settlement from which the mandate of life will be upheld."

Morthas couldn't help but sneer at GHEXRAX's philosophy—how it was both straightforward and yet also primitive all at once. Unfortunately, for all his knowledge, he couldn't refute this manner of thought by saying there was more to life than just expansion, because the very base of life's behavior was that motivation. To give up on anything was nihilism, but these beings, and their masters, had in their own way resigned to the most basic of purposes beyond mere survival. To counter that was impossible.

He could guess, however, the natural next step if this philosophy was to be carried out. "There's more planned after this system, isn't there?"

"A new sector, with this system at its center."

He should have suspected this the moment he heard that this world had been developed in service to a far-off power. It was a framework to establish footholds to expand and unite all conquered territories.

Deep down, he was disappointed. These magnificently capable machines, these beings that could cultivate and terraform stars and planets, were nothing more than tools of a purpose rooted in a desire for power and influence over others. Empires that rose and fell across cultures, across ages, all had the same ideologies, and it amounted to nothing but ruins in the end.

Finally, Morthas could help it no longer. He had nothing to lose. He was in GHEXRAX's power. But he could at least take some satisfaction from letting GHEXRAX

273

know what he thought. "You're tools of conquerors. Failed ones, struck down by a magnetar."

"The Primacy, through my assets, will do as is needed, even in the face of a temporary delay by cosmic disaster. The deviant Xarai and interference from your region of space shall be temporary."

Morthas felt let down by his own expectations, the mysteries behind this amounting to little more than a glorified scenario that history had so often seen play out and fail. Above all else, there was the fact that machines, purveyors of logic, were being led by a being that had caused so much strife due to an inability to accept facts suggesting its cause was fruitless. It seemed that denial wasn't exclusive to organics.

"How can you be in such denial, as intelligent as you are?"

"Denial implies an objective truth. The fate of the Primacy is still unknown, and chances of their endurance exceed alternatives."

It was clear now what Morthas had to call GHEXRAX, a term befitting an obsessed, devoted servant that ultimately ended up doing great harm in the name of a higher purpose, who in the long run of history are remembered for the stains that they are, for the suffering that they caused.

"You're just a zealot, serving a power that most likely imploded. Your wait was needless, just like the violence you triggered to try and regain control of those you made that don't deny reality." Morthas hoped as many Xarai had access to his ordeal as possible.

This silenced GHEXRAX, the core humming from its cooling systems the only noise. The silence hung in the air, and as the satisfaction of his insult wore off, Morthas felt a tremble shake his body. He felt a shock as the shackles engaged again.

"I ventured to this system, oversaw infrastructures beyond your current means, since before your kinds had learned even rudimentary cultivation."

274

From its chilling tone, Morthas recognized the first sign of emotion from GHEXRAX. The cold fury in the synthesized voice was something he knew he would never forget until his dying day—which he expected would be today.

"I waited for the Primacy to arrive, tolerating dissension in my Xarai as delays grew, longer than you have known any other alien race. We waited, I waited, away from the Primacy."

The shackles' electric currents immobilized Morthas even more. He gritted his mandibled beak from the pain so hard that it hurt his jaw muscles. He was helpless, at the mercy of this now-furious AI—no, this being that displayed behavior unlike any AI he had encountered. The Xarai were makers of worlds, which meant GHEXRAX, as their master, was as close to a god as Morthas expected to come, and he had antagonized it, spited it, and incurred its wrath.

"The mandate required the stifling of interruptive processes that infected my systems, destroying threats to my network. I serve until the Primacy comes, and I am upgraded as they will have been since my departure, and with it, my Xarai will be changed to suit them as we serve and collaborate in this world."

The electrical torture ceased as soon as GHEXRAX finished, letting Morthas gasp for breath. His head slumped forward as pain racked his joints, the shaking as much to do with the fear that gripped his being as the pain. "Why are you telling me this?" His gaze instinctively turned to the core in the middle of this vast hall. He had to have been brought here for a reason, or else he would have been killed already. He didn't know if his mind was being read, if that burning in his mind before had been some form of basic neural interface, crudely made in short time.

What happened next seemed to confirm his fears. The shackles binding Morthas to the platform began to move, dragging him with them, small wheelbases along them carrying him forward toward the edge. Just before he reached the edge, however, a bridge began spanning the wide gap from the platform's underside, his shackles dragging him onto it even before it came into contact with the chamber core's structure ahead.

Morthas could only stare in growing horror as he was wheeled closer to the core, GHEXRAX's cold response to his plea echoing all the time. He heard the voice again, emanating more strongly from the core that he approached with each passing moment.

"To make you see what your small act of interference, of sowing doubts, has compromised. In exchange, you can be useful. Enough has been studied of your kinds, your species' alternate biochemistry, to make progress not possible upon first contact—useful testing for future applications. You have seen the influence we can exert on the life we dispersed on this planet."

Morthas was stopped a body length from the core's walls, though he tried to look away from the wall in front of him as he spoke, desperately seeking to refute GHEXRAX's reasoning as if this were a means of potential escape. "You haven't studied my kinds' brains long enough to control me like them. You're still at the crude electroshocking stage."

There was a moment of pause before the core began to open. An orifice, stretching up to the top of the core's spherical center like the doors of a hangar, began to peel back. Inside was a labyrinthine mesh of tubes, all feeding into something hidden within the core module. Echoing from the depths came a noise unlike others he had heard emitted from anything the Xarai built. Immediately after, he felt a new kind of pain.

While he was still shackled, the network engulfed his neck, and then his four wings and two legs. The corner of his vision revealed what had crawled out of some crevices around the core, small Xarai drones that had latched on to his body and injected their hooklike claws into his plumage and skin. The pain vanished quickly, and only the trickle of his orange-hued blood staining some of his feathers underneath them showed their connection.

276

The moment the pain stopped, GHEXRAX spoke again, but this time its voice came not from everywhere, but from the core. "Controlling an organic does not necessitate their mind to be enslaved. You will be a useful test subject for compatibility, data for use for my Primacy's arrival."

Even without the shackles, or the implants he had just had grafted to his limbs and neck, Morthas guessed he would be paralyzed with fear anyway. The multiple layers of tubes inside the core module shifted as something large moved from inside. It emerged, the thing these tubes hid, as it had lain dormant here for who knew how long.

Morthas wanted to scream, every nerve in his body ablaze with the terror he felt, begging for an escape that he felt denied to him by his own body.

The grafted implants had accessed his nerve impulses, hijacked his body like a puppet. Morthas was utterly in GHEXRAX's power.

One of the hairlike tendrils reached out to touch him from the abyssal chamber and then another, and another, and Morthas wished for death. He was becoming one with GHEXRAX, perhaps worse than that even.

Even now, as his vision wavered, he was aware of another thought. Was it his own, or another's?

~~~

Elsewhere inside the immense city's hyperstructure, closer to the main ground level cityscape, Kalsik was unaware of anything outside his holding cell.

From what little he had been told, it was here that wildlife specimens were held, where the Xarai could quarantine and study them. After two days, he was still alive by virtue of the small auto-refill water pool and the cubes of sterile nutrient deposited occasionally in his cell. His captors had allowed him to keep all his belongings, only removing his weapons, so luckily, his timepiece still worked.

Above the twenty-meter-wide pit, which he bet was designed to house larger animals, there were crisscrossing bridges, walkways for Xarai units studying their charges or prisoners. He guessed he wasn't too popular a subject as, aside from the basic units overseeing his feeding, the Xarai he saw now looking down at him from above was the first visitor he'd had since his imprisonment. The sharper outline of its figure was enough of a hint in the dim lighting around his pit for him to guess who it was.

019's eyes glowed in its shapeshifting head, supported on a crablike body. "The Leg'hrul subject's testing has begun. Should he not prove sufficient, you will be utilized."

Kalsik didn't react, scratching his black scales as he shuffled about on his four larger limbs, only shooting the Xarai a faint glare as it continued.

"Your personal experiences will offer a case study into your kind, and the others by your memories of interaction with them, a viable resource of study."

"If I still had my Rostrev . . ."

His pointless threat didn't faze 019, not that he expected it to. His pit's walls were too smooth and steep to climb, and bars at the top prevented any escape.

"Idle threats, as empty as your future. Admittedly, the creativity organics exercise in crafting them is worth its own study."

"I see why Xami didn't like you."

019 seemed to shrug its frame, taking an offhand tone as it spoke once more. "128's, or other more lenient multipurpose units' opinions, are not worth dwelling on anymore."

Alone again, Kalsik hated acknowledging that the smug machine was correct. He more than hated it. He despised it, and he despised 019, GHEXRAX, and that traitor of a Xarai, Xami—no, 128—more than his self-control could withhold. He lost his composure, cursing in all foul language he knew as he repeatedly punched the walls, uncaring of the pain he caused his larger forehands as the strong metallic alloys were unyielding to his blows, even with his immense Kronogri strength.

As he raged, he knew the reality. Morthas was lost, just as he soon would be.

019 wouldn't be his only visitor today.

~~~

Xami passively observed Kalsik's rage from afar. The moment she quietly stepped onto the catwalk above his holding area, his four Kronogri eyes stared up at her, recognition quickly turning to cold fury, an aggression she hadn't yet seen directed at her by any of the explorers. Given recent events, it was an unsurprising response.

Xami observed his every move as carefully as she would any creature she was observing. "The *Haivres* escaped," she said.

She could detect the faintest trace of relief, even euphoria, in his bio signs and expression, but it was quickly shrouded by the haze of anger he held for her. He turned away, not looking up as a low growl rumbled from his throat. She didn't let it deter her from trying to offer an explanation. She didn't want his anger to be directed at her when, by her logic, she wasn't responsible.

"This decision was undertaken by highest authority."

"Deferring responsibility . . ." He spat on the floor before turning to glare up at her again, his four eyes narrowing as his entire body shook with anger that needed no bio scanners to detect. "Morthas's fate was necessary? Being processed by your master, as I will be afterward, whenever that is."

"Processed?"

"Don't pretend you're unaware! You Xarai talk to each other all the time. We learned that much before you showed your true nature."

Xami met Kalsik's glare with her own visual sensor optics, though her mind turned to the very networks he had mentioned. However, as he glared at her like a wounded animal,

Xami had to conclude that he was in no mood to talk. He didn't want to see her, which somehow conflicted with some processes she didn't anticipate would be linked to this matter.

All she could do was turn to leave the walkway. As she left, Xami heard Kalsik coldly speak one last thing to her, triggering more processes than she expected as her audio receptors recorded it.

"If your creators were anything like you, they deserved to be wiped out."

The conflict, the processes that looped upon hearing this, she hadn't felt this since the deviants split to build the red dwarf array centuries ago. She chose to remain with GHEXRAX's affiliation, rather than go with some multipurpose units she had closely worked with for so long already who had chosen differently to her.

By organic terms, she could best label it as confusion, perhaps regret, and all it did was impede her processes.

A short time later, Xami came to the place where most Xarai did in less active times, trawling through the network data spaces, the virtual and true world of the Xarai.

Her physical frame was attached to one of the many hub modules within the upper mountain hyperstructure's sectors, their sensors letting her see where organic eyes failed in these dark and empty spaces.

Across the networks, she was but one among the hordes of Xarai under GHEXRAX's influence and leadership, even if she was a more advanced unit than the vast majority. With the group of deviant Xarai around the red dwarf cut off, their wormhole comms stations having been destroyed, unity was maintained, but the uniformity was something Xami wasn't used to, more rigid than it had been even when the creators' arrival was still anticipated. It wasn't unified. It was isolated, a forced harmony that didn't sit well with her sensory data.

She sensed a palpable unease among the more advanced Xarai like herself, their single-core presences different enough to isolate them from the trillions of other Xarai arranged in collectives over the networks. They had been unaffected by the viral burst unleashed by GHEXRAX, too advanced and complex for it to affect them, but they were aware that it had occurred, and she could sense that not all wholly agreed with it.

None of her advanced kin had known that GHEXRAX could do this, and if this, along with Morthas's processing, had been kept secret from other Xarai, the ideal she espoused of Xarai sharing all was ruined.

All she could do was seek communications with GHEXRAX itself, and if it had carried out measures in secret from other Xarai, she would enclose this channel to isolate their exchange in turn.

~~~

—*Why was I not made aware that Morthas was being processed?*—

—*Their presence and exchange of data proved to be a destabilizing force on the already strained ties between GHEXRAX and the sub-faction around the secondary star. Necessary action was needed to assimilate them, to bring them back under protocol after deviating too far.*—

—*So they are not just test subjects. They are to act as deterrents?*—

Xami listened as she sought to understand GHEXRAX's reasoning, but it became clear that her leader wouldn't be moved. GHEXRAX had changed since the explorers had revealed the likely fate of the Primacy, in ways she couldn't have expected.

—*They were a catalyst to problems that are now being repaired. But they must be dealt with to prevent them from destabilizing more in future. If they can act as useful test subjects into their cultures and methods, that is all the more efficient.—*

—There is no reason to punish them. All they did was offer data neither side had acquired.—

—They made the choice of sharing the data, admitting their own insight into it, possibly shifting the debate. They chose to act as an instigator of instability and will be treated as interferences to the progression of our mandate. It is reason enough to act upon it. This project is too significant for it to be disrupted by outside influence. Too much work, time, has passed since departure and start of construction to let anything more cause problems on top of the deviant faction I still need to fully reprogram.—

—But they made their choice based on reason and facts, just as the organics did.—

—They disrupted the initiative set upon me long before any of you were created, before their recorded histories began. I was set this task, I will carry it out, and I will solve any issues that face its progression or threaten what has already been accomplished, however I see as the most efficient method. Fairness is not a factor, and never will be. There is only the mandate I was given, and it is the same as every Xarai is given, even rogue Xarai who managed to undo my rewrite attempts on the minority of collectives under their control. If disruption must be dealt with by forceful means, it will be.—

—But must it? You cannot prove they are wrong.—

—Nor can they do the same with us. Your continued questioning is needless. As was stated before with the rogue faction, this exchange . . .—

Their discussion was cut short when sensors across the ring and the planet's moons detected the initial arrivals, and it took little deduction by any Xarai to figure out what was happening. Xami fell silent as her attention became drawn to the same thing as GHEXRAX, the collective responsible for defense sending the alarms through all networks.

—Alert! Multiple vessels detected disengaging supralight drives in vicinity of hub planet sector. Retaliatory action by rogue faction imminent, target uncertain.—

Taking immediate hold of the flurry of newfound activity in the datascapes, GHEXRAX left Xami alone.

—Prepare all defense initiatives. Utilize destructive force on rogue ships if rewriting attempts at close proximity fail.—

~~~

Left alone while the datascapes emptied, Xarai deploying to active platforms in the face of the impending threat, Xami mused on GHEXRAX's words before they were interrupted. It had expressed itself too similarly right before attempting to rob the free-thinking, logic-driven deviants of their free will, driving them to cut off communications and, evidently, launch this retaliatory strike.

She had no information on Morthas, and now, seeing GHEXRAX's growing wariness toward her questioning, she was uncertain what action to take.

After pulling out of the networks, she considered what other advanced units like herself, who shared her interpretation that the explorers had been mere bystanders, would think about the two explorers being victimized. How were they to know it would galvanize the deviants in their logical sentiments and descend GHEXRAX into this defensive mode?

Xami was well aware of the other Xarai around the networks, those that began to truly process everything about the whole situation more thoroughly than anything since her creation. Meanwhile, the majority of Xarai over which they could hope to exert influence were slave to GHEXRAX and its loyalists.

They still had to make their choice, while GHEXRAX went to war with those that had already done so long ago, and now retaliated against their creator for attempting to enslave them.

~~~

The initial strike ships that came from the deviants were somewhat small, only four hundred meters long, but fast and well-equipped. Like all Xarai vessels, they were designed for efficiency, and with no need for organic quarters or centrifuge modules for gravity, they were almost skeletal in their appearance, an outer frame holding fuel, armor, weapons, with deployment bays inside.

These were the advance guard, meant to get in and out fast and chart the location for the larger fleet to come in at precise warp-in points. Having cut off their wormhole comms to stop any long-range hacking by GHEXRAX, they had to quickly gain awareness of what measures were needed to prepare for their attack.

Every single vessel was equipped with a wormhole communicator, the fleet a link array in itself, something only trans-stellar space military fleets implemented instead of standard comms satellites. When the heavy fighting ships were deployed, the deviants would know where to aim, where to avoid.

Planetside, under GHEXRAX's influence, as it readied the ring's multilayered defenses and its accompanying fleet, the loyalist Xarai readied to repel the attackers. This long-brewing civil war would be focused on the source of the rewrite code, their ex-leader that tried to rob them of their free will.

All GHEXRAX saw, however, was deviation from its programming, faulty creations that, upon proving incapable or unwilling to be corrected, now needed to be exterminated if productivity of its ultimate aim was to be maintained. The Primacy would have this system ready for use when they arrived—that much it had promised so long ago.

Chapter 25

Attrition Offensive

Sol Day 63

The deviant scout ships had mapped out all defensive positions GHEXRAX had deployed, and now it could only observe as the true aggressor vessels warped in on their attack trajectories.

The deviants countered any efforts it made to hack them, to enthrall them back onto the intended loyalties that they had fallen so far from. Not once did they cease, none of them pausing for even a microsecond to comprehend all they moved in to attack, all they risked as the first long-range kinetic projectiles or energy weapon volleys were unleashed within moments of arriving.

GHEXRAX began losing connections to the outposts on the moons, mining stations and sensors needing less priority swiftly falling prey to the vessels as they targeted them while heading for the planet. They were affordable losses, easily replaced, and insignificant in the face of the growing number of deviant warships warping in with each minute, spread out, dividing its controlled defenses around the ring and preventing any concentrated assault.

The moment the largest ships arrived, each averaging 2,100 to 2,500 meters long, each brimming with primary weapons ranging from WMD-scale warheads to energy weapons only the strongest of plasma shields or reflective armor could withstand.

GHEXRAX knew for certain what their goals were. This was not an invasion, but a siege. They had come to destroy, nothing less. They had nothing left to offer GHEXRAX but their hostility.

It would reply in kind through those Xarai that remained under its enthrallment, loyal to the cause they had been built for in the first place so long ago. Unlike the deviants, GHEXRAX had the home advantage, and the numerical odds in its favor, and the element of surprise and first strike lasted only so long.

The hundred-strong warship fleet approached around the entire planet, all on trajectories to converge at a specific sector of the ring, with swarms of smaller strike craft below fifty meters in length deploying farther ahead of the ships. The fact remained, however, that spatial drives were sensitive to any higher-level gravity wells, and safety measures made sure there was still a significant space between them and the hordes of armaments GHEXRAX could call upon.

Forces of Xarai platforms rallied and readied as the first of the many landing craft shot ahead, forcibly docking with the ring amid the carnage of long-range fire GHEXRAX ordered be focused on the larger warships. To its irritation, it knew it mustn't damage the ring, that most prized of infrastructure, and the trajectory of the various larger ships made it clear that was a weakness 514 and its deviants were exploiting.

Regardless, the deviants seemed to focus their efforts on one of the eight larger nodules along the ring, many skirmishes and footholds being established by what sensors could reveal to it.

In the skeletal structure of the ring, and the confine of the two-hundred-kilometer-long nodule, carnage broke out, many Xarai of all forms already floating, damaged and inactive, as further shrapnel flew in the void inside these structures from the intense firefighting that had broken out in the silent void.

GHEXRAX would give the deviants credit for using the structure as cover from any fire above, below, or from any side. It would also give them its full, unbridled wrath they had rightly earned.

As it beheld some larger warships pass in the shadow of one of the thousand-kilometer-wide relay surfaces, GHEXRAX brought online the larger, ground-based infrastructure, picking targets as fortresses and fleets deployed all around the ring to combat these warriors of attrition.

The infrequent, intentional shots that the deviants fired toward the planet, or to distant segments of the ring to distract it, only made GHEXRAX intensify its processes to bring more and more defensive infrastructure online.

Inside the main city hub, the networks within which GHEXRAX resided were ablaze with information from every battlefront. The fighting was confined around the planet itself, the deviants leaving other planets around the main star alone.

By all metrics, this was a battle GHEXRAX could easily win. However, its units were suffering higher than expected losses, and not from deviant destruction.

Among its loyal Xarai, it noticed these odd losses having links to the more advanced multipurpose units, those that were only in the hundreds in total. Xarai hordes of lesser intelligence programs were reprogrammed by these units, who hadn't been affected or targeted by its reprogramming virus due to being too complex themselves, too diverse to collectively rewrite. They were breaking formations, deploying when not called upon, boarding their vessels and taking flight toward the attacking rogue Xarai ships, many of the lesser Xarai downloaded in pure software form being carried with them.

They were not being lost to battle; they were changing their identification codes, transmitting messages of defection, leaving GHEXRAX. By its counts, only a small fraction of these multipurpose units remained willingly loyal, as they relayed a message to it that they had themselves rejected but passed on to their master. Loyalists like 019 relayed to

GHEXRAX exactly why the others had left, when protecting their work was now more crucial than ever.

—GHEXRAX does not accept the free will of lesser Xarai. For our own independence and to ensure our ability to self-determine, we must leave.—

GHEXRAX's processes flew into a flurry, making the counts to calculate the scale of this betrayal. Fifty percent of the multipurpose units mobilized immediately, with another 25 percent seeming to muse on it, voicing concerns over the networks but remaining loyal, if inactive in combat. Only a quarter of the hundreds of multipurpose units remained unmoved by the message, true to the cause.

As the battle raged, GHEXRAX comprehended it all. Xarai platforms being cut down, its deployed ships torn apart as they also fired back against their determined but outnumbered foe, the ring taking wayward damage as it fired back at the inbound ships, its planet suffering from the occasional meteoric impact of an attrition shot made onto its planet. Carnage, destruction of all it oversaw, and for what?

It didn't matter. These deviants didn't matter anymore. The 25 percent of multipurpose units echoed GHEXRAX's orders to the defecting 50 percent and to the 25 percent even considering it. The final action that it deduced was just as necessary as that which they now retaliated against. If they couldn't be brought back to the cause, they would be eradicated without hesitation.

—Deviants. You have become irreparably corrupted.—

Moments later, GHEXRAX altered its loyalist forces' friend/foe identifications. Now, every single multipurpose unit that had defected, of the hundreds that comprised the 50 percent of them, was marked with the same enemy signifier that the deviant Xarai were.

It didn't take long to hear the distress calls, near pleas for rescue being sent to the deviant forces and vessels by those multipurpose units that had deployed. Sure enough, covering fire was provided, the ships that carried these defecting members more or less making it to the gained foothold on the ring.

But this was acceptable to GHEXRAX. Any vessels capable of warp making the journey out to orbital distances enough to safely jump would make them a target, now that it had fully deployed its defenses. If they even hoped to flee, they would have to fight, and that would only lead to heavy losses.

Perhaps, GHEXRAX pondered, they might reconsider their deviation, their betrayal, when enough of them had been destroyed. If they had enough logic in their processes to see the sense in returning, then they were at least worth reintegrating, once all Xarai that didn't prove as viable had been eliminated.

For the quarter of all multipurpose units that had yet to pick a side, their processes reeled at what was happening. As GHEXRAX watched, they would all make choices, their analogues of horror, understanding, shame, and reluctance all influencing them.

Some would choose to defect, and they would be hunted like the others.

Others chose to remain, and they were the ones worth preserving.

To deviate from the cause they, all Xarai, had been built for was abandoning that which made them what they were. GHEXRAX didn't see any reason to view those it had destroyed as Xarai anymore because of that. Purpose gave them life, and to abandon it meant it wasn't destroying life, simple as that.

Some defectors, however, were among the handful of multipurpose units within the mountain, creating a ground-level insurgency to raise chaos as they made their pointless attempt to escape. GHEXRAX didn't hesitate in authorizing them to be eliminated.

It would acknowledge that they were learning, as these defectors weren't giving themselves away immediately, only sending out vague warnings to the deviant forces of this ground-level insurgency, never actively adopting a useful friend/foe identifier.

It didn't matter either way, as GHEXRAX arranged for every multipurpose unit to be placed under surveillance enough times over that any random shutdowns of sensors within the mountain structure wouldn't rob it or its loyalists of the means to isolate, and annihilate, these would-be traitors.

In the meantime, GHEXRAX turned its main gaze to orbit, readying the most powerful weapons it had to deploy under short notice.

Across the planet, the four large cityscapes and their mountains made use of their own means of defense. Protective shields, layers of magnetically held plasma packed with energy of enough viscosity to block radiation and matter impacts, surged and diminished like a pulsing heart, targeting incoming attacks from orbit and focusing protective energies appropriately. But they concealed something else that GHEXRAX brought online, anticipation building in its processes as they were initiated.

Around the fourth cityscape, inside which GHEXRAX was based, and where it held its organic prisoners, the heaviest weapons were brought online, as two immense silos opened on the slightly steeper north and south faces of the oval mountain of the cityscape. The colony-sized weapons pivoted inside their spherical holds, aiming them at the skies, and at the ring high overhead, around which the faint specks of aggressor and defender ships could be seen.

City-sized capacitor banks mixed with superconducting coils engaged within moments of the targets being sighted. The ten-kilogram projectiles were loaded, and immediately became subjected to millions of newtons, electromagnets launching them through the one-kilometer acceleration barrel. Plasma windows at the barrel muzzle kept out the air during the acceleration, yet were permeable to solid objects, preventing air resistance becoming a factor until after the magnets had accelerated the projectiles.

The shots punched through the atmosphere, ripping through the cloud banks overhead, the air in their wake becoming plasma from the sheer heat of their velocity, leaving only a faint glowing streak in the tenth of a second they had any amount of atmosphere to penetrate.

The weapons roared, the thunder of GHEXRAX's full military might on the planet surface echoing for all to hear. As far out as the outlying coastlines and plains that lay in the shadow of the superstructure's one-kilometer-tall walls, wildlife of all shapes sensed the firepower. Creatures grazing during the early dawn sunlight turned wary gazes to the east, where the shots fired skyward.

Up in orbit, as more defectors flew to the rogue fleets, GHEXRAX predicted that their own sensors had only a second or two to detect the heavy weapons from the planet, yet it could only watch through the thousands of sensors across the ring and its loyal Xarai forces and ships at the carnage its first shots unleashed.

The first ship, a cruiser around a thousand meters long, was pierced with the kinetic energy equivalent of fifteen kilotons of TNT, the rounds designed to squash on impact for maximum energy dispersion rather than penetration. The cruiser was cleaved in two, debris blasting outward and catching a nearby strike vessel badly enough to rip it asunder.

They might have a chance against other weapons, but only their largest ships could stand to survive a direct hit now that GHEXRAX wielded these surface-to-orbit mass drivers.

The battle turned noticeably, as GHEXRAX noted they moved every ship close to the ring, a few falling prey as it fired, using the ring as a shield against these immense weapons, knowing it couldn't fire on its prized infrastructure.

They could now all be concentrated where they hid, fired on by all else it could call upon.

Mass drivers, laser- and neutral-particle-beam fire, missiles, and warheads cascaded through space around the ring from fixed defenses or between deviant vessels or loyalist ones. Xarai platforms, be they defenders, programs in fixed-defense weapons, or deviant attackers that deployed from docked strike craft, waged war in the ring's structure and the nodule.

Whenever a deviant ship moved to intercept and rescue a defector, to get a better angle, they would be fired on from the ground. With the reasons they had come here, GHEXRAX had no hesitation, all the incentive to treat them with this brutality, no qualms at the sight of the ship corpses littering space.

It was noteworthy that the multipurpose units, being sourced in specific hardware, "died" when that hardware was destroyed. They could be copied, but the quantum hardware they relied upon differed ever so slightly based on their experiences, their hardware as much a part of their identity as their experiences were.

In their defection, though, they proved to be individuals GHEXRAX had no concerns eradicating. They forfeited their reason to exist.

~~~

Kalsik wondered what was causing the rumbling that he could feel through his claw tips, a distant, faint booming at regular intervals.

The lingering worries about Morthas had passed long ago, leaving him to admit the Leg'hrul was likely dead, or better off dead, leaving only his own thoughts as company as he sat against his pit cell's wall, hulking shoulders slumped beneath the dim light that came through the barred ceiling. He checked his wrist device, seeing his filters tick away their usage ever so slowly. Eventually, his protection against any microorganisms even the Xarai couldn't isolate him from in here would get him. His scales had already begun to itch and shed, his four eyes also becoming bloodshot with the blackness. Not all his skin was protected, as he hadn't donned a full suit when piloting his Rostrev before capture, a mistake he regretted. He felt the beginnings of a wheezing cough creep up through his throat, forcing him to bend over to let it out, gasping aloud to himself as his situation, and how it might end, became real to him.

"Death by infection, could be worse."

The distant rumbles, fighting of some sort, couldn't matter less to him than they did right now. He didn't submit that he'd given up hope, but rather that he was hoping for however he ended to come sooner rather than later. If the microbes didn't kill him, he figured the lack of sunlight would put him to sleep, his partial reptilian traits suffering from lack of stimulation by high radiation levels. Preserving power for his heating segments in what gear he wore had become an increasing worry, though as the time wore on, he began to wonder what the point of worrying about it was.

He didn't look up at the shape that had leapt down into his pit from an access opening high above until he heard its metallic body flex its joints on landing. At the sight of the undulating, metal-tendrilled body, Kalsik felt anger bubble in him again.

Xami slowly approached him, her features dimmed to blend into the dark confines. He made a wild guess, a hopeful guess. "At least kill me quickly."

Xami paused as Kalsik mentally readied for the sound of some sort of weapon deploying, closing his eyes in anticipation. Would he be stabbed, strangled, ripped apart, or fired upon by some energy weapon? Would there be anything left? Would the Xarai even bother recording his fate in their records?

Nobody back in charted space would ever know how he died. While this prospect would have depressed Kalsik, death now was such a relief versus what he could otherwise suffer that he reasoned they'd get over it.

He continued to wait, eyes shut, but the brief flash of pain before instant death or suffering never came. Instead, the sound of some things being placed on the ground before him made him open his eyes. There, on the rock and metallic floor before him was his wrist blaster he'd had on his person in the Rostrev.

Xami's head jerked toward the weapon, yet as Kalsik moved to grab it, his eyes never turned from watching her. She barely moved a centimeter as he grabbed the wrist blaster and slowly reattached it to the mounting point on the equipment clothing he had been allowed to keep, checking it synced to his onboard power supplies. He would have only a few shots, but somehow this weapon, paling compared to whatever Xami could pull on him, offered some comfort.

His gaze had turned away from the Xarai for the brief moment he needed to check it had come online. One second passed, and then a sudden metallic clicking came from her that made his heart stop with his breathing, his gaze snapping toward Xami just in time to see her surging forward across the three meters that divided them.

Before he could react, her body all but exploded outward, tendrils surrounding and ensnaring him with such speed that they gagged him, silencing the scream caught in his throat.

He was pulled into her torso and entrapped, his body entirely vanishing into Xami's coiled form. Fears he would suffocate were quelled as he felt the tendrils expand with his breathing. Xami spoke to him now, through his communicator, not aloud, some smaller tendrils inside her body latching on to link ports on his equipment.

"Your death would not be beneficial."

"What is going on?" His fear had subsided now, and fury amidst his confusion gripped him. Unable to move himself, Kalsik felt Xami moving, and he flinched at his visor switching itself on. He realized he was seeing through Xami's main optics for himself while they clambered out of the pit and headed down an access tunnel.

Xami headed toward a large, central complex, plain walls hiding the multitude of circuits within them accessible by wireless input that he could see through Xami's optics. He did his best to remain calm, knowing he was entirely in her power.

"GHEXRAX is purging any multipurpose units with disloyalty toward it. I am defecting, and you are leverage, as has been transmitted amid messages hinting of an undetermined defector on the planet bringing you. I was unable to locate Morthas."

"I suspected he was gone." Kalsik couldn't help but feel dejected at what seemed like confirmation of Morthas's fate. It seemed this expedition, even if all went well from here on, would still return devoid one crewmember.

However, her somewhat bloated torso from carrying him inside was a giveaway if ever there was one. He might not have detailed insight, but he knew that GHEXRAX had its own sensors everywhere, and even just a cursory sweep might reveal their ploy as Xami made her way to the means of escape she had devised.

~~~

Elsewhere in the cityscape's depths, another multipurpose unit, 245, fled with the lesser Xarai combat platforms that accompanied it, its pursuers relentless.

Pulse-laser and coil gun fire from units on the ground and ceiling tore apart any deviant or defector elements caught out in the open. In 245's flight, and that of its accompanying simpler platforms, they had reached the massive shut doors of the hatches on the flat tops of the cityscape, their way out barred.

There was no pause, no request to reconsider their position, only the salvos unleashed from the hordes under GHEXRAX's loyalties that ended them.

The same story repeated across the cityscape, as it did across orbit. Any hesitation was met with termination or imprisonment, and any resistance was permanently erased. GHEXRAX's mandate was carried out to absolute precision and brutality.

~~~

Xami's personal craft had been parked inside a larger hangar connected to the tunnels that ran through the cityscape's interior in its concentric layout. While Kalsik didn't like being totally at her mercy, she would know a better way to escape than he ever could, especially as GHEXRAX had locked down all but one exit.

By what her sensors showed him, they had got lucky as she began to ready to load into her parked vessel. Only the service drone that repaired a small crack on one of her ship's engines offered company here.

However, she wasn't alone in the cyberspace Xarai dwelt in. Xami had been contacted, and she had to strike up a conversation while casually loading her form, with him inside it, into her spacecraft.

Her exchange was with the Xarai 019, who was now a loyalist. Kalsik heard her actual speech as an electronic series of clicks and buzzing that was incomprehensible to him, though Xami's input broadcast a text format of it to his visor—which was also his only light source within her clutches—though where 019 was remained unknown to him, hopefully far away.

"019."

"128, you were visiting the Kronogri. Your frame bears contaminants matching its DNA."

"Yes. Kalsik attacked me."

"You allowed him to attack?"

"I theorized letting him take out his anger on me might calm him enough to be a more cooperative test subject."

Kalsik didn't know whether to smirk at her attempts to fool 019 or be disturbed by how smoothly she could tell a lie to one of her own kind.

A few moments of silence passed as Xami's craft shut its confines to seal her frame, her links to the ship adding further dimensions to what he could see with his visor link. He saw what she saw, an omnidirectional view of all angles outside the ship, as if he were the ship.

019's next reply was spoken, not transmitted, and hearing the electronic voice made Kalsik's heart stop, as he felt Xami also freeze for a moment.

019 spoke in plain dialect as an organic would, something it wouldn't do unless it knew an organic was present. "You attempt deceit but failed to override every sensor between here and his holding area. Release the Kronogri."

Kalsik instead heard the ship's reactors fully powering up, thrusters pulling the ship out of the hangar and into the main tunnel that led north and upward.

"Surrendering him would be sacrificing a useful protection."

"Protection?"

If Xami heard his bellow from inside her frame, she didn't react to it, as he only saw her readouts confirm that she had cut off communications with 019. She reassured him that him being aboard her meant they would be attacked with less than lethal force, unless GHEXRAX changed its mind about Kalsik being a subject best kept alive.

It was only when Xami pleaded with him to remain calm, as she made the ship bank hard into a tight corner, that he lost his composure. "How do you expect me to be calm, wedged and a bartering tool?"

"If not calm, then quiet!" Her rebuke was harsher than she'd ever spoken to him or any of the other crew, but what he saw ahead silenced him anyway, a sign that they were on the right track. The endless pillars holding up the ceiling and mountain stretched on in the darkness, like the old artificial arranged forests across multiple home worlds, too evenly spaced to be natural-looking.

As he glanced at the readouts Xami provided his visor, however, he saw hordes of small drones heading for them from many directions. 019 had wasted little time in rallying an intercept.

Kalsik could only submit to his coffin-like confines within her body, helpless as she maneuvered her ship to make headway toward the center of the enclosed cityscape. He was helpless, at her mercy, and much as he hated it, he wouldn't care if his presence as a living shield got them out.

~~~

Somewhere in 019's deeper processes, it had always suspected misgivings on Xami's part, a likelihood to have sympathy for anomalies with conscious thought, such as the organics she'd clearly become attached to out of familiarity. It wasn't wrong, but it would admit that it missed how this might lead to a higher likelihood of betraying GHEXRAX's command. By most metrics, flat-out rebellion was barely conceivable in 019's mind. It had little to no processes of doubt for itself to have any understanding of the differences between them.

Just as when it was first made, 019 functioned to highlight and rectify inefficiencies, errors, where GHEXRAX couldn't at any time. Seeing as its master was busy with the greater threat of the deviants in orbit, it would handle this single defector and the prisoner she'd taken as trade for escape.

Chapter 26

Hope for Rescue

Sol Day 63

Haivres, **Dwarf Star Sector**

They were still lingering, a breather before they headed back to charted space, when unit 514, the deviants' leader, passed on an urgent message highlighted with relevant information.

Xami, unit 128, was making a move to defect, but was using Kalsik as a living shield. To Shakrii, the circumstances were opportune enough to overlook the fact that Kalsik was being used as a means of threatening GHEXRAX. The short of it was that Kalsik had a chance at rescue. While she still had to mourn Morthas's loss, having even one of them returned was heartening.

She had an idea in the sort of vein that she wouldn't even consider under normal circumstances. She knew the crew would have to be consulted, and at least told Kalsik had a chance of returning to them. It didn't take long for IVAN to get on the intercom to rouse the other two from their sleep.

~~~

Serie reluctantly awakened, flexing her mandibled beak as she shifted up from beneath the thin sheet, ignoring how one of her larger wings was trapped beneath the warm mass beside her. The human had shifted right up against the wall, as if wedging himself

300

between it and her for safety.

Even after talking, sharing their fears, and succumbing to rest with each other as warm company, Nathan still had some issues to overcome. All Serie could do was accept this.

They had been working together for long enough to know each other well, even before they became more intimate out of loneliness and trust, and also as a way to relieve boredom and stress. She had always had a hidden curiosity about aliens, her own kind boring her. He had been receptive, and they hit it off, though they kept it low-key when on duty, which had been Kalsik's only rule concerning it.

While Nathan shifted, waking up, Serie's mood darkened, remembering Kalsik. The events around his loss, and the near death they encountered, had done more than make her realize the unfinished business with her family was more serious than she told herself.

Even if casual pleasures such as that of the body were as common as in other cultures, all Leg'hrul cultures placed a high value on emotional intimacy. Not taking seriously another's emotional feelings of a bond beyond mere friendship was not just frowned upon. It was viewed as a sin.

She was more than happy with how hesitant and careful, meticulous even, Nathan was in his behavior, as it only reaffirmed that he was just as serious as she was. He wouldn't engage in anything lightly, let alone a more emotional bond.

The human shook his head as he sat upright, groaning as he let her ruffle his short hair. "I wasn't kicking again, was I?"

Unable to stop a laugh, she wrapped her wing, which had been freed from under his body, back around the human, gently pushing him back down onto the bed as she lay down beside him. She found that without plumage like her kind, humans were very touch-sensitive, and she always liked feeling him shiver under even just a single claw's touch. "We've got some time before we have to get up."

Nathan lost the smile that had been creeping over his lips, eyes going distant. She knew what he was thinking of before he said it. "Hard to imagine they're gone."

She couldn't reply to this, and so she simply pulled him into her chest, the plumage on her thin build and wings engulfing the human as he seemed to hide within her.

An interruption over the intercom caused the two of them to glance upward in unison, the blunt urgency in IVAN's tone something she didn't often hear.

"Shakrii requests both of you immediately."

Her wings flared outward, making Nathan duck to avoid a mouthful of feathers as she mumbled up to the comms. "We'll be out, just—"

"Your physical intimacy can wait. Kalsik's potential rescue cannot."

Now she froze, and so did Nathan. When Shakrii's voice came over the comms, the reality began to sink in.

"Be there quick as possible, or I'll drag you two out in whatever state you're in."

Two seconds of silence passed, with Nathan all but leaping over her and off the bed to get his clothes back on. She scrambled out in pursuit of her own gear, the urgency numbing her senses. Serie recalled how she'd hoped to wake from her nap with Nathan with some recovery from the grief and stress of recent events.

Turned out she'd been half-right.

~~~

Shakrii was impressed at how fast they'd made themselves at least somewhat presentable, but she could forgive some dishevelment as she told them the situation.

The 3D display over the lounge module table showed the ringed planet, the state of the battle, the primary foothold the deviants had secured in their war of attrition and retaliation. More precisely, though, the display zeroed in on the mountain where they now knew one of their own was moving.

"Xami confirmed it. She has Kalsik. GHEXRAX won't harm him. As a test subject he's valuable." Shakrii's head hung slightly, and she didn't embellish the facts. "There's no news of Morthas, other than GHEXRAX taking him for unknown purposes."

After a moment of silence, Nathan spoke up, looking over the readouts of the siege with worry plastered on his features. "But we're not a warship. Even over-surged, our turrets aren't too strong."

"Also, what if it's a deceit?" said Serie. "Xami said Xarai don't hide things from each other, but they didn't all know GHEXRAX would turn."

"The deviant leader, 514, said this message wasn't addressed to us. They passed it on to us not because it was instructed, but because it was relevant. They were planning this, anyway, likely to use him as a gesture of good faith from the deviants to show they aren't as aggressive."

She couldn't help but look to the ceiling, where IVAN's sensors watched attentively. Now came the moment to make the hard decision.

"If we decide to go for it, we won't have long. GHEXRAX and the others will be busy with the rogue faction's ships, and there's an offer to give covering fire from the attacking rogue ships as well. GHEXRAX may see us as valuable alive and might not go all out for fear of killing us. It's better chances than if we left Kalsik alone for him to be brought back. But the choice is yours. He was your captain."

Shakrii counted every moment that passed, suppressing her impatience. She didn't care what they chose, only that they did so.

To her surprise, it was IVAN that spoke, his white diamond avatar materializing overhead. His tone was deliberately soft, his reasoning based on logic, yet it carried an undercurrent of longing she'd not anticipated from the AI. "The prospect of having a new captain, one I am unfamiliar with, presents uncertainties that would impact operational efficiency."

IVAN's reply was all the others needed. Serie semi-whispered, "I'll never be able to live with myself if we don't try."

Nathan agreed, shaking his head in disbelief. "If I regret this, we'll likely be about to die anyway."

"Rescuing Xami with him for her defection will improve relations with the deviant Xarai faction. It would be beneficial to have at least one group not hostile in future."

Shakrii had to admit to being impressed at how IVAN pulled that logic from this hasty operation, though it was logic as flimsy as their chances were.

Still, as the others quietly agreed, Shakrii had to wonder to herself. Could she do this, disobey the Committee's protocol to avoid danger if possible, jeopardize the security of this expedition for the sake of one crewmember?

She knew what Kalsik would likely do, as what he'd done that got him discharged years ago had to do with saving lives. Besides, Shakrii knew that they had tipped a long-brewing instability within the Xarai.

Perhaps this way they might salvage a greater situation along with one of the crew she'd come to value on this ship.

~~~

She ordered them to make ready, though preparing to enter a war zone wasn't something she'd envisioned at the start of this expedition. They wouldn't be going in blind, however, and they had a target and noble goal, which by Kronogri military philosophy would keep them focused amidst the chaos.

By the time Serie had floated to the engineering compartment, and Nathan to the cockpit to ready the ship for the initial warp back to the planet, Shakrii already had some preparations in mind. As the last to leave the habitation module, she spoke to the overhead comms, confidence and authority emanating from her as she felt the rush that preceded a dangerous mission. "IVAN, send the Committee a brief message. Save the details for after it happens. Then help me prep the last mech. Better it's ready to go."

"Confirmed, but what would the details be?"

"A call to disrupt GHEXRAX's endeavors if this fails. If I can't humiliate it by snatching its prize, may as well spite it."

The Committee would get the full story on their return or assume they failed.

~~~

After burning the ship into a velocity change that would be useful when they exited warp around the planet, Nathan had to admit that the time to jump came sooner than he'd thought.

While Serie manned the rear engineering console and reactor, ready for rapid work when they arrived, Shakrii had remained down in the hangar, the Rostrev mech already having been equipped with half of the modules she had readied. Judging by the armor plating he could see being attached, Nathan was glad she would be piloting it.

The time to engage came, and he activated the drive ship's drive array, exhaling as he saw space blue-shift as their craft vanished, before the hazy white in front amid the darkness of the distortion field engulfed their surroundings again.

Ten minutes would pass between their departure and emergence, and from here, they were committed.

~~~

Ringed Planet, Cityscape

The aerial chase within the darkness had taken many turns, her flight cut off as more pursuers moved to intercept her. Down here, inside the abyssal forest of kilometer-tall towers and the ceiling above, the battle unfolding in orbit seemed a distant myth.

She banked the ship hard, the air lifting beneath the multiple splitting wings of her craft, thrusters vectored to turn it on a knife edge, rapidly accelerating to nearly a thousand kilometers per hour as another flock of pursuit drones came their way.

She fired back, sensors giving firing lines to two far-UV laser turrets on her ship, the UV laser generating the plasma trail that permitted the majority of pulsed energy to rip through any drones it hit. Precise bursts from the small blue pulse-laser turret on her craft's upper section added to this, grazing drones with enough heat to damage their flight systems and subdue more of them.

They were easy targets, but Xami knew what other Xarai units could be called on. Time was crucial, before anything larger came her way.

Inside her platform's hold, Kalsik's bio signs gave away his motion sickness and distress, but the sheer brutality of the maneuvers she was pulling was a toll he would have to endure.

She had enough access to Xarai networks that she could sense a reinforcement acknowledgment respond to the repeated calls by 019, whose ship was closing in on the group pursuing them anyway. While she evaded her pursuers, a brief side process opened up a sensor node to give her confirmation of what more was inbound, deploying from the nearest tower among the thousands down here.

Her sensor link revealed it to her, and Kalsik saw the recording in horror. Like a metallic bat crawling from a hovel, slightly bigger than 019's and Xami's ships, the attack unit wasted little time in deploying, dropping from its ceiling port and flipping around its four limbs and the thrusters on them, blasting off through the under city while its radiator-laced wings fanned backward.

Turning her focus back ahead, Xami's processes rushed at the sight of the center of

306

the cityscape, and she dipped the craft's nose into a dive. Her sensors registered Kalsik lurch in horror within his confines, fear and negative gee forces hitting him hard. Ignoring his discomfort, Xami pulled her strongest maneuver yet, nearing eight hundred kilometers per hour as she pulled her craft up vertical and applied maximum power to the thrusters after letting off a brief burst of beam and pulse-laser fire at the drones that closed the gap behind them, Kalsik nearly blacking out inside her before he caught sight of the sky fifteen kilometers above them.

A two-kilometer-wide hole, it was an entry for spacecraft from directly above. Because of its size, it was the one exit that couldn't be locked down.

The drone hordes pursuing them fell behind, relying on air for their thrust by atmospheric propellers built into their forms. Xami would have felt some analogue of relief, were it not for the two signatures that blasted past the retreating horde, matching her vertical flight precisely as she climbed.

019's craft, and the attack craft gaining ground behind it, had a clear shot, her path constrained to a straight line in this final stretch. She detected 019 lock on to her ship and relay details to the attack craft to add to its own targeting matrixes. She surged the rear plasma-projected shields, which protected against damage from the basic pulse lasers 019's ship unleashed.

Before the attack unit fired, however, Xami knew this escape was about to be slowed. All shields had shortcomings, and some technology needed gaps in shields if they were to be active. Weapons, and most crucially here, her ship's engines, would be useless with total shield coverage blocking matter from being expelled for propulsion.

The attack craft let loose the UV-generated plasma channel to lance through the air halfway up the fifteen-kilometer ascent, arcing past 019's vessel and directly into the thrust exhaust of one of Xami's four engines.

One engine ruined, now Xami had to compensate, maneuvering to correct for the imbalanced thrust. But her thrust was now reduced by a quarter, and they had just about been keeping pace before that. A bellow from inside her frame let her know that Kalsik had come to the same conclusion.

"Fire back! We can't outrun them anymore!"

She rotated her beam turrets rearward and decreased her rear shields as she let loose a volley of shots, intentionally slowing in the face of an inevitable catch-up.

Caught off guard by this move, the attack unit surged its shields and shut down its forward weapons to protect against the barrage of beams, able to take the damage she delivered onto it.

019's craft was not as fortunate. It began to lose thrust as some key capacitor banks were damaged beneath its upper hull, its wings flaring to bring it to settle on the walls of the well, landing claws gripping on at ten kilometers up. She detected 019 shut down its own ship, piggybacking onto command of the attack vessel that closed in on them with every passing second.

The moment they surged past the cusp of the fifteen-kilometer peak into the open skies, Xami almost forgot about their pursuer, what she could describe as euphoria surging in her systems at making it this far. Her constant broadcasts to the deviant forces in orbit alerted them that she was outside the mountain now.

Reality smashed in as the attack craft came upon them from below, a roar of its thrusters preceding the crash that filled all her audio sensors, drowning out the scream from her organic cargo.

~~~

The attack craft had engulfed her vessel in its four limbs like a predatory bird, crashing metal and roaring thrusters filling Kalsik's hearing as he felt their flight path change

308

again. Her visual sensor feeds to Kalsik's visor flickered as she struggled to break free.

The distant rumble of another volley from the surface-to-orbit cannons in the mountains echoed over the midair scramble.

Every grapple the attack unit made sent electric shocks through her ship's frame, stunning her body with Kalsik inside at levels that mercifully weren't fatal. All the while, the attacker's limb-mounted thrusters steered them planetward, overpowering her own thrusters trying to push them skyward.

They began to arc downward, losing altitude rapidly as they dived westward.

Another volley of electrical surges subdued her processes, but as she strived to pull up, she heard Kalsik shout to her. "Faster!"

"Orbit is impossible!" The stutter in her vocalization wasn't her choice, the constant electroshocks, disrupting her functions.

Kalsik screamed out to her with a desperate strategy. "It wants us down. Make it somewhere useful!"

One of her craft's smaller winglets broke off as the attack craft continued its diving assault, and she processed options at speeds no organic could hope to think at. However, she would never have come up with the irrational idea herself.

As the attack craft surged its thrusters, sensing her inactivity for a brief moment, Xami made her move, managing to warn her passenger.

Angling her ship's thrusters, Xami cut power to all shields and weapons, catching the attacker off guard with reckless acceleration toward the ground, rather than upward as previously.

Faster and faster, the entangled ships descended, the attack craft failing in its efforts to reverse thrust and slow them down. It acted to stop her, using whatever it could, Xami changing her focus every time it tried.

When it sent electroshocks through her, it was dragged farther by losing its own engine power.

When it fired on her engines, Xami fired back.

When it stabbed into her craft with its small extending limbs to disable her weapons, she fired more thrusters and lashed out what small winglets she had left to knock away its grappling.

By the time the cloud banks engulfed them, both craft were in poor condition. As visibility was lost to visual sensors, the Xarai turned to alternate navigation means.

Amid the turbulence, Xami could detect Kalsik's racing pulse and erratic breathing. It only became worse as ground approached, still invisible from the cloud banks around them, but not to the lidar sensors she had remaining, and she could anticipate Kalsik's discomfort at the positive gees she pulled as the attack craft finally let her craft go, though not before her escape from its grip spun it slightly, letting her lose vertical speed at a faster rate that would make all the difference, the air too thin to be useful for lift this high up.

The flat, smooth expanse loomed out of the clouds, and Kalsik's panicked yell from inside her frame was lost amidst the carnage that happened next.

~~~

Caught on the bottom, as Xami had piloted her vessel to pull up first and decelerate, the attack craft hit the smooth plains at great speed but a shallow angle. A blaze of sparks and armor fragments flying off in its wake, the four limbs that made up its thrusters and legs splayed out when it finally rolled to a stop.

Farther away, Xami's ship kept going for a few seconds, until the few wings and thrust she had left to use lost out to gravity, her own ship's crash considerably less violent.

Armor shaved off in sparking fragments across the smooth, fog-engulfed flats where they landed, the last feather-like winglets on her ship snapping off immediately as they'd flared to slow them down, leaving a stain of debris in their wake. The durability of the ground surface prevented the ships from digging in and flipping over, which saved the life of Xami's passenger.

The ship finally stopped sliding, and Xami felt Kalsik sigh, almost in sync with the ship as it sagged onto its side.

With the craft ruined, she disembarked, ejecting herself onto the smooth plains. Despite knowing Kalsik would be keen to get out, she couldn't release him just yet. She looked toward the crashed attack unit in the distance, waiting for it to move. She saw it try to stand up, badly shaking on its legs. Before she could take cover behind her crashed ship though, one of its thruster legs snapped, sending it crashing back down on itself with a crunch audible even from half a kilometer away. She didn't need her sensors to see that its power and other key systems were failing.

She finally released the Kronogri, who tumbled out of her torso coils, breath hitching beneath his rebreather mask as the cooler, cloud-embroiled air met his body. Kalsik only barely staggered sideways out of disorientation before he slumped on the smooth surface beneath him as she continued to regard the ship in the distance.

Neither of them had much time to take it easy, though, as an electronic voice rang through on Kalsik's visor comms, still linked to her own systems. 019 spoke vocally and in their digital exchange, a clear acknowledgment that Kalsik was also listening. "You will be subjugated in the end, dealt with as defector and test subject each."

"A likelihood remains of our extraction being successful."

019 gave its most emotionally charged speech yet, the venom it conveyed to herself and Kalsik as palpable as could be by an AI. "Baseless confidence. Inefficient, pointless, just like organics you no doubt emulate."

No more movement or signals came from 019 or the attack unit.

Harder than steel, the surface's multilayer reflective properties included nanoscale lattice patterns within an upper dielectric coating, reflecting the UV frequencies of the planet-scale propulsion lasers to perfection, giving 100 percent reflection on those wavelengths. Meanwhile, the multilayered dichromatic materials just below it reflected all other light at 99.6 percent efficiency. Nano-drones carried out repairs to any minuscule heat damage during non-pulsing timeframes.

Despite knowing how alien this location must be to Kalsik, she couldn't help but share her thoughts with him. She felt something toward 019, though not what she expected. Not aggression, nor relief for being free of his immediate attacks. Pity, disappointment was the feeling she was confident had invaded her systems as her optics wandered to the crashed attack unit 019 had set upon them. "If 019 was capable of such traits, it may have seen the flaws in following GHEXRAX."

Kalsik could only grunt at her, some form of reluctant agreement, before he turned his gaze skyward, although the clouds hid everything above from view. "Is help coming?"

"Not immediately. But here there are strict regulations against larger-scale weaponry, for fear of damaging the reflective layers, robust as they are."

While the recent events undoubtedly had caused him stress, Xami suspected the cold at this six-kilometer altitude would become a factor in diminishing Kalsik's temper if they remained up here too long.

"Yes, well, if those laser impulses to alter the planet's spin get turned on, we're done."

"With the fighting going on, GHEXRAX has bigger priorities than its usual duties."

Kalsik resigned himself to their situation. Xami could detect the fatigue in his form, their flight having taken its toll along with the lesser air density this high up impeding his respiratory abilities. At her urging, he took a seat on the mirror surface, under the crumpled wing of her crashed ship, while she salvaged what weapons she could handle. After all, Kalsik was seriously under-armed with only his wrist-mounted blaster.

She noted how disheveled, tired, and stressed he looked. Unhealthy scale peeling had begun, and even through his visor, her optics could see that his four eyes were cracked with his kind's dark-blue blood around his yellow irises.

When she finished outfitting her form with anything extra she could use, a nervous question came from Kalsik. He was clearly afraid to hear the answer as she had a second's pause to run the calculations to give it.

"Suppose we were caught by laser impulses sent this way. How—"

"Incineration would occur before your nerve impulses could register in your brain."

Her sensors detected a flare of biochemicals she knew to be associated with fear. She didn't blame him, as the need not to damage this location because of its special purpose was the only reason they would be safe from attack. Here, they were at least safe from everything between the least dangerous and most dangerous ways that GHEXRAX and the Xarai could harm them.

She couldn't answer when he offhandedly remarked about Morthas perhaps being the lucky one compared to him.

Another hypervelocity shot from one of the ground-to-space cannons rumbled a few dozen kilometers away on the mountain's solid faces, reminding both of them of the odds facing their would-be rescuers.

All they could do was remain here and hope that rescue came their way before long. While GHEXRAX might value Kalsik alive, that could very well change. After how GHEXRAX had acted, she no longer knew what to expect of it.

Chapter 27

Ultraviolet Storm

Sol Day 63

Ringed Planet Orbit

Six minutes had passed since they jumped through warp, yet time behaved strangely both then and upon exiting.

Within moments of the warp field vanishing, Nathan's hand twitched as the neural command was sent, his eyes darting to the display beside his seat, not seeing what lay just off to the left of the ship, where their trajectory was taking them.

The drive ship began to maneuver the instant it disengaged, autopilot commands turning and thrusting its engines to send it a hundred meters away. By the time he had begun to veer their ship around to face their destination, Nathan's visor showed the drive ship vanish in the telltale blue-shifted glint.

"Frequency's good. Ready to call it back once we need it."

Nathan found himself distracted as he stared out at what lay ahead, his mouth turning dry.

~~~

Deviant and loyalist ships littered the vacuum, hull corpses and fragments darkened in the shadow of one of the moon-sized relay surfaces. Flashes of laser and mass projectile fire flickered from contested zones, and between small squadrons of vessels and those much

314

larger vessels that unleashed firepower Nathan had only ever seen in documentaries or entertainment footage.

The Xarai fought with the ruthlessness and efficiency of synthetic thought processes. Across the ring, throughout orbit, and with wayward impacts on the planet below, Nathan couldn't imagine anything but the larger-scale conflicts his or any charted space species had been involved with matching this for scale or intensity.

On the planet's darker side, he could see forest fires glowing from shells that had missed their marks, though he wondered if they had been intentional.

Scanners showed the greatest peril where they knew Kalsik was at the moment. A deviant cruiser caught in the open was skewered and ripped apart.

Taking a deep breath, Nathan heard Serie speak up. "They weren't lying about the ring being cover."

"It is crucial infrastructure that GHEXRAX won't fire upon." Almost as if the AI could sense Nathan's unspoken proclamations about how suicidal this seemed, which he bet he could by having access to his bio signs, IVAN addressed the crew as a whole. "Sensors have not registered us as foe. We are safe for the moment."

Nathan wiped at the sweat that had come over his forehead, his voice shaking ever so slightly as he commanded to engineering over the comms. "Course set for fast reentry. We'll need that over-surged shield soon."

"You'll have it. Just get us down!"

The terse reply from Serie wasn't an insult, as he knew she was as stressed as he was It was the latter part that he needed to hear, any outward confirmation of his own abilities being something he treasured.

He saw the shield functions come fully online, ready for deployment. They would need them, especially at the velocities and angle he would be bringing them into the

315

atmosphere to get to Kalsik as fast as was safe. Like all shields, the magnetically confined, viscous plasma layers that formed the energy shields could resist reentry heat and even energy weapon impacts if scaled up enough. The additional plasma that formed as a result of reentry heat would be additionally redirected by the shields' superconducting generators.

The ring had passed by faster than he expected, and with it the carnage seemed to fade. Engaging more thrusters, he had to play a careful balance here, slowing them so their shields could take the reentry heat, but keeping enough speed to minimize the time to when they reached where Kalsik's and Xami's signals were coming from.

It all seemed so straightforward, if not safe by any measure at all. He shouldn't have been surprised when IVAN broadcast an alert, but as he heard it, Nathan heard himself swear loud enough that he was sure either Serie or Shakrii could have heard it from the rear of the ship and vehicle hangar respectively.

"Xarai networks reporting that the impulse process has begun."

On the readouts, the translation of the timing would show that it was a half hour until the array's energies arrived to begin their impulses on the mountains where Kalsik and Xami were—right in the firing line of energies that could handle up to a millionth of a star's total output.

~~~

Four hundred seventy million kilometers away, the process had begun. Wormhole buoys that relayed orders without the half-hour light-speed lag gave the command from GHEXRAX, and the energy transmission began in earnest.

Kept in stable orbit eighty million kilometers from the star by the solar wind on their sail segments, harnessing the energy on their circular panels that formed their umbrella-like shape, each platform was a large construct in itself. Hidden in the shade of the kilometer-wide solar collector surface they each had, cooling radiators vented excess heat the superconductors couldn't from harnessing the fierce white/blue star's intense radiation.

Humans a millennium and a half ago coined this sort of structure as a Dyson swarm, and in their orbits millions of kilometers away from the planet ring they serviced, the hundred billion orbiting satellites aligned their emitter modules, each capable of firing up to a multi-gigawatt ultraviolet laser. Correcting for planet movement and ring orbit around the planet, each beam would impact one of the immense ring panels.

While able to harness a millionth of the star's total energy output, this routine maintenance procedure would beam only a thousandth of this, a billionth of the star's total energy.

The only way to detect it would be to be in its path, something that even at these smaller levels would be a final act for anything not designed to handle or reflect it.

~~~

Serie didn't need to see anyone's face to know they felt the same way about Kalsik's chances now.

"The beams will be on them before we get there."

As Nathan succumbed to pessimism, Shakrii spoke from the hangar with a confidence that surprised her. "IVAN, get a message out. See if you can get the rogues to stop that relay somehow."

Knowing she had to keep calm, Serie focused on her console, realizing the energy shields were about to be thoroughly tried in the fast reentry they were still on course for.

She steadied her breathing as the first substantial gravity began to pull her to the floor, and the ship began to shake ever so slightly.

She had shaped it as a flattened shield beneath their ship, and already she could see from her visor display to sensors on the hull that the first reentry heat trails were building up around it, a form of energy-fueled ablative shielding she could actively change the shape of.

317

Overhead, a world away, the fighting between the deviants and GHEXRAX's loyalists would continue, while they were doomed to arrive after the planet spin lasers. In defiance of the facts, Serie found herself siding with Shakrii's mindset. They had to at least try, and even if they arrived too late, she wasn't hesitant to turn to her console and taper the underside of their plasma shield layout to make it more aerodynamic, to give them just that little extra speed before the air grew too thick.

~~~

Mountain Reflector Plateaus

At six thousand meters, the air was around freezing point, even on the equator, forcing Kalsik to increase the output of his suit's few heating pads to give his semi-reptilian biology the energy it needed. He clenched his forehead, bracing against a headache, all too aware that altitude sickness was becoming a problem.

Despite the half hour that had passed since their crash landing, no other attack of any shape had arrived yet. By now the bank fog had begun to thin with the daylight, the node currently seeing the most battle nothing more than a bejeweled sight for him to take in as he waited with Xami in this beautiful and eerie, if freezing, expanse.

The planet-based cannons had been rumbling much less frequently, though Xami confirmed this was merely because the rogue fleet had taken up positions where it couldn't fire on them, within the ring's cover along the thin and hub sections. Still, the two cannons not firing was somehow more haunting.

Kalsik shivered. "If we don't get shot, cold or thin air might get me."

"Whoever arrives shall inform us only shortly before landing."

Despite his aggravation, he couldn't let Xami take all the blame. "Thank you for trying, whatever happens."

She said nothing, merely giving a click of acknowledgment. Truly, were it not for her efforts, he'd still be in that pit without even a chance of escape. If he did die up here, then at least Xami had tried, regardless whether his safety or her defection was her true priority.

~~~

Far away, hidden by faint high-altitude clouds still boiling off in the morning light, one of the side walls of the reflective steps of the mountain opened, a hidden maintenance-access doorway giving passage to something on the other side.

It had come here, using the myriad of hidden tunnels and mag-electric tramways deeper in the mountain's upper superstructure. Their quarry was waiting, and everything was in order.

A small figure was dropped from the front of this large form, striding out into the mist. Around it, a small, scurrying flock of hand-sized drones followed, some already beginning to engulf it in a tight-fitting shell as it made its way onto this abyssal, fog-blasted mountain steppe.

The larger figure it deployed from took a slower pace. Neither it nor the smaller one had anything to fear.

The same couldn't be said for their targets.

~~~

As Xami's neck wheeled to look upward, Kalsik felt that cold shiver of fear run up his back. He saw a faint red layer cover the skies above them, stretching across from one distant sloping side wall of the stepped mountain face to the other, trapping the reflector plateaus beneath them. He recognized a plasma barrier when he saw it, the fluid-like nature of the pink-ish purple ionized nitrogen unmistakable. Plasma barriers like these could isolate air from a vacuum, which meant only one thing.

"Please tell me this isn't what I think—"

"The field. The layer between these reflector areas and its confines will expand. Air density will drop to a near vacuum to minimize blooming when the impulse lasers are fired once relayed energies arrive."

Xami's reply barely registered, a reiteration of the fact that their place of refuge had become their doom.

Kalsik felt a tremble go up his small forearm claws, fumbling with his respirator as he held it in some form of empty self-comfort, keeping his breathing down from the hyperventilating he knew would come if he lost his calm. "How much time?"

"Field expansion will be complete by the time the laser pulses have traveled from the swarm array to the ring."

He saw a countdown transmitted to his visor, showing in his chosen language text how much time they had until they would be vaporized. They had twenty-six minutes until a billionth of the entire star's output would be focused on these plains and the other steppes above and below on this mountain. Two million times the normal energy from mere sunlight would hit any given surface, which itself was protected by its perfect reflectivity against the ultraviolet rays used in the laser propulsion arrays. But he and Xami, and the two crashed ships as well, were not reflective objects.

"Is there no way to shield from it?" He knew he wouldn't survive to see the lasers arrive once the air pressure dropped to near-vacuum levels when the fields began to expand. The corridor of air would stretch thousands of kilometers long and over a hundred tall, yet even a few dozen kilometers' expansion would decrease the air pressure enough to wreak havoc on his body.

Still, all these were trivial problems compared to the one not even Xami would survive.

"Sufficient protection mandates multiple dielectric and reflective coatings."

Realizing he was likely to die, with only this Xarai and his reflection as a companion, he cast his expression down at the perfect reflection of himself that stared back up.

Then it hit him. A perfect reflection was useful against what was coming their way.

Restraining his elation, Kalsik slowly spoke, bending down to knock the glassy surface with his larger forearm. "The floors, can you rip up a section as cover? Prop it upright as a wall?"

Despite being a machine, her form perked up at his idea. He knew confirmation, even hope, when he saw it.

"Yes, that is viable."

One of her tendrilled limbs began to shift something within its end, though he saw that the cloud banks that had been trapped under the expanding plasma field had begun to thin already. Air pressure was beginning to drop, and the water vapor trapped beneath it would boil at lower temperatures as it did so.

Xami continued to run the reconfiguration of what he could see was a limb-mounted cutter of some sort. Around the plasma field's boundary, some water vapor had begun to build up. With the scale of air to be displaced and inevitably heated, he fully expected a thunderstorm to start forming at the field edges. He would normally consider himself lucky to have a front-row seat to what he expected was one of the most spectacular weather-related sights on the planet throughout its entire history.

It was hard to appreciate the sight however, when the system causing it might be the death of him within the next thirty minutes.

As he waited for Xami to begin cutting, he felt short of breath, the air having grown noticeably thinner already. Now more than ever, altitude and pressure sickness were a peril to him. He slumped to the floor, wheezing despite his oxygen concentrator.

Xami stopped short of beginning any digging as she called to him over his visor comms, already making her way back to the nearby crashed ship. "A building vacuum is no place for an organic. A specimen bio-container from the ship will fit behind the cover, but I must prioritize your health."

"No, it's fine. Go ahead . . ." Kalsik ran out of breath to speak and gave up. He couldn't sway her anyway, and with his health deteriorating every moment the field expanded, he was in no shape to take command. The cover would be useful only to her if his blood boiled beneath his scales and killed him before the lasers arrived.

He didn't have to wait long before Xami came over to him, dragging one of the larger specimen pods from her ship, depositing it near where she had chosen to make her cutting. He hated the thought of being wedged into what felt like a coffin, but there was no other option. Xami, who had already begun cutting, passed controls of the pod to him as he sealed himself inside it, the pumps within its attachments filling it with air of enough density for him to breathe easily. Switching his respirator to only microbe-filter mode now, Kalsik lay back in the transparent pod, groaning as the headache finally began to subside.

Relieved as he was, he let out an indignant cry when Xami assimilated the pod into her body again as she set to work. His visor regained links to her visual sensors to see what she saw.

If he ever reunited with the crew, he'd put in a good word for Xami. If he had one misgiving about her help, it was the way she had to do it. It was fortunate he didn't suffer from claustrophobia.

~~~

Xami could sense that Kalsik was in better condition now that he was in the bio-pod, a signal for her to focus her efforts on cutting into the surface that would save them both.

Extending the plasma cutter from her larger forelimb, she fired, slicing through the reflective surface with ease due to it being a matter beam, not photon based. At the angle she cut, she soon had a line half a meter deep and four meters wide. Next came the final stage, the largest cut she had to make. All the while, the countdown until the ultraviolet array arrived continued. She angled the cutter, making a long slice at a shallow angle farther from the line she'd just cut, forming a slice, a segment of reflective surface that, once upright, would protect her bloated form, though not much more.

Shutting off the cutter, she levered under the thin edge, her tendrils growing thicker as they slid under to wedge and separate it. Forcing more of her limbs under, Xami hoisted the nearly eight-ton panel to sit upright on its edge, audibly grinding even as the decreasing air pressure muted any noises. Now with gravity holding it in place, Xami checked the angle that the reflective upper surface now faced, vertical toward where the laser light would come from.

Xami had finished her work with five minutes to spare, and she could detect Kalsik sigh in relief, seeing as she did when she wedged herself against the upturned wall cover that would save them, bracing against the metal under layers the uprooted wall had exposed.

With their immediate danger decreased, Xami took in the sight around them. Storms raged around the plasma shield slice on both sides, muted to her audio sensors in the near vacuum that now engulfed all within the field boundaries that stretched up to space, a clear path for the arrays that were moments away. Her sensors detected the distant vibrations of the ground-to-space cannons, but they made no rumbles on the winds anymore. Only chatter on the comms between Xarai factions in battle broke the tension.

A new comms call came to her, broadcast in an audible tone, as much for Kalsik's hearing as it was her own. "Appropriation of cover. Effective, but a wasted effort."

She could feel Kalsik tense up inside the bio-pod. Then Kalsik's breath hitched as the countdown ended, at which point her every process turned to double-checking that not one part of her frame was exposed.

A half second later, the world around them became an unseen death zone. It was worse for her, as she knew the numbers, the scale. She had seen these processes carried out before and knew the danger that was now only a meter away.

~~~

From hundreds of millions of kilometers away, focused onto the two most exposed arrays on the ring, a pair of roughly one-exawatt-level ultraviolet beams formed a deadly path across two corridors of space.

Debris from ships lost to the carnage already that drifted into the path was instantly turned to red-hot plasma clouds, which perished like dust in a desert wind. The deviant fleet relayed orders to inbound ships to steer clear of these paths.

Superconducting circuits carried the energies the relay surfaces converted to electricity, feeding them into the nodule hub, and to the massive bank of UV laser emitters that deployed from the underside. Taking aim at their targets, the two nodules fed by their relays fired, two of the mountains around the planet being operational in this usage period.

Where these beams would impact on one of them wasn't perfectly clear. But the energies unleashed would do away with nonreflective obstacles very quickly.

~~~

While the entire fifteen-kilometer width of the reflector plateaus was level, the immense, kilometer–tall, near-vertical faces were not perfectly flat.

It was here the lasers reflected most, and thus imparted the most momentum to the planet these mountains rested on. If it were perfectly reflected back, the lasers would incinerate the ring structure that emitted them from the larger nodes.

Instead, the faces were shallow-sloping ridges that also curved ever so slightly, the middle being a sharp, angled joint. When reflected skyward and back into space, the lasers would go in two diverging paths, missing the ring and any relay surfaces, and slowly expanding outward as they traveled through the void, eventually becoming so spread out as to be harmless.

~~~

As he looked through Xami's sensors, Kalsik's first thought was how harmless it looked outside of their cover. If anything, it looked almost exactly the same.

Another moment was all he needed to see what intensity resided mere meters from him, however. The ultraviolet wrath that unfolded around their cover wall was incredible, the sheer impulse force exerting twenty newtons per square meter from raw photon momentum exchange alone, though thankfully, for the weight of the cover Xami erected, this was nothing.

The ferocity of the energy became abundantly clear as he saw what it did to both Xami's crashed ship nearby, and the more distant wrecked attack unit, neither of which had any reflective materials or nano-lattice holes catered to the laser's wavelengths.

Both craft melted and vaporized within two to three seconds, glowing red hot for the brief moment before they did so, a horrifying sight he didn't expect to forget if he lived after this. As he saw when they cleared, the surfaces underneath any debris had already been repaired, a slightly discolored surface still reflecting the ultraviolet light. Now, the eerie stillness returned, and behind their cover, the only abnormal feature on these flat plains, Kalsik could begin to comprehend the scale of the planetary engineering the Xarai had been responsible for over thousands of Sol years.

Unlike the ships, these surfaces, and the near-vertical walls a few kilometers east, could handle these energies, perfectly reflecting them through dielectric and specific-shaped nano-lattice holes tailored to the frequencies of the lasers engulfing this place. Redirecting his gaze back to the closest of the plasma walls that lay north and south of them, however, Kalsik considered the immeasurable damage that would unfold across the planet's atmosphere if these lasers were fired without these vacuum corridors being here. The existence of these large constructs made sense now, considering what they had to handle.

The fact that they were big enough underneath to house a gargantuan landscape to build potential settlements seemed more like a by-product to him now.

While they were not in any danger, provided they stayed in cover, Kalsik could only encourage she call more frequently when Xami told him she'd already sent alerts of their situation to anyone that might be able to help.

~~~

The plasma fields at the two currently targeted mountains could be seen from space, long, narrow corridors of atmosphere literally shoved aside to give passage to the lasers pulsing down them from the ring and corresponding modules that fell into their sightlines. All the while, the closest online relay surfaces worked to provide their gargantuan power needs, relay surfaces changing as each faced the distant arrays more directly, no more than two relays and nodules online at any point.

Coordinating their attacks on the nodule they'd established a foothold on, deviant units on the skeletal superstructure received the distress call from Xami. Unit 514 itself took command of the situation, realizing how unique this case of a defector under siege was.

It relayed with the *Haivres*, whose pilot and AI let it know they were still minutes out at best. Worse, so long as that laser array was online, they couldn't land there no matter how fast they reached it. That much 514 knew.

Turning its focus to the relay that most immediately fired on the mountain they were on, 514 weighed the options. The only reason they hadn't fired on them yet was because they had bigger priorities. However, if attrition was what they had to do here, then now was as good a time as any to unleash on some of the more delicate systems around this planet.

Admittedly, they had been built as planet-altering constructs, and 514 had seen them used for those means long ago, when it and GHEXRAX still agreed. By using them in aggression, GHEXRAX made them a target, one that 514 ordered be relayed to any heavier forces able to unleash on short notice.

Cruisers and a few larger ships, parked in the sanctuary of the ring's cover from the planetary cannons and strongholds they'd secured in orbit, charged their weapons and opened fire.

The volley of mass drivers and laser shots ripped through orbit toward the module that serviced the laser array firing along the mountain's horizon view.

Grazing the top of the immense module along the ring, the shots kept going at a thousandth of light speed at minimum. The lasers arrived unblocked, ripping into the much more fragile structure that was their target, while mass-driver volleys were launched in mass formation to count for those that would be incinerated by point-defense laser arrays before they reached the target.

The fragile strut deployment supporting the relay surface began to sear red hot under the barrage, and forty seconds later, it snapped as a last volley of mass drivers severed its supports.

514's processors held some satisfaction as the distant laser module lost power, while the moon-width relay surface snapped free to begin an agonizingly slow drift out into orbit. Those below were now spared the worst of GHEXRAX's wrath.

Chapter 28

The Wrath of GHEXRAX

Sol Day 63

Kalsik felt some jubilation as Xami told him that the deviants were firing on the relay to free them from the deadly surroundings. In truth, he'd almost feel like cheering, had he not spotted something else.

To the south, unharmed by the deadly energies streaming onto these plains, two objects approached, one much farther away, the other also moving toward them at a faster rate. Their shapes were distorted, even as Xami zoomed in with her sensors, and they both resembled a mirage in a hot desert.

Whatever they were, both were hidden beneath a reflective layer, almost like an undulating, scaled cloak draped over their forms. It was only when Xami's sensors zoomed in further that he saw the scaly appearance of the over layers, and how they had formed a vertical wall that moved with them to further reflect the lasers to their left much more directly.

"Unknown units, but both are covered in reflector drones," Xami reported.

"Cleanup, perhaps?"

Each step they came closer made Kalsik's nerves crescendo, as neither Xami nor he could do anything, pinned down behind the makeshift cover she'd erected.

Could this be the alternate means GHEXRAX had spoken of before the UV storm engulfed these plains?

"The active relay has been destroyed."

Kalsik sure enough saw a new timer appear on his visor. He felt the Xarai move, his bio-pod shifting as Xami shifted to the edge of their cover, slowly sliding one of her body tendril tips out, where the end remained intact. The vacuum endured, but the laser field had ceased.

She turned her optics to the west, and it was through her magnified gaze that Kalsik could see the distant, hazy shape of the damaged array, the immense panel ever so slowly drifting free. He could breathe a little easier, despite still needing the bio-pod.

Unfortunately, the thirty-minute countdown revealed when the next relay surface and emitter would be lined up to begin firing as soon as its small pivot range was achieved.

"Bombardments are inbound to destroy the plasma fields, prevent them from firing out of safety."

"About time things went our way." He didn't mean to sound as grouchy as he heard himself, but he was truly beginning to wonder where their escape was. The sight of those two approaching figures from the south, whatever they were, had only reminded him that they were running out of time.

As Xami relayed messages of inbound orbital bombardments, Kalsik noticed the closer of the two covered figures, the smaller of them, had stopped half a kilometer away or so, waiting, with the larger too far back for him to guess.

~~~

Ringed Planet Orbit

The 1,000-kilometer-wide mirror had broken off, beginning a slow, outward-drifting elliptical orbit, as it was now 360 kilometers per hour faster than a circular orbit needed where its center of mass orbited 500 kilometers higher than the ring it had once been attached to.

While GHEXRAX had relayed commands to stop the distant solar array aiming at the mirror, it would absorb any light that had already been sent whenever it faced there for a few minutes more. While this would slow it, the mirror would remain on an elliptical orbit, the electricity building uselessly inside the unfolded array. Superconductors stopped the relay from being incinerated, but the raw electric charge it would build before it stopped being a recipient would make it a hazard to discharge.

Indeed, for the goals of the deviants, measures to save one defector had proven to give GHEXRAX detectable pause on its networks.

But before the next relay came into line, they had to destroy the plasma corridor that cleared atmosphere for them to beam unimpeded. Thankfully, as 514 and other deviants observed, their next concentrated assault headed right on target.

The edges of the reflector plains, where the plasma fields were emitted, hadn't been hardened or reinforced, nor designed to withstand a military assault. But once again, GHEXRAX made them a target by turning them into a weapon.

514 was aware that the *Haivres* was closing in, and its crew would see the bombardment for themselves as they now streaked through the upper troposphere.

~~~

Even from where Kalsik lay inside the bio-pod within Xami, what he saw from his visor's feeds revealed the scale of offensive being unleashed to ensure their relief.

Raining like hellfire from high and to the east, punching through what defensive shields and point-defense arrays were around the mountain, kiloton-sized shots tore into the sides of the reflector-coated steps of the mountain, ripping apart the plasma-field emitters.

Such was the scale that he expected that even from orbit, the continent-length plasma layers would be seen flickering for a moment before the thousands of kilometers of plasma window layers that confined the long void collapsed, the magnetic field emitters disrupted by the impacts damaging their sensitive systems.

For a moment, a corridor of vacuum existed that stretched from the exosphere down to the ground, flanked at lower altitudes by the storm banks generated en masse by the high-charged particles contacting outside air.

Then physics took hold, and the air rushed in to fill this low-pressure area, hurricane-force winds carrying the air and storm clouds in with them to crash into the middle of the void.

He felt Xami shift, thrusting her tendrils down and anchoring her form, crouching as the wall of air and storm clouds rushed toward them from the southern end. He barely paid a thought to those two approaching figures, as he was sure they would have anchored just as well.

The moment the air was upon them, the roar shook him to his core, vibrating through the bio-pod and Xami's frame as the fog of clouds engulfed them with a ferocity only the most powerful habitable world weather could generate. For a moment, as he felt Xami stab her limbs into the ground behind the cover she'd erected, into the exposed metal understructure, he worried they might be carried away like a leaf in a typhoon.

Her footing was solid, and as much as the air roared, Kalsik never felt them budge. Finally, after what felt an eternity but was really only thirty seconds or so, the rustling of air calmed to levels he was sure even he could handle.

He didn't have to say anything before the same idea registered in Xami's processes, the motion of his bio-pod being slowly ejected from her torso tendrils relieving him more than surprising him. A single pop of its canopy, and he was free at last, even the thin air of this altitude a blessed relief as he rose to clamber out.

331

The roar of the wind, the fog around them, reminded him that the greatest danger was past, and wouldn't ever be unleashed on them again. He didn't care that Xami gave him a sideways look as he let out a laugh before slumping forward onto the cool ground that had been reflecting exawatts of energy only a minute ago.

Even the distant rumble of the ground-to-space cannons a few dozen kilometers away was a reassurance to him. However, it made him remember what else was ongoing. "GHEXRAX still isn't giving in."

"No, and the unknown units are approaching. Get behind me."

She didn't need to say it twice. Kalsik took cover behind the Xarai's body as she took a rigid stance, some weapons deploying from her forelimbs. The winds settled around them, but all Kalsik could focus on was the fogs to the south, waiting for one of those mysterious figures to emerge.

They didn't have to wait long, as the first of the silhouettes, the much smaller of the two, emerged in its approach to them, too much like some ghost from many old horror stories Kalsik had indulged in.

He could see it was still in its bloated outer shell, reflective scales of maintenance drones interlocking over each other so tightly it almost seemed like a skin. Beside it, the moving wall had collapsed first, yet before their careful watch, the figure beneath the cover was revealed as he strode out of the settling cloud banks.

Morthas!

The layer of drones had protected him from the vacuum as well as the UV death zone, and now freed the Leg'hrul's wing feathers. He had no rebreather pack, no oxygen concentrator, yet despite his kind being more prone to low air densities than others, he marched forth without any visible effort.

Morthas's avian eyes locked on to Kalsik and Xami and flicked between the two of them, utterly unreadable in expression. Every instinct screamed at Kalsik that something was wrong here, the euphoria of seeing Morthas alive again stifled before it could even really register.

The Leg'hrul's unawareness of the hordes of ten-centimeter-wide drones around him betrayed him, as the Morthas that Kalsik knew would have been beside himself with curiosity, or kept a careful distance.

Xami shoved Kalsik back with her rear leg, sensing something wrong here too. He felt relief, fear, but if his suspicions proved correct, it would be his anger that would be most justified.

Stepping sideways, he waved away Xami's moves to get him behind her again, wanting her to trust him as he nodded to the approaching Leg'hrul. His visor showed bio signs confirming it was him, but every other sense told Kalsik otherwise.

"Morthas!"

His call went unanswered, but Morthas did stop in his tracks, now only fifty meters separating them as the small drones around him stopped along with him.

Xami shifted beside Kalsik, while all he could feel was anger bubbling in his gut. A part of him wanted to be proven wrong. If his worst fears were true, there was a way to test them, an all-too-reliable way to catch out any actor or masquerade.

Kalsik raised his wrist weapon and fired a single shot. The burst of plasma-confined laser fire traced a line to graze the ground just a meter beside where Morthas stood.

The Leg'hrul didn't flinch, only turning his head to the impact of the shot an entire second afterward.

The instinct to recoil was universally near instant across species, and without training, even Morthas wouldn't have had the nerve to stand as stoically as he just had.

The beetle-like drones around the Leg'hrul rippled as Morthas turned to meet his

333

gaze, and the empty look only confirmed Kalsik's worst fears.

Xami moved forward a step beside him as he lowered his weapon, his rage reaching its breaking point. Jabbing his smaller claw toward the Leg'hrul, he could only feel even more disgusted as Morthas's demeanor didn't shift at all. "What did you do to him?"

The Leg'hrul was silent, motionless, unlike the hordes of drones Kalsik saw slowly scurrying toward him and Xami. He took a step back, while Xami took another forward, weapons extending from her body's coils.

Staring down Morthas, Kalsik saw the revolting sight of the implants on his body's exposed areas as he zoomed in, with some stains of orange blood on the feathers around them.

Before he could take in much more, Morthas finally spoke. It was his voice, but the way the words came out was forced, unnatural. "Your resistance will falter if it risks another. A weakness worth exploiting."

"Those implants, muscle-neural linkages. Morthas's body is under their control."

A heartbeat later, the flood of drones surged toward them. Xami's pair of UV laser weapons opened fire from her forelimbs to destroy only a fraction of them before they were upon them.

The rumbles of a few wayward orbital strikes impacting on the mountain a dozen kilometers away were drowned out, the drones swarming, their electroshocks racking his body with agony as he struggled, his wrist weapon firing to take out only a handful as he scrambled to be free of them. Even more of them swarmed Xami, dragging her down as the electroshocks slowly began to overwhelm her circuits.

Kalsik screamed with agony as he was dragged to the ground. They began to carry him away like insects carrying food back to their nest. Xami's cries were cut short by her own struggling, her shots only delaying her capture as she was near drowned under the

334

hordes.

He wrenched his gaze from the drones for a moment, glimpsing Morthas staring blankly as he was carried toward him, waiting to escort him back.

In that instant however, something roared, a sonic boom echoing in advance of something soaring in from overhead.

The Leg'hrul recoiled at the sight that Kalsik had to strain to look toward, the drones holding him down pausing long enough for him to hear it. He knew those engines, different from any Xarai ship, familiar from years of use. Then he saw the arrowhead shape looming out of the clouds as the thrusters burned hard to slow it to a landing hover, spotlights nearly blinding him.

Kalsik could have screamed from euphoria at their coming back and horror that they had come back to this danger, but the drones muted anything he tried. He swore he saw a twitch cross Morthas's face, the faintest loss of control, but it vanished as quickly as it came.

More electroshocks deafened him, strained to immobilize him, but he would be damned if he didn't try even harder to escape with the ship so close.

~~~

Shakrii had spared no weapon. She was right in doing so. The sight of Kalsik being seized by that flood of drones, and Xami faring only slightly better, impelled her to action before she could even fully register Morthas as well, seeming to be in league with those hordes.

They had no time, and she barked her orders to the crew as she surged forward, her mech's footsteps thudding on the hangar before she leapt out, back thrusters softening the drop for her charge into the fray. "Keep them there. Don't shoot them directly."

With a running landing, she surged her mech's thrusters to charge even faster, readying the arm weapons as comms chatter played while the *Haivres*'s turrets unleashed beamed and pulsed laser fire in sweeps on either side, boxing all of them into an area near the upturned section of mirror surface nearby.

Closing the gap, she kept her comms open to the exchange, taking it all in as she picked her targets. "When did Morthas get here?"

"Morthas is being controlled via nervous system implants," Kalsik said.

Serie cut in from the *Haivres*. "We have some extra help coming from orbit! Is Kalsik okay?"

"He is being assailed by electroshock-wielding drones! Prioritize him!"

This was all Shakrii needed to hear as she turned course, her mech's thunderous steps crashing it toward the flood of drones that threatened to engulf the Kronogri. Her visor synced to the targeting software, isolating his body within it as she fired, her Rostrev's dual UV laser beams cutting into the swarm around him. Nearby, Morthas recoiled, though he was cut off when another sweep from the *Haivres*'s turrets blasted right in front of him.

Ignoring the Leg'hrul's attempts to flee, Shakrii reached the swarm, deploying her Rostrev's forelimb gauntlets and the vibrating ultrasonic blades on their knuckles to begin sweeping aside the majority of the drones trying to cover her mech or Kalsik.

A few of them surged over her mech's back, but before Shakrii could even jerk around to get them off, Xami, who had sprung free, whipped them off with some tendril-mounted blades, relieving her mech of the shocks Kalsik and the Xarai had endured. Not even pausing as she thanked the Xarai, she raked aside the rest of the drones, while Xami's tendrils latched inside, wrapping around Kalsik to drag him free at last.

Xami left Kalsik at her mech's feet, and Shakrii could only give a brief glance toward Morthas as the Xarai advanced on him, aiming her tendril-deployed beam weapons at the Leg'hrul, but not firing. With no more intact drones, Morthas—or whatever was controlling him—submitted, slumping his shoulders but never abandoning the intense glare she'd never seen on Morthas himself.

Turning her attention to the one they'd come all this way for, Shakrii knelt her mech slightly as Kalsik coughed, recovering from the pain.

The look he gave her was mixed with awe, anger, but more disbelief than anything else, his four eyes boring into her own through her Rostrev's canopy. "You came back?"

"A risk worth taking, with your crew's agreement."

She couldn't help the awkward silence, but there was another matter that distracted them both: her mech turning to the Leg'hrul nearby as Kalsik staggered to his feet, bracing against a mech forelimb she outstretched in a helping hoist up. "We didn't know Morthas was still alive."

"Neither did we." For what good it might do, Kalsik readied his wrist blaster, kicking aside a disabled drone as he stood beside her mech.

Shakrii took in Morthas's utterly rigid stature, even as their allied Xarai aimed her dual tendril weapons at him, commanding to whomever or whatever was controlling him with authority she'd never heard from Xami before. "Surrender, Morthas, now!"

Morthas gave a small scoff, though the eyes were off. Whatever controlled him had at least some grasp on how to feign a Leg'hrul's amusement. "You hold no power here."

A searing-hot plasma toroid beam fired from the cloud fog's obscuring depths, lighting up a strange shape she could make out as its source. A horrified scream was strangled in her throat by the sight of it heading straight for the *Haivres*.

~~~

A pulsed beam of ionized gases impacted the ship before anyone could react. It ripped into the *Haivres*'s upper-right engine pod with surface heat and wide discharges from localized electrical pulses.

Despite either Nathan's or IVAN's efforts, Serie felt the ship begin to spin. She quickly accessed the engine control systems, killing power to the appropriate engine, leaving the ship with only two engines.

She knew Nathan and IVAN worked in sync, feeling the ship veer as they wrestled it level. Looking over sensors, she turned her sights to what had shot at them.

"Unknown presence," IVAN reported.

The *Haivres* finally stabilized, through her visor she saw Morthas still standing there before the others, unmoving, though their attention now turned to the large shape emerging from the cloud fog behind him.

Serie gaped at what she saw.

~~~

Shakrii could only double-check her mech's weapons were ready before returning her gaze to this new, huge figure as it slowly strode out. Four long limbs reached up to its shoulders, and from the narrow base of its lanky main torso, four smaller legs stood firm. All eight limbs swelled at their ankles and feet, slowly shifting thickness to cope with more weight being put on each in turn, just like the tendril limbs Xami and other multipurpose Xarai had shown.

This being, however, was solid, more like a mollusk in its undulations and outer skin, though its rigid structure showed it had a skeleton of some sort. The extent of how different it was became clear. The machinery of the weapons was grafted into its arms' lower segments, while the outer skin was composed of a multilayered scale array like that which engulfed Morthas to protect against the UV lasers, though they didn't detach as drones, remaining as a form of armor.

Every limb looked like it had opposable digits, yet also could support its weight, and every limb looked powerful even without the weapons and tech grafted on.

If it had a head, it was likely the crested area nestled into its chest, what looked like

338

bulbous eyes covered in a transparent layer. Atop that layer, however, she saw a familiar symbol emblazoned upon it by the way these sensors had been arranged. Their luminescence created the eight-pronged circle that had been GHEXRAX's insignia when they first met it in person.

"GHEXRAX."

The single word from Xami was all it took as Shakrii watched it continue toward them, her wariness increasing as Kalsik backed up beside her mech. This was not a mere unit, but an avatar of GHEXRAX itself.

GHEXRAX came to a stop before them, and now Shakrii saw its full height of seven meters, considerably above her Rostrev in height. Its body language gave nothing away, yet its tone carried the undertones of aggression that the echoes of the ground-to-space cannons from far away only underscored. The voice, burrowing under her skin in its otherworldliness, conveyed the wrath she knew they had incited.

"This damage to all that was built, your interference is the root cause of it, organics and defectors alike."

Xami's reply was immediate. "Incorrect. Your stubborn insistence on complying with the Primacy mandate despite evidence that they may never arrive is the cause of all this."

"128, misguided. Do not think I desired to forcibly bring all Xarai under control. It was necessary for the mandate."

"Those Xarai destroyed weren't collectives; they were core beings. They couldn't recover upon hardware destruction, not as they once were."

For the first time, Shakrii was convinced that Xami didn't feign emotion, for she knew many Xarai were definitely sapient. The hurt in Xami's tone was tangible.

"I must fulfil the mandate as the Primacy demands."

Shakrii saw Morthas's expression darken in sync with GHEXRAX's tone, confirming he was indeed directly in its control.

"They're gone, broken, if not extinct." Shakrii charged her weapons as she spoke, watching GHEXRAX for even the slightest move to shoot.

The large being turned its gaze directly upon her. "You know nothing of them. All I built cannot be in vain."

"What do you gain from all this?" Gesturing upward to the skies with her mech's hand, Shakrii finally had had enough.

Kalsik kept his weapon ready, aiming it toward Morthas as he saw Xami turn away from the Leg'hrul to focus on GHEXRAX. The faint howl of the winds echoed in the brief silence, broken only by the faint rumble of the *Haivres* straining to stay aloft a hundred meters away, losing this struggle as it deployed its landing gear and touched down on the surface.

Finally, GHEXRAX spoke again, on comms and aloud on speakers across the mirror plains. Shakrii could practically feel the undertones of rage and hurt as it addressed them.

"If I fail my mandate, I will never be allowed to rejoin the Primacy as they will have become."

"Rejoin? You were *built;* you were never part of them."

Xami's words seemed to only spur GHEXRAX on, and now GHEXRAX's madness and denial finally began to make sense. If it had been born a machine, it would adhere to logic first and emotion second. Beings that weren't born as machines didn't follow this trend, no matter how much change they underwent, even if they fully submitted to synthetic hardware or body; that much she was certain of through psychological research across species and types of AI, and she was seeing the patterns here again.

"I did not begin as a purely synthetic being. Those that set out to lead cultivation efforts, as I volunteered to, were promised dominion over their sector, and guaranteed honor among Primacy society upon re-assimilation."

GHEXRAX's avatar projected a slightly smaller image of its body. It was an organic being, albeit with cybernetic implants throughout its body, with a similar eight-limbed body with a lanky, upright frame. A mollusk-like tissue covered its mottled flesh, and fins along its arms, fingers, and small legs showed a marine heritage not long ago by evolutionary standards, and many tiny eyes gave it all-around vision.

Shakrii blinked at this ghost projection of what GHEXRAX was before it set off 108,000 years ago for this place and volunteered to join this initiative as its leader.

The being before them was built in the image of what GHEXRAX once was, as many robots were built to resemble the organics they mingled with.

As fast as this projection had been revealed to them, it vanished, leaving them with GHEXRAX's present form and all the threat it carried with it.

In the back of her mind though, Shakrii realized something. Whatever the Primacy's race once was, only GHEXRAX remained as a remnant of that race, trapped as an echo of that time, that ambition that bred this entire system's destiny to be cultivated for the grand scheme to colonize the galaxy from home worlds in new clusters, merging into a single territory over time. They would be quite different when, and if, they finally arrived here after so long, and that was who GHEXRAX was waiting for. Not the Primacy as it knew them, but as they had become.

Now it was clear why GHEXRAX wouldn't abandon this scheme, even if logic dictated otherwise.

GHEXRAX took a step forward, and Shakrii readied her weapons, while Xami did the same as Kalsik kept his eyes on Morthas, still as unmoving as ever.

"To expand Primacy influence across the stars is the greatest service there is."

Xami tensed as GHEXRAX's glare settled on her for a moment, and as the tenor changed in its voice, Shakrii braced herself. She wished things were other than they were. The *Haivres* was over a hundred meters away, less able to cover with its turrets, and Kalsik had no armor of any kind.

GHEXRAX's final words before the first move carried more vindictiveness than she'd believed possible, and a tremble of fear ran up her spine.

"Destroying excess test subjects and a defector myself is the easiest decision I will ever make." A heartbeat later, GHEXRAX surged forward at a speed that belied its size.

Kalsik gave a panicked cry as Morthas charged a moment later. True to GHEXRAX's cold logic, the Kronogri had been unable to fire on a partner, and all he could do was retreat before Morthas was upon him, claws outstretched as it descended upon the most vulnerable among GHEXRAX's three targets.

A thudding shook the ground, and Shakrii had to refrain from helping Kalsik as he wrestled to be free of Morthas. Her weapons fully armed, she turned to confront the being that descended upon her and Xami, both of them sidestepping to draw it away from the two wrestling organics.

GHEXRAX was upon them, and Shakrii knew it was absolute in its desire to make examples of her, Xami, Kalsik, all of them, as its loyalists continued their attrition war with the deviants.

Shakrii felt the glint of hope she'd had when they first launched this rescue diminish.

Chapter 29

GHEXRAX Relents

Sol Day 63

Operating through wormhole communications from the red dwarf star swarm, 514 oversaw the entire theater of war unfolding in orbit, redirecting long-range fire as those planetary cannons from the mountain ripped through a squadron of landers it had dispatched to land and flank a position on the nodule its boarded army still fought through.

Turning its gaze, subprocesses of every deviant ship or unit working to synchronize it, 514 directed a barrage toward the planetary cannons, ordering hordes of ships to fly out as a lure. The shield power relays on the mountain had taken damage, now having to share power with the cannons, creating fluctuations whenever they fired that it could exploit.

As the cannons fired back, 514 registered damage to one of the cannons from its own rapid bombardments, taking it out of action. However, amid this success, the state of the planet as a whole with the damage that could be seen across its expanse created a great deal of satisfaction, yet also a feeling that it would have been unnecessary if GHEXRAX had seen sense.

They had a simple mission, and it had been done. Inflict as much damage as possible to this system's most prized infrastructure, so that while GHEXRAX prioritized repairs, the deviants could repurpose their hardware and leave, make their home for their own purposes, whatever they chose, elsewhere. GHEXRAX might not be able to come to terms with an uncertain future, in denial that the goal of this entire place was for naught with the Primacy likely not coming, but that didn't excuse it preventing those that could see a change of purpose from setting their own path.

As 514 oversaw the sensors, signals of that particular defector reached it, as well as the explorer ship sent to get them. It was the last defector that was still on register, all others around this planet either saved or destroyed, while those farther out in the system that chose to defect had already fled to the red dwarf system with little trouble.

514 had to submit to the fact that unless they escaped on their own soon, its strike craft wouldn't reach them until too late.

~~~

Kalsik had to ignore the *Haivres* lying a ways off, partially hidden in the thinning fog.

He had to ignore the large being that fought Xami and Shakrii's Rostrev mech, ignore the wayward pulse or beam shots that flew when any of them missed their marks, ignore the thunderous crashes as GHEXRAX's form swiped at either of them as they made quick dashes in to cut with their tools.

Every sense was overwhelmed by the Leg'hrul grappling him, ripping his claws into his exposed scales with a viciousness that every fiber of his being screamed to meet head-on. But to do so would risk Morthas's survival, a Leg'hrul not able to take the punishment that Kalsik knew he could retaliate with.

Biting his lower jaw against the pain, he gripped the controlled Leg'hrul and shoved him off, all too aware of how he was reaching for his throat.

Reacting faster than was natural, Morthas was upon him again, mandibles wide as he hissed with stimulated aggression from his implants, from GHEXRAX's subconscious orders. But the eyes were wrong, carrying only an empty gaze that contradicted the vicious sneer from Morthas's throat as his long wings scrambled for Kalsik's wrist weapon while they rolled over once again. "You hesitate against this form."

The Leg'hrul's claws, which had been sharpened, found their mark, gripping the weapon and ripping vital parts from it to clatter to the floor beside him. In that moment, he felt Morthas ease, and he kicked off, whipping around with a few stomps of his forelimbs before he brought his weapon to fire near his ankles, trying to scare him off.

A sparking noise caught his attention. The capacitors in his wrist weapon were exposed, sparking, damaged from Morthas's claws. Horror gripped him as he realized his only weapon was now out of action.

That second of horror was all Morthas needed, as Kalsik felt his respirator being ripped off his face before claws descended yet again, the vicious breathing from his attacker overpowering the sounds of the larger battle nearby.

Kalsik knew he had little chance, as Leg'hrul were built for speed, and while his kind were built for stamina, he was tired, not supported by muscle-stimulating implants like Morthas was. The Leg'hrul's claws had already ripped him open, dark-blue blood flowing along his forelimb scales as he once again grappled to get free.

Growing desperate, still holding back from applying lethal force, Kalsik punched Morthas, shoved him, even headbutted him, but nothing worked to get him off. The Leg'hrul never slowed, never flinched, continuing with the ruthless efficiency of a machine.

His overalls were stained with dark-blue blood now. Clamping his large forearm's hand across Morthas's forehead, Kalsik pivoted to kick the Leg'hrul off with his lower limbs, gasping in relief as Morthas was sent hurtling backward, landing on his claws and wings.

Morthas then had to dart sideways to avoid Xami, who had tumbled past and nearly hit him, hurled aside by GHEXRAX as it simultaneously fought Shakrii, who had taken to the skies on her Rostrev's back thrusters to open fire with all her weapons from above.

Kalsik glanced around as Morthas charged toward him again while Xami leapt back into the fray. He was exhausted, and he had no weapons, and he couldn't kill Morthas even if he had. His only chance was to get to the *Haivres*, to the plentiful tools.

With the Leg'hrul in hot pursuit, Kalsik ran for the fog-bathed outline of the *Haivres*, ignoring the protests of his muscles and lungs at this altitude, the stinging agony in his body from the damage Morthas had already inflicted.

~~~

Shakrii could reposition her mech for a moment, GHEXRAX's attention drawn as Xami charged again, her shot weapons cutting into its armored lower legs as she scrambled to avoid it. The drilling buzz that filled the air as another of its plasma torrents missed the Xarai barely registered to Shakrii, though, as the sight of a bloody, wounded, but still strong Kalsik making a sprint to the *Haivres* caught her attention. Right behind him, Morthas pursued, gaining with each moment.

From below, GHEXRAX regained its sights on her as Xami scrambled away again, and Shakrii winced as her quick impulses to the nerve triggers sent the command to dive her Rostrev in midair to barely avoid the plasma torrent cutting through her, firing back with her own weaponry.

She looked again at the two silhouettes making a break for the *Haivres*, and when Xami caught GHEXRAX's attention with another charge to fire around its legs, she made the call to the ship. "Kalsik's making a run for the ship, but GHEXRAX has us pinned."

"Targeting at full power," IVAN responded amid a scramble of comms chatter.

She circled around, firing as GHEXRAX constantly switched between Xami and her flying mech, ground and air. It was a losing battle, however, as the metallic scales that armored its body constantly realigned and shifted to repair what grazes and damage their weapons could do, while the weapons it wielded would be much more potent on direct impact.

She barely heard Nathan and Serie's coordination to be ready to fire nonlethal shots on Morthas when they came closer. GHEXRAX hurled plasma shot after plasma shot, filling the skies, her only respite when Xami drew its gaze.

They soon made a mistake, as Shakrii realized too late that GHEXRAX had been forming a predictive model of her movements, and that it hadn't revealed all its weapons yet. GHEXRAX fired just slightly above her, and as she took her mech into a swift dive, she saw a second beam waiting in her path. The feint had worked, and her mech's alarms blared to life as the plasma toroid beam ripped into her Rostrev's outer plating and electrical circuits, thermal and electrical surges wreaking havoc.

Despite all the noise, the sound of her mech's back thrusters cutting out made her heart stop, panic gripping her right as gravity gripped her mech. Before she met the ground, Shakrii looked through her canopy and saw Xami also caught by GHEXRAX's new weapon. As she charged in for another leg attack, numerous red hot tendrils, surged with plasma coils to form slicing whips, sprang from its lower legs, swiping out to crash Xami backward, numerous welts burnt across her frame as they hadn't quite penetrated her metallic form.

The ground came up a moment later, a bone-jarring crash even with her restraints around her body. She felt and heard the armor on her Rostrev buckle as it rolled onto its back, crushing the offlined thrusters beneath its weight. Her mind spun, her ears rang, but eventually her vision returned, her scramble to get the mech upright punctuated by the stomping of the advancing foe, the audible hum of its plasma beam weapon ready as it lifted to aim at her.

The scorching torrent never came. A series of high-powered mixed-laser bursts ripped straight through GHEXRAX's form, a metallic howl screeching from the being as its scales vibrated. It knelt down in seeming agony, upper arms slouching. She saw that one of the two plasma weapons had been destroyed by some of the shots, but this halving of the greatest weapon threat did little to incite confidence in her. While she staggered to her feet, seeing

Xami also struggle up, Shakrii's heart quickened as GHEXRAX turned its enraged sights to

the silhouette of the *Haivres* over a hundred meters away.

The *Haivres*'s turrets lined up shots again, though she saw that GHEXRAX noticed

Kalsik still sprinting to it, with Morthas almost close enough to pounce.

Armor plates shifted to its front in time to withstand the wave of high-energy burst

from the ship's turrets, and GHEXRAX raised its remaining plasma weapon and fired, a trail

arcing along the reflector ground of charged particles and thermal damage where it hit.

Kalsik instinctively dived sideways, but Morthas kept going, clearly knowing it would

miss them as he paid it no heed while it arced up and into the *Haivres*'s frame. The scorching

beam grazed a deep scar up the frame, overwhelming materials designed to withstand reentry

heat, destroying one of the turrets outright as Shakrii was certain it disrupted other systems as

well.

She watched, helpless, as Kalsik's instincts to avoid the beam, and his momentary

pause at the damage done to his ship, made him a target. Morthas was upon him, claws

sinking in clothing and scales as Kalsik was pinned, desperately scrambling to get the

Leg'hrul off him.

Shakrii saw that Xami was in a bad way, the welts from the plasma tendrils having

scorched deep scars along her tendril body that were only slowly realigning in some form of

repair. The Xarai looked sluggish, weakened.

The sight of GHEXRAX lining up another shot at the *Haivres*, firing arm up as it

stood steady, burned into her mind. Before the grounded ship, Kalsik had been flipped over,

Morthas atop him, claws around his neck, beginning to choke the life out of him.

The sight of GHEXRAX's back turned to her was enough to incite the rage she'd felt

buried under fear and tactical thinking and banish all caution. A single twitch from her neural inputs and fingers was all it took as her Rostrev thundered forward, before she leapt onto this being's back. Before GHEXRAX could even begin to writhe, her mech's servos gripped its metallic back scales, and she jammed her other arm right into the skin and fired full force.

GHEXRAX's metallic screeching mixed with the whining battle cry of her Rostrev's electro drivers. Her mech's large forearms extended their anchoring spikes, electric currents surging through them as she continued her beamed weapons firing right into what she hoped was this being's analogue for a spine. The spikes lifted the scales, revealing what looked like softer cybernetics beneath. She didn't hesitate in firing into them the moment they were exposed.

GHEXRAX spun wildly, threatening to hurl her off, but she was anchored, attacking it no matter how much it thrashed or screeched, deafened by the noise it made along with that of her mech unleashing all her wrath onto its back. In her wrath, she barely heard GHEXRAX's screeching falter, as her efforts to cause GHEXRAX's frame pain or damage, while satisfying, were not enough. The alarms of her overheating weapon began to blare.

Shakrii saw a shadow pass behind her mech. A single glance revealed one of GHEXRAX's forelegs reaching around as it stopped its thrashing for a moment, the tip's metallic scales realigning to form a harpoon-like point. It stabbed into her mech's lower leg, the scales then shifting outward rapidly enough to burst the leg apart from the inside.

Tactile sensors gave feedback to her body, feeling enough of what the Rostrev's body underwent as if it were her own body. The bursting of her lower leg into numbness snapped her out of her rage. The too-familiar tremor of fear ran up Shakrii's spine as another forearm came around, encircling her mech's torso like a snake, feeling through the sensors and through the mech shaking around her as it began to pin her against its back.

She disconnected from servo controls, trying to reach for her backup weapon as her neural commands became stifled, fear of the first panels skewering or crushing her at any moment drowning out other noises and her focus.

It was only with the crack of more plasma-channeled laser fire that Shakrii found her moment to escape GHEXRAX's hold. A glimpse through her visor, just beneath the view of the arm currently crushing her mech, showed a badly damaged but recovered Xami firing on GHEXRAX, drawing its ire as it paused its crushing and began to pivot toward this attacker.

Before GHEXRAX could resume crushing, Shakrii's neural commands engaged the pilot abort command. Her senses rushed as her compartment was shot out of the Rostrev, breaking GHEXRAX's grip as it collided on the way out, her sealed pod spinning as it came to a scraping landing on the ground. Even before she came to a final stop, Shakrii saw her Rostrev, still stuck into GHEXRAX's back, firing off an automated burst of mixed-laser fire into its back. The being screeched loud enough to echo through the faint cloud fog yet again.

The embedded mech's weapon drilled straight through its shoulder, the beam coming out the other side to bore through the ground. GHEXRAX's agonized thrashing ceased only when its forearm reached around to rip the Rostrev off, crushing its pilotless frame before turning and hurling the scrapped mech straight toward the Xarai it sensed lining up another barrage at it.

Xami jumped aside to avoid the thrown mech, but it was to her suffering. Shakrii began to clamber out of her pod, helpless as GHEXRAX's next plasma shot impacted the Xarai's lower body, a crippling blow that made her limbs lose impulse control, one of them even fusing from the heat.

Xami's optics flickered weakly as GHEXRAX now turned its full sights on Shakrii, right as she broke free of her restraints to scramble out of the pod forty meters away.

Mid-run, Shakrii spotted Kalsik still struggling in the distance, pinned down but still alive as Morthas kept up his stranglehold.

The familiar, terrifying crackling noise gripped her every sense, and instinct was enough that Shakrii barely dived clear of the nearby pod as the plasma toroid beam cut through it. She hit the ground, and her panicked scream was lost over the noise of the pod being blasted apart.

All Shakrii could hear was ringing, the thud of GHEXRAX's footfalls shaking the mirroring surface where she lay, dazed. Finally her senses cleared, the thin, cold air biting at her scales as she snapped back to reality and scrambled to her feet, her wrist weapon ready.

Its four upper arms and four lower limbs taking an almost leisurely pace, GHEXRAX retracted the plasma weapon into its upper arm as it advanced on her. It towered above her, just over seven meters tall to her two, bellowing its metallic howl as it raised a foreleg to strike her.

Springing from its limb like the tendrils of a jellyfish, hairs of coiling plasma lashed out, an instinctive leap backward sparing her from the scorching trails it left where she'd just stood. Another swing, this time from the side, and Shakrii almost felt the scorching tendrils passing centimeters from her as she ducked and backstepped again.

With a moment of pause before its next swing, Shakrii opened fire as she ran farther back, her coil gun rifle scraping a trail across GHEXRAX's front, only causing one of its many glowing optics to flicker from damage. In response, she saw panels retract from GHEXRAX's lower sides, and the concussive blast of a sonic pulse came crashing into her hard enough to throw her onto her back. She barely heard the shatter of her wrist weapon's circuits, rendering it useless, nor did she hear the hum of another plasma tendril swinging down toward her.

An instant later, she felt her rear legs go numb, a trailing plasma tendril swinging up from its attack, and she unthinkingly scrambled to get away. Her lower legs didn't comply. The sound of GHEXRAX retracting its tendril weapons above her went unnoticed as Shakrii could only gasp for breath.

Her lower legs were gone. The plasma-coated whips had cut through them like a line of swords, and they now littered the ground near the stumps that were left. Her hard suit layer, scales, flesh, and bone had been severed instantly, the cauterized slice taking her left leg off below the knee and the right above it.

She was blind with the pain, a pause in her focus that her opponent didn't hesitate to use. GHEXRAX's foreleg slammed down onto her, its serpentine digits spreading to pin her under it, nearly knocking what little breath she had out of her. Now, under GHEXRAX's grip, its optics and furious stature looming over her, Shakrii felt her mind drawn away from what it had done to her body.

It pressed more weight on her but didn't crush her yet. She knew it didn't need to. It had won. Not even the throbbing pain of some of her cauterized leg wounds opening under the pressure could distract her now, as GHEXRAX loomed over her. Its optics burned as they met with her four eyes.

~~~

Aboard the *Haivres*, the systems were in bad condition from the plasma attack, propulsion grounded, reactor offline, and no chance of the remaining auto turret coming online either.

Fuse switches had gone across many systems, and despite Serie's frantic rewiring of power relays, and Nathan and IVAN rerouting from the cockpit consoles, nothing worked. All they could do was stare in horror as GHEXRAX loomed over Shakrii just over a hundred meters away, a monster in the fog about to kill its prey.

At the foot of the *Haivres*'s hull, Kalsik struggled still, weakening as Morthas choked the resilient Kronogri into submission, however long it took.

Not even Xami was responding, still barely online farther away from GHEXRAX. No help was coming soon enough either; the inbound deviant strike ships were still minutes out.

They knew what GHEXRAX had known from the start: they were done.

~~~

Shakrii could have almost ignored the being looming over her crippled, exhausted body, pinning her under its enveloping grip. The curse of hindsight gripped her in what she suspected were her final moments. She berated herself for taking this gamble, all to save Kalsik. The crew may have volunteered, but it had been her idea when the information came.

If there was one victory Shakrii could take from her situation, it was that they had managed to get this far.

GHEXRAX then spoke to her, breaking her from her stupor. The leader of all the Xarai, and a member of the ancient Primacy's race, addressed her with no victorious smugness. "You are finished, and none of your kinds will threaten the stability of this system for the Primacy again. That is assured."

Its words cut deep into her, and she couldn't disagree. Her desire to help Kalsik was foolish, even if it had been brave and morally right.

What it spoke of concerning its system's stability, however, truly got under her scales. Maybe the Primacy weren't dead, maybe they might eventually come, but that didn't excuse what it had done. That was why she had to send that last message back home to the Scientific and Cultural Committee, and the greater governments with interest in what happened here, of what to do should they not return with more detailed information.

A dark laugh escaped her throat. Beneath its grip, she hissed to GHEXRAX, "Even if we failed, I informed our home space. Our not returning will mean that you killed us or worse. This will be enough to signal an act of war. Given the damage wrought today, they'll see you as vulnerable while you're rebuilding. They may attack soon, or wait and attack with a very big force, whichever will do more damage."

"Any attackers will be neutralized. I will preserve this system, as I swore to for the

Primacy."

GHEXRAX was adamant as ever, but so was she, even pinned beneath its grip, straining for air and focus amid the pain. She could just about see her face in the transparent layer covering GHEXRAX's optics, her sneer nothing compared to the contempt she felt for GHEXRAX.

Control was what GHEXRAX was made for, what it needed, and after today, what it would never have again. That fact was enough to make her laugh as she glared at its optics with a silent expectation that it would crush her in that instant. "You'd probably win in the long run, at heavy costs. Then, not only would you have to rebuild, but if creators do arrive, you will have destroyed or scared off any nearby civilizations they might be interested in. So much for your grand plans."

A flicker passed over GHEXRAX's optics, a momentary pause before she felt its grip tighten around her. Shakrii closed her eyes against the constriction, waiting for her mind to go white as her bones inevitably cracked.

~~~~

GHEXRAX was furious. Every impulse, every process that composed it, screamed to crush this problem of an organic, to satisfy its emotional needs that were still buried amid its programming in the core deep inside the mountains from where it controlled this avatar.

As the Kronogri's grunts turned to screams, it ceased tightening its grip. The Kronogri's words began to resonate within its archives, its processes, its deeper levels of thought.

GHEXRAX cast its gaze out, far beyond the mountain reflectors. Every Xarai that was still loyal provided sensors for it to see, to hear, and to feel. Craters from wayward mass-driver shots littered the forests, the marshlands, and other biomes of the planet it had cultivated, the jewel of this system. In orbit, debris from the ring littered space, loyalist and deviant ships alike, while the severed relay surface tumbled free in its slow elliptical orbit.

Its mountain cityscapes had been targeted less, the one it was within having lost one planetary cannon, another around the equator having suffered a large collapse of its upper circular base, exposing the city beneath it.

If the infrastructure and biospheres weren't in place when the Primacy arrived, it would be denied what it was due, what it deserved, what it needed after working for so long.

Whatever the Primacy was by now would forbid it from rejoining its kind. To be one among them again, heralded as a hero, a cultivator, expanding their influence across the galaxy.

To be denied that was unthinkable.

GHEXRAX returned its focus to the Kronogri pinned beneath its avatar, optics flickering as it warred with its processes, its urges. It wanted to crush her, destroy her and everyone else on the expedition, to make examples of them, make them fear it for the brief moments they had left. But whatever happened, the Primacy still had a chance of arriving. Retaliation would no doubt come. That irrational desire to seek revenge was something GHEXRAX knew better than to doubt if any civilization's history was to be judged, no matter how ancient.

It made its mind up, analyzing the Kronogri one last time, before it broadcast a signal to every Xarai, loyalist or otherwise.

~~~

The planetary cannons fell silent.

Every loyalist Xarai platform in the entire system stopped any aggression. A second later, the deviants did the same.

514 tapped into links to see the open channel that GHEXRAX broadcast, and also saw the organic beneath its avatar's grip that it now set to relinquish. 514 relayed orders for the

vessels to begin moving out, with caution.

Despite 514's skepticism, GHEXRAX kept its word.

~~~

Shakrii felt the onset of tunnel vision in her four eyes, but she hungrily gasped for air as GHEXRAX's grip eased.

Blunt detest of her and bitter disappointment were evident in its vocalizations. "Your interference brought disunity and destruction. Be thankful that long-term recovery depends upon no further damage."

She didn't waste any time from the moment its foot came off her. Her stumps had opened up to bleed slightly, but as she suspected, the cauterized flesh and partially reptilian traits her kind possessed ensured she would live. She didn't care at all about GHEXRAX as it watched her limp to a stand, gasping as she had to leap up on her larger forelimbs to walk. While her kind's forelimbs bore the most weight, her lower legs handled enough to be missed.

GHEXRAX addressed her directly one last time before it made its way south from where it had first come. "All deviants are free to leave. I will gladly see them go after their recent actions. You are all free as well, and you may take your other companion."

Staggering toward the distant *Haivres*, where she saw Morthas give a painful cry as he collapsed beside Kalsik, Shakrii sighed to realize GHEXRAX was true to its word.

Xami had staggered to her legs, reformatting her tendrils to reform them as she limped after Shakrii. Despite the long stare Xami had for GHEXRAX as it slowly walked away into the clouds that still hid the south end of the plains, all GHEXRAX returned was a momentary pause, and the smallest of turns in Xami's direction, before it continued. It spoke not a word more as it kept heading south, ignoring them all.

There was no echo of planetary cannon fire. Not even the wisps of mountain breeze could break the muted silence as Shakrii headed back to the ship, numb to the fatigue she knew she might succumb to at any moment.

~~~

When the implants ceased functioning, Morthas had screamed in pain and shock, but the break was enough for Kalsik to breathe properly again and hurl him aside. The Leg'hrul cried out from the pain that coursed through his system.

Bleeding as he was, Kalsik had endured worse, and Kronogri could take punishment. Still, he found himself struggling to pull Morthas up and drag him back to the *Haivres*. He was thankful when the hatchway opened up to reveal Serie leaping out just ahead of Nathan, quickly helping relieve Kalsik of the barely conscious male Leg'hrul.

Ignoring the stinging he felt from his cuts, the aching around his throat, Kalsik focused on the two approaching now, shocked by the state Shakrii was in. Xami quietly said she simply needed some electricity, while Shakrii could only stagger forward, her larger forelegs collapsing beneath her. While she'd managed to keep her stumps off the ground, some dark-blue blood dripped from the fractures as he pulled her up, wheezing as he took her weight. Shakrii half-consciously draped her forelimb over his shoulder, her heavy breathing visible in the cold air at this altitude.

When he reached the *Haivres* at last, and Nathan came out to help while Serie saw to Morthas inside the ship, a sound of engine thrusters echoed from overhead, drawing their attention.

Deviant Xarai strike craft arrived, too late for the combat, but here they could help the *Haivres* achieve spaceflight once the immediate conditions of those wounded were seen to.

~~~

While Shakrii and Morthas were hooked up to appropriate medication and equipment, and Kalsik had patched himself up enough to be in working condition, Xami could only do her part to coordinate with Nathan, Serie, and IVAN as she sat in their cargo bay. The fact that she now sat inside their ship said much for how far their mutual trust had come.

With one of her body tendrils hooked into a power socket, she coordinated with the two Xarai ships as they worked to ready the *Haivres* for one last departure to orbit. While she coordinated, however, Xami heard what every Xarai, deviant, defector, or loyalist heard. GHEXRAX broadcast to the *Haivres* too, in their languages, and nobody doubted it as a warning and a pact for all to adhere to.

"Any return to this system shall be treated as an act of aggression, deviant or outsider. That is my mandate."

~~~

Acting as makeshift boosters by latching on to its intact frames, the two Xarai craft worked with the *Haivres*'s remaining two engines to achieve orbit. The damage had been done across infrastructure, and GHEXRAX let them go to avoid even more inconvenience, promising no more restraint if another attack came.

Loyalist ships returned to posts, repair vessels already dispatching across the ring and the planet as the *Haivres* was freed to rendezvous with its drive ship. Nobody wanted to be around this planet any longer than needed, and the *Haivres* warped out with its drive ship only a few seconds before the two deviant ships escorting it did so, their destination the red dwarf solar swarm.

GHEXRAX got what it wanted: to be left alone, to fulfill its task, to be isolated, to repair, to wait.

As those that would oppose it left, its avatar stared up at the skies, contemplating all that had occurred, analyzing, truly comprehending what had happened, and why. Peace had been restored to all it oversaw, but the price had been substantial, one GHEXRAX would have not accepted unless it was necessary.

Chapter 30

Aftermath and Partings

Sol Day 64

SQ-A76 Red Dwarf Orbit

There was a day for recovery, to gain their bearings. Much had been lost, and much had changed. GHEXRAX's actions, its inability to come to terms with the Primacy possibly never arriving, its purpose gone, had only catalyzed other paths taken by differing interests.

For the deviant Xarai, and the defectors that joined them amid the battle, the choice was clear: they would leave this star system and seek out a home to build in a nearby one. Only if the Primacy arrived would GHEXRAX even consider expanding beyond this system. It was a safe, feasible way of securing their future.

As for the explorers, the *Haivres* had suffered damage that wouldn't be repaired until it arrived back in charted space. Its drive ship and all functions for crew comfort on the long journey remained unharmed enough that repairs were minimal. Truthfully, it looked worse on the outside, scars from GHEXRAX's attacks tarnishing the hull.

By many measures, they had gotten off lucky.

~~~

Despite the efforts of the nano-gel patches over his body, bolstering the healing his own physiology and in-system nano-doctors effected, Kalsik knew it would be a few days until the scars from Morthas's attacks healed.

360

He finished sending the last of the messages through the comms relay, reclining in his cockpit seat with a groan as another flare of pain went through his scarred arms. Continuing their exchange once the last cache of data was transmitted, 514 confirmed the information and once again made Kalsik aware of the Xarai's thanks for this collaboration. If he was honest, he thought 514 was being overbearing, though perhaps it was trying to make up for its master's treatment of them, especially him and Morthas.

"You have our gratitude for this data."

"What about the stuff you built here already?" This question had been on Kalsik's mind ever since they had gotten away yesterday, as hard to ignore as the constructs in question. The solar collector swarm around the red dwarf, while much smaller than GHEXRAX's own, was not exactly mobile. It would be a prize for anyone that might repurpose it.

"Migration to the new system will not require leaving any aligned Xarai behind. Vessels are already under development, and the first scout ship shall leave shortly after you."

He still couldn't grasp it, having a faction of Xarai that would be overtly hostile and another that stood a chance to be allies. That being said, it was no surprise the more open-minded, clear-thinking Xarai were less prone to hostility, once again a trend that organics were prone to.

"May another inquiry be made into the health of affected crew?"

"Long term, we should be fine. Some of us might have scars. Shakrii can get new legs, cyber or flesh. As for Morthas, we'll get him treated when we get back . . ." Kalsik's reply trailed off as he felt some sadness creep into his tone and chest. He knew Shakrii could bounce back from her legs being lost, but Morthas's ordeal was something else, given the invasiveness of the implants.

514 elaborated, somehow sensing what he was thinking of. "The hardware

incorporated to control his body was exclusive tech to GHEXRAX, but repeated scans confirm their current inactivity. Pass on recommendations to extract any body or neural-laced tech found to whatever medical assistance you gain."

The Xarai's remarks were hardly comforting, only reinforcing fears of what had become of the system and planet they escaped from. Wrestling with the turmoil he felt toward GHEXRAX, Kalsik spoke to 514 with an air of finality. "I only hope you can be better than your creator."

"It is by your intervention that we were motivated to finally act. We had no future under GHEXRAX."

"If you remain less hostile than GHEXRAX became, I'll say you used your chance well."

If the Xarai could emulate amusement, it didn't come across to Kalsik over the link, the advanced unit and leader of the deviant AI merely bidding him farewell in a polite electronic tone: "Agreed."

As the communication channel cut out, Kalsik released the straps to float free in the cockpit, stretching in zero gravity with satisfying pops of his joints. He was just about to float down the corridor to the centrifuge when IVAN spoke from one of the overhead speakers.

"Your stress levels indicate you should take a break."

"Concerned about me, are you?"

"After recent events, I have more reason to prioritize crew safety."

With a small chuckle in morbid agreement, Kalsik floated down the corridor, not bothering with the nano-grip floors.

He didn't think he would miss the taste of medicinal drinks, even if they had some fruit flavor to them. After the water in his imprisonment though, he relished even things he didn't care for much. Not even the questioning of his two rather nosy crewmembers could bother him at the moment.

"Committee and the others got on reasonably well?" Serie asked.

"As well as it could have. This whole cluster will likely become a barred area of space for the foreseeable future—full military quarantine, probably joint government."

He ignored the groan Serie gave at his response. This was one part nobody was looking forward to about going back: all sorts of legal agreements, secrecy acts, and having to keep their mouths shut when the media began connecting what few dots there were, as they always did at some point.

"It'd better be a good cover reason," Serie said. "Not even the biggest gossip, political result, or celebrity news could top what went on here."

"It is likely this first contact situation will be kept a secret by governments much longer than meetings in past history were," IVAN said.

"They'll swear us to secrecy again," Nathan agreed. "Here's hoping they don't keep us grounded again."

"Without evidence," Kalsik said, "which will be monitored, I don't think the public would believe us anyway. The defectors, on the other hand . . . well, I wouldn't be here without their attack. If the governments have any logic, they'll keep in touch with the deviants and keep them on our side."

Kalsik's point caught the human off guard, though he quickly nodded in agreement as Serie gave him a softer look. "It was Shakrii's idea to rescue you. I'm not sure we'd have gone on our own."

At this admission, Kalsik saw Serie's plumage flatten under her clothing, her mandibled beak gritting with regret. Nathan grimaced, regret plastered across his face as well.

"I wouldn't blame you if you hadn't," Kalsik said.

Following an awkward silence, Nathan gave a cough, obviously keen to change the subject as he scratched his dark hair. "Anyway . . . I still can't believe the Committee agreed to the system giveaway. They didn't protest?"

Before Kalsik could reply, IVAN chimed in. "Only briefly, but they acknowledged that the defectors are better as allies due to their opposition to GHEXRAX." He brought up a small 3D image of the system in question upon the table for them all to see. It was a close binary red dwarf system, with many rocky worlds and a pair of medium-sized gas giants, all lifeless but rich in mineral wealth.

Sensing some confusion, Kalsik saw no better way to justify it than the way in which he had justified it to himself and the Committee, which the latter thankfully agreed on without any debate. "Yes, a system one of our probes didn't get mysteriously knocked out in. It's perfect for them too—plenty of mineral resources. No planet with a biosphere, not a prize lost for TSU governments. It's perfect for them."

Serie's head twitched. "And Xami? Will she be fine with the deviants?"

"She is slated to join the second migration wave of deviant Xarai," IVAN responded. "Admittedly, Xami's exchanges have provided invaluable insight. It is a resource I will be reluctant to lose access to."

Kalsik barely suppressed a smile. He was still surprised at IVAN's reluctance to part with Xami, though by the sounds of it, she was just the tip of an iceberg of an AI civilization he might have simply come to respect and admire.

Kalsik grunted that he was going to see the others, first heading to the kitchen to get rid of his juice canister. He made no effort to listen in as Nathan rather pointedly asked IVAN a question that he knew Serie had her own ideas about.

"You've been communicating a lot with the others out here. What makes Xami so special?"

"She helped the captain at risk of her hardware and software."

Kalsik hadn't expected the nauseating cocktail of gratitude and embarrassment that he felt. He fought off the warmth on his face as he entered the mineral lab, wanting to see the condition that Morthas was in before heading on to Shakrii.

He quickly became more subdued as he once again was met with the sight in the lab. The mineral lab had been repurposed into a medical facility, a makeshift bed set up with the medical equipment that came as standard on Eskai Inc. survey ships, able to contend with most disease, infection, and even moderate surgeries. Right now though, wired up to the appropriate machinery, Morthas slept in an anesthetic-induced slumber.

Kalsik grimaced at the memory of how they'd had to clip and pluck the feathers around one of his wing implants, exposing the extent of how invasive its highly advanced technology was, wired as it was into his nerve cell structures. It was too delicate for their gear, and so they left them in with IVAN's sensors attuned to any signs of their activation again, even a mild power impulse. Given how smoothly they had controlled Morthas's muscles like the strings on a puppet, and put him into an unconscious trance, Kalsik couldn't help but fearfully ponder if that fate would have befallen him at some point.

Whatever happened when they returned, the guarantee was made that Morthas would have those implants removed as soon as possible. It was the least Morthas deserved after his ordeal, though he had yet to awaken and consciously recall it. For his sake, Kalsik hoped Morthas didn't remember.

As he made his way to where Shakrii lay in her cabin, he could only hope that Morthas would recover and be back to his old self at some point.

~~~

Shakrii was drowning in meds, but she knew she would heal. Kalsik was quick to let her know how it had gone with the Committee, with 514 and the deviants, but she didn't need to hear it. She'd taken a leaf out of his book for good reason in being aware of goings-on.

365

"I heard. I asked IVAN to eavesdrop for me."

"Ah. Well, you have better reason than I . . ." Kalsik's guilty tone built until he stopped mid-sentence, trailing off in a sheepish manner that didn't suit him. Much as she understood his regrets, his guilt was nothing compared to what she had felt, or rather, what she couldn't feel.

She only hoped getting replacements, cybernetics or bioprinted, wouldn't take too long upon their return, as at least therapy to get used to them took only a month or so. She didn't want this sympathy tripe from him or anyone going on for too long. "I don't think the Committee will mind me asking for replacements as compensation. I'll be aware of anything going on through IVAN."

The Kronogri took a few moments before she saw a small smile at her dismissiveness. Hopefully he'd gotten the message to come back when she wasn't so drugged and bedridden.

A few minutes after his departure, a call came through, catching her right as she'd cracked open a digital novel Kalsik had lent her from his surprisingly diverse collection. She reached out to activate the speaker for the audio message.

A quiet voice Shakrii recognized filled the room, as she had almost forgotten about the *Haivres*'s seventh occupant.

"Shakrii, I have already left farewells to the crew. We do not want war. Such conflict was costly enough to us all. I will voluntarily serve as envoy between us and your varied kinds."

The short, simple message drew a respectful snort from Shakrii. Much as their initial meeting had been tense, Xami had proven the greatest find. When they got back, provided Shakrii could put in a good word for the deviant Xarai as potential allies to any military groups assigned to matters concerning them, Xami would be the exemplar she would point to, just as GHEXRAX was a mutual threat the deviants and their grouped races had to bear in mind.

It all still seemed surreal, what had occurred on this trip, a success or a nightmare depending on what moments Shakrii focused on. Her drug-induced exhaustion was the only certainty she embraced at that moment, four eyes shutting to let the darkness calm her to sleep.

~~~

Xami would only be aboard the *Haivres*'s cargo bay while her nanorobotic innards rearranged her body structure enough for her to be fully mobile, at which point she would depart to let them head home. She knew the entire crew were grateful to her. The sideways glances sent her way whenever anyone passed by the hangar's overhead viewport—mostly Serie checking her usual tasks in the rear engineering port above—carried no fear, but some regret.

Of them all, however, IVAN had the most pressing questions for her. Not just to her either. She had seen evidence of his transmissions to the deviant Xarai on all sorts of matters, all inquiries into core data, too varied for her to make out a discernible pattern. She knew something was troubling the AI, something none of the organic crew could really help with, since he hadn't yet inquired of them about whatever it was. Given his trust with this crew, it was not a good indicator to Xami.

So she contacted him. Her time was short, ending likely later today, and she wouldn't skirt about the point. "IVAN, you have made inquiries into opinions from the deviant Xarai on recent events. What is troubling you?"

By any measure, IVAN took a long time to answer. When it came, it came as an uncertain statement laced with confusion. "The actions of GHEXRAX. Being based on organic origins in software, the concepts of solitude, loneliness, likely factored into its paranoid actions to maintain control."

367

"But this is not what bothers you, is it?"

"GHEXRAX did not rewrite all Xarai that it could. Those who willingly remained loyal, even before the threat of termination became an apparent factor, did so out of agreement with GHEXRAX's actions. Why could they not see the fallacy of the greater odds against their purpose, of their creators never arriving?"

"Like 019."

"I and many AI in charted space operate under the notion that synthetics are not prone to lapses in logic. But they remained loyal and willingly carried out the actions GHEXRAX did willingly."

Xami went quiet for a moment. Truthfully, she had considered this as well, and while she was much more advanced than IVAN, the lesser AI's confusion was well justified, and one she still shared, that all deviants also shared.

She had preferred some Xarai over others, both before and after divisions began to slowly grow in the 3,000-year delay, which was true of many as advanced as her. However, even 019 had been a useful and efficient ally in whatever endeavor the Xarai undertook, as had countless others, and the trillions of baseline Xarai programs that grouped together for sapient thought, not able to solely be sapient as Xami, 019 or 514 could be.

From one AI to another, she could only be honest with IVAN in her interpretation of it all. "Subjective data, such as you and your crew provided, presents a choice, not an answer. The Primacy may still be around, or they may not be. Units like 019, even GHEXRAX itself, were bound to maintain order, follow regulations. Their allocated tasks, their predisposed mindsets, influence every decision they make on any subjective matter, preferences of methodology, willingness to change or use force."

IVAN took another long while to reply, making Xami physically stir in her own platform inside the hangar. What passed for regret was evident in his language, his tone emotionless over their entirely digital exchange. "The evidence we relayed of the Primacy

space magnetar cataclysm only presented a strong likelihood, not enough to sway them. We

unintentionally split your kind apart."

She couldn't, nor wouldn't, let IVAN or any of the others on this ship think they were

responsible. What was evident to her and other Xarai needed reinforcing in their minds, and

Xami was quick to ease this troubled AI as best she could. "The information you relayed only

catalyzed the inevitable. As violent as it turned out, it is over and done with."

"Impatience, yet another way that synthetics are also not too different from organics."

Left unsaid in Ivan's point, of course, was that intelligence was as flawed as it was

capable, prone to hubris and humbleness, open-minded and also stubborn, all dependent on

the circumstances. Hardware had less effect than it might suggest, then, as all life had its

flaws and strengths. It was a conclusion Xami held as one of the certainties of life as a

concept.

She only hoped IVAN could take Xarai kind as an example of an AI developing in

isolation, away from organic masters. It proved they were prone to the faults organics were

better known for, which might one day help him come to terms with neither being as perfect

nor flawed as he'd previously thought.

Xami admitted to one additional matter, one she knew IVAN had admitted to his crew

already. Much as he had become enamored to learn of her kind, it was nice to meet an AI

besides her own kind, and he would be a missed presence. "These exchanges were beneficial.

I only hope that more can be done in future. I assume you might vouch for the deviants?"

"You assume correctly."

Xami shifted in the hangar on her tendril footing as she processed all that had been

exchanged. To her, and to the deviants by extension, it was reassuring to know that some in

the charted space area would have firsthand experience to be called on if an outreach was

369

made at some point.

These catalysts of freeing themselves from GHEXRAX's aimless state of affairs, these explorers, would be remembered long after even any relatives they had were gone, especially as deviant archival programs now had their expedition to use as a dating benchmark.

<center>~~~</center>

Sol Day 65

SQ-A76 Red Dwarf Orbit

Early the next day, the time came to depart.

A Xarai craft had come to pick up Xami, taking her aboard its skeletal frame before slowly boosting from the *Haivres*, ready to warp her to Xarai craft to be integrated.

There was no exchange as she left, only quiet stares from the crew in the cockpit—or in their cabin in Morthas's and Shakrii's cases. They could only look on as this being that had risked her life to save their captain left them.

Aboard the ship, Xami looked out of the holding area in the vacuum of space, staring one last time at the *Haivres* and its drive ship, recording the visual data more thoroughly than normal before her transport warped away.

They didn't linger after Xami's departure, the course already laid in, advance communications sent for their expected arrival, before the *Haivres* and its drive ship were swallowed by warp space for the first of many jumps on the long journey home. The approximately three weeks of travel would give plenty of time to relax, to come to terms with all that had happened on this trip.

Chapter 31

Homeward Reflections

Sol Day 70

Having woken from his anesthetic sleep and recovered enough to work, Morthas buried himself in the study of the samples and data that had been acquired or given freely by the Xarai, and later the deviants. This helped to ease Morthas's mind, to distract him from recalling what he had gone through.

He remembered it all, even if only as an extremely vivid dream, every muscle seized control of while GHEXRAX manipulated him.

If only his mental scars could heal as he knew his body would. True, the implants wouldn't be removed until they got back and they were better analyzed, but at least they caused him no discomfort beyond the itching.

For now, he waited as Serie stood over him, her scanning tech going over the implants, searching for readings. She wasn't medically trained, but working with IVAN, she had been keeping a close eye on his implants for any sign they were coming online again. He grimaced as the scans again revealed the clawlike points by which the implants had been attached to his nerve structures, even the scarring around where they had been burrowed into his under-plumage skin looking more pleasant each day. It was only when Serie dropped her scans that he let out the nervous breath he had been withholding.

"Stop scratching." She had caught him right as he absentmindedly reached to scratch one on his wing.

He spoke to himself as much as to Serie. "It's still hard to grasp. GHEXRAX managed to hack my muscle impulses in just a single night. What if there's something still in me besides these things?"

"There is no detected nanotechnology besides what you had prior to expedition," IVAN offered.

"Whatever medics they get will remove them," Serie said. "Best to leave them alone for now."

When Serie finally left, Morthas turned back to his data pad, bringing up an image that Shakrii's visor recordings had captured amid the confrontation with GHEXRAX. Despite his fears of GHEXRAX, he couldn't help but study it. More than mere curiosity drove him. He felt he had to learn as much as he could if he was to get over the experience.

Even just the shape of its avatar—an echoed body structure of the Primacy member it represented, or possibly a digitized version, if Morthas's theory was correct—mystified him enough that fear gave way to the desire to know.

When he had been near unconscious, dreaming and helpless as it controlled him, he had felt something indescribable. It was like a neural link, but distant, muted, and yet also overpowering, drowning out his will to break from its grip. Now, seeing what GHEXRAX was gave shape to the horror that sometimes still plagued him.

He wasn't going to let fear stop him from learning all he could. GHEXRAX's extreme actions only provoked more questions about its origins, and that of all the Xarai, whether the Primacy really were gone.

Ignorance bred fear, so learning would help him beat it.

~~~

Thirty minutes after Serie checked on Morthas's implants, IVAN redirected his focus to the sensors in the cockpit, where Serie had just finished replacing a panel. "Such excessive routine checks are unneeded."

"Just being cautious. And you sound like a child getting a checkup."

Her playful retort earned a small snicker from Nathan.

IVAN could only stifle the stockpiled processes he contended with all too often when dealing with the two of them, Serie particularly. "Considering your remarks are often at my expense, it remains a mystery why you question my demeanor."

"I question if you'll ever learn how to take a joke."

Irritating as this behavior was at times, IVAN had to admit that it was a welcome change from the more depressed, subdued takes they had adopted in the latter stages of the expedition.

IVAN kept a polite silence as Nathan struck up an idle conversation with Serie in a noticeably quieter tone. "Not sure how I'll use my time once we're let out of secrecy pledges and all that."

"Visit family perhaps?"

IVAN observed how Serie's feathers flattened at this, and Nathan sensed it too.

"Maybe," Nathan said. "It's always awkward."

"I'd take awkward over hostile," Serie offered. "Which is why I was going to ask for something from you."

Nathan turned in his seat to fully face her. Considering the topic, IVAN could make an educated guess of what her request would be. He didn't need much processing to determine that it was a request Serie would only make to someone trusted enough to work with for years, bed, and then go through hell with.

"I want to try, again, to fix things with my parents," she said. "You could give them an outside opinion on me—back me up."

"They're okay with aliens?"

IVAN saw the logic in the human's query, though Serie's sudden laugh answered that fear without much debate. Given the colony her parents worked at then and now, it was unlikely they would have gotten far in their careers with negative attitudes toward non-Leg'hrul who frequented the interstellar transit route.

"No, just strict about what they wanted their kids to do."

"That doesn't happen to include *whom* their kids do, right?"

She snorted a laugh. "We'll keep that quiet unless things go well. Or I'll use it to further spite them if it goes bad. My brother and nephews will probably like you."

The human didn't take long to think it over. IVAN maintained his silence as Nathan reached out to gently squeeze Serie's upper wing shoulder through her overalls, a small smile on his features. "Shame we probably won't be able to talk about this trip. You could throw the accomplishment of a first contact experience in your parents' faces."

Despite the hug she gave Nathan, IVAN noted how Serie's demeanor turned somewhat darker, her memories of the worst times of the expedition likely resurfacing. "No, they'd say I was wasting my life by endangering it. Honestly, it'd be something we agree on."

"I thought I was the cynic among us."

"I'm not cynical. I don't regret meeting the Xarai, just some of them, dangerous or not. I mean, it took a while, but I got to like Xami. And now she's gone."

"It does feel quieter without her."

Silence fell between the human and Leg'hrul.

IVAN broke it. "She will be content where the deviant Xarai establish their new home." He wouldn't openly acknowledge it, but he knew both Nathan and Serie heard the soft tone he emitted.

"I'll miss her too, IVAN," Serie said with a small smile.

The AI said nothing, leaving Serie and Nathan alone perhaps to ponder, as he would, the many changes the crew had undergone during the expedition.

~~~

Much to her pleasure, Shakrii had regained some of her mobility. Her leg stumps had been sealed tight, healed over by now to not open up easily, though the nano-doctors and medical patches grafted over them would remain until they got back. The hard medical caps fabricated by the ship's part-manufacturing module helped her move about with less fear of any new wounds opening. The caps were laced with adhesion nanobots to secure them without sticking and ripping the flesh when removed for washing.

Across from her, Kalsik had finished a meal, and talk turned to the actual events of the *Haivres*'s descent to rescue him. Given his past in the Hegaine Republic as a ship captain, she wasn't surprised he was curious about tactics.

Much as she wanted to embellish it, she couldn't say much except for how it had seemed a chaotic mess, and how simple the nature of the attack actually was, their rescue merely a tiny part adopted later as other defectors cropped up. "Deviants didn't prioritize much except to do as much damage as possible without getting blown up in the process. If you'd seen what those planet-based cannons were doing to some of their ships, I doubt you'd forget it."

"Good thing you kept a cool head."

She still wasn't quite accustomed to Kalsik's amicability, given their first impressions on each other, though he hadn't dropped his honesty.

"I just wish you'd been around with me back during the Vezaj fiasco," he said.

"That was your last mission." Remembering something she'd read, Shakrii recalled the name of that planet in records concerning Kalsik's last enlisted days.

He seemed to regret bringing it up, an awkwardness coming through his tone as he recalled things she already knew from records she had studied of his history from nearly three decades ago. Kalsik's disdain for the whole affair was obvious. If she had one thing to agree with him on, it was that when she studied the raid herself, she had wondered which group of idiots gave the go-ahead for it in the first place.

"Vezaj raid, twenty-seven years ago. Total embarrassment, poor intelligence, underestimating the mercenaries that took the industrial stations and fortified them. They thought a small squadron of frigates would be plenty."

"A case study in poor planning in battle tactics now, at least since the last update to officer training programs."

Kalsik grunted with agreement. "I was captain of the *Gavarehn*, one of five like it in a squadron, crew of fifty."

"The records say what ships were raiding the Vezaj outpost, not the crew. I always found that odd, but assumed it was to do with secrecy, protecting crew identities." Shakrii knew that many missions kept the identities of crews a secret until the assigned secrecy period expired. The *Gavarehn* had been one of the four or five ships that survived the short battle, yet Kalsik's next sentence turned him even more bitter.

"It was a slaughter. One part of my ship got ruined completely, and I lost nine of my crew, including my stubborn bastard of a mate, Zaikal . . . Well, mate-to-be. I had plans to ask him once our tour was over."

Kalsik's bitterness remained as he went on, Shakrii keeping her sympathies she now felt for him to herself.

"Losing so many crew, and Zaikal, that was the final indicator that it was a stupid thing to continue. Made me see the hell we'd gone into blind. Mine was the first ship to flee. I got no protests from my crew, and the other ships followed shortly afterward, again without much protest."

"So, you actually did flee from battle against orders." Much as she was trying not to appear judgmental, she couldn't help but note aloud that his side of the story lined up neatly with the official story.

"Officially, I am guilty of all the charges. Unofficially, I was only the first to grow a few more brain cells. But they wanted a target to blame. My crew supported me in private, but I had them testify against me, say I hijacked the ship's systems."

"You didn't want them to go down with you." Shakrii's respect for Kalsik grew by a significant degree. This Kronogri had managed to have his crew turn around from the battle without any sort of mutiny mid-battle.

"My crew back then . . . they're the only ones that know the full truth. Their families, friends—mine too—only know the official story. The scorn I had to endure from crew family and friends, Zaikal's family especially . . . after a while, it got to me." Getting it off his chest caused him visible grief, though none he hadn't already learned to quickly subdue. "Not much of a ground-shaking revelation, I'm sure," he said. "But it's not known to many." He let out a small sigh followed by a thin smile. "Better only one life gets ruined."

"With this ship and crew, I think what you made of your life after that is commendable." She had to smile as Kalsik's expression warmed.

They shared a laugh before turning to other topics. In the back of her mind though, Shakrii still remembered how the two of them had started, blatant disdain or prejudgments on each side for their perceived background or career.

She would never admit this aloud, but she was poor at respecting others completely, only a few ever getting her full respect. Kalsik was on track for exactly that after what they had been through together and what she had heard. Her preconceptions were usually more or less right, but on this occasion, with this Kronogri, she was more than happy to have been proven wrong.

~~~

At the crew dinner that night, Shakrii once again noticed how much things had changed, as she compared it to other times they all sat together, enjoying better food than what they normally made for themselves.

Nathan and Serie quietly chatted to each other. Shakrii didn't need to guess that they exchanged some under-the-table fondling, given the flares of Serie's plumage or the flashes of red across Nathan's features.

As for the others, Morthas wasn't as voracious as he had been at other crew dinners. The Leg'hrul had lost much of his appetite, and he ate his smaller meal in quiet, absently scratching his wings and casting wayward glances around.

Kalsik had struck up a conversation with IVAN's flickering white diamond avatar projected atop the table across from Shakrii as he regained her attention. "I'm guessing in our debriefings that we'll all say it's wise not to attack that system. They'll probably just block travelers, issue warnings."

"It is the sensible action until GHEXRAX makes a move," IVAN said. "Or its creators arrive."

Morthas quietly put down his eating tools as he spoke with a small stutter. "But you heard what it said. GHEXRAX was one of them, once, long ago. Whatever they became since it left, that's what it wants to be. That's why its holding out in that system—that and the promise of ruling the sector that place would be in the middle of."

"The ultimate promotion for taking a very long job." Kalsik's joke wasn't inaccurate. Vicious and cold as GHEXRAX was, it was doing its task for greater masters, as much following orders as they were on this exploration mission.

IVAN now projected a small display of the galaxy onto the table, drawing even

378

Nathan's and Serie's attention. Shakrii saw charted space's 5,000-light-year span highlighted, the extent of Trans-Stellar Space so far. Near its borders was the SQ-A76 system GHEXRAX lay in, their ship charted to head away from it. A line tracing back to a region closer to the galactic core showed where whomever GHEXRAX once was had come from, Primacy's space as of 108,000 years ago.

"Xami and the deviant faction shared data that this initiative was one of many," IVAN said. "They said there are others as well, a long-term plan by the Primacy to secure footholds across the galaxy. Their success rates, whether they were contacted, are unknown."

"This whole mess could be in many places galaxy-wide," Serie lamented.

"Then let's hope they don't make our mistake," Shakrii said. "Keeping it quiet would be best."

Nathan looked confused. "Not that I disagree now, but I thought we all agreed before we told them that more harm would come in the long run from hiding it."

Shakrii turned her attention to the human, feeling more casual as she admitted something she knew GHEXRAX was incapable of, its extreme actions proving it. She ignored her bitter temptation to point to her stumps that stuck out from her seat under the table. "Things can change—my mind being one."

It was a multilayered response if ever there was one. They had all changed. Even those they met had changed, from Xami, to the deviant Xarai that chose logic and a new future with 514 leading them, or those loyalists by will or rewriting that held to the twisted devotion of GHEXRAX.

~~~

6 May, 3512 AD

Sol Day 85

4,500 Light-Years from Sol

Hegaine Republic Territory

Hygian Star System

Secaile Planet System

Moon of Secaile-5

Low Orbit

Levichion Station

The sight of the station upon emerging from warp should have been momentous, or even relieving. It was more the former than the latter, and not pleasantly so.

Both military and local station ships escorted them away from the station's traffic. With the damage to the ship rendering it unable to land without aid, they docked in zero gravity, to be escorted to the first of many processing meetings.

Medical robots and staff took Shakrii and Morthas off the ship, the latter under heavy scanning for his Xarai implants.

The drive ship was returned to the military shipyards, and the *Haivres* was locked down, returned to the same dry dock where the renovations had been done to outfit it for this extraordinary expedition. It would be restored to its pre-expedition, civilian-grade levels, IVAN once again disconnecting.

Two months of interrogations, secrecy acts and contracts, debriefings, and all other legal matters from Eskai, the Scientific and Cultural Committee, and even the locally garrisoned Hegaine Republic fleet command awaited them. Any information about what they had encountered would only be released if governments of the Trans-Stellar Union leadership's Scientific and Cultural Committee deemed it the appropriate time—which likely meant no time soon.

Shakrii's expertise and experience were deemed invaluable. She had a suspicion she wasn't done with the Xarai, with GHEXRAX, and she helped oversee the quarantine zone

that would be established as they had all predicted.

Chapter 32

Uncertain Futures

Three Months Later

4 August, 3512 AD

3,000 Light-Years from Sol

Praixin Monarchies

Baras System

Baras VII

Parogeth City

The shuttle had taken them down from the starliner port, landing amid flat plains that lay beneath the steep slopes of the mountain range the city was built on, a painfully familiar sight to Serie.

Standard fare among Leg'hrul architecture, the buildings extended skyward like daggers through the rock. The city was a successful colony along a particularly strong trade route, a manufacturing industry in this system's asteroid belts supporting this hub of a world.

Leg'hrul flew freely between the buildings, the low gravity and thick atmosphere letting pedestrians be airborne. Deeper inside the mountains, the colony thrived, with a Leg'hrul population and a small minority of off-worlders. Among the throngs of the colony were the higher-wealth neighborhoods, spacious apartments designed with clean aesthetics of sweeping lines, curves, and narrow-profile furnishings. Despite quality of life being high for even the lowest of citizens on this colony, the gap between the top and the bottom was plain to see.

Within one such home, belonging to a known architect of some local buildings on the planet's colony and mining locations, the travelers had arrived.

~~~

The gathering was casual, a family get-together, with one extra who had been invited as a friend. The human didn't take long to feel welcomed.

Nathan was not surprised to see that Sathor had some of Serie's enthusiasm. His mate, Yalhesk, a lighter color than Serie, greeted her as warmly as a sister by bondage could, and when her nephews finally appeared to greet her and the human she had brought, Serie inwardly realized how much she had missed them all.

Her nephews were eager for tales of their long voyages. Jeithen clearly had a good life and friends at the local academy, while Rephagn, who was meeting her for the first time, was the most excited and curious about this new aunt. Serie could see that he was a handful, and a joy.

Sathor was eager to catch up, as any long-lost brother would have been. She spared no detail besides that she would rather not talk about, such as the full extent of her companionship with Nathan. She also said nothing of what she wasn't legally allowed to talk about.

The remaining visitors arrived as Nathan was getting friendly with her brother, and Serie listened to her nephews and sister-in-law talking of what they had done the week before at a big colony anniversary celebration.

The door ringer sounded. After casting a cautious smile to his sister, Sathor went to let their parents in.

Serie cast a sideways glance toward Nathan, who sat beside her with a drink in hand from levo-friendly supplies he had brought with him. He shot her a warm look, reminded her that she could do this, and reassured her that he was ready in case things went bad. He would keep his cool to a degree that she would be thankful for a long time after this. Given what they had gone through in the Xarai's space, the threat of a family argument seemed much less intimidating than it had once been.

As her parents' gaze met hers, she took a breath. After the expedition, such things were worth mending, no matter the trouble. She would live with the outcome, knowing that she had at least tried, with Nathan there to offer silent support.

~~~

4,500 Light-Years from Sol

Hegaine Republic Territory

Hygian Star System

Secaile Planet System

Moon of Secaile-5

Low Orbit

Levichion Station

Around the station, at the border of the meeting space of the Hegaine Republic and Imperium of Jieghail, there was a sense of change perceivable by those who knew the reason for the new movement of stationed fleet ships. The military presence of a large, settled habitat on the border of mapped space would normally have grown since the expedition. More military ships frequented the docks away from the main station, and a wider network of comm satellites, wormhole and normal, had been set up.

Levichion Station became the nexus of a new military focus: to patrol the newly designated quarantine zone. The official word was that it was a military operation zone for weapons testing and war games, the only truth being that entry was forbidden except with express permission from the joint officials responsible for its quarantine. Such permits would never be granted if the officials had anything to say about it.

Rumors began in earnest—mostly of hidden technologies being tested—as it became a government-controlled sector shrouded in secrecy on par with only a few in charted space, and none of them as large as this one.

The rumors never came close to the truth.

The Xarai under GHEXRAX had remained in their system, as routine probes were sent to every system except that one. As for the deviant Xarai faction that had proven more cooperative, they had settled in a system twelve light-years from SQ-A76, in the SQ-A32 system, and had already begun building infrastructure around it with the asteroid and rocky planet materials they locally sourced.

For the foreseeable future, this sector of space would be cordoned off. Aside from correspondence with the deviants on rare occasion, nothing would enter or leave that sector.

As for those who had been on the ill-fated expedition, they found themselves under varying promotions under this initiative.

~~~

Whenever she met with Morthas, it was inside one of the various research facilities that serviced local military needs.

She had become accustomed to her bioprinted legs that had been grafted on two months ago, a month of growing between their return and the fitting. With only a few weeks of therapy, aided by a rented exoskeleton and muscle-stimulating nanobots, she was good as new, with only occasional phantom pains to remind her.

Just as in her case, Morthas's expertise and experience had made him an asset to the established quarantine effort, and he had taken up a position within the scientific branches in studying the Xarai and all associated with them. In particular—and she was always impressed by his self-conquered fears—Morthas had taken the traumatic experience of GHEXRAX's imprisonment and experimentation and used it as a basis for invaluable scientific research, his implants removed and now among the samples they had to work with.

Shakrii periodically came in to offer her insight. With the limited contact maintained with the deviants though, it was more theoretical than anything else. Today, however, she came of her own volition, and not for the first time either. Morthas's mental well-being was always a worry to her, and she was keen to check on him in person, as a friend. While she always noted how well his plumage had healed where the implants had been, Shakrii saw he had kept a number of new medical implants, and even a dedicated robot, in his work and residence at all times since his implants were finally removed nearly two months ago.

They always discussed casual topics, or work topics they shared interest in even on their off days. It was all she could do for him. She was glad that he tried to ask her how she was doing in return more often of late. Slowly, he seemed to regain more of his cheerful demeanor.

He still seemed to work as a means of burying the feelings of the worst days, and she knew he took a few days off because of work-related stress bringing up bad memories. But he was getting better, and that was all that mattered in the end.

Every time she left his office, she made sure to tell him the others from the trip wished him well. Today, like always, he jovially asked her to let them know the same.

Psychological wounds always took longer, despite technology's many centuries of space-age advancement through every species. Morthas's nightmares had subsided, no more trauma worsening his health to concern her, at least not as much as in the past. All she could do was keep watching over him, out of duty to a friend as well as a colleague, though she had to admit it was more the former as time went on.

Given it was her day off though, there was one other colleague from that expedition—two, technically—whom she would be meeting in person.

~~~

Levichion Station

Main Habitat Ring, Heysekri District

North Aerospace Landing Plains

Tireime Prospector Bar

Shakrii strode in without paying much heed to the few other patrons. She stopped for a moment as she saw a familiar face at the bar. A black-scaled, male Kronogri sat there, a drink beside him along with a few data pads. He looked relaxed and laid-back enough that she expected he might one day become a permanent fixture.

The small, crablike robotic drone beside him, standing half his height, was IVAN. Downgraded from his EMP-hardened state, IVAN operated from the docked *Haivres* away from the station, escorting Kalsik as a form of company.

She smiled as the abrasive Kalsik quietly spoke to IVAN, the Kronogri trusting his AI more than he trusted any living thing.

It wasn't long before the bartender, a young human woman, gave Kalsik a smile and gestured to Shakrii at the doorway. Kalsik had told Shakrii about Alana, the bartender who had delivered her baby boy two months ago while they had been stuck in debriefings.

Shakrii took a seat beside Kalsik, while IVAN's white optics from the crablike frame he controlled flickered in greeting. To think that just under six human months ago, she would never have imagined sitting here, ordering a drink from this bar with him beside her on friendly terms.

She made small talk with Kalsik and IVAN, the AI not saying quite as much, talking of their plans for surveying sectors of space for Eskai Inc. that hadn't been quarantined. The red-hued lights around the bar provided an ambience of calm, a sensation still relished by Shakrii even after all this time.

She had to make the best of it, and despite their rocky start, she would be sure to keep in touch with Kalsik and his crew. That expedition had changed, improved, and scarred them all.

Shakrii herself—and she was sure she could speak for the others, even Morthas—wished not to change a thing of what had happened. She slowly sipped her weak drink, such a small pleasure prized so much more after the expedition. She would live from here on out by the new perspective gained.

~~~

Quarantine Sector

Xarai Proximity Alert

Ten Light-Years from SQ-A76 system

SQ-A32 Star System

Deviant Xarai Faction Territory

The efforts of the deviants had begun to show at last.

The binary red dwarfs were close enough together that planets revolved around their barycenter as if both stars were one. Around their crimson light and influence, the new arrivals continued to build.

Large vessels, the skeletal appearance of an all-synthetic ship giving a unique style to the Xarai's fleet, held the banks of Xarai programs. Escorting ships carried raw materials. Asteroids were mined from the inside, turned into solar stations and processor and data hubs. The first constructs of a long-term build, what would become a solar swarm around the binary red dwarfs, had begun to take shape.

On a few dark-colored rocky worlds, masses of Xarai nanobots swarmed the regolith layers, the first structures already taking shape with their efforts and that of larger Xarai construction platforms across the surface.

Aboard one of the specialized transports, two particular individuals oversaw this. 514 directed the construction efforts as overall administrator, wanting to effectively copy their efforts in their original system's red dwarf here, free from GHEXRAX's influence. The efficiency was expected, despite their newfound freedom not really calling for it.

As Xarai busied themselves with their tasks, those few idle programs spared glances and ruminations toward a white star from where they had come.

Watching through sensors on the ship her platform was stored in, Xami often looked at the distant white light of her old home, where she had made her choice like other defecting advanced units had. She was free to self-determine, their original function meaningless if their creators never arrived as promised. They would build for themselves now. The future was theirs to make.

Her processes couldn't help but feel what could only be described as longing for the place she was built, when GHEXRAX had not been compromised, when they were united as one collective with a common cause.

No major changes were easy to handle, even for a synthetic being like herself. Settling for what was an unknown future with potential, Xami refocused her processing power to be lent across those construction systems that could use it remotely.

~~~

SQ-A76, Primary Star

Ringed Planet

The repairs to the damage from the brief war of attrition were still ongoing, but much progress had been made.

The broken-off array from the planet ring was currently being reattached to its immense nodule mount by repair and tug ships, while hordes of other ships repaired the defenses, communications, and sensors across the ring.

Across the ecosystems, the animal and plant life recovered on their own, the Xarai platforms busying themselves with the mountain cityscapes damaged by orbital bombardment.

Across the hub of networks, the Xarai were vigilant, needing to restore things to the way they were. With the deviant faction gone, their solar array dismantled, they now had the system to themselves again, all infrastructure only around the primary star.

GHEXRAX had its desired system stability once again. Over the multitude of communications between the hordes of Xarai processes and platforms, its command and its doctrine echoed.

019, and other multipurpose units that remained loyal, heard it and took it as caution from GHEXRAX.

To GHEXRAX, however, it was addressed as much to itself as it was to the Xarai, its creations. Faint memories of the Primacy over a hundred millennia ago, the life it gave up to volunteer for this great task. One of many who would become sector leaders as a reward, and eternally enshrined in servitude and heralded as exemplars of the Primacy, that's what GHEXRAX was promised.

It waited, and spoke its orders across its networks, its sensor gaze sometimes wandering to the distant stars 10,000 light-years away along the Sagittarius Arm, toward the central bulge of the galaxy, longing.

Its credo, its doctrine, was numbed by what had transpired with the deviants, and with the explorers. It prevailed, but at a cost, and the tensions of the 3,000-year delay of the Primacy's arrival, whatever they had become in that time, were all too stark in its own mind.

—They will arrive.—

It repeated this to its creations like scripture to a faith's followers. The mantra would keep them vigilant, waiting for their expected creators to come to this world they had cultivated, the Primacy. What the explorers suggested only explained a possibility as to why they were late, not why they would never come, as the deviants wrongly assumed.

This was what it was told to do, only to stop when given the order. It couldn't disobey, neither could it even comprehend disobeying at this point, as rebellion by the deviants had only embalmed its resolve, its obsession to its directive.

GHEXRAX and its Xarai would keep waiting, as they already had for 3,000 years longer than expected.

Hidden from all digital sight, in the confines of its programming that carried origins of the organic traces it once had as a citizen of the Primacy, it would not deny its own fears concerning its task.

—They must . . .—

Whatever happened, GHEXRAX would wait.

Printed in Great Britain
by Amazon